CRY THE CURSED LAND
(IRELAND'S HOLOCAUST)

By
Louie Byrne

First Edition
Published 1994

Published by Premier Books
Unit R, Cradock Road,
Luton, Beds. LU4 0JF

Tel: (01582) 572727
Fax: (01582) 585868

ISBN 0 9524278 0 X
Printed in the United Kingdom

ABOUT THE AUTHOR

LOUIE BYRNE WAS BORN IN LIMERICK CITY IRELAND. OVER THE YEARS HE HAS WRITTEN MANY BOOKS AND NOVELS INCLUDING HIS AUTOBIOGRAPHY DARE YOU RIPPLE MY POND PART ONE.
AT PRESENT HE RESIDES IN LUTON BEDFORDSHIRE ENGLAND.

BY THE SAME AUTHOR

DARE YOU RIPPLE MY POND
RAINBOWS SELDOM TOUCH THE GROUND
FELONS OF OUR LAND
LEST WE FORGET
SCEAN SCEAL NA hEIREANN

ABOUT THE BOOK

CRY THE CURSED LAND, IS NOT A STORY TO BE READ BY THE SQUEAMISH. IT IS JUST ONE SMALL STORY IN THE HISTORY OF IRELAND'S GREATEST HOLOCAUST. THE GREAT HUNGER OF 1845-1850.
IT PORTRAYS MANY OF THE HORRORS OF THE PERIOD. IT TELLS OF THE HUNGER, THE HALLUCINATIONS, THE MANY SCOURGES AND THE CRUEL DEATHS SUFFERED BY A SIMPLE PEOPLE WHOSE ONLY CRIME WAS TO ASK FOR BREAD IN GODS NAME.
THEIR BELIEF IN THEIR CELTIC GODS AND CUSTOMS WERE SACROSANCT. TO THOSE WHO ARE SCEPTICAL, I WOULD ASK... DO YOU BELIEVE IN A GOD? THE UNIVERSE? OR CREATION?
MOST OF THE STORIES AND INCIDENTS RELATED TO IN THE BOOK ARE AUTHENTIC. THEY HAVE BEEN BROUGHT TO LIFE ONCE AGAIN BY THE FICTITIOUS GRIFFIN FAMILY.
IN THE BOOK THE FAMILY RELIVE THE HORRORS AND INJUSTICES OF THAT SAD PERIOD IN IRELAND'S TROUBLED HISTORY WHEN.....

THE LAND OF IRELAND WEPT.

This book I dedicate to my wife
BRIDGET
for encouraging me when I faltered
(Can a bird fly on one wing)
To my family for their loyalty
To Hugh who rallied to all my needs.
God bless you all.

ACKNOWLEDGEMENTS

TO MARK DOUGLAS WHO EDITED THIS BOOK.

TO SHEILA HEATH WHO PROOF READ IT.

TO MARK HEATH WHO TYPESET THIS BOOK
& DESIGNED THE DUST JACKET.

FOR YOUR HELP AND SINCERITY MY THANKS.

FOREWORD

THE STORY OF THE GREAT HUNGER WILL NEVER BE FULLY TOLD, FOR THERE ARE A THOUSAND STORIES YET TO BE TOLD OF THIS INJUSTICE.

STORIES THAT HAVE BEEN HANDED DOWN BY WORD OF MOUTH AROUND THE TURF FIRES OF IRELAND, THE CITIES OF BOSTON, NEW YORK, PHILADELPHIA AND ACROSS THE VAST PLAINS OF CANADA. THROUGH NEW ZEALAND AND THE EMPTY WASTES OF AUSTRALIA.

THE CRIES OF THE MILLIONS WHO DIED IN IRELAND'S GREATEST HOLOCAUST, THE GREAT HUNGER WILL ECHO FROM THE FOUR CORNERS OF THE EARTH.

MILLIONS OF IRISH MEN WOMEN AND CHILDREN DIED IN WHAT CAN ONLY BE DESCRIBED AS ETHNIC CLEANSING. THERE WAS NO FAMINE IN IRELAND JUST A GREAT HUNGER PERPETRATED ON THE PEOPLE BY AN INDIFFERENT UNCARING GOVERNMENT OF THE DAY.

MOST OF THE INCIDENTS OF THE GREAT HUNGER RELATED TO IN THIS STORY ARE AUTHENTIC. THE VICTIMS HAVE BEEN GIVEN FICTITIOUS NAMES AS NO INDIVIDUAL NAMES WERE EVER RECORDED. ONLY STATISTICAL RECORDS PRESERVE THEM FOR POSTERITY. IT IS TO THEM AND TO THEIR MEMORIES THAT I DEDICATE THIS BOOK.

In the early 20th century, a construction company by the name of **Messrs. Peto Brassey & Betts** were carrying out construction work on **Grosse Island**, situated in the **St. Lawrence** river, **Canada**. During their excavations they discovered many mass graves.

At first they were shocked and puzzled by their discovery. The truth soon emerged, for these were the remains of **Irish immigrants**. When fleeing from cruel landlords in Ireland and weakened by pestilence and hunger they found not hope, but a grave in Canada.

The text on the front cover are but a few of the inscriptions put over the graves by the
"Ancient Order of Hibernians of America"

It is midnight, but what is midnight?. it is neither to day nor is it to morrow, it is the time when the fairies are most vulnerable to the human, when they can be captured within that time lapse. But dare a mortal be so bold as to risk all in the hope of obtaining that elusive Crock of Gold. Once captured there is no escape from their underworld, the world of the undead.

The rowan, the hawthorn, the mistletoe and the yew, all magical trees that stand beside the cleansing waters of the crystal stream. They grow in the sacred places. Places made known to Anne Griffin by the Sideog Ri, the fairy king.

It was she and she alone who knew the secret ritual of the Crann Mor and the Crann Beag. It was she who could interpret the messages left by the Sideog Ri in the music of the babbling waters and it was she who invoked his help in time of need or when a pishogue had been inflicted on a person or their farm.

Anne Griffin lived in an age when such beliefs were common, respected and feared. On her death bed, she did not call on her Christian God to take her into his Paradise. No. She called on the Sideog Ri, for was it not the Sideog Ri who had spared her and her family from the Great Hunger, the evictions and the hangings. She left her earthly home on the stroke of midnight on Halloween the most sacred of all Celtic festivals.

This is a story from that period when

THE LAND OF IRELAND WEPT

Extracts from a letter written by Nicholas Cummins a well respected magistrate from Cork to the duke of Wellington and to the Times of London in December 1846; pleading for help. Regretfully without success...

My Lord Duke,

Without apology or preface, I presume so far to trespass on your grace as to state to you, and by use of your illustrious name, to present to the British public the following statement of what I myself have seen within the last three days. Having for many years been intimately connected with the westerly position of county Cork and possessing some small property there. I thought it right personally to investigate the truth of several lamentable accounts which have reached me, of the appalling state of misery to which that part of the country was reduced.

I accordingly went on the 15th inst; to Skibbereen, and to give the instance of one town land which I visited, as an example of the entire coast district, I shall state simply what there saw.

Being aware that I should have to witness scenes of frightful hunger, I provided myself with as much bread as five men could carry, and on reaching the spot I was surprised to find the wretched hamlet apparently deserted. I entered some of the hovels to ascertain the cause and the scenes which presented themselves were sure as no tongue or pen can convey the slightest idea of.

In the first, six famished and ghastly skeletons, to all appearances dead were huddled in a corner of some filthy straw, their sole covering what seemed a ragged horse cloth, their wretched legs hanging about them, naked above the knees.

I approached with horror, and found by a low moaning they were alive- they were in fever, four children, a woman and what had once been a man.

It is impossible to go through the details. Suffice to say, that in a few minutes I was surrounded by at least 200 such phantoms, such frightful spectres as no words can describe, either from famine or from fever.

Their demonic yells still ringing in my ears, their horrible images fixed upon my brain. My heart sickens at the recital but I must go on-

In another case, decency would forbid what follows but it must be told. My clothes were nearly torn off in my endeavour to escape from the throngs of pestilence around, when my neck cloth was seized from behind by a grip that compelled me to turn.

I found myself grasped by a woman with an infant just born in her arms and the remains of a filthy sack across her loins- the sole covering of herself and her baby. the same morning the police opened a house on the adjoining lands, which were observed shut for many days, and two frozen corpses were found, lying upon the mud floor, half devoured by rats.

A mother, herself in fever was seen the same day to drag out the corpse of her child, a girl of twelve, perfectly naked, and leave it half covered in stones.

Yet in another house within 500 yards of the cavalry station at Skibbereen, the dispensary doctor found seven wretches lying unable to move, under the same cloak. One had been dead many hours, but others were unable to move either themselves or the corpse

NICHOLAS CUMMINS [MAGISTRATE.]

SKIBBEREEN REPORT
NOVEMBER/DECEMBER
1846

To Mr HEWETSON (COMMISSARIAT) LIMERICK CITY.
WINTER 1845-46.

I saw three dead bodies in the street and buried them with the aid of the constabulary.

One hundred and ninety seven persons have died in the workhouse.

One hundred bodies have been found dead in lanes and derelict cabins half eaten by rats.

A woman wandering the streets begging for non-existent food and with a dead infant in her arms. She was unaware that it had died.

Guard of the mail found a father and three children lying dead by the road side.

Half of the children in the workhouse are now dead.

In a cabin was found a woman and her two children half eaten by dogs which we shot.

In a room in a cottage we discovered five corpses.

We found a room full of people, the husband still showing signs of life. His wife and two children, a boy and girl so it seemed, dead in the bed, while their starving cat had dragged the dead infant from the bed and was eating it on the floor.

These reports made no impact on Lord Trevlyan who suggested that they should look to their landlords who were bleeding the people dry for relief.

NO RELIEF SUPPLIES WERE EVER SENT TO SKIBBEREEN.

DOCUMENTED REPORT FROM
ELIHU BURRITT
AN AMERICAN PHILANTHROPIST WHO VISITED COUNTY
CORK IN 1847.

"I SAW MEN WORKING ON THE ROADS THEIR LIMBS WERE SWOLLEN TO TWICE THE SIZE OF THEIR BODIES. WE CAME ACROSS A BODY OF MEN SOME 500 IN ALL. THEY WERE NAKED AND WITHOUT SHAME AND STARVING. THEY STOOD PATIENTLY WAITING FOR THE SOUP TO BE DISTRIBUTED. A DOCTOR PRESENT NOTING MY SHOCK REMARKED....

" IN THREE TO FOUR WEEKS TIME NOT A SINGLE ONE OF THESE WILL BE ALIVE. WE SEE 50 DEAD BODIES OR MORE DAILY.

MANY WE DON'T SEE FOR THEY BRICK THEMSELVES AND THEIR FAMILIES UP IN THEIR CABINS. THERE THEY DIE TOGETHER WITH THEIR CHILDREN ASHAMED TO BE SEEN BY ANYONE.

SKIBBEREEN

Oh father dear, I've often heard you speak of Ireland
Her lofty peaks, her valleys green, her mountains rude and wild
They say it is a lovely land, where princes might dwell
But why did you abandon it, the reason to me tell

My son I loved my native land with energy and pride
'till a blight came over all our lands, and my sheep and cattle died
My rent and taxes were too high and I could not them redeem
Sure that's the cruel reason why I left old Skibbereen

'Tis well that I remember that bleak December day
When the landlord and the sheriff came to drive us all away
They set my thatch on fire with their cursed English Spleen
And when it fell the crash was heard all over Skibbereen

Your mother too, God rest her soul, fell dying in the snow
With poverty and desolation growing all around
She never rose, but passed away from life to mortal dream
And found a quiet grave me boy, in dear old Skibbereen

And you were only two years old and feeble was your frame
I could not leave you with my friends for you bore your fathers name
I wrapped you in my coat a more [big coat] and at the dead of night
I heaved a sigh and bid good bye to dear old Skibbereen.

Right well do I remember too that year of '98
When we arose with Erin's men to battle against fate
We were hunted through the mountains, as enemies to their Queen
And that's a very good reason why I left dear Skibbereen

Oh father dear the day will come in answer to our call
When Irishmen with hearts so stout, they'll rally one and all
I'll be the man to lead the band beneath our flag of green
And with hue and cry revenge we'll cry, remember Skibbereen.

Unknown I die; no tongue shall speak of me;
some noble spirit, judging by themselves,
may yet conjecture what I might have proved;
and think life only wanting to my fame.

Tragedy of Douglas

The Travels of Phelm Griffin During the Great Hunger

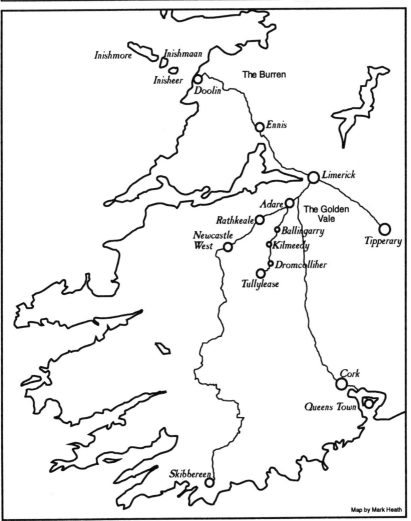

Inishmore

Inishmaan

Inisheer

Doolin

The Burren

Ennis

Limerick

Adare

The Golden Vale

Rathkeale

Ballingarry

Newcastle West

Kilmeedy

Tipperary

Dromcolliher

Tullylease

Cork

Queens Town

Skibbereen

Map by Mark Heath

Family and Home

This is the story of me, Phelm Griffin, and that of the thousands of Irishmen, women and children who are unable to tell their story. It is a story of survival that evokes both pathos and anger in turn. I write it hoping to exorcise the ghosts of the Great Hunger that still haunt my consciousness. The Ireland that I lived in has been obliterated from the pages of history. It is to right this injustice, that I tell my story......

My father, Patrick Griffin, was born and raised on a small farm in the village of Castlelurgan on the outskirts of Limerick city in the south west of Ireland. Mother often reminded me that he was a broth of a boy in his younger days.

There was no mistaking my father. He stood at least a foot above the tallest man and had the longest pair of legs this side of the Galtee Mor mountains. There was always that mischievous look about him. He had big bushy eye brows and a Cows Lick of a hair style. Mother was forever scolding him for the way he kept tossing it out of his eyes with a shake of his head.

"You're like a fisherman casting a line." She would chide him. She warned him on numerous occasions that she would cut it off him one day. She never did, and he retained it. Although in later years it was getting thin and grey.

I remember him as a big strapping man, who found little problem in hoisting and carrying a hundred weight sack of corn on his shoulder with ease. He was always ready with a laugh and a joke. Rarely did he take offence and when called upon to help a neighbour in need he was never found failing.

My mother, Anne O'Grady, was a real saint and the Belle of Castlelurgan.

She was a proud woman and walked with the haughty gait

1

of a Peacock. Her hair was as red as the sinking sun and just as striking. Her eyes were a deep blue and as searching as the waters of the river Shannon itself. There was something mystical about them, always searching, as if they were reading ones mind.

Father maintained that they were two crystal lakes that one could swim in. He was as proud of her as she was of him. It was said, that as sure as God made them he matched them. Mother had the gift given to her by the Sideog Ri and the Tuatha De Danann. It would be the brave one indeed to cross her path.

Up to the time of her demise, not that long ago, she still retained that rare Irish charm that endeared her to so many. I am conceited enough to think that my parents were perfect in every way. My thoughts are with them both as I put pen to paper.

Castlelurgan village is situated in the parish of St. John. It contains some two dozen cottages, occupied by tenant labourers. The cottages and the smallholdings belonged to Captain Singleton, late of the Coldstream guards, and were under persistent supervision of his bailiffs. It was their duty to collect the rates and taxes from the tenants on his behalf. They also had the sole right to evict any tenant together with his immediate family and possessions.

There are two churches, one Protestant and one Catholic and the ruins of a much older monastery. This was built by the monks of old and destroyed on the orders of King Henry of England. Its ruins are now used as a burial ground by the Catholics.

It is a typical Irish village full of warmth and yes the occasional upset.

It is there that my father, mother and grandparents are buried. The cottages are built of stone and wattle with thatched roofs. At the end of the village is a bridge that is patrolled regularly by the Royal Irish Constabulary.

Towering over the village on a hill is the rambling, now deserted mansion of the late captain. Its dark grey foreboding walls overshadow the village like the dead carcase of some monstrous parasite.

The high clock tower stands like a sentinel ringing out the

2

hours.

The huge bell, situated at the highest point in the tower, called the servants and labourers to and from their daily toil. My father was very proud of his house. Forever telling me that it had been built by his grandfather on his own lands.

"Why Phelm let me show you," he constantly reminded me. Crossing the floor to the old kitchen dresser, he would open the drawer and retrieve the family documents.

"Here it is. The written proof that this house and land is legally mine. Yours when we are both gone." The old hand written deed, tattered from constant inspection, together with its well thumbed plan would be produced.

"That was before the ancestors of Captain Singleton came and took it all without so much as a"How do you do."

He would continue to enlighten me as to how the house was erected.

"My grandfather with the help of his neighbours, God be good to them all, built every stone and sod in it with their own hands." He would tap the plan to emphasis its importance.

"They had to put in small windows if you must know, to avoid the window tax. Another curse put on us by England. It was better known as the"Typhus Tax" because the people used to develop the disease from the lack of light and air but granddad and his neighbours were no fools. Not so them. He would nod his head in that knowing way.

"They added the half door. Did I tell you that the idea came from them? This would allow light and air into the house and at the same time avoid the tax."

It was in my father's cottage that I was born in the year 1827 and it was to that same cottage that I took Shelia McNulty to meet my parents before she became my bride. My story really begins in the spring of 1845.

Spring comes to Castlelurgan

Anne looked down at the long neat drills of potatoes and noted that the young shoots were showing above ground.

She was pleased with what she saw. It was a good return for the labour of those long winter months spent in clearing and preparing the field ready for the planting. She herself had burnt many late candles cutting and preparing the seed and covering it in soot.

Now, thank God their labour would be rewarded, of this she was sure.

It was well worth the fine fat chicken she had given the Priest in payment to bless the setting of the crop. Not that her husband Pat was over zealous at her generosity and chided her for it.

This year she prayed that the crop would be successful. There had been shortages and hunger for the previous four years. Still they could not complain, in parts of the country the crop had failed completely.

There was no use in trying to chastise a merciful God, he was after all powerful and all seeing.

The men would have to cover the drills again to prevent a sudden ground frost from damaging the tender shoots.

"I would have thought that Phelm would have seen to it and not waited to be told." She remarked to herself.

Instinctively she covered a few of the buds with fresh earth. Turning her back on the field she went up through the long meadow and on towards the house. The men would soon be home expecting their meal to be on the table.

The hens were already there as well she knew they would be. Kicking a hullabaloo around her feet in noisy anticipation of their supper.

She shooed them away from her door, entered swiftly and closed the lower half behind her. The cacophony of sound rose as the insistent hens had by now been joined by the

4

hissing geese and the handful of ducks on the farm. Several hens took advantage of the open half door and settled themselves on the ledge forcing her to close the main door to deter them.

Picking up a wooden bucket from the back scullery, she half filled it with cold potatoes and scraps from the table. To this she added sour milk, bran and the contents of a pot of nettles she had collected and boiled the night before. Taking down the scrubbed pounder she reduced the contents to a mushy mash.

Returning to the door she opened it and was soon surrounded once again by hungry hens, geese and ducks. All in competition for their share of the bucket. Some of the hens flew on to the rim and tried to steal from it only to fall to the ground unable to keep their balance, as the bucket swung freely to and fro in Anne's hands.

Not content with feeding her own fowl she had also to contend with the jackdaws, crows and the occasional magpie, who would swoop down from the large chestnut tree.

She took a liking to the crows. They reminded her of the women of Limerick covered in their jet black shawls.

The magpies, well, they were nothing but thieving rogues. Yet they were God's creatures and were put on this earth for a purpose.

Going to a small green sward some distance from the house she spread the food in a long thin row on the grass. Hens geese and ducks fought and squabbled over the food.

The wild birds took every advantage to avail themselves of the feast on offer.

Leaving the poultry to their supper she crossed to the coup and collected the days egg production. Her hens had surpassed themselves.

She was more than pleased as she found the bucket slowly but surely filling with eggs. She still had to collect from the geese and ducks.

Her God was more than generous. The returns were ample proof, although her husband said that it was all in the mind. There would be enough for an egg for herself and two each for the boys. They needed all she could manage to sustain them now that the crops needed constant care.

"Why, she thought I'll go as far as to give them two each for supper with their gruel." She was in a generous mood as she continued to search every ditch and barn for any eggs laid by wayward clucking hens.

Not only did they have to sustain themselves from the income of the farm, they also had to pay rent and taxes to Captain Singleton, the usurper.

Although the farm rightly belonged to her husband's people for generations. It was seized and given to the Singleton's together with the village and surrounding lands as a reward for their loyal services rendered to the English during and after the siege of Limerick. Blood money Pat always called it, and rightly so. Were not his people butchered in their defence of their home and country.

Anne was using a pair of tongs to transfer the red hot turf from the fire to the lid of the griddle pot, when she heard her husband and son enter the kitchen.

"I've made a few soda scones, but I doubt if they are cool enough yet, this is the last one." She pointed with the tongs towards the oven sitting in the hot coals.

"Hot scones, my very own favourites." Phelm went across to the fireplace and took one from the griddle. Breaking it in half he blew on it to cool it before stuffing it into his mouth.

"God bless the work," Pat intoned as he removed his caubeen and hung it on the back of the door.

"Have you wet the sup of tae yet? I'm ravished." Phelm leaned over the table and made a grab for another of the hot scones. As usual he was thinking of his stomach and failed to spot his mother's ever-sharp tongs. All he received for his effort was a set of sore knuckles.

"It's more than ready, if you'll just be patient and let me finish putting the coals on the pot."

Taking the linen cloth containing the five hot eggs from the hob, she placed them on the table next to a scone of soda cake she had baked some time before. Some salted butter from her churn had been placed on a large cabbage leaf next to the jug of milk fresh from the family cow. The final offering was a scalding pot of sweet tea.

She looked down at her neat, well filled table and thanked her God silently for all the blessings he had bestowed on her

6

and her family.

She took her place at the table and waited for her husband to say grace before the meal.

Prayer's finished, Pat opened the linen cloth and looked at the five eggs.

"What's the occasion then, Anne! And why five eggs?" He studied her face.

"Oh sure, I thought that I would give you all a treat, seeing as the hens are so generous." She smiled in self satisfaction.

"Why five eggs when there are three of us?"

"I can only manage one, the rest are for you two. Now get on with it before they get cold."

Phelm wasted no time in cutting off a quarter of the large scone.

Breaking it in half he took a knife and smothered it in butter. It began to run down the sides of his mouth as he took a liberal bite.

"Did I tell you that the potatoes are shooting and will need covering as soon as possible? It was lucky I was down the long field and noticed them. I've never known them to shoot so early in the season." Anne informed her boys.

"Did you not take the very words out of my mouth? Why I was looking at them on my way up and you are right, they do need a covering. Pray God we don't get a frost this night." Her husband agreed with her.

She smiled, 'so at times he does call on God to help him,' thinking of how he chided her over the blessing from the Priest.

"We have to go to Limerick tomorrow with the heifers for the mart. By the time we get home we will have lost the light," Pat scratched his head.

"Look here, if you could manage the heifers, I could bank up the spuds no bother on my own." Phelm told his father.

"No! There is no way that I could manage the pair of them. Why the road will be filled with sheep and cattle and all sorts. That rhone heifer would try the patience of St. Francis himself."

"Wouldn't Tady Quin give you a day? I could let him have a dozen eggs and a slice of the salted pig," offered Anne.

"Do you know that's a grand idea make no mistake. Sure

7

they could do with all the help they can get. What with the bailiffs evicting them from their cottage and they hungry along with their other problems.

"Phelm! away you go after supper and do the calling."

About an hour later, Phelm made his way to the rough booley erected by Tady at the side of the road.

"Tady, if you are not too busy would you ever help himself with the drive to Limerick, we'll see you alright."

"Phelm, your family were always good to us and I'll be only too willing to help."

"Thanks Tady we'll be beholden to you. Will you call and see himself in the morning?"

"I will to be sure, I'm sorry Phelm that I cannot be more sociable and ask you in, but....." Tady looked away as a lump built up in his throat.

"There's little need for an honest man to apologise, Tady, it's well we understand." Phelm took his hand and held it tight. "Don't worry Tady, your day will come. Of that have no doubt."

A day at the Fair

There was a frost in the air when Anne rose early next morning to prepare breakfast for the three men. Ignoring the fire, her poultry, even her bare feet she opened the door and ran down to the long meadow as fast as she could. Terrified that the frost may have affected the potatoes, she could only hope and pray in gasps as she stumbled her way to the field. Breathless, she sank to her knees and examined the tender shoots of first one and then another. The crop, it appeared, had been spared. There was relief in her voice as she prayed her thanks to God and gently caressed them.

Making her weary way back from the field, she opened the coop door and was greeted by the babble and bustle of the hens as they rushed out and followed her to the house.

Returning from the scullery with her bucket she made quick work of feeding them before turning her attention to the fire and the preparation of the breakfast.

As the big iron kettle came to the boil she placed six eggs inside and replaced the lid. Only then did she go to the bedroom and awakened her husband.

She heard Phelm moving around in his room.

"So you are awake then." She called as she passed the door. Returning to the kitchen she looked across at the half door and saw the tall, gangly, red haired figure of Tady, ash plant in his hand, coming across the field.

"Good morning mam," he called."God bless the house. Is himself ready?" Tady was his usual good humoured self with that jovial smile that said it all.

"Will you come in and sit yourself down and rest, it's a long drive to Limerick." Anne greeted him as she continued with her preparation of the breakfast.

"The roads are full. You didn't mind me taking the short cut over your meadow?" Tady asked as he made his way through the half door into the kitchen.

"Sure the meadow will be there long after you and I have

passed on Tady. Will you have a bite of breakfast?

"That's more than generous of you, I brought a bite to stave off the hunger in the city." He produced a small linen cloth with a hunk of cake in the centre.

Anne looked at the meagre meal. She knew that his wife had sacrificed her own breakfast to let him have it.

"My! but you are the early bird." Pat entered the kitchen.

Going to the fire he tipped hot water from the kettle into his shaving mug and motioned to the scullery.

"I'll just have a quick scrape of the razor."

Anne set the table and called on her boys to come and eat the meal before it got cold.

"Will you sit down and eat Tady, you're making the place look untidy," Anne laughed, gently pushing the big man towards the table.

"That's more than generous now, but if you don't be minding I had a belly full of good porridge oats earlier." He rubbed his stomach.

"Will you sit down man and not insult the table. Sure a sup of tae and an egg never hurt anyone," Pat entered the kitchen rubbing his face with the towel.

Phelm came from his room, his mouth wide open as he scratched and yawned.

"Will you look at yourself? Anyone would think that you were up all night," His mother scolded.

"Now make sure you all eat enough, you'll not be getting much in Limerick, I have no doubt."

Leaving the men to get on with their breakfast, she took a linen bag from the dresser and began to fill it with home made scone, eggs and a generous helping of boiled bacon. Taking a tin can, she scalded it and filled it with sweet tea. She replaced the lid and put it inside a woollen sock to keep it warm.

"That should keep the hunger off you both," she placed the bag and can on the table in front of her husband.

Pat rose from the table and picked up the bag and slung it over his shoulder. Tady picked up the can of tea.

Anne placed herself between the two men and the half door.

"Now before you go, I don't want to hear of you getting into any trouble in the city. If you must have a drink, then for

God's sake go to a respectable hotel." All three managed to look suitably humble as with a smile she let them past. At the door Pat paused and took the holy water, followed by Tady. Picking up their ash plants they left the house.

Phelm, true to his word, undertook the covering of the potato drills. He had the task completed by the time that his father and Tady returned from Limerick.

Anne, for her part, had succeeded in covering her small patch of potatoes in her kitchen garden. The potato crop was now safe from any late frost that might occur.

On entering the city, Pat and Tady made their way to the centre and found an unoccupied corner near to where the market was in full progress. There they hemmed the two heifers and awaited for potential buyers.

Pat lit his pipe and sat on the sill of the building. Tady pitched stones into the nearest puddle of water.

"Here Tady, try a handful of this in your pipe, it's not the best. Still it is a good drag." Pat got up from his seat and handed Tady his tobacco pouch.

"Thanks Pat, that's more than decent of you." He reached into his coat pocket and removed his pipe.

Together the two men sat on the sill, sending wafts of blue smoke skywards. A few minutes into their pipes a gnarled, stumpy figure came on the scene and began to look the two heifers over. Dressed in his high hat and coatamore, he handled the cattle with a practised feel.

"Are these two for sale by any stretch of the imagination?" He asked removing the almost obligatory clay pipe.

"If we can agree on a price, then they are," Pat replied amiably.

"Hmm, I see." He walked round and round the two animals, once more examining them closely. He looked at their feet, then at their flanks, he even lifted their tails. Finally he looked them straight in the eyes before he crossed the road and again studied them from a distance.

Tady leaning on his ash plant looked at Pat and spat on the ground.

"I'll tell you this Pat Griffin, there's one man looking for a bargain."

"What did you say you were asking for the pair?" The

potential buyer called as he crossed the road.

"I'm not asking at the moment. What kind of offer had you in mind?"

"Well now, I was thinking of their worth to me." The buyer scratched the stubble on his chin and looked to Heaven for guidance.

"Tell you what. I'll take the pair off your hands and let you get home. Eight guineas and not one penny more, and I'd be looking for a luck penny at that." With that he gave the rhone heifer a belt on the rump that made her jump.

"Eight guineas did I hear? No! I'll not be taking up your time." Pat turned his back and returned to his seat on the sill. The potential buyer shrugged and walked away.

"He'll be back Tady, have no doubt. He liked the looks of them," Pat looked after the man.

"Course he will, sure they are the best that I have seen today."

The day wore on and several other bidders came forward to haggle over the heifers, but Pat wanted to test the waters first as he said.

Finally the original stumpy figure returned with a deal maker and approached Pat. The bidder took Pat's hand and that of the potential buyer and held them together.

"Eleven guineas, and that's a fair price, shake on it." Pat eyed the buyer but once more refused to accept the offer.

"What price then are you willing to agree on?" asked the deal maker.

"I'll take seven guineas for the rhone and eight for the other." The buyer snatched his hand from the deal maker's,"Ah come on now man, be sensible. Sure there is not a beast in the market worth that. Will you tell your friend to have some sense? Sure I'd be the laughing stock of the country if I paid that," the buyer looked to Tady.

"Tell you what," the deal maker interrupted,"I'll not leave you both until you settle. Make it twelve guineas for them both and we have a deal," Once more he grabbed both their hands and tried to make them shake.

Pat calmly removed his wrist from the deal maker's grasp, turned his back on both the buyer and the deal maker and walked away.

This show of defiance did not deter either the buyer or the deal maker in any way. They both moved past Pat and blocked his way. Once again they upped the offer.

"Now I want no shenanigan. Come here both of you." Once again the deal maker grabbed their right hands.

"The deal is this, twelve and a half guineas and we'll forget the luck penny." He was no more successful this time than last. The buyer cracked.

"Damn but if this isn't the most stubborn deal I've had to suffer this day. Fourteen guineas then and not a brass farthing more."

Pat looked at Tady and smiled."Take them and good luck to you." He spat on his hand and offered it to the buyer.

The deal was now struck. The buyer counted out the money. Pat took the money and returned a half sovereign to him.

"There is no need for that," said the deal maker intervening. "The deal was made without the luck penny."

"Let it not be said that Pat Griffin ever reneged on the luck penny. Good day to you both." Pat pressed the coin into the buyer's hand.

"Come on Tady. We'll bid you both good day, may the sun shine on your faces and the rain be to your backs." Putting their ash plants under their arms they made their way to the nearest alehouse.

The familiar sounds of crunching footsteps and banging doors announced Pat and Tady's return.

"How was it then?" Anne asked as she came out of the scullery. Pat had a sack of flour on his shoulder. Tady had another containing the rest of the days' purchases.

"You'll be the proud woman to have married such a fine man", boomed the big man."I made a bargain that would be the envy of the village if I told them," Pat managed to drop the sack in a corner and reached into his pocket.

"Open your apron woman."

Anne giggled and taking the hem of her apron held it out in delighted anticipation.

Pat let the sovereigns trickle slowly from his hand into her apron.

"There now, add them to the nest egg." Pat went to the fireplace and removing a glowing piece of turf lit his pipe.

"Things are not all that good if I may say so, are they Tady?"
Pat's voice took on a more sombre tone and catching his tone
Tady laid the sack on the table and nodded his head in sad
agreement.

"On the way we saw many more cottages abandoned and
tumbled. We were told that the bailiffs had evicted the
occupants for non-payment, poor souls. I have no doubt that
it will be the open highway, or if lucky then the emigrant
ship for most of them and their young families, God be good
to them."

"You call that luck? God help them."

Anne listened to her husband tell of the state he had found
their country to be in, all the while watching Tady and his
reactions. She made a half pleading, concerned gesture to her
husband as Tady hunched over the sack on the table. Pat
stopped his observations in mid flight and was immediately
contrite at his own thoughtlessness towards his friend.

"Sorry Tady, we got carried away, selfishness would you say,"
Pat laid his hand on Tady's shoulder apologetically.

"Oh, don't you go bothering yourself with that It's common
knowledge that I am on the highway with little shelter, sure
you meant no offence now."

"Of course not and none taken I'm sure." Tady managed a
smile at his old friend but the slump of his shoulders told Pat
the true story of his plight.

"Sit down you two, you must be ravenous with the hunger."
Anne broke the uncomfortable silence and motioned the two
men to the table. She went to the hob and wet the tea, calling
Phelm as she did so.

"Tady will you tell Anne about that drover from Clare, now
there was a character." Pat clumsily changed the painful
subject.

Tea was spent recalling the day's bargains and successes.
Anne and Phelm listened as the two men took turns to
recount the characters and events of the day.

"You know Anne how the market works, the best of the
animals are bought up by the end of the day."

"Is this the tale about the drover"? Anne interrupted.

"The very same." Tady continued eating as he related his
story.

"Well this old drover, a well know character. Somehow he got hold of an old dried up milch cow. In all probability the farmer gave it to him in payment for the drive. Shure the poor creature was so weak that it had to lean against the wall to stand up.

A knacker from the city came across and looked over the dozing animal and then at the drover.

"I'll tell you what I'll do for you. I'll give you a sovereign for her and put her out of her agony."

"She is not for sale but I would be willing to give her to you for nothing if you give me three sovereigns." The drover replied without a bat of an eyelid.

"Three sovereigns is it. Sure she's nothing but a cripple."

" A cripple did you say and you in ear shot of her. An insult to a fine beast. She walked all the way from Parteen, if you must know."

"She may have walked all that way but I doubt if she will walk from the market." The knacker remarked as he walked away.

"What happened then."

"Sure we don't know, do we Pat? We left them arguing."

Tea finished, the three men adjourned to the hearth, Pat claiming his sugan chair by the roaring turf fire.

"There's always a warm welcome in this house, God bless it and all its occupants," Tady reached into his pocket and withdrew his half clay pipe.

"Mind if I have a drag or two?" He showed the pipe over his shoulder to Anne.

"Will you not be troubling Anne with such niceties. Sure if it makes you feel better I'll join you myself." Pat took his pipe from the mantle piece. Reaching into the grate, he removed a smouldering kindling and lit his pipe before passing it on to Tady.

The two older men chatted away about the Hunger and reminisced on better times, whilst Phelm was gradually lulled to sleep by the warmth and the voices. Later, Anne brought them three hot mugs of broth.

"Ah! God bless you Anne Griffin. Sure I always said it, you are a real angel bless you," Tady reached out for the cup.

"Tady, I'll say this for you, you have more blarney than the

15

Blarney stone itself," She laughed, delighted with the compliment.

The eight day clock on the wall struck out the hour of eleven. Tady looked up at the brass pendulum as it swung to and fro.

"Is that the time Pat? Sure am I not an awful blackguard, keeping decent folks from their beds so I am?"

"Finish your broth like a good man, sure there is no wedding haste." Pat assured him.

A half mug of broth and some more idle chat later, Tady made ready to leave.

"I'll be off now Pat. Should you need me again, feel no compliment in the asking for sure." Tady rose from the chair and going towards the door collected his cap.

"Don't forget your parcel Tady. I left it on the table for you," Anne came in from the scullery, picked the packet from the table and pressed it into Tady's arms.

"Thanks for everything Tady, we'll be beholding to you."

Pat went to the door and taking Tady's hand shook it warmly.

"Ah sure are you not the awful spalpeen, Pat Griffin, but I'll not be insulting you by refusing. It is more than generous of you, a decent man you are at that. There is no denying it but you and Anne have made your bed in Heaven. I'll be making the indulgence for you, not that you need them."

Struggling with his parcel, Tady continued his rhetoric as he opened his palm and looked at the two sovereigns sitting in the palm of his hand. Tears of gratitude welled up in his eyes in appreciation of their kindness.

"Will you forget it man, what are friends for?" Pat tapped him on the shoulder. Opening the door for him Pat watched as Tady made his way across the hillock.

"I'll leave the door open to light your way," Pat called after him.

He watched as Tady raised his stick in final salutation before disappearing below the brow of the hill.

"Is he gone Pat, did you see him alright?"

"Yes, for sure. I feel such a fool, bringing up such a painful subject. I could bite that blubbering tongue of mine so I could." Pat was all remorse for his earlier remarks about the

16

evictions.

"Don't you worry about it. Yarrah! it was only a slip of the tongue, no harm done and none taken I'm sure. He was more than grateful for the few sovereigns and the food." Anne reassured him.

"We had more than a good bargain with the heifers, and what with the showing of the potatoes, we should be well able to pay our rent and taxes and have a bit over." He was more than pleased with his day in Limerick.

"I hope that you won't be bragging about our good fortune, you know what the bailiffs are like. If they get a smell of any extra money, then they'll want it," Anne warned.

"There's little fear of that Anne love. I'll be like our parish Priest and put on the poor mouth, how about that?" He laughed as he saw the grimace on his wife's face.

Going over to her he put his arms round her waist. "Sure I was only joking love," then he kissed her on the cheek.

"Let go you silly old fool, I know that." She cuffed him gently with the dish cloth she had in her hand.

Phelm, waking from his doze began to rise and make for his bed. Smiling coyly at her husband Anne called to her son.

"Phelm, in all the excitement I forgot to tell you that Mary Welsh called to see you, what's it all about?" She asked innocuously.

She had hoped that he would divulge the reason as to why the matchmaker had called. Intrigued, Pat watched as his son entered his room.

"It's nothing for you to concern yourself with, I'll go and see her myself next evening," he mumbled.

Whatever it was about he was keeping it close to his chest.

Strangers in the Bog

Phelm finished his chores early next evening and hurried through his supper. Having had a quick wash he emerged from his room dressed in his Sunday clothes.

"I'm going over to Mary's place this evening and I'll take the broken slan to the forge on my way," Phelm told his father avoiding the questioning glances from his mother.

"That's a good idea, we'll need both of them for the bog." His father was by now relaxing in the sugan chair, his clay pipe stuck in the side of his mouth.

Phelm left the house and retrieved the broken slan, before making his way across the small hillock to the village.

"Do you think there is something he is not telling us?" Anne asked.

"Look woman, it's best that we leave well alone. He'll tell us all in his own good time."

"I wonder who she is? Do we know her?"

"Know who? Will you let it be." Pat fidgeted in his chair, avoiding his wife's gaze.

"What makes you think that it is a girl anyway?" he asked.

"Will you not be so blind Pat Griffin. Why else would he be dressed up to the nine pins in his Sunday best?"

"Well whatever it is, we had best let him tell us in his own time. Now remember, leave it be woman."

Leaving the slan at the forge, Phelm made his way to the home of the Welsh family.

Opening the door, he entered the kitchen where Mary and her husband sat before a roaring turf fire.

"God bless all here," Phelm sauntered across the kitchen floor and turned his back to the fire. Rubbing his hands across his buttocks he began to appreciate the warmth of its heat.

"Good evening Phelm." Mary's knowing glance barely hid a suppressed smile. She had obviously expected his visit.

"I was over to your place yesterday afternoon, I suspect that is why you called, fancy a sup of tae?"

Without waiting for his reply she went to the dresser and

taking down a cup filled it with tea from the pot.

"Mother told me, I'm glad that you didn't tell them too much for now." Phelm tried to assume an air of casual interest.

"What did Shelia's parents say anyway?" Mary's grin got larger.

"I done my best for you as you asked, but her parents feel that she is a bit young as yet. If you wait till the harvest they will again keep you in mind. It looks good for you Phelm Griffin, so be patient." Mary smiled her assurance.

Phelm had the distinct impression that Mary wasn't telling him everything. He felt sure that the old matchmaker derived most of her pleasure these days in the pleasant torture of withheld information. He couldn't help himself, he had to know more.

"Do they think me a good match then?" Phelm turned and began a careful study of the front door. Mary caught his almost pleading tone; his desire for the forbidden fruit of knowledge mixed with the desire for his Eve.

"A good match? Why I'd marry you myself tomorrow were it not for Tom there."

"You can have her and more than welcome. Why I'd even throw in a luck penny, the Lord knows you'd need it," her husband laughed.

"Ah, weren't you the lucky man to get me and no mistake," Mary waggled her stumpy finger at her husband. Phelm stood apart whilst Mary and her husband continued their own good natured banter. Eventually, he made his excuses and left the pair. As he made his way through the door he could still hear the dying echoes of the good natured banter. Judging by her joyful tone he guessed that Mary had won, not for the first time. Phelm left the house far more confident and happy than he had been when he arrived.

Returning across the hillock, he collected the slan from the forge and made his way home.

His parents had long since retired to bed by the time he arrived at the house. Taking a poker from the side of the grate, he poked life into the fire before adding a sod or two from the creel.

Using a taper, he lit the candle and went to the scullery. He removed the cloth from the milk churn and filled a mug from the contents.

Sitting contented in his fathers sugan chair, he removed his clay pipe from the mantle piece and filled it with tobacco, lighting it he relaxed before the fire.

He knew that his mother was curious as to his visit to Mary Welsh. She was no fool his mother, and would put two and two together and realise that he had not gone to the matchmaker for nothing. He would have to tell them sometime but not just yet.

Next morning Phelm was up bright and early. He needed to be for his parents were now getting on in years and needed his strength and energy on the farm.

The weather was still holding good and the potato shoots were again showing above the soil. A good sign and the promise of a healthy harvest.

The oats in the three acre field were fattening and moving like a gentle sea in the fresh morning breeze of that early summer.

Phelm leant on the gate, looking over the field of oats. He again reflected on his life. God had been good to him and his parents.

September would not be that long in coming. Then he could approach Mary and remind her to mediate once again on his behalf, for the hand of Shelia McNulty.

"Good morning." His father's voice interrupted his day dreaming.

"Your mother sent me to find you, your tae will be getting cold."

Breakfast was a somewhat muted affair. Phelm gave the food his complete attention, shutting everything else out. As a consequence he missed a whole unspoken conversation between his parents, his concentration only being broken by his mother's repeated attempts to pour him more tae.

Phelm's reticence was not entirely due to his reluctance to speak of his visit the previous night. A day's turf cutting was something that he had to work himself up to. Many tasks were necessary on the farm and Phelm could, at worst, plod his way through them. But his own personal hate was a day spent in the bogs cutting that damned turf.

Breakfast over, they went to the barn and collected the two

slans and wended their way up the road towards the communal bog. On their way they met other neighbours bent on the same task.

The common bog was the property of Captain Singleton, like everything else in the area. Each family was allowed a limited cutting once each year and no family was allowed more than two cutters in the bog at any one time.

Widows and families unable to do their own cutting had to depend on the generosity of their neighbours.

Although there were many families on the bog most spring days, it was still a lonely and mysterious place. Passing through it in the dusk one was bound to meet"Jack O lantern", the keeper of the bog. The fact is that Jack is no more than a cloud of bog gas that rises from the depths of the bog and floats freely. A glorious sight to watch yet to the superstitious people it had supernatural powers.

In the early morning with limited vision, a man depended a great deal upon his sense of hearing. One could hear the call of the Fox going back to his lair from his night of destructive carnage. The lonesome shriek from the Snipe, forever calling to his mate. The sheep like bleat of the Jacksnipe and the cry from the Curlew, not forgetting the Frogs with their dawn chorus. These eerie sounds encouraged the cutters to whisper as no one wanted to have their talk overheard by Jack, who might still be lurking in the mist. As the early morning sun burnt off the mist, so the conversation rose in volume and tempo.

The bog was a wonderful place to think and meditate. A place where history remains buried until one of the sleadoirs inadvertently disturbs its resting place.

Something would always be uncovered. Sometimes it was the body of some long forgotten chieftain or more often, no more than a long forgotten box of butter. The bog preserved all until it was disturbed.

Pat Griffin was one of the best turf cutters in the county and nobody could ever call him a clod hopper. The area that Pat rented was lowland, flat bog. Consequently, he could cut that much more turf compared to the upland bog which was slow and narrow cutting.

Phelm and his father spent most of the morning cutting and

throwing sods on the bank for drying. The blacksmith had done a first class job on the slan. The new ash handle suited Phelm, he was cutting through the sods like a knife through hot butter.

His father lent on his slan admiring the speed at which his son worked.

"Phelm, I only wish that I had the strength to match you, but the years are telling and that's for sure." He resumed pitching the sods on the bank at his own pace.

Around midday, Anne came on the bog with the more than welcome meal and together as a family they sat and ate. The meal over and grace said, they began to spread the cut sods for drying.

Anne went to the edge of the cutting and looked over the edge into the bog.

"What are you looking for there? We did not find the crock of gold yet," Pat laughed.

It was believed that the fairies kept several crocks of gold hidden deep within the bog. Should a sleadoir happen upon one then it became his property.

"Laugh you may but I was making sure that you did not bring the curse of St Columcille down on us."

It was said that as St Columcille was crossing the bog he fell into a bog hole and was trapped all night. He was not rescued until next day when a passing cutter saw his plight. Subsequently he put a curse on any sleadoir, who failed to cut three escape steps for any unwary traveller, unfortunate enough to fall into the hole to escape. The three steps would also remind the cutter of the three divine person in the blessed Trinity.

The Irish saints were forever putting curses on the people and their towns. No county got more curses than Limerick did.

Father and son stood several sods upright and placed them against each other. More sods were placed on the top to support the small pile.

The piles grew and looked like miniature beds of Diarmid and Grainne beds or megalithic tombs or Dolmens. These are the burial places of prehistoric Irish people and are found throughout the country.

The forming of the coirceogs was left to Anne whilst the men continued cutting and footing.

There the sods would be left to dry throughout the summer, the winds whistling through the piles. In the autumn the dried sods would be put in creels and carried on the backs of the men down to the house. Others, more fortunate than Pat's family would use a donkey to transport the backbreaking creels. The donkey would also be able to manage two creels placed pannier style on its back. One good cutting would be more than adequate to see the fire kept burning for the full year.

There were days when the weather was poor and the cutting had to be postponed for another day.

However, this year the weather had held and no such problems had occurred. The cutting and the stacking had gone well and there would be some time to help a neighbour or a widow woman struggling with theirs.

There were those who could not afford the price of a cutting and would come to the bog begging for the fum. This was the first cutting to open the bog and was a poor substitute for turf. It being mostly reed grass with a thin layer of poor quality turf underneath. Still it kept the hovel warm during the long cold winter nights.

On the road home the bog cutters tired wet and weary, Pat and Phelm in their midst, were confronted by a mounted detachment of Red Coats. It was most unusual to see them so far away from the city. More so on an old bog road which was of little importance. Their presence became the immediate subject of a lot of speculation and gossip.

"There must be a good reason for them fellows to be out here so far." Pat remarked, removing the pipe from his mouth.

"I don't care much for the bastards," whispered Phelm vehemently.

"They never done us a good turn and that's for sure. It's the landlord sent for them, of that I have little doubt." Phelm looked across at the mansion silhouetted against the evening sun.

"I hear that the Ribbon men or Whiteboys, whatever they are called now, are active again in the area. I thought that they had died out in the 20's." Pat glanced around, assuring himself that there was nobody within hearing distance.

The news soon spread that the Red Coat's were in the area and it was not too long before the reason for their presence became local gossip.

Captain Singleton, had ordered that a widow woman and her children were to be evicted for non-payment of rent and taxes. Her home was to be put to the spleen.

Whenever the bailiffs went to carry out this duty, they were met by the ribbon men armed with cudgels and makeshift pikes.

Storage barns outside the protection of the walls of the estate were set alight nightly. This rebellious conduct was a threat to the landlord and to all the other landlords and had to be eliminated.

Such defiance of the law would not be tolerated in British territory.

Notices were posted on each and every door in the village warning the occupants of the dire consequences to any giving shelter to the ribbon men. Anyone giving help to them or failing to inform on them would find themselves before a summary trial after which they would be taken to Limerick and hanged on the gallows green. Then their homes would be given to others or put to the spleen.

Much as the ribbon men tried to protect the innocent people they were no match for the forces of the crown.

Eventually the bailiffs were successful, as usual, in evicting the widow and her family and putting the house to the torch. There was nothing that the people could do to help the widow and her family. Should anyone be bold enough to offer her and her family shelter, even for one night, then they too would be evicted.

The widow was left with little choice but to take to the road and beg sanctuary in the workhouse.

Anne counts her dowry

It was a few days later as Phelm and his father were attending to the potato crop, that they saw a stranger coming over the hillock. Both men stopped what they were doing and shading their eyes looked to see who was trespassing on their land.

As the man came nearer they saw that it was non other than Joseph O'Brien. Joseph was a distant cousin from West Clare. If he had come via the bridge at Avondoun he was a long way from home.

"Well Joe, we haven't seen you since the day that cousin Mick was married. What brings you here?" Pat reached out his hand to greet him.

"Anne said you were out in the fields, and I had to go to Limerick anyhow, so I called to see you all."

"You're more than welcome Joe, come on up to the house and tell us all the news."

Phelm, glad of any excuse for a respite from the back-breaking work, quietly followed.

At the house, Anne wasted no time at all wetting the sup of tae and buttering the scones. Soon what news there was had been conveyed and the conversation neared exhaustion. It was then that Joe exploded the bombshell.

"Did you know that there is sign of a blight in my county? It is causing many the anxious glance at the potatoes I can tell you," Joe told them.

"Oh Blessed Jesus!" Anne whirled to face her husband.

"Are they sure that it is the blight? Sure we would have noticed any sign and we working most of the day weeding the spuds." Phelm's voice took on a pleading tone. He looked as if he had seen a ghost.

"Now I don't wish to be the bringer of bad tidings, but I thought, well Delia thought, that it best I tell you."

"No, you done the right thing. There is no need to feel upset, and we are grateful," Pat assured Joe.

We'll go down the field now and make a thorough inspection of every leaf and stem." Pat rose from the table.

"Will you not finish your tae first?" Anne asked.

"No, sure the cake would stick in my craw, I must make sure."

"I'll come with you," offered Joe.

The three men left the house and went down to the potato field.

Phelm started at the right hand of the field, his father at the left and Joe went to the lower end of the field. An hour of careful searching proved fruitless. They found no sign of the dreaded blight.

"There's no sign, thank God," Pat assured them after the inspection.

"Amen to that Pat. But keep your eyes open. You know how quick it strikes." Joseph warned as the men left the field.

Phelm looked back over his shoulder at the potato flower swaying gently in the breeze. He was apprehensive. He knew that blight had no respect for boundaries. It could appear overnight like the fairy stools and devastate the whole crop, as it had in his father's and grandfather's time. Should it strike, and heaven forbid that it should, would they be able to weather it as had granddad?

The following morning, Joe began his long journey home leaving his relatives to worry as to the outcome of their crop. Unlike Phelm, who ate ravenously as usual, Pat toyed with his breakfast.

Anne could not help but notice the worried frown on his face as his fork weeded and hoed his food. He was not chatting about the days work and the plans for that day as he usually did.

"Pat! I know that you are worried, but did not Joe tell you that it might not be the blight, there's no certainty."

"You're right of course, everything is fine. Did we not prove that, Phelm?" He looked across at his son for reassurance. However, his tone of voice spoke far more eloquently of his true feelings.

"Will you not be trying to convince yourself that all is well. Did we not make sure, what more do you want? Now eat your breakfast and leave well be." Phelm, like his father, was struggling to impart confidence in those present. He returned to clearing his plate.

"Take no notice of me, it's just that I'm under the weather."

"Pat Griffin, how many years have I known you? Under the weather my foot! Come on now, a worry shared is a worry spared." Anne took his cup and filled it with warm tea.

"What will we do if it does get this far?" Pat voiced the nightmare that haunted them all.

"Once and for all will you stop worrying about the potatoes! If the blight does come, and God forbid that it should, then it will be too late. The crop will be saved and that's that." Anne in her frustration banged the cup on the table.

Despite the encouraging words, Anne knew in her heart and soul that it would not be that simple. Should the blight strike it wouldn't matter what state of growth they were in, the crop would be useless.

"I suppose you are right. Anyhow I had a good look at the oats and they are doing well, thank God." Pat's melancholia seemed to lift somewhat much to the relief everyone.

Yet deep down they all worried and feared that the blight was too near home not to worry.

Spring gave way to early summer, the worry over the potato crop had come and gone.

Anne stood looking over the crop. Where in the spring she had seen the drills and the budding stalks, now there appeared the purple and white flowers of the potato. Another six weeks or so and the leaves and stalks would die to denote that the crop was ready to harvest. There was no further talk of the suspected blight in County Clare.

Phelm went to see Mary Welsh to remind her of her obligation to put his proposal to the parents of Sheila McNulty. She had not forgotten she assured him. How could she? Every time he passed her door he pestered her on the subject.

Phelm's mother knew that something was afoot and suspected that he had gone above her head and been to the matchmaker himself. She had thought of all the eligible girls in the district and in her mind's eye tried to find the one most suitable for her son.

It was a situation close to her own heart. She often

reminisced of the day she eavesdropped on the matter of her betrothal to her Pat. When the matchmaker came to her parent's door pleading for her hand to be placed in that of Pat's. Not that she minded really, for had she not a secret crush on him long before they met?

Did she not secretly watch him from behind the hawthorn hedge, not once but time and time again? He swinging his scythe through the meadow grass. To make matters even worse she never uttered a word of it in her confession, much to her shame.

There had also been the envy that she had felt when the other girls, prettier than her she thought, looked shyly at him as he sat on the threshold stone of his father's cottage.

"Will you not be such an old nincompoop," she chided herself. Though she still let slip that beguiling smile of hers, as she recalled the events leading up to her own wedding.

They had been blessed with only the one child, her son Phelm and what a treasure he turned out to be.

The salt of the earth and a credit to them both. They could hold their heads high with their chick.

Whilst God in his infinite wisdom had denied them a large family, he had amply compensated them with Phelm.

He would make a fine husband for any girl, and her dowry would be little compensation in return. She would be that much richer getting her son.

In her mind's eye she saw him and his shy bride cross the threshold of the old house and bring new life into the hearth. Crossing the floor she closed and bolted the door. Returning to the scullery she moved the salting barrel to one side.

Lifting a loose slab she removed a tin box from the recess below. Opening the lid she spilled the contents on to the table.

There were thirty seven sovereigns and a sheet of parchment in the box.

Some of the coins were part of her dowry, given to her by her grandmother on the day of her nuptials. The rest she had saved in the good years.

Like her mother, and her mother before her, Anne was one prudent woman. Pat knew nothing of her little hoard and she had no intention of telling him.

She counted all thirty seven sovereigns into her hand. She would have had thirty nine but she gave two to the Parish Priest for him blessing the crop.

Pat's mother had passed away some two years before her own marriage, God give her peace. His father was little more than a cripple in the ashes and half blind then, no disrespect to the souls of them both.

Pat's father died shortly after that and was buried beside his wife by them both under the old yew tree that grew down by the stream.

There they both rested. With nothing but the babbling brook and the singing of the birds to disturb their long sleep. No better and no worse than burying a dog. That would not happen to her and her Pat.

She had bought the rights to be buried inside the consecrated ruins of the old monastery, in a spot where she knew the high altar once stood and where the feet of the saintly monks walked and where they knelt in adoration to her God.

She made sure that there would be no mistaking the plot she had bought. She went all the way to Limerick to have it noted, witnessed and signed both by a solicitor and the priest himself. That document would remain in the box until God in his mercy decided to call one or both of them to his heavenly mansion.

When their time on earth elapsed they would lie together, proud and unashamed, where all going to and from the church could look and remember them, and of their charity would say an Ave Dei for their souls. Sure no God fearing Christian would leave the Holy Souls hungry for a prayer.

"There lie Pat and Anne Griffin, no finer pair lived in this parish, God grant them both rest," Anne predicted.

There would be a cross of the finest Connemara marble at the head of the grave with their names carved deep into it and outlined in lead.

If they could not own enough of their own soil in their own native land to make a living on, then they would own the little plot below the gable end of the monastery.

Having carefully stacked the coins she removed the deed to the plot from the box, and again read it's message.....

THIS DEED AND DOCUMENT WITNESSED BEFORE ME DO

CONVEY TO ONE ANNE GRIFFIN OF THE PARISH OF SAINT JOHN IN THE BARONY OF HOSPITAL IN THE COUNTY OF LIMERICK. ALL THAT PIECE OF LAND IN THE GRAVEYARD OF SAINT JOHN AND SITUATED IN THE VILLAGE OF CASTLELURGAN. MEASURING SOME TWELVE FEET BY SIX FEET OR THEREABOUTS IN FEE SIMPLE FOR THE SUM OF TWO SOVEREIGNS AND IS COLOURED RED ON THE ATTACHED PLAN.

WITNESSED BY ME JOSEPH SPILLANE A MERCHANT OF NOTE

GIVEN THIS DAY 22ND FEBRUARY IN THE YEAR OF OUR LORD 1822 IN THE CITY OF LIMERICK.

She looked at the measure of land and thought how wise she had been. Did she not buy enough land for Phelm and his family, should they wish to lie beside them when their time came?

There would be no common burial for her and her Pat, in a field in which they would never own a stick nor stone. Why the landlord could evict them from the farm, then what.?

Yes, she thought as she counted the money back into the box, she had made the right choice and no mistake.

She looked once again at the document and emphasized the word"FEE SIMPLE." The solicitor had told her, had he not, that this meant it was their's now and forever.

The coins in the box were for Phelm when she and Pat had passed on. It was not a lot to leave their son but then God was good. She had a few more active years left if she were spared and she could add a few more sovereigns to make it all the more respectable.

They could not leave him the cottage and land, that belonged to Captain Singleton by default, stolen from her husbands family. Though he still kept the deed safe in the portmanteau. They would leave that to Phelm, hoping that the day would come when justice would be done and the farm returned.

One thing was certain however, they would not be offered the chance to buy the cottage and land. Catholics were forbidden to own any land. Not that they would be able to raise that kind of money anyway.

Phelm would make good use of the money she was sure of

that.

Returning the document and coins to the box she secured the lid and returned it to the recess. Replacing the slab she covered it with the salting barrel.

The cursed blight strikes

The weather that first week in June was excellent. The people thanked God for his many blessings, especially on the potato crop which at this time of the year was susceptible to the elements. Any major change in the weather could spell disaster.

The Griffin family spent more time nursing and praying over the potatoes than they did for their own souls.

Anne lent on the half door that evening and watched the myriad stars in the sky.

A fox called to his vixen in the woods to the east. He would have to go hungry this night or else catch one of the many pheasants that had escaped from the grounds of Captain Singleton's estate. He could well afford it, she thought to herself. Her poultry were safely locked up in the barn out of harm's way.

Closing the main door she returned to the kitchen and turning her back to the window she closed the drapes. She would not look through the window this night, for to look at a full moon through the glass would bring bad luck. She would not tempt fate.

That night as the village slept, storm clouds were gathering far out in the Atlantic ocean. Heavy weather was building up around the country.

Phelm tossed and turned in restless sleep, and finally awoke to find that he was sweating profusely. Thinking that it was no more than a bad dream, he rose and went to the water barrel outside the house and sponged himself in the cool soothing water.

Although it was very early in the morning, he decided that the sleep had left him. He dressed and left the house taking the road down by the stream. There he vaulted the stile and entered the meadow where he knew good mushrooms grew for the picking.

By the time he returned to the house his mother was up and

about, preparing the breakfast.

"You're the early bird then. I see that you have been busy."
She looked down at the mushrooms lying on the table.

"I had a restless night and as the sleep had left me I decided to make myself useful."

"It did get ever so hot in the night, I felt it myself and took a blanket off the bed."

The weather was holding good that morning. In the afternoon the storm clouds began to gather.

"There is little doubt about it but the weather is about to break." Pat predicted as he looked up at the slowly darkening sky in apprehension.

It was now past midday and the sun was obliterated behind black clouds. At times, it sent long fingers of light from behind the clouds that imprisoned it and grappled with them as if trying to escape.

By evening large drops of warm rain began to fall but as yet no real showers. The weather was now murky and viscous, a real bad sign for the potato crop.

By nightfall the weather had deteriorated further. A warm fog of mist was rising from the fields and leaving a glutinous dew on the potato leaves and stalks. If the weather were to break now, they knew that it would spell disaster for the crop.

That night instead of the usual gatherings in neighbours houses or on the bridge below the village they assembled in the church anticipating an apocalypse.

The Priest heedful of their justifiable fears and no doubt worrying about his own crop at the same time, answered their call for guidance before God.

Entering the church through the vestry he donned the sacred robes of Benediction. Kneeling before the high altar he led his congregation in pitiful prayer.

Would that God in his infinite mercy spare his village from this pestilence. He accepted that whatever was to happen was the will of God. He elucidated to God that were it to happen then the people would starve. He mentioned the potato crop especially, to convince God, if that were needed, that it was the potato crop that they were worried about.

As if in defiance to their prayers and pleas, the rain began to gain in momentum. Firstly there was the occasional large spattering of rain and then a lull. Lightening lit up the night sky, Thunder roared across the heavens. Christ on his large cross looked down disconsolately at the people assembled before him. The night sky darkened deeper and deeper as the rain grew in intensity. The angel Gabriel in his stained glass window blew his trumpet of hope, as the demonic crescendo of thunder ably assisted by the ostentatious lightening drove his efforts into insignificance.

Inside the church the congregation prayed louder and louder, trying to overpower the rain. But the rain would not be silenced. It grew in intensity, challenging the people to leave the sanctuary of their church at their peril.

Clouds of mist rose from the fields and the roads, this was indeed a bad omen.

Satanic lights lit up the old graveyard and illuminated the Celtic crosses and tombstones. As the rains cascaded down the engraved names of the dead, it appeared as if they were crying in sympathy with the living.

There was a sickly sweetness in the air. Not like the sweet smell from the hawthorn after a shower of spring rain. The elders of the village knew that smell. How could they forget it? Had it not left them with a full churchyard in the not too distant past?

The people were filled with apprehension as they left the church and returned to their homes.

The rain continued relentlessly all night. There was to be no respite as it pulverized the fitful sleep of the villagers.

By next morning the rain had eased. The lull allowed the anxious people to go in trepidation into their fields to inspect their precious crops.

It was pathetic to see the women with their children, huddled under their shawls, like cygnets under the protective wing of a mother swan, and they weeping silently as if they were tranquillized. The crop was totally destroyed. All that remained of the once majestic potato was a putrid mass of foul smelling green slime.

Yet what protection could they offer? Their prayers had gone unanswered. The innocent children would have to suffer together with their parents. Their God had deserted them and left them with this pestilence.

Any stalks remaining were now turning to dross and were vomited down the sides of the drills even as the people watched. Streams of putrid green slime flowed sluggishly between them.

In the flat fields it formed into small uncanny green incandescent lagoons. The crop had been completely obliterated overnight.

Pat looked in utter despair at the desolation growing before their eyes.

There was an eerie silence about the place. The people were paralysed with foreboding.

"Should we collect dry bracken and kindling and place it round the field? That may save the crop." In all the adversity Phelm was trying to be the proverbial optimist.

"We will try anything that may help." His father was across the field and heading for the woods before his son caught up with him.

"We had best be careful, the captain will be none too pleased should he find us stealing from his wood," Phelm warned his father.

"Damn the captain, we must try and save the crop. If we don't then not only will we suffer but so will he."

Together they gathered bracken from the hill and dead wood from the forest. They lit several fires around the perimeter of the field. It was a desperate attempt to save their crop but without success.

Defeated in their efforts, they decided that as soon as the field dried, they would open the drills and salvage what they could of the crop. No useful purpose would be served by leaving it to rot.

But the rain did not stop. It returned and became a deluge without interruption for ten more days. The fields were turned into a quagmire. There was now no hope whatsoever of saving any of the crop.

The fetid stench coming from the potato fields was proof of that and now it was spreading nausea throughout the village. Yet the crop of oats still had its ears showing above the water, bringing some consolation.

After fourteen days that seemed more like fourteen years the rain finally stopped and the fields began to dry slowly.

As the fields gave up the water to the stream, it left behind a mass of smelling putrefying vegetation. Where once the majestic stalks of the potato crop swayed in the gentle breeze there was now a mass of obnoxious slime.

Pat and his family surveyed the damage. Would there be anything worth saving under the drills?

Phelm took the slan from his shoulder and dug it deep into the soil.

Opening the drill, he was confronted by a rotten putrid stalk with a few miserable potatoes clinging pathetically to it. As he held them in the palm of his hand, they too were reduced to a slimy mass of decomposing evil pulp.

"Take them, take us too, what kind of a God are you anyway, go on take us all now, why don't you"?

Covering his face and hair in the stinking slime he prostrated himself over the drills and cried uncontrollably.

An old hag hobbled on her stick towards the stone wall. Curiosity getting the better of her on hearing Phelm she looked over. Raising her stick above her head she began to beat at the stones crooning and wailing, swaying as if in a trance.

One by one other women joined her in her unarticulated dance. Their wailing grew into a crescendo that echoed like the banshee wail through the mountains and valleys.

Tearing the stones from the wall, they charged through the breach, they too prostrated themselves in the stinking slime. "God of mercy and compassion! Ochone! Ochone!" they cried as they covered their heads in the slime in an unconscious act of contrition.

They wept, the children wept, the mountains and valleys wept even the heavens themselves wept. And still the rain fell.

It was on this day that the...

LAND OF IRELAND WEPT.

The hanging of Thomas Carey

Captain Singleton stood in a nonchalant manner before the foliage bound windows of his conservatory. His hands clasped behind his back as he surveyed his well kept lawns. His favourite peacock stood on the stone balustrade ostentatiously displaying his plumage to a gullible peahen.

Although the potato crop had failed, all the other crops had survived and their yield was satisfactory.

These would soon be harvested and his share would be taken to his barns.

His wine cellars would be filled with the finest wines from Europe, when the ship docked in Limerick on route from his French vineyards.

The ship bringing in his fine wines would take away the cereals collected in rates and taxes from his tenants.

The hard currency return would pay for the life style to which he had become accustomed.

Yes, God had indeed been good to the captain and he would duly thank him when the cleric came calling.

The coming winter held no fear for him and his family, the people could starve for all he cared.

The old were nothing but an ever exhausting burden, the cold of the coming winter and the impending hunger would put paid to many of them.

He was scurrilous to the Priest when he asked him to relinquish his demands for rent and taxes until the situation improved itself.

They were willing to pay what they could afford, any more would result in starvation or the coffin ships to America and Canada. The priest told him, that this would result in great deprivation to the village and a greater loss to the captain in labour for the coming season.

All pleas fell on deaf ears, what cared he for pleas made in the name of God, and by a Papist Priest at that. It was easy for the Priest to be generous with other peoples money, let him look to his own flock.

Pat was lucky indeed, for he would be able to pay his rent and taxes from the oat crop and the sale of the geese and ducks, plus he would bring down one of the boxes of butter from the bog where it was buried to preserve it. Others were not so lucky. They were faced with eviction and starvation, there would be no reprieve for them.

One such unfortunate was Tom Carey. He had lost all in the famine of 1845/46. With his wife and two young children to support and with no food to fill the gnawing hunger in their bellies where was he to find his rent and taxes and food for them.

He decided that he would go personally to the captain and make overtures to him. There was little use in talking to his agents, they were heartless.

His luck was holding as he entered the long drive into the manor. Who did he see walking down the drive with his two dogs but the captain himself.

The dogs on seeing the stranger coming up the drive ran towards him barking. With his heart palpating, he held his position. He called to the dogs, they responded to his friendly greetings and wagging their tails they jumped all around him trying to lick his face. The captain called the dogs to his side and chided them for being disobedient.

Removing his cap in respect Tom approached the captain.

"Could you spare me five minute of your valuable time your lordship." He pleaded as he grovelled before the arrogant captain.

The dogs were far more friendlier to Tom, than was their master

"Sir, my family are starving, you know that the potato crop has failed. Would you consider waiving my rent and taxes until next year. In return I'll work for you for nothing. I'll work my fingers to the bone." He followed at the side of the captain who was ignoring his pleading and begging.

Surely his desperate plight would win some reprieve.

Walking on sedately, never looking right nor left he dismissed Tom and his plea for a stay of his payments with a curt brush from his walking stick..

Tom did not return to the bosom of his family that afternoon, what was there to return to?

He hid in the woods until nightfall. Then under cover of darkness he crossed the orchard, finally entering the courtyard. There he remained concealed in one of the many outhouses until he assured himself that all the servants had left.

Entering one of the large storage barns, he procured a jute sack and began to help himself from the captain's store.

Having filled the sack, he hoisted it on his back and began to leave.

At the gate leading into the orchard he was confronted by one of the bailiffs. who held a long bladed knife in his right hand.

There was no doubt but that he had heard or seen Tom and was determined to apprehend him.

Tom dropped the sack as the bailiff lunged at him with the knife, shouting for assistance at the same time.

Tom stepped to one side and the bailiff slipped and fell. Hearing people running towards him shouting, screaming and waving cudgels, he stood Petrified. There was no escape.

He was apprehended and taken to the cellars beneath the mansion awaiting arrest by the constabulary. He would be detained in the sponging house awaiting his secure incarceration in Limerick jail.

He was unaware that the bailiff had fallen on his knife accidentally and died.

Some days later he found himself before the magistrate charged with trespass, theft and the murder of the bailiff. He would be remanded in Limerick jail to await trial.

At his trial he swore that his only intention of entering the captain's estate was to beg for some food for his starving family.

He stated that he had called on the captain earlier in the day to plead for food but that this request was rejected.

The captain instead of showing some mercy dismissed his plea and demanded in full the rent and taxes due for the year. He had no food and no money to give and without food both he and his family would perish.

He swore that he never killed the captain's bailiff, he surely fell on his own knife in the dark. He did not know that the bailiff had died until he was charged with his murder.

The arresting constable swore that there was no blood on the person of Tom nor were there any traces of blood on his clothing. It was his experienced opinion that Tom was telling the truth and that the bailiff had indeed fallen on his own knife.

This was a brave and commendable statement by the constable and should have resulted in the immediate release of Tom.

Captain Singleton took the stand and told his version of what happened that day and the events leading up to the night when the bailiff died.

He related how Tom Carey came charging up the driveway with a cudgel in his hand, demanding that he be given food and a reprieve from all his rents and taxes.

He had tried to reason with the ruffian who was in a foul temper. Were he to concede and waive the dues on one tenant then he would be expected to give the same concessions to all his tenants.

This would not help anybody and would only succeed in bankrupting the estate. This logical explanation did not please Tom Carey. In a violent temper he raised the cudgel over his head and struck him a vicious blow on the temple. Although dazed and bleeding from the unprovoked assault, he fought the uncouth lout off bravely with the riding crop that he was carrying. He was lucky to be alive and able to give his evidence before the court he declared.

Tom Carey, he swore left him in a distressed and bloody state and made no effort to seek help for him. He was sure that he was being left to die. Carey retreated to the safety of the woods and from there he shouted threats and abuse at him. He threatened to come back and finish the task of killing the captain and his staff. He would call on the ribbon men for assistance to carry out this mission. This was indeed damning evidence were it to be believed.

Tom confident in his innocence conducted his own defence and cross examined the captain. If he were attacked so viciously why then did he not have any marks or bruising whatever on him. This line of questioning was dismissed by the sitting magistrate.

He asked why the captain did not seek help from one of his many bailiffs to apprehend him. This question too was dismissed by the magistrate.

In desperation he pleaded with the captain to tell the court the truth of what really happened. The captain reiterated his evidence briefly once more.

Tom was asked if he had concluded his examination of the witness. There was no use in pursuing the captain for the truth.

He knew that this was no more than a show trial like many others and resigned himself to his fate. All the proof and all the pleading fell on deaf ears. He was remanded to appear at Limerick court on a charge of murder before a judge and jury. Tom was sentenced at that trial to be hanged at the fair green outside the city of Limerick come two weeks hence.

The day before his execution several soldiers arrived with a wagon and chained Tom to the centre seat. Then the cortège with armed soldiers each side of Tom set out for the cottage. He was allowed to say his farewells to his wife and two children from his seat on the wagon before he was once again driven away between two soldiers.

Villagers watched from the hedge rows as the sad cortège wended its way across the bridge and on into the countryside, his wife looked after it doubtful if she would ever see her husband alive again in this world.

Tom looked back at her for the last time. He could not wave his goodbye for the chains were tied round his hands and coupled to his feet.

Slowly that evening the wagon was driven towards the city. The red coats leaning on their muskets, slept throughout most of the journey. The moon, the guardian of the night cast the shadows of the trees along the road like sentinels.

He watched the rabbits and hare run freely past the horses heads making them shy. He would never run free again in the land of his birth.

Slowly the darkness of the night gave way to the dawn. He saw the sun rise for the last time. The moon having kept vigil all night was now slowly waning and making way for the early morning sun.

"What crime did I commit he thought"?. I only asked for a share from what I grew with my own hands to feed my starving family and for this I must sacrifice my life."

His thoughts were interrupted when he heard one of the captains peacocks noisily heralding the dawn in the distance, as if to mock him.

'Was the just God, that the priest told him about allowing this to happen to him'?

Before him stood the small hillock and the gibbet. This was to be his final destination. Slowly the wagon turned right into the field and near to the gallows.

The soldiers dismounted and stretched wearily before lifting him bodily from the wagon. Tom cried out his innocence as the soldiers removed his chains.

Little if any notice was taken of his pleadings. Had they not heard it all before.

He turned to his God and swore his innocence but he too it seemed had deserted him, depressed he fell silent and awaited his fate. He looked hopefully towards the road out of the city leading to his old home. Would his wife, Philomena come in time with the children to bid their last good byes to him in this life?

He made a silent act of contrition and blessed himself. Two red coats stepped forward.

"Can you not wait until I bid my last good bye to my family?" He took a final look up the long road, it remained deserted. Perhaps it was for the better. What husband would want his wife and young family to see him swing from the gallows. No! let them remember him as he was. He was taken minus his chains up the steps and on to the trap door. The noose placed round his neck, the signal was given......... Tom Carey was publicly hanged on the gallows at the time, place and date set by the court.

It was some two hours later that his wife Philomena together with their children arrived foot sore, weary and hungry at the outskirts of the city. In her arms she carried their infant son, not yet twelve months old.

"Could you tell me please where they are keeping my husband Tom Carey." She asked a sentry guarding the Ballineety road.

"If you go across the road to the guard house the sergeant will be better able to help you than I can." He pointed to a stone building some yards away.

"Come on now children we'll soon see your father." She encouraged them to make one last effort.

The children rose wearily from the side of the road and joined their mother. Entering the guard house she saw the sergeant sitting before the fire asleep.

"Excuse me Sir, I'm told that you know where my husband Tom Carey is being held."

"What!, what's that you say." The sergeant awakened lethargically from his sleep and began to scratch himself. Philomena repeated the question as her children collapsed on the dirt floor.

"Did you say Tom Carey, and who might you be?."

"I'm his wife Philomena and these are our children"

"I see, will you follow me." The sergeant rose from his chair and rubbed the sleep from his eyes.

Once again the children rose from the floor and joined their mother. He opened the back door to the guard room, Philomena followed with her children in tow.

"No! they cannot come, you had best let them here, I'll get one of the soldiers to look after them." He stopped the children who were trying to get out of the doorway.

He shouted to one of the soldiers and told him to take care of them and under no circumstances were they to be allowed past the door. She held the infant close to her bosom, he would accompany her.

Philomena looked after her children apprehensively as they were escorted from the guard house. Why should they want to separate her from her children, she thought. The sergeant noticed the worried look on her face and assured her.

"Don't worry about them, they're as safe as if in God's pocket." Opening the door he invited her to follow him.

Together they walked down the road in complete silence until they reached a bend in the road. Here he stopped and called her to one side.

"Do you really wish to go on Mam, it's not a very pleasant sight if you must know." He warned her.

"What's not a pleasant sight,?" she asked as she continued

43

walking on ahead of the sergeant. Passing clear of the bend in the road she saw before her the gibbet and hanging from it the body of a man swinging to and fro.

"Oh Jesus, Mary and Joseph have mercy on the poor soul." she blessed herself and covered the infants face with her shawl..

The sergeant stood for some moments looking at the hanged man before he turned towards her.

"Mam, I did warn you, did you not know that your husband was hanged no less than two hours ago." he felt embarrassed as he told her.

"The man on the gibbet is Thomas Carey, your husband, mam, I did warn you."

"It cannot be, it's some mistake no! no! not my Tom. They hanged my Tom and me not there to say my last good bye. They could never, never be that cruel."

"I'm sorry mam but the only hanging this morning was of your husband." The sergeant played with his waxed moustache and shuffled from one foot to the other. He tried unsuccessfully to avoid her pleading eyes.

Composing herself she moved closer to the gibbet but the sergeant restrained her.

"Please! try and remember him as he was." They both looked across at the body swinging slowly to and fro on the gibbet. The hook and eye holding the rope making a grating noise as they ground together under the weight of the body.

"Can you please have him taken down, I want to take him home." she pleaded as she stood before him spell bound.

"I'm sorry mam, don't you understand, your husband was hanged as a murderer and a felon. You have no claim on his body. Please return to your children and forget this day"

"Forget this day you say!. Don't you understand? You have deprived an innocent man of his life. You have condemned his widow and children to the mercy of the elements and you say, Forget this day. Have you no pity? no sense of shame?." She faced the sergeant, her tears streaming down her young face in sorrow and anger. Taking her rosary from her pocket she knelt on the rough ground and began to pray. The sergeant left her to her sorrow and returned to the guard house.

Taking one last look at her husbands body, she rose to her feet, held her infant to her and walked slowly back along the road. Her children saw her coming and called to her through the window.

"When is father coming home." They asked, she did not reply nor did she shed any more tears.

"Come children, we must leave this place." She heard the grating noise of the gibbet, mocking her. Perhaps it was her Tom calling to her. She did not look back.

She bartered his few possessions for a scone of bread or two. There was not much to barter. The scythe he had used to cut the few ears of corn and hay, together with the sharpening stone. His well worn slan that had seen better days would not fetch very much. Was it not too long ago that he was planning to visit the forge and have a new one made.

She knew that it was only a matter of time before she and her children would be evicted from their home, she was resigned to her fate.

The bailiffs arrived on her door step some days later. There was to be no reprieve or mercy as they evicted her and her children from the cottage. She picked up her infant son from his crib and wrapped him in her shawl. As she left the cottage the crib was thrown, together with her other chattels through the door. She did not resist nor did she protest. She was, as her late husband was, innocent in the eyes of a merciful God. For their suffering on earth they would be rewarded in heaven.

She and her family were to be banished from any town land in the county of Limerick.

To the islands in search of seed

Pat had succeeded in paying his rent and taxes by stringently managing his paltry income and savings. There were, however, prices to pay. There would be little butter on the table. The hens were not laying all that well as there was now little food with which to feed them. The ducks and geese had long since been sold.

As summer came to its close the situation had improved somewhat. The root vegetables were doing well and the oats had cropped enough to pay their dues. By now he was planning next year's crop searching all the while for a way to prevent a repeat of this year's losses. It was more a case of survival than living.

There were many who had not been so lucky. They now stared death in the face, or take the coffin ships to Canada and America.

September proved to be an idle month for Pat's family. The frenzy of activity created by the harvest had not occurred, the weather had put paid to that. To try and offset this year's losses, Pat and Phelm would take the two day trek by road to the west coast. There, they would barter their passage and board a fishing boat. Their final destination would be the Aran Islands, just off the west coast. Here they could barter for seed potatoes as the crop on the islands had escaped the blight. If they were to get there before anyone else, who may have the same ambition and procure their needs for the new season, their chances of a healthy crop the following year would be greatly enhanced.

On an early morning in mid-September they left the house, unknown to any of the neighbours. They took with them a portion of the salted bacon, one of the slans and several pots and pans. These were the goods they hoped that the islander's would be willing to accept in exchange for the seed potatoes.

On the evening of the following day they arrived at the

village of Doolin Point in the north of county Clare. The first priority was to find a fisherman willing to transport them to the island's. This was by no means an easy task. The seas were running high and strong north easterly winds had kept most fishermen from even attempting the crossing to the islands. The usually treacherous journey was now one which only the foolish or desperate were willing to make.

The fishermen and their families were also suffering. The elements were denying them their living.

Several negotiations, and hours later, they finally managed to flatter and persuade a captain into making the short trip, for a small price.

With Pat at the tiller and Phelm helping to man the oars, the three of them eased the boat out into the ocean. As the boat rounded the mainland, Pat was astonished to see men, women and children on the beach building a pyramid of stones. There were several of these strange pyramids scattered along the shore line. Curiosity getting the better of him, he asked the captain what they were building on the beach. Surely with so much hunger about, they should not be using up energy on what appeared to be a useless task. The sea would wash them away. What was the purpose of it all? he inquired.

"They are not building up stone monuments, they are burying their dead," the Captain informed them.

"Burying their dead. Was there some kind of epidemic then, how many are dead?" Pat looked at Phelm in shocked surprise.

"How many?" The Captain's face looked gaunt and haunted. "You may as well ask how many angels in heaven? that's how many. They are the victims of the great hunger. There are not enough graves for them, so we take them to the beach. Each body is carefully placed and gradually piled into a pyramid. Then we cover them in stones and sand. This is their final resting place, God be good to them one and all. Their souls will find a little comfort in the company of the Maighdean Mhara.

"Oh my good God be merciful to them!" Pat's bewilderment changed to astonishment.

"Were you not informed of the incident that occurred on

Doonbeg Strand? The captain looked intently towards the pyramids.

The story was related to us by Gerry Donneely, a local fisherman, as are all the men hereabouts.

He told us that, as true as God is his judge, he saw the Murrughact.

Once they left the ocean they formed upon the strand. Then joining hands they completed a circle around the pyramids and began crooning. Every few minutes some would leave the circle and rush into the ocean. As they done so the waves increased in size and began lashing the shore and cliff face."

"Are you sure that they were indeed the Murrughact." Pat interrupted.

"They were the Murrughact alright, for did not each and every one of them have Cohullen Dearg on their heads. They crooned and they crooned drowning out the very noise of the ocean itself. They kept running into the circle of the pyramid and kept arranging and rearranging the bones.

Gerry being curious crept nearer to the cliff face to get a better view of the proceedings. At the same time he said a silent prayer to his God to protect him. He knew well that he had to be cautious. should one of the Maighdean Mhara (Mermaid) see him she would lure him on to the strand with her sweet singing. Once there she would cast her spell on him and put a Cohullen Dearg on his head. She would then take him back to ocean home and keep him for her own. His only escape would be if he could come out of the trance and knock the Cohullen Dearg from off her head before she swam with him beneath the waves. Without it her spell would be broken and he could escape.

He watched as they collected large oval stones of equal size and lay them along the shore line. Returning to the pyramid they removed the skulls from each and every one of the corpses, God be good to them one and all. These they took to the shore line and carefully placed one on each stone.

When the task was completed they lined up in a long row facing the ocean and behind the row of skulls Then joining hands they began to croon in unison.

'Oh! Tir-na-nOg' Oh! Tir-na-nOg

We cry for you Ochone! Ochone
We place these pillows beneath your heads
In the ocean depths their story tell'

They repeated this chant over and over again as the waves grew higher and higher. Finally they were engulfed in a huge wave. When the wave receded and the ocean calmed of the Murrughact there was no sign.

On hearing Gerry Donneely's story the villagers went down to the strand. To verify his story if you get my meaning. There, true enough, before their very eyes in a thrie-na-helah were the skulls. Of the stones there was neither sight nor sign. It took the villagers most of the afternoon to collect all the skulls and return them to the pyramids.

We were not aware that the hunger was so severe here. Can you not catch fish?"

"Will you use the sense that God gave you. We had to sell our nets and boats to pay our taxes. The few curraghs left are not sea worthy. What man could take a curragh out in that swell? The seas have been like this for months, and worse. There is no incentive here to risk ones life against the elements, no matter how hungry he is. When and if he does catch any fish he has to surrender them to pay his rates and taxes."

To add to our misery the landlord's have confiscated many of the boats and nets in payment for rates and taxes.

Pat could only stare at the mournful procession on the beach. Phelm pulled the oars with even greater force than before. His grim silence and determined pull of the oars betrayed the fact that he knew he was somewhat out of his depth. He was witnessing death's final act and had no desire to become one of the leading players. The strain of the oars had increased his respect for the strength and hardiness of the fishermen. The burial mounds had also increased his respect for the dead.

The Captain voice once more intruded on Phelm's musings. "We have never witnessed seas so high and fierce, this many year. Several have drowned taking out the frail curragh in the hope of catching some fish. We reached America in our boats when manned by a crew of four, that was hard enough. But casting fishing nets over the side of a curragh, that's impossible.

"They are living on sea weed and grass, you can see the results for yourselves. Go tell them that in your fine city. There are more ghost villages back there crying to Heaven for vengeance, than fish in the sea."

The fisherman dipped his oars deeper into the water as if trying to distance himself from the ghastly ceremony on the beach.

An hour after their journey had begun, they beached the craft in a little bay. Both Pat and Phelm had suffered with seasickness throughout the journey and now were merely glad to have dry land beneath them once more. For the moment all thoughts of starvation, death and suffering disappeared into the background. All their concentration was spent on trying to stop their worlds from rolling and rocking. After receiving much sympathy, advice and directions from their Captain, they made their way to the house of the vendor.

As was the custom, Pat made his deal with the farmer and he and Phelm stayed as guests for the night. The following morning, they left in search of their Captain, their precious cargo of two sacks of seed potatoes carried between them.

They returned some days later with the two sacks. The islander's had been more than generous and for that they would be rewarded in heaven. The precious seed potatoes were not stored in the barn, where the rat's and mice would eat them. They were stored in the loft above the bedrooms until the time came to cut them ready for planting.

The matchmaker springs a pleasant surprise

Phelm had not forgotten that Mary Welsh had promised to approach the McNulty family. Today was the day that he would find out if he had been accepted or rejected. No sooner had he donned his best clothes to go and see her than she was at his door.

Anne looked up as Mary entered the kitchen. She knew that it was courting time and that Mary was here to arrange the match for her son's betrothal, though she was still ignorant as to who the fortunate girl was.

"I was just wetting the tae, will you take the weight off your feet, Mary." She motioned Mary to take a seat.

"Well why not. Tell me, is Phelm at home?"

Phelm came from his room before his mother could answer. "I suppose you know why I'm here Phelm Griffin?" Mary rose briefly from her seat before she sat down again.

"I was on my way to meet you, when I saw you come across the high meadow,"

"The news is excellent for I have made a good bargain for you Phelm Griffin. You are to have the hand of Shelia McNulty after the lent. She will be bringing a fair dowry, if you must be asking." Mary folded her arms and looked at him with that sense of achievement

Having gained an impassive response she revealed a little more of the deal.

"She will be bringing twenty five golden sovereigns and her own china left to her by her grandmother. All that together with a fair cutting of the bog from her father and brothers. Not a dowry to be sneezed at. It's the best match that I have made this many a year, don't you agree."

She drummed her stumpy finger's on the table and awaited his reply. His mother went to his side and held her son close, this was indeed a joyous day. There would be new life at the hob and she knew Shelia and her family. A fine upstanding God fearing family and they without a blemish to speak of. Mary had made a good bargain for her son and they would not be the ones to forget it.

"Will you say something to me and not be standing there with your mouth open catching all the flies of the day." Mary's portly midriff waddled as she took on a fit of laughter.

"Ah go on Mary Welsh, leave the poor boy catch his breath, sure he just cannot believe his luck," Anne again hugged her son.

"Sure I'm only joking, I get this all the time, an old hand at it as they say."

"Well, do I tell them that you accept or will I make a bargain elsewhere?" Mary rhythmically drummed her stumpy fingers on the table.

"You'll do no such a thing. Phelm agrees and so do we. We'll be more than proud to accept Shelia into our home, is that not so son?"

"Well it's agreed then. I can tell the McNulty's that the wedding will be the week following lent. Now there's the question of my payment as agreed," Mary stopped drumming her finger's and rose from the chair.

Phelm was still recovering from the shock.

"I'll be paying you now Mary and glad to do so. You have been a God send to me and that's the truth," he stammered. He went to his room and returned with three sovereigns which he laid on the table in front of Mary.

"I only hope that you will be thinking the same of me in two year's time, should she turn out to be a bad one." She picked up the three sovereigns. Spitting on them for luck and placed them in the pocket of her skirt.

"I'll be off now, thanks for the tae. I'll call in and let Mr McNulty know the good news on my way. I'll be seeing you all again at the wedding no doubt." Humming softly to herself, she left.

Pat came across from the scullery where he had quietly observed Mary's announcement.

"Well Phelm, so it's to be an Easter wedding for you, and to Shelia McNulty of all people," He took his son's hand in his and held it tight.

"Are you not the bold one, never letting on to a soul that you had been to the matchmaker yourself." His mother said with that knowing twinkle in her eyes.

"Look, if it had been left to me, I could not have made a better choice for you." Pat, beaming with pride, was delighted that his son was to settle down.

"You don't mind me doing it on my own then?" He had not expected such enthusiasm from his parents. He was relieved that all had gone well and now he could plan for his future. The following evening he went to the home of the McNulty family to meet Sheila and her parents.

"Come in Phelm Griffin and welcome," Shelia's father was half way across the floor to greet him before he had crossed the threshold.

"It's a pleasure to meet you Phelm," he said gripping his prospective son in law's hand.

"Likewise Sir," Phelm replied, albeit somewhat nervously. His attention was attracted to his fiancée sitting in the corner by the window.

"I suppose you will want to get acquainted with our daughter." Joan, Sheila's mother, greeted him without leaving her chair.

He looked again at Shelia, their eyes met momentary. She looked away and blushed. He ran his hands round the rim of his caubeen. He fidgeted from one foot to the other.

Her mother rose from her chair and placed a chair at a discreet distance from her daughter and invited him to sit down.

"Will you be going to see the Priest soon to make the arrangements?" Joan asked.

"That's why I came. I suppose we will both have to go and see him."

"Well! that is the way it is done. You can make arrangements whenever you like, but there's no haste."

"What do you think of your new man then Shelia?" Her father asked.

Discreetly she tried to hide her blushes behind her hand. She kept her gaze lowered and stole a shy glimpse at Phelm.

She had always had a crush on him. She had hoped that he

would be the man her father would agree to be her husband. Now, here they were some years later discussing her marriage to the man she had secretly loved since childhood.

An hour or so later Phelm made his excuses. His initial task of acquainting himself with Sheila and her parent's had been accomplished. There would be a lot of preparation to be made later on for the wedding but for now, this was enough. He would now be welcome to call at the cottage and court her, though only in the presence of her mother. It being the custom that they should get to know each other that little bit better before the final nuptials.

In the meantime there was the land to prepare.

Phelm and his father ploughed the ground and planted the potatoes in the meadow some fields away from where the crop had failed last year. As it had a long slope leading to the stream, they felt that any rain would soon drain away. They were taking every precaution that they could.

Anne sacrificed one of her hens and gave it to the priest in return for blessing the planting.

The priest had not been too pleased when he saw the emaciated excuse for a bird that he was offered for his services. Why he had seen more flesh on the dead than on the scrawny hen. As a consequence, he had not felt too charitable to Anne Griffin as he weighed the bird in his hand. "Sure if nothing else Anne, it will give a little body to the soup, God help us," had been his only sarcastic remark.

Pat felt sure that now with the new seed and the different location the crop would succeed.

When the appointed day came, the Griffin family together with the neighbours of the district went to the local church to pray for the success of the crop. They offered up the suffering of the black famine of 1845 to his holy will.

Surely, Jesus in his divine mercy, would care for and protect the potato crop and consider their predicament. They were not content with the prayers in the church alone.

A solemn novena would be made to their patron saints in the form of the Stations of the Cross. All fourteen stations would be mentally visited and prayed at. They would walk in bare feet to St. Bridget's and to St. Patrick's well in the village of Singland outside the city and recite ten decades of the rosary together with the five sorrowful mysteries of Christ's death.

Having fasted from midnight that Saturday they set out in bared feet the following dawn on the rocky road to Limerick, singing hymns in praise of God and of his blessed mother.

The rain dripped from their rosary beads as they took it in turn to lead the prayers.

There was no stopping them. They would fast all the way and at the church of St. Patrick they would receive the sacred host. The more the sharp stones cut deep into their bare feet, the greater their faith. Each bloody cut was offered up to their God, as an atonement for their sins. A humble offering indeed in return for his sacrifice for them on the cross at Calvary.

What were their few scratches compared with what Christ suffered for them? What indeed.!

On the road they were joined by others from neighbouring villages. On they went growing in numbers until finally, soaking wet and shivering with cold, they reached their destination at the holy well of St. Patrick at Singland.

There they knelt; each one in turn, in the grooves left in the bed of the rock by the knees of the saint himself. Where he too had knelt in humble prayer all those hundred of years ago.

Finishing their pilgrimage to the shrine, they adjourned to the stone church and received the sacred host before once again taking the long road back to their respective villages.

The wedding

Lent had passed and Easter had now arrived. It was time for Phelm and Shelia to be joined in holy matrimony.

The morning of the wedding, Shelia left the house on the arm of her father. Together they walked the short distance to the church where the whole village had assembled to wish them good luck, long life and that their marriage would be blessed with many children.

Both mother's were as proud as punch at the union of two such respected families. The father's preened themselves and strutted like peacock's, some were wearing Cravats of various colours. It was obvious that they were not comfortable in them. Hands were continually seen to be running around necks trying to loosen collars, only to be chastised when noticed by a wife. Praise was however expected on such occasions as this and was duly given.

With the wedding service concluded the congregation assembled on the road outside the church. Paddy Fay took his place at the head of the procession and he with his trusty fiddle tucked under his chin ready to tickle the strings. Behind him came the trap in which sat Phelm and Shelia with the bride's brother Patrick at the reins. He had secured a large bunch of white heather between the ears of the pony for luck. Sitting precariously on the seat at the back of the trap was Spud Murphy with his well worn melodeon at the ready awaiting the cue from Paddy to strike up the music. Beside him sat young Tony Donovan with a mischievous grin, and he jumping up and down off the cart like a jack in the box giving tempo to the march on his bodhran to the assembling congregation. Paddy scraped the bow across the fiddle, Seamus picked up the key on his melodeon and the whole village with one whoop were off to the home of Pat Griffin singing and dancing to the mellifluous music as Tony kept the tempo swinging on his Bodhran.

They danced and they sang all the way to the threshold of Pat's house. Here they lined the route to the door. The men and boys to the right and the women and girls to the left. The single girls wearing the white heather to denote that they were virgins..Nobody would enter the house until Pat and Anne followed by Shelia's parents had invited them.

Respect to the house had to be observed. On his arrival, Pat as head of the household, called on the assembly to greet the new life into the hearth as tradition would have it. Phelm and Shelia walked between the two rows accepting the good wishes for a long and fruitful life to them both.

With these formalities completed the guests were invited into the house there to partake of the refreshments on offer and to join in the celebrations.

There was no standing on ceremony when a hooley was in the offing in Castlelurgan and none more so than at a wedding.

Sure was not going to a wedding the makings of another, nobody would alter this fact. And who could? What with Mary Welsh the matchmaker, sitting in the corner and she noting all the eligible bachelors and spinsters. There was many the girl and boy trying to catch the eye of Mary in the hope that she would speak to their parents this day or at least notice them for another time. She would make many the match this day.

Did not Rose Kelly approach her and she neither shy nor ashamed as she offered collateral to Mary. Could she find a man for her daughter Monica who was getting on in years? Sure was she not a fine catch for any man? Their only daughter who would inherit their small holding when they passed on providing that she was married.

"Will you do your best this time Mary before Monica is past child bearing years?" Rose pleaded.

"I feel it in my bones Rose Kelly that before this night is passed I'll be making a decent girl of your daughter," Mary reassured her.

"I know, I know Mary, but Michael is putting in the years and praying for a grandchild to take over the farm before the good Lord calls him."

"Did you not hear me, Rose Kelly? Will you put away your

worry beads. Your daughter will be wed within the month or else my name is not Mary Welsh."

"It's the good flagged floor that makes the dancing, and there's not a floor in the county to match that of Pat Griffin" Rose looked nostalgically at the dancers.

"Rose, geal mo croide! I wish I had the God given strength to take you in my arms and twirl you around the floor." Michael shuffled his feet awkwardly and gazed into the fire.

"Sure I was only thinking out loud, Michael."

"I know, I know Roes but...."

"We must thank God, Michael Kelly, that he and his blessed mother spared you from an early grave and me from widowhood.

"Amen! Amen Rose love, but all the same." Michael stopped in mid sentence.

He remembered the day so long ago now, when the ancient wall of Castlelurgan came tumbling down.

He was taking their milch cow to pastures new beyond the hungry hill when it happened. Climbing through a gap in the wall, it collapsed on top of him.

He lay trapped for several hours before being rescued by a neighbour. The weight of the stones biting deeper and deeper into his back.

It was all but a painful memory now. A cross that he would carry with him to his grave.

Couples set aside their inhibitions as they took to the floor and danced the buckles off their shoes.

Round the dresser they danced, across the flagged floor and on into the yard. Many the hen trying to retrieve a few crumbs off the floor lost her tail feathers in the mêlée for floor space.

Young Donovan cheekily stepped up the tempo which was quickly followed by Paddy Fay as he raced the bow across the fiddle and tapped on the flagged floor and he with that knowing twinkle in his eye. Not to be outdone Seamus Murphy took a quick swig from his glass and was off racing up and down the keys of the melodeon with nimble fingers. The pace mattered little to the dancers, they too with a cheer stepped up the tempo another beat challenging the musicians as they did so. Sure there was no stopping them for as one couple retired in sheer exhaustion another took their place on the floor.

Then came a lull as the dancers outdone and exhausted finally surrendered to the challenge and retired to the nearest seats. Now it was time for those who knew most steps and disciplines of the Irish dance sequences to take to the floor and show off their prowess. There was none better than Anne Griffin when it came to the intricate steps. It was said and seen that her feet hardly touched the floor as she moved gracefully like a feather in the breeze.

"You never lost it Anne Griffin all credit to you girl."

Tady McGuire a dab hand himself when it came to the steps, encouraged her. Lightly she hopped around the floor until the dance sequence had been completed.

"Come on, out you come Tady, we'll show them. Paddy put a bit of life into the fiddle and lets have 'The Rake in the Rafters'." Anne stood in the middle of the floor and practised a few steps.

"No sooner said than done Anne, I'm ready if you are."

Tady took the floor his long legs carrying him in two strides to the side of Anne.

"Come on then Paddy, we're as ready as we'll ever be." Tady linked arms with Anne as Paddy began to play and the guests began to clap in time with the music.

"Swing her Tady, swing her like a good one." Tady swung Anne round and round the floor increasing the swift movements with every twirl. Yet he was no match for Anne as she followed him step for step.

"Go on Anne show him a neat step or two, you'll not beat her Tady," the good-natured baiting continued.

"You're one fine dancer Tady, I'll give you credit for that." Anne panted as the music stopped.

"Tell you what Anne. We'll give them one Hornpipe just to mark the occasion then we'll both call it a day."

Together the took the floor once more and the sight of them and they dancing toe to heel in sequence. They with their hands on their hips would take the very sight from ones eyes.

"That's that Tady, I'm not as agile as I was and that's for sure." She placed her hand on her chest and vacated the floor.

59

"Now Pat! what about a song from yourself, keep the craic alive."
Anne, flushed from her triumph on the dance floor, was now in great humour.
"I will of course and why not? It's not too often that I get the chance to sing at my son's wedding," he laughed.

As I went out one morning, in the merry month of May
A farmer and his daughter I spied upon my way
And the girl sat down quite calmly to the milking of her cow
Saying"I will and I must get married for the humour is on me now"
Ah, be quiet you foolish daughter and hold your simple tongue
You're better free and single and happy while you're young
But the daughter shook her shoulders and milked her patient cow
Saying"I will and I must get married for the humour is on me now"

And, sure who are you to turn me, that married young yourself,
And took my darling mother from off the single shelf?
Ah sure, daughter dear go aisy and milk your patient cow
For a man might have the humour but the humour is off me now.

Well indeed, I'll tell me mother the awful things you say,
Indeed I'll tell my mother this very blessed day;
Och, now daughter have a heart dear, you'll start a fearful row
So I will unless I marry for the humour is on me now.

Och, if you must be married will you tell me who's the man?
And quickly she did answer, there's William, James and

John,
A carpenter, a tailor, and a man to milk the cow,
For I will and I must get married for the humour is on
me now.

A carpenter's a sharp man, a tailor's hard to face,
With his legs across the table and his threads about the
place,
And sure John's a fearful tyrant and never lacks a row,
But I will and I must get married for, the humour is on
me now.

Well if you must get married will you tell me what
you'll do?
"Sure I will", the daughter answered,"Just the same as
Ma and you"
"I'll be mistress of my dairy and my butter and my
cow",
"And your husband too I'll venture for the humour is
on you now."

So at last the daughter married and married well-to-do,
And loved her darling husband for a month, a year or
two;
But John was all a tyrant and she quickly rued her vow
Saying"I'm sorry that I ever married for the humour is
off me now."

The Farmer's Daughter (Trad.)

Songs and ballads followed in quick succession as more and
more guests came forward to entertain the company.
Mary Welsh crossed the floor to where Rose Kelly and her
husband Michael were sitting enjoying a pipe between them.
"Rose! you are not going to believe this, but do you see your
nabs over there?" Mary gestured with her eyes to a middle-
aged man seated by the fire.
"You mean him with the glass in his hand by the fire?"
"The very one, what do you think of him?" Mary looked into

Rose's face.

"A bit long in the tooth if you ask, why?"

"Well I have it on very good authority that he is seeking a wife." Mary pulled up a stool and sat closer to Rose.

"You mean himself? He looks as old as myself," Michael interrupted, removing this clay pipe.

"Is it the drink that's talking now Michael Kelly, remember your manners. Let Mary speak. Go on Mary we're all ears."

"I can promise nothing but he has recently buried the last of his parents and is in possession of a fine farm of land in the Golden Vale no less."

"Did you say in the Golden Vale Mary? Grand land that. Why I'd give my eye tooth for a field of that land so I would." Michael was now all ears.

"Well I'll make no promises so I won't, but if you wish it I'll be making the calling. Discreetly mind you on behalf of your Monica." Mary folded her arms and awaited the reply.

"What do you think Michael? Is it one for the matchmaker?" Rose left the final decision to her husband.

"A farm of land in the Golden Vale," Michael scratched his chin and a far away look came into his eyes.

"Aye Mary! away you go and do the calling. Monica, I feel sure will be obliged to you."

"You heard Michael, away you go Mary and do be prudent if you know my meaning. We don't want him to think that we are pushing him."

"Don't you fret about my approach. I promised to marry off your Monica and I'll do it if only to uphold my reputation."
They both looked after Mary as she rose from her stool and left their company.

"Our Monica married to a man from the Golden Vale what a catch that will be." Michael hugged his wife.

"Behave yourself Michael Kelly whatever will the neighbours think?" Rose brushed his arm away. Yet deep down inside she was as pleased as her husband at the prospects.

"Will you look at who has arrived unnoticed ?" Michael nudged Rose.

"Good God! it's the sagart himself and he with a glass in his blessed hands." Rose looked across the floor to see the priest holding the centre of the floor.

"I'll not be making any sermons now, but I'll bless the house and all within." At this the women left their chairs and knelt on the floor. What men had caubeens and hats on removed them and placed them against their hearts.

Putting his glass to one side and removing his hat, he raised his right hand making the sign of the cross.

"Benedicat vos omnipotens Deus, Pater, et Filius, et Spiritus Sanctus."

"Amen" replied the assembled people as they blessed themselves.

Anne ran to the scullery and brought back a bottle of Holy water.

"Father! just to be sure, will you do the honours."

"For you Anne Griffin nothing is too much." With that he took the bottle removed the cork and once again called God's blessing on the house, as he sprinkled the holy water around the room.

"And now before any of you pester me further, I'm going to sing one little song out of respect before I must go."

Retrieving his glass, he took a drink and began to sing.

Not far from old Kinvarra in the merry month of May
When the birds were singing cheerily, there came across me way,
Oh! as if from out the sky above an angel chanced to fall
'Twas a little Irish Cailin in her ould plaid shawl

She tripped along right joyously, a basket on her arm
And Oh, her face, and oh, her grace, the soul of saint would charm;
Oh her brown hair rippled o'er her brow, but her greatest charm of all
Was her modest blued eyes beaming 'neath her ould plaid shawl

I courteously saluted her,"God save you Miss," says I;
"God save you kindly, Sir!" says she, and shyly passed me by.

Off went me heart along with her a captive in her thrall,
Imprisoned in a corner of her ould plaid shawl.

Enchanted with her beauty rare, I gazed in pure delight,
Till round an angle in the road shure she vanished from me sight;
But ever since I sighing say, so I that scene recall.
The grace of God about you and your ould plaid shawl.

I've heard of highway robbers that with pistols and with knives
Make trembling travellers yield them up their money or their lives,
But think of me that handed out me heart, my hand, and all,
To a simple little Cailin in an ould plaid shawl.

Oh some men sigh for riches and some men live for fame
And some on history's pages hope to win a glorious name
My aims are not so ambitious and me wishes are but small
You might wrap them all together neath her ould plaid shawl

I'll seek her all through Galway, and I'll seek her all through Clare,
And I'll search for tale or tidings of my charmer everywhere;
Oh peace of mind I'll never find until my own I call
That pretty Irish Cailin in her ould plaid shawl
That pretty Irish Cailin in her ould plaid shawl.

Mo Ros Geal Fain.
The Ould Plaid Shawl

(Francis A Fahy)

There's no need to tell but this singer was greeted with acclamation and applause. Was it not the sagart himself who had graced the threshold of the house.

Another song was called for, then a hush fell on the assembly as the priest raised his hand.

"One more then and no more, I'll have little voice for my sermon if I dilly and dally."

Songs, poems and recitations were sung and spoken many fastidiously.

To Limerick on their honeymoon

Later that evening, as the dancing, singing and story telling continued, Shelia's brother, Patrick arrived with the pony and trap. He would drive them to their honeymoon hotel in the city of Limerick.

It was dark by the time they reached the outskirts of the city, Patrick knew that he would have to light the lamps on the trap to avoid any interrogation by the peelers.

Calling the pony to a halt by the side of the road. He looked back at Phelm and Shelia cuddled together in the back of seat the trap.

"Just going to light the lamps, won't be too long now to the city." He jumped lightly from the trap.

Opening the glass doors at the sides, he lit each candle in turn before closing the door and resuming his seat. Encouraging the pony into a gentle trot they resumed their journey.

Although the hour was late the city was its usual busy self. Merchants were doing their final bargaining before the city retired for the night. Sailors were singing their shanty songs as they drifted from one alehouse to the next.

Children on seeing the fine trap enter the city ran after it begging for coppers.

Finally Patrick called the pony to a halt outside the biggest building they had ever seen.

 Cruises Royal Hotel, Shelia looked up at the notice, so this was to be her home for the next few days.

Patrick alighted from the trap and going to the rear turned the big brass handle and opened the door.

Taking his sister's hand he helped her alight.

"Will you be coming in for a drink?" Phelm invited Patrick into the hotel.

"I will not! Thanks anyway, I must be getting back. There's some drinking that I must catch up with," he smiled at them both.

"Are you sure now? It's a long way back without some kind of refreshment," Phelm half insisted.

"You know Phelm Griffin, for a married man you have little appreciation of the situation. Don't you know that two is company and three a crowd, especially on an occasion such as this." He nodded towards his sister.

Patrick climbed back to his seat. As the carriage moved off his voice could be heard singing an old song, gradually fading into the distance.

The hotel was something that neither of them had quite expected. Apart from all the finery and decoration, it seemed that there was always somebody bustling about their business.

They were met by a porter who took their bags and escorted them to the reception desk. The days events were all brought home to Phelm there and then. He signed the register as Mr. and Mrs. Griffin.

Having completed the formalities, the porter selected a lamp from a nearby table and removing the globe, lit it. Replacing the globe he turned up the wick and motioned to them to follow him.

Their bedroom was on the first floor. Placing the lamp on the table he handed the key to Phelm and asked if they would like to partake of supper. Politely declining his request Phelm surveyed their new, albeit temporary, home.

The porter crossed the floor closed the door and left them to their privacy.

They were now alone for the first time in their lives. Like two statues they stood in the middle of the room unable to move so it seemed. The silence was almost eerie. Here they were, practically strangers, man and wife alone in their bedroom. For one of the few times in his life Phelm was unsure as to what he should do next. Finally, more for wanting to break the silence, he told her he would get some refreshments. Moving uneasily he made his way back downstairs, leaving Shelia alone.

When he returned to the room a short time later, he noticed

that the lamp had been dimmed and that Shelia was already in bed. Putting the small tray he was carrying on the table, he called to her. There was no reply. All that was visible was her glorious auburn hair spilling across her pillow.

More than a little nervously he removed his clothing. Gingerly pulling back the covers he climbed into the bed and snuggled up close to her.

Shelia lay still, her young heart pounding in her breast as she wondered just what it would be like. Then she felt his hand reach down and lift up the hem of her nightdress and push it slowly up her body. Very gently he cupped her young breast in his strong hands, first one then the other. His hand spent some time fondling her breasts and nipples.

Then he moved his hand ever so slowly down her body, stopping to explore every part of her.

He paused for a moment before gently turning her on her back, his hand continuing to explore. Gently he parted her legs and explored her most intimate secrets.

She felt him move closer to her. Looking up, his body towering over her, she felt his loins pushing against her.

Parting her legs further with his she felt his manhood slowly entering her.

She did not encourage him nor did she resist. She had expected it to be a painful experience, why she did not know. Yet he was gentle with her. With a final thrust he took her virginity. She felt a slight stabbing pain but that soon receded and she felt herself beginning to enjoy his movements inside her. Moments later he began to moan and quicken the pace. She felt his entire body stiffen as his seed entered her for the first time.

They lay together, motionless, for a few moments before Phelm turned on to his side. Minutes later he was sleeping soundly.

For the first time she felt really happy, the man she always desired was now hers.

She woke next morning to find that Phelm was no longer in the bed, nor was he in the room.

As she wondered where he was, there was a knock on the door. A girl entered carrying a large jug filled with hot water. Bidding Shelia good morning, she placed the jug on the wash stand by the window. After pouring a little water into the bowl, she left closing the door behind her.

Shelia rose from the bed, went to the basin and filled the bowl. Removing her nightdress she washed herself all over. Standing before the long mirror attached to the wardrobe, she looked at her nude body and wondered just what Phelm thought of her.

She caressed her young body and felt proud, she had never before seen herself fully naked in front of a mirror. Yet she was apprehensive for somehow she thought that she should not be so vain. She dismissed her feelings of guilt, after all this was her honeymoon, had she not been given to Phelm by God himself.

She heard the door open and grabbing her night dress tried to cover her exposed nudity.

She had no time to hide her modesty. She stood there blushing as Phelm walked in. He closed the door and turned the key in the lock.

Reaching out he gathered her in his arms. They stood for some time, not speaking. Shelia could feel his heart pounding, the latent power in his body. Slowly he began to caress her body. Picking her up, he took her to the bed and laid her down. He stood admiring her as she tried to hide her modesty with her hands.

Removing his clothing he lay down beside her. He was in no hurry and spent a long time kissing and caressing her. Shelia felt a tingle of excitement at his every movement. Yet she could not return his love making although her whole body cried out to respond.

She was ashamed of her feelings. She longed to participate in his love making, but could not overcome her inhibitions.

Finally, he brought her legs up around his body and entered her again. This time there was to be no resisting. She felt herself climax as his seed once again entered her womb.

With words of endearment, they rose from the bed and dressed. Unlocking the door, he went downstairs leaving Shelia to continue her ablutions.

The servant girl again entered the room and emptied the contents of the basin into a slop bucket. As she was leaving she turned and addressed her.

"Your husband would like you to join him in the dining room," The girl genuflected and left.

Satisfied with her attire she went downstairs to the dining room. Phelm was sitting at a table set for two, reading a newspaper. She took her place opposite him at the table. He folded his paper and called the waitress forward. She felt proud of her new husband.

They had heard so much about the city and its history, that they wanted to see as much of it as possible during their short stay. Although they had lived in the county all their lives, they had never toured its capital.

Across from the hotel were several shops and millinery stores, Shelia wanted to visit them and see all the latest fashions.

"Come on then, I can see no harm in looking." Taking her by the hand he guided her across the busy street.

Approaching the store the door was opened to them by a man in livery and a top hat. Unlike the village, where a bell attached to the door rang to announce a customer.

She was fascinated as she entered the store. The array of garments set out on display seemed endless. There were hats of all shapes and sizes. Some had exotic feathers on them from birds of foreign lands. There were fox furs complete with head and tail and a clasp below its jaws to tie it round ones neck to keep them warm. Phelm picked up a fox fur and teased Shelia with it much to the annoyance of the ladies present.

There were reams and reams of cloth, in all the colours of the rainbow.

Phelm saw a staircase leading to the first floor and persuaded her to follow him. Laughing, they ran up the stairs and found themselves in the gentlemen's department.

A floor walker approached them haughtily and asked if there was any particular item of clothing that they wished to see. He even addressed Shelia as 'Madam', much to her delight and amusement.

The walker dressed in a tight fitting suit with starched collar and cravat took little notice of her as he guided them to the counter.

There she was offered a chair as Phelm was taken to the counter and handed over to one of the assistants.

He was shown top hats, tall hats, caps, walking sticks, boots and shoes, jackets and cloaks.

Shelia giggled as she watched her husband's increasing embarrassment as they tried several coats and hats on him.

There seemed to be no end to the array of merchandise on offer. However, they had little money to purchase such fancy clothing and anyway when would they wear such haberdashery in the village.

Their parish priest would have a few words to say about the sin of pride if they turned up in his church in such fancy accoutrements.

There are horses for saddles and horses for straddles, Shelia thought, as she rose from her chair and signalled for Phelm to join her.

Leaving the stores they went down Custom house quay and on into Arthur Quay, where boats and ships of all sizes were loading and discharging their cargo.

Men and boys sweated, as they carried heavy bales and sacks down the steep gantry to the holds of the ship. This, despite the fact that there was a distinct chill coming from the Shannon.

Phelm went to the edge of the quay and looked into the bowels of one ship. In the dust coming from the hold he could see boys stacking the sacks of corn, port and starboard under the strict guidance of a crew member. The sacks were being carefully placed in position in order to keep the ship at an even keel.

"Come here Shelia and look at these boys."

She declined, saying that she was frightened that she might fall in to the hold.

She left Phelm who seemed to be fascinated by the ships and walked along the quay. There was a notice board on the wall of the quay near the bow of one ship. Reading it, she noted that it was a notice of the coming and going of the ships and their cargoes. The ship anchored opposite her was the"S.S. Sara Anne Jane" out from Philadelphia with timber, tea and general cargo. It would return to New York and Canada the following Thursday on the full tide carrying emigrants and general cargo.

Phelm came across and joined her, she pointed to the notice.

"I wonder if anyone from our village will be on that boat?."

"God I hope not, it looks so small and dirty. How could it carry passengers?" Phelm put his arms round her as if to offer her protection.

At the end of the quay they saw the castle of King John, its grim walls silhouetted in the mirror waters of the Shannon river.

"Should we go over there and have a look at it? We could also look at the cathedral." Shelia was more than anxious to see all she possibly could during their short stay.

"Come on then. But remember, we are not allowed into the cathedral, and I doubt if you will get permission from the garrison to see the castle."

Hand in hand they walked up Francis Street and on into Rutland street. Before them on the other side of the bridge stood the cathedral of St Mary.

"I hear tell that it is lovely inside," said Phelm."Tis a pity that we are forbidden by the priest enter."

"Well! it was ours in the first place. Built by Domhnall Mor O'Brien, the king of Munster. That is until King Henry took it from us," She intoned.

"King Henry or no King Henry, it is now a Protestant church and we must not enter it. You don't want to start your married life in a state of mortal sin, now do you?" Phelm squeezed her hand and pulled her gently away from the gate.

Reaching the castle of King John they looked up at its massive gates protected by high walls. On each side of the gate stood a sentry in scarlet with a gleaming sword by his side.

"Do you know that the walls were far higher than they are now. They had to be lowered in order to carry the new cannons?" Phelm informed her.

Leaving the castle, they went on towards the bridge at Thomond. At the quay Shelia looked across the Shannon and noticed another large stone building. This she mistakenly took to be another military establishment.

"What is that barracks for?" she asked.

As he did not know the answer, he asked a ferryman who was on his way down the slip way to the river.

"Sure you must be strangers indeed to this town, That place

is no barracks, it is the workhouse. Nobody goes near it unless needs be, God bless them,"

"Do you think by any chance that Tom Carey's wife, Philomena and her children are there?"

"I suppose there is no harm in asking, seeing that we have time on our hands."

Phelm wondered how they would get across the river to the home on the other side. They could take the toll bridge and go along the strand, but that was a long walk.

"Would you ever take us across there please?" Phelm asked the ferryman who by now had begun to remove the rope holding the boat from the railings.

"I'll take you and your good lady there and back for three pence," he would no doubt be glad of the fare.

After some haggling the fare was agreed at two pence.

Phelm helped Shelia into the boat and together they took their seats in the bow.

The ferryman placed one foot in the boat and with the other pushed it clear of the castle wall. Taking his seat in the centre he dipped the oars deep into the river and was soon making headway towards the far shore. It was only a matter of minutes before they arrived at the slipway in front of the workhouse.

"I'll wait here for you," Try and not be too long, the tide here is far from generous when it is on the turn."

They made their way up the stony slipway to the gates of the workhouse. In reply to their knocking the door was opened by what could only be described as a foul mouthed governor.

"Who is it you want, and did you bring any money?"

"We wish to know if the widow of a Mr Thomas Carey sought refuge here in the fall of last year," Phelm asked.

"Come on in and I'll look in the entry."

He motioned them inside the building and out another door which led into a large courtyard. On seeing the strangers, several inmates came forward, begging for alms.

"Get away with you before I put the strap across you," the governor roared as he picked up a long whip lying behind the door. The inmates scattered, retreating out of his reach.

"They are worse than the water rats that we get here, whenever they see an opportunity." He scolded as he returned to his office.

"Now, what did you say the names were?" he had a large hard-backed book open on the window ledge.

"Carey, C.A.R.E.Y," Phelm spelled out the name looking over the shoulder of the governor at the book.

"Do you mind? this is confidential" He half closed the book on him.

"Sorry, I was only trying to help." Phelm apologised.

"Trying to help? Snoop more as likely," he wiped his nose on the cuff of his filthy sleeve.

"There's no Carey here, wasting my time if you ask," he closed the book.

"Are you real sure? It's important to us," Shelia implored.

"I told you that they are not here. Don't you think that I know the inmates of this place?"

"Oh well, that's that then. Thanks for your time anyway," Phelm guided Shelia to the door.

"Thanks for your time, is that all you have to say? What about a donation then?" He held out a dirty palm.

"I'm sorry but we don't have any money," Phelm pushed Shelia a little harder towards the door. He wanted to get as far away as possible from the dreadful place.

They were grateful that Mrs Carey was not in that repulsive place, yet disappointed at not finding her.

"We did try anyway," Phelm consoled Shelia.

That evening they returned to their hotel. After dinner, they retired to the lounge and sat for some time talking over their adventures of the day before going to their room.

Phelm entered the room first and went across and adjusted the wick of the lamp. The dimly lit room was now filled with light, casting their shadows high on the wall.

Closing the heavy drapes, he crossed the floor to where Shelia was standing and embraced her. She clung to him as he kissed her and stroked her hair, her face and her neck.

Slowly he removed her clothing, before picking her up in his strong arms and laying her on the bed. She lay there exposing her nakedness to him.

Removing his own clothing, he came forward and lay down beside her and they both embraced.

He kissed her lips, her eyes and her neck. Reaching down

and took one of her young breasts in his hand and caressed it. Taking the nipple in his mouth he kissed and suckled it like a baby.

First one, then the other, she felt her nipples swell and stretch between his lips. As he explored more and more of her body with his kisses she responded.

Shelia remembered, in some far recess of her mind what the good priest had told her in confession. Her function in life was the procurement of children. To enjoy the company of a man in her bed was a mortal sin, for which she would be condemned to Hell fire.

That was a long time ago, tonight her whole body was aching for him. As he reached out to her and held her close, she made up her mind. There was nothing that she could or would refuse him.

Reaching down she took his penis in her hand and began to stroke it. Her response both surprised and exhilarated him.

She stroked and weighed each testicle in her hand as he continued to explore her with his hands and mouth. This time she was not passive. She may burn in Hell for all eternity but she would deny neither herself nor her husband. It was there, lying in her husband's arms that she finally pledged her soul to this man, come what may. When they climaxed together, it seemed that all her desires had indeed been blessed.

It may only have been just two nights and three days that they spent alone but to them it was a life's dream come true. They would always cherish the love and affection that they held for each other.

On the afternoon of the third day, Patrick returned to the hotel with the trap. He took their case and placed it in the trap before taking his place in the drivers seat.

Phelm squeezed Shelia's hand as they both looked back at their bedroom window.

The matchmaker keeps
her promise

Mary Welsh arrived at the cottage of Michael and Rose Kelly some days later.

"Is it yourself Mary"? Rose looked up from her seat by the fire.

"None surer Rose, and me with the good news."

"What news might that be then."

"What news indeed, it's about your Monica and Mr Frank Quin from the Golden Vale. Now let me take the weight off my feet and have a drop of tae before I start."

"Frank Quin is that the fellow we saw at the wedding." Michael was all ears.

"None other, who else might I be talking about?" Mary intoned.

"I'm here to negotiate the settlement here and now. What are you offering to take Monica off your hands"

"Don't be so crude Mary Welsh. Monica is a fine girl and we will be sorry to let her go."

"I know, I know an empty heart is no consolation for losing a daughter."

"When will we be for the Walking of the land"? Michael was being shrewd and did not want to disclose the dowry until he was sure of what Frank Quin had to offer in return for his daughter.

"You and himself can do it after we settle the question of the dowry."

"Well now, I m not making an offer at the moment, but there are twenty two sovereigns guaranteed. The brass bed of her grandmother's and the full of a house of best furniture. You have my word on that Mary."

"Indeed, indeed. Your word is more than enough for me to approach the other party."

"You could go over to Hospital town on the pretence of looking for a beast. Once there you could walk the land with Frank Quin himself." Mary suggested.

"I'll go as soon as I can Mary and thanks again," Michael returned to his comfortable chair.

"Will you get yourself off that chair Mick, you've been glued to it for far too long. Away you go this instant and look over the land." Rose demanded.

"For one who is worried about losing her daughter you are in one hell of a hurry to get her off your hands." He rose from his chair with the aid of his blackthorn stick.

"Take no notice of him Mary, he's like a cock, loves crowing on his own dung heap."

"I know Rose, I have one like him myself at home."both women began to laugh.

"Well you two might talk and skitter, it's well to remember that...

You haven't caught the fish until you've landed it. He left the house pleased with his remark.

That afternoon found Michael in the town of Hospital Co Limerick.

Discretely he asked where the farm of Frank Quin might be. Having located the Farm he vaulted the style and began to take a note of the quality of the land.

In the distance he noticed a fine two storied house with a slate roof.

If all this belongs to Frank Quin, I had best meet the man now before someone else makes a better offer. He thought as he hurried towards the house.

"Good day to yourself." Frank Quin came to the door, a questioning look on his face.

"God bless the house and all within." Michael crossed the threshold.

"You wouldn't know me now. I'm Mick Kelly from Castlelurgan. I've come about the dowry arrangements"

"Come in man, come in and a cead mile failte to you."

Some time was spent over a pipe and a meal before Michael opened the negotiations.

" I suppose that Mary Welsh has spoken to you by now."

"She has indeed and so has the Parish Priest. I believe that you have a daughter of marriageable age."

"I have a daughter that is blessed. I can assure you this with out contradiction." Michael began to exalt the qualities of his daughter.

She is ripe for marriage and brings a fine dowry. There are twenty two golden sovereigns." Michael paused and looked at Frank intently.

"Then there is a fine big brass bed with no less that two feather mattresses and five, if you don't be minding, five down feather pillows. There's more to follow, a house full of the best of furniture. Could we be more generous now, tell me?" Michael rose from his chair and hobbled towards the fire.

"It is indeed a fine dowry and more than generous. Is there something wrong with your leg?"

"It's my back really, but it's a long story. Now forget about me.

I have left the best for last if you don't be minding. The nearer the bone the sweeter the meat, if you take my meaning." Michael leaned heavily on his stick with his back to the heat.

"Our Monica is blessed with the Gift no less.

"The Gift did you say?"

"I did indeed! you heard me rightly the first time. She can cure broken bones, mumps and most if not all complaints. I tell you this in all modesty."

"They are rare gifts indeed Michael. They run in the family, I have no doubt"

"Not on my side of the family, sorry to say. They come from the wife's family, on the female side. Monica bless her is the last in line."

"Shame that, the gift is so important, is it not?"

"Now don't be hasty and get me wrong Frank. You don't mind me being impertinent, first names are less formal. Should she be blessed with daughters, I have little doubt but that they too will inherit the gift."

"Daughters did you say?. Are there no sons in your family?" Frank was looking to having an heir at a later date. Daughters were an expense to say the least.

"Of course we have sons Frank. There's Willy and Joe in the

family." What Michael did not tell him was that they were his brothers sons. He did not want Frank to have second thoughts.

"Well, I'll give real serious thought to the matter and will let Mary Welsh know my feelings on the matter."

"You do that Michael but remember, 'The helping hand is the hand faulted'."

"True enough, true enough but..."Examine the river carefully before you trust yourself to the current." With a final hand shake both men departed.

Michael full of excitement at the prospects of a son-in -law from the Golden Vale, hurried home to tell Rose of their good fortune.

"There will be a wedding in the house before too long I have no doubt." Rose predicted on hearing the good news.

Frank did marry Monica and much to Frank's delight and satisfaction and no doubt to the relief of Michael their first born was a boy.

Phelm finds the Carey family

Phelm had reason some days later to take the short route across the hill to Tipperary, where the travelling tin smith was camped.

His mother needed some new utensils for the kitchen and dairy. If he did not go now then he may find that the tin smith had moved to more fertile grounds. That would not please his mother and it would be many the long day before he heard the last of the matter.

Passing through a wood he was surprised to hear the voices of children at play. Curiosity getting the better of him, he followed to the place where the voices came from.

After a search, he found hidden in a well concealed spot a booley.

Around it several children were playing, Phelm knew them at once and called to them.

Startled by his sudden appearance, they ran in panic to the shelter of the booley.

He tried to call them back assuring them that there was no need to fear him. They would have none of it, for not one appeared outside.

Going to the entrance he pushed the makeshift door open. As his eyes got accustomed to the dark, he saw the widow of Tom Carey in the farthest corner, her children huddled round her.

"Is that yourself Philomena? It's me, Phelm Griffin." He came deeper into the dark interior.

Philomena Carey came out from the shadows slowly with her children still clinging to her.

"Well God bless you Phelm Griffin, aren't you a sight for sore eyes," she held her hand out to him in greeting.

For some moments they looked at each other in complete silence, then Phelm spoke.

"I was on my way to Tipperary to meet up with the tin smith, when I heard the children at play in the woods. Sure curiosity got the better of me and here I am."

"It's not that long since I went to the workhouse in Limerick expecting to find you there. Now don't tell me, is this what it has come down to? Philomena Carey living in a Booley on a hillside in county Tipperary, God help you and yours." He shook his head in disbelief, as he looked around the sparse makeshift home.

"What else was there for us, Phelm? I feel no shame whatsoever. What with my poor, innocent husband Tom, hanged as a common criminal and me and the children banished from our own county. It's not shame I'm feeling, may God forgive me."

"What else indeed, I meant no offence and none taken I'm hoping. It's a diabolical shame that we have to meet under such circumstances. I sometimes wonder if there is a God in heaven."

"Let's not dwell on what is done and past, nor blaspheme by blaming it on God. Come on in and tell me all the news. Is there a lot of starvation and evictions?" Philomena invited him to rest on the dead stump of a tree that she used as her chair.

"When I tell you what my eyes saw on the north shore of Clare you just won't believe me."

He related how he saw the people taking the dead; men, women and most pitiful of all, the children and piling them in pyramids on the shore line, there to be covered in stones and sand.

"Sure there's plenty of food in the country. I was in Limerick and I saw with my own two eyes ship loads of food from the Americas being taken to the warehouses and stored. God be praised but I fear that they intend to wipe the Irish off the face of God's earth. To add insult to injury, they were loading Irish cereals into the holds of other boats for export. Now does that make sense?"

They remained silent for some time brooding on the tragic news.

"Do you mind if I have a drag on the pipe?" Phelm took his clay pipe from his pocket.

"Yarrah! There's no need to ask, go ahead." Philomena got up from the floor and went outside to her fire. She soon returned with a glowing stick from it and handed it to him. Sticking the taper in his pipe he slowly drew on it. Soon a blue perfumed smoke began to fill the booley.

"The smell from the tobacco brings back memories to me," Philomena stood before him her eyes closed as if in a trance.

"Here! Sure I almost forgot to tell you, I got married myself this Easter." He removed his pipe from his mouth and tapped the bowl against the side of his boot.

"You don't say? Well aren't you the one Phelm Griffin, and who was the lucky girl?"

"I married Shelia McNulty, you must know the family, they come from the other side of the old castle."

"Know Shelia? Come off it now. I know her and all her family. A fine girl, and a better family. You done yourself a lot of good there, so you did."

"Don't I know it, I'll be sure and tell her that I met you and that you were asking for her."

"You do that now, and don't you forget, do you hear me."

"Tell me," asked Philomena,"are the potatoes showing any promise the year, seeing as your family are the experts, so they say."

"To tell you the truth, I wish that I had never seen or heard of the potato. I am on tenter hooks, what with four of us to keep now and father getting stiffer by the day, God help him."

"Is it like that now? God be good to you," Philomena laid her hand on his shoulder to console him.

"And to you Philomena. Sure what right have I to complain, look at yourself."

By now the children had gathered round the entrance of the doorway. He called the youngest to him and took him on his knee.

"You're getting to be a fine strapping man, just like your dad, I have no doubt." He bounced the child up and down on his knee.

"It won't be too long, God willing, before you are bouncing one of your own."

Ignoring the intended compliment, he returned to discussing the potato crop.

"Talking of the potato crop, this year we went to the islands and got clean seed, that's how we saw the burials in the mounds on the shore. You know mother, she had it blessed by the priest. It is now in the hands of God." Phelm removed his caubeen and blessed himself as a mark of respect to his God.

"Amen to that," Philomena blessed herself in return.

"I must be away now, else I'll miss the light." He lifted the child from his lap and handed him to his mother.

"Before you go, Phelm Griffin, swear to me before God that you won't tell a living soul where we are."

"There was no need to ask me that, I'd no more betray your whereabouts than I would a Priest at the Mass rock."

This referring to the times in Ireland when the Priests were hunted by the English and had to say Mass in secret at rock stones.

Reaching out he took her extended hand in his and placing his left hand on top shook it affectionately.

"Whatever is this Phelm." She retrieved her hand and saw sitting on her palm two half sovereigns.

"Just a little something for the children, I'm sure you will understand."

"We're more than grateful to you, Phelm Griffin, but really you shouldn't. God bless your journey. May he keep the sun on your face and the wind to your back."

Promising to return in the not too distant future Phelm made his final goodbyes to Philomena Carey and her children and left for his business in Tipperary.

As he left the hill side and came down on to the road, he was once again reminded of how bad the hunger was.

There were whole families on the move, some were going to Limerick, perhaps to the poor house. Others were going in the opposite direction, begging and pleading for a little food. Most of the wanderers had a green saliva discharging from their mouths. There was not a nettle to be seen in the hedgerows, they had been picked clean of anything edible. Some, unable to endure any more suffering, just lay down and awaited their fate.

Anne's optimism is unfounded

Anne could not restrain herself any longer, she was anxious to know just how the potatoes were progressing under the sod and now was as good a time as any to find out.
She dug up a bucket full from the ridge in her own garden between the two blackcurrant bushes.
She was more than surprised to see that the potatoes she had brought to the surface were clean and free from scab.
The Priest had earned his chicken, she thought as she piled the potatoes into the bucket. Why if the potatoes in the big field were only half as good as these then their troubles would be over. Up the lane she went towards the house and began singing. She was pleased with her discovery. She continued to sing as she washed the clay from the potatoes and placed them in the big pot.
Filling it with clean spring water she placed it on the hook of the crane and pushed it over the fire. Leaving them to cook slowly, she left the house to see to the poultry.
They would be ready in time for supper and would come as a pleasant surprise to her boys.
Pat returned wearily from the fields, he came home early for his pains were getting far worse. Phelm would have to finish off the chores. As he entered the kitchen he was overcome by a powerful stench permeating from the fireplace.
He called to Anne, thinking that she might be in the back scullery, there was no response. Going to the fire place he pulled the crane from over the coals.
'Was she too getting forgetful like himself?' He thought, leaving a pot on the coals to burn.
As he removed the lid from the pot the room was obscured in a foul smelling steam. The potatoes were not burnt, as he had at first thought. They were still covered in boiling water. The smell was so obnoxious that he felt sick.
Taking the putrid smelling pot by its handle, he took it out of

the kitchen and on into the yard.

On leaving the haggard Anne was joined by her son. Together they returned to the house. Pat was standing in the yard awaiting them with his hands on his hips and his half clay pipe stuck in his mouth and it sending out plumes of smoke. A sure sign that he was in a temper.

"The potatoes Anne, can't you smell them? Whatever have you done?" He pointed to the pot with his pipe.

"Something does smell foul, but I can assure you there is nothing in that pot but new potatoes and clean spring water. What were you expecting?" Anne placed her hands on her hips in indignation.

"No offence now, and none taken I'm sure, but the smell is coming from the pot." Pat apologised for his lack of perception.

Phelm went to the pot and removed two of the offending potatoes and broke them in half, a repulsive odour permeated from them. Crushing one in his hands he smelt it, he let it fall to the ground.

Several hens rushed forward to partake of the free meal, but retreated after the first peck, scratching at their beaks trying to remove the offending mash.

"O blessed Mary, will you just look, the curse has struck again." Phelm fell on his knees in despair and raised his hands to the heavens.

Composing themselves they went to Anne's garden patch and opened another drill and examined the potatoes.

Seeing that the potatoes were showing no sign of the dreaded blight should have given them some encouragement. They knew from past experience, that a healthy looking crop could be very deceptive.

They returned to the house in a despondent mood. What if the crop should fail again this season? Not only did they have to meet crippling rent and taxes, they were also compelled to pay for the upkeep of the Protestant Church and its clergy. All this was in addition to the upkeep of their own church and its Priest.

It was early morning when Phelm, unable to sleep, rose and dressed without disturbing Shelia.

Going down the long meadow to the potato field, he paused

for a moment and looked back at the home of his birth. Would they too have to suffer the same fate as Philomena Carey and her family?

Finally he reached the hill field where the potato crop was growing. He looked along the straight drills that he and his father had ploughed. The drills into which his mother and Shelia had dropped the potatoes.

He was not surprised to note that several of the stalks had collapsed into the drills. On examination, several had black spots on the underside of the leaves.

The ones in the trenches were covered in a fine white powdery substance. He was not mistaken in his findings, he wished to God that he was. The blight had once again attacked the potato crop dealing a hand of misery, terror and death to the innocent people.

The women were up and about when he returned. His father had gone to the byre to milk their one cow. He saw no valid reason as to why he should not disclose his findings there and then. It would be far better to tell them now than to let them build up their hopes and expectations of a good harvest.

"Sit yourself down," his mother called as she stirred the pot of porridge. He watched the reflection from the fire in her eyes, as yet unaware of the devastating news that he was about to break.

Taking a soup dish she filled it from the pot and placed it before him. Phelm collapsed into the chair his shoulders hunched, his mind confused. Picking up the spoon he began to stir the porridge round and round, making no effort to eat it. Shelia noticed that there was something amiss and came behind him and placed her hand on his shoulder.

"Oh! Good God Shelia, whatever is to become of us all?" He dropped the spoon into the dish and placed his hand in hers.

"It's the blight, is it not?" His mother continued to stir the pot over and over again as if in a trance.

They looked towards the door as Pat entered carrying the milk.

"Did Phelm tell you?" Anne continued to stir the pot.

"Tell me? Tell me what? By the looks on your faces perhaps it would be better that I never knew," he continued into the scullery.

"If only it could be that simple Pat, God help us all. It's the potatoes," Anne let the spoon fall into the pot and picking up the hem of her apron she burst into tears and covered her eyes.

"Is it true Phelm? For God's sake man tell me, you're not mistaken now are you?" Pat crossed to Anne and placed his arm around his wife to comfort her.

"Mistaken? No father! I wish to God that I was." He looked across at his father and mother who were now comforting each other.

He saw his father's hands slip from her side before he fell to the floor in a dead faint. He rose from the table and picking his father up in his arms took him to the bedroom.

Anne grabbed a cloth and ran to the water barrel outside the door and soaked it in the cold water, before wringing it out and running into the bedroom.

Bad news travels fast so they say, and it was not long before the neighbours became aware that the blight had struck again. Next morning, Pat was insistent that he should be up and about and had to be restrained by Anne and Phelm from rising.

"A long lie in will do you the world of good. If we need you, then you can get up," Anne told him.

Phelm returned to the potato field and was not surprised to note that the blight was spreading at an alarming rate. He watched helpless as the stalks collapsed in the trenches before his very eyes. It was as if God was punishing him for his lack of faith. He wanted to open the drills and salvage what he could of the crop, yet he did not wish to upset his father by making the decision on his own.

He returned to the house and asked his mother to put his suggestion to his father, this way there would be little upset.

"Phelm it now looks more likely that you will have to make the decisions around here, so lift the crop. Let your father alone," his mother told him.

Next day, he returned to the field accompanied by his mother and Shelia. He opened the drills one at a time and spread the potatoes on the ground. There they were collected in buckets by the two women. The crop seemed to be in reasonable condition under the circumstances, but would they be edible? Phelm spread the potatoes out on the barn floor to dry. He would return next day and clamp them.

On the evening of the same day, his mother went to the barn to milk her cow. She was about to lift the latch when she was overcome by an obnoxious smell coming from inside. There was no need to confirm what had happened. The potato Cholera had struck down what was left of the harvest.

Shelia tells Anne the good news

When Shelia awoke next morning she was surprised to find that her husband was up and about. Entering the kitchen she noted that he had eaten his breakfast and was preparing to leave the house.

"You seem to be in a great hurry this morning. Is there something that I should know?" Shelia looked to her husband. He was totally dejected, no mention of the potato failure crossed his lips.

He then let it be known that he was going to Limerick in search of work. There were the rates and taxes on the land and cottage to be met.

"Phelm I can see no good reason for you going there, why there must be thousands with the same idea,"

"Did I hear rightly, you're going to find work in Limerick?" His mother came into the kitchen, smoothing the front of her dress.

"Do you know of any better ideas?" He approached Shelia and gently kissed her before taking his caubeen from the peg. He paused at the threshold as he was about to dip his hand in the holy water.

"Shelia has good news for you both." He looked across at his mother.

"Well you may as well know it now as later, we are expecting our first child," Shelia broke the news to his mother.

Anne went immediately to her side and called God's blessing on the new baby.

"I must after all agree with you Phelm, there is little to do here. We will need all the money that we can lay our hands on." His mother was in a more conciliatory mood now, her thoughts having been skilfully deflected.

"I'm away then, wish me luck." He took down his coat and

slung it over his arm. Dipping his hand in the holy water, he blessed himself, placed his caubeen on his head, and wended his way down the boreen.

Pat, weary of his bed, got dressed and entered the kitchen. Anne placed his breakfast before him and told him the good news. Finishing his breakfast he rose from the table and left the house without uttering one word. Some time later he returned to the house and sat down wearily on the nearest chair.

"Sorry for my bad manners love but I went off to think. Can you tell me Anne, what is to become of us? We will have to give the cow to the captain in payment and that may not be enough, nor may it be acceptable," he looked questioningly at his wife.

"Pat Griffin, I told you before, not to worry, God will provide." This was her answer to every crisis.

"You and God! If he were all that merciful and good, why then is he allowing tens of thousands, the length and breath of the land to die of hunger?" Pat wanted answers, not prayers.

She did not scold him for what she considered blasphemy as she would have in better times. She was sure that God was testing their faith and that for their belief and love of him they would be rewarded. All they needed was patience and all would be well. She was aware of Pat's concern for the family, she would ask God to try and understand him. Pat would worry all the more now, with his new grandchild due in the near future.

Anne waited until she had the house to herself before she went to the front door, closed and bolted it.

Returning to the scullery, she removed the salting barrel covering her hiding hole. Picking up the loose slab she removed her tin box.

Opening it she counted out thirteen sovereigns. before returning the box to the recess in the floor.

Putting her shawl round her shoulders, she crossed the floor, and left the house closing the door behind her.

She paused at the long drive into the mansion of Captain Singleton. Then with a dep sigh she proceeded to the office of the estate manager. Pausing at the door of the estate office, she studied the brass plate on the door.

Mr Thomas Roche Esq.;

Estate Manager

In black lettering underneath was written,

Please knock and Enter.

So this was where Tom had got to, she thought as she approached the door. She hesitated for a moment before knocking on the door. With a deep sigh she turned the large polished brass handle and entered the office. The room was sparse enough for such a rich estate. The wooden floor was bare of any covering. Books of all shapes and sizes cluttered the many shelves along the wall. At a large roll top desk sat Tom Roche, a life long friend of her family. He had lost a lot of his roaring red hair of which he was once so proud and he was that much fatter around the gills. Still she could not mistake him, it was himself down to a tee.

On seeing Anne enter the office, his face lit up in a friendly grin as he rose to greet her.

"Anne, you're more than welcome, do please come in and sit down. What brings you all the way out here, nothing amiss I hope?" He studied her face intently.

"No, there is nothing wrong, as such." She paused and took a deep breath.

"What with the failure of the potato crop this two years running, and that we cannot pay our rates and taxes in kind everything else is fine." She remarked sarcastically.

"Ah, these are bad times in Ireland, and between you and me you won't get a lot of sympathy from his nibs," Tom pointed towards the door.

"Still, you've done the right thing in coming to see me, what are friends for? Now let me see." He reached behind him and removed a large hard backed ledger, and placed it before him on the desk.

"I see your Pat has the lease of the small holding below the woods, Is that right?" He ran his finger down the page.

"That's the one Tom, would you let me know what the rent would be in money?"

"The rent in money is it? Well according to the records, and they go back a long way, you always paid in kind."

"There is no crop worth talking about this year, no more than last, to pay with."

"Of course I can accept payment in money, but can you afford it?"

"That I won't know until you tell me, how much,"

"The annual rent is fifteen sovereigns, or half the produce. Didn't Pat know?"

"Pat is not in the best of health and knows nothing of my coming here and I would be obliged, if you did not tell him."

"'Tis sorry I am to hear that Anne, but he's bound to find out. He'll wonder why the bailiffs are not knocking at his door."

"Leave Pat to me, Tom. I know how to handle him, after all I married him," She half smiled.

"I only have....." then she paused.

"What's the matter Anne, is there something that you want to tell me?"

"To be honest Tom, I already told you that we cannot meet our taxes from what little harvest there is. If the bailiffs come and take our cow, then there will not be any milk for Shelia and she with child."

"You know well Anne, that were it in my hands alone, then I would forgo the rent, but like Pat I am answerable to the captain.

"The captain!, the captain! that's all we ever hear, but what of us? I'm sorry Tom, I should know better. It's not your fault, I apologise, for my outburst."

"No need for apologies Anne Griffin, I'm not inhuman if you must know."

"Will you take a dozen sovereigns that I have here in my hand? I know that it is not the full rent, but it is the best that we can do." Anne held out the money. She had no intention of giving more than she intended to the captain, that is if she could avoid it.

"Anne, I must be getting old, my lamps are not as good as they used to be." Tom picked up his pen and dipped it in the ink pot. Running his hand down the ledger he stopped at the name Patrick Griffin, then he deleted the sum of fifteen sovereigns and amended the figure to read twelve.

"The rates and taxes for the farm will be twelve sovereigns or half of the produce Anne, see for yourself, the ledger states so." He blotted the amendment and turned the ledger round for Anne to see.

"Tom Roche, you'll get your reward in the golden book, have no fear of that." With that she counted out twelve sovereigns and placed them on the book.

Tom turned the book round and entered"Paid in full, this 23rd day of August 1846, under the tenancy agreement of one Patrick Griffin.

Phelm seeks work
in the city

Phelm canvassed several venues seeking work in the city, without success. He returned to Custom House quay, where he sat on a bollard watching several ships being unloaded.

Two of the ships were unloading grain, another timber, perhaps they were in need of workers, he thought.

Seeing a man standing above the grain ship with a board in his hand, he approached him.

"Excuse me, I am seeking work, do you need any more men"? The clerk ignored him and continued counting the sacks of grain as they appeared on the quay side.

Without taking his eyes away from the ships hold he asked, "Ever worked a ship"?

"No, but as you can see I am big, strong, and hungry enough." Phelm removed his caubeen and half smiled.

Laying the board on a bollard he looked Phelm up and then down.

"Very well! get down there and bring up the sacks as they are filled. You'll be paid by the sack."

"My name is Phelm Griffin if you must know."

"Your name is of little importance to me, you are number twelve. Don't forget it if you wish to get paid." The clerk handed Phelm a piece of paper with the number written on it.

Phelm went down the gang plank and into the bowels of the ship.

Men laden with the heavy sacks of corn walked slowly up the steep gang plank. Their backs bent double with the heavy strain of the constantly moving grain.

In the hold a pernicious dust haze hung over the wheat as it was shovelled into the awaiting sacks.

He felt a chocking sensation in his throat as he inhaled the dust and began to cough.

One of the men, seeing that Phelm was having problems with his breathing, stepped forward.

"Cover your face with your cravat and hold the sacks open like the others are doing, you'll soon learn."

Phelm covered his face and crossed to where young boys were shovelling the grain into sacks. Taking an empty sack from the pile he stood in the queue.

This he placed on the wooden platform with two handles each side, as he had been instructed and held it open.

When it was filled the two boys twisted the neck and tied it with a string. Placing their shovels against the bulk head they took hold of the platform by its handles and helped him to hoist the sack onto his back.

Phelm walked slowly up the gang plank and deposited the grain on a waiting cart.

It was back breaking work, Phelm was not used to this kind of work and that made it all the harder. At midday a halt was called to the work for a meal and a well earned rest. Joining up with one of the other labourers, they went to the nearest and cheapest eating house.

"Would you ever tell me, with all the hunger about, why they are storing all that corn in the warehouses?" Phelm quizzed his companion.

"It's kept there to keep the prices high."

"Do you know where I come from people are dying from hunger"

"Dying from hunger did you say, what in the name of God, do you think is happening here? Look my friend, the grain that you are unloading comes from America to alleviate the hunger. The people see little if any of it for the simple reason that they cannot afford to buy it."

"But if the people have no money to pay for it, what difference does it make. It would make better sense to let them have it for nothing."

His thoughts returned to the day he witnessed the people burying their dead in giant pyramids on the beach in north Clare. Had the grain stored in the warehouses in Limerick, and no doubt elsewhere been released to the people of Ireland, then there would have been little hunger or death.

He could not obliterate from his mind the sickening sight he had witnessed on the beach in Clare.

By night fall the ship had been cleared of it's cargo and the workers paid off.

He waited until the others had left the quay side. Then he approach the captain. He offered to sweep the hold clean on condition that he could keep the corn that he swept up.

Agreement was readily given, after all it saved the crew from carrying out the task. Phelm swept up the wheat and filled the sack. Tying it by the neck he hoisted it on his shoulder and left the quay side.

As he crossed Ellen street on his way out of the city he was stopped by a platoon of dragoons.

The sergeant in command demanded to know what was in the sack. He accused him of stealing it from one of the warehouses. Phelm swore his innocence and explained how he came to have the wheat. As Ellen street was less than a few hundred yards from the quay side, he was ordered to pick up the sack and return with him to the ship. He was held captive on the quay as the sergeant went up the gang plank and entered the ship. Returning he ordered that Phelm be released. The captain had confirmed his story.

"Don't you know that you must have a pass to leave the city with grain?"

Phelm was too tired after his days work to answer.

The sergeant scribbled a pass and handed it to him,"Take this and go."

Phelm once again hoisted the sack on his back and left the city. On his journey home he was in luck for he met up with a dray returning with stores to a village on the outskirts.

He reached his home late that night. Tired but happy that he had earned some money and had a bag of precious corn into the bargain.

His parents had retired by the time he crossed the threshold . Shelia was dozing in a chair by the fire, when she heard the lifting of the latch. Looking up she was surprised and delighted to see her husband silhouetted in the doorway. The sack of wheat still on his shoulder and a broad grin on his face.

She jumped out of her chair and ran to greet him.

"Hold it, let me get rid of this first." He removed the sack from his shoulder and rested it against the wall of the kitchen. Reaching out he took her in his arms and kissed her. "I'll make us something to eat, then you can tell me all about your day." She went across to the fire place and settled the kettle over the glowing turf.

Phelm came from the scullery, having washed the days grime from himself. A bowl of hot gruel was sitting on the table together with a mug of scalding hot tea. He did not realise how hungry he really was until he saw the food.

"Tell me how are the old couple? He worried for the welfare of his parents. More so now because his father was not looking too good this last week.

"Your father retired early, he tries not to show it but his steps are not as lively as they used to be." She joined her husband at the table.

Phelm related his adventure in the city and told her how he was arrested. He thought it funny, Shelia was concerned telling him how serious it could have been.

"I brought a sack of wheat. We could get the miller to grind it for us."

Finishing the gruel he rose from the table and retired to their bedroom leaving Shelia to tidy the kitchen. He was sleeping soundly when she entered the bedroom. Turning the wick down to a low glow, she undressed and retired for the night.

A Pishogue strikes

Phelm woke late, he heard Shelia humming a lullaby as she moved about in the kitchen,

He rose from his bed, as he did so every muscle and bone in his body ached. Although he was fit and strong, thank God, he never had reason to use the muscles required to work in a ship. Slowly he dressed and entered the kitchen. Shelia was busy making a scone.

"I must have been dead beat last night, I don't remember a thing after my head touched the pillow." he scratched his head and yawned.

"A good night's rest won't do you a bit of harm, there is little for you to do here. I'll make you something to eat." Shelia finished the cake and placed it in the oven.

Phelm watched as she put the lid on the oven and took it to the fire. She placed it on the crane and taking up the tongs selected glowing cinders placing them on the lid of the pot, before she swung the crane over the fire.

"That's the last of the flour, and no prospects of any more." She dusted her hands together.

"Did you say something?"

I said that there is no more flour." She repeated.

"What do you mean no more flour, what do you think that is?" Phelm pointed to the sack of wheat next to the door.

"Do you know I forgot all about it." Shelia was contrite for her forgetfulness.

"I'll take it down to the mill and have it ground to day." He told her.

Setting the breakfast table, she took her place opposite her husband.

"Where is mother and father?, he asked.

"Your mother went to early Mass and no doubt is gossiping with her neighbours by now. Your Father, I heard him go out some time ago. No doubt but he is down one of the fields.

After breakfast, Phelm took his caubeen from the peg. Picked up his ash plant and left the cottage.

In the distance, he saw his father walking along the edge of the wood. Crossing the field he joined up with him, and together they strolled along the boundary of the Captain's estate.

Whenever his father saw a hazel nut or crab apple tree, he would leave his son's side and search for any signs of the coveted nuts and apples. Returning empty handed for the umpteenth time, he looked at his son and opened his hands wide.

"I tell you son, this will be a lean winter, there's not a peck to be found," he predicted

"It cannot get any worse than it is now." Phelm thrashed at a sapling with his stick.

Having reached the perimeter of the boundary the two men retraced their steps back towards the house. Phelm was his usual hurrying self, striking out with a spring in his gait. He had travelled some distance across the field before he noticed that his father was no longer by his side.

Stopping he looked back and saw that his father was lashing out at something with his stick. He raced back to where he was standing.

"What's the matter father, did you find something?"

"You might well ask, so you might, look at this."

Several sharpened willow sticks were stuck around the field in the shape of a star.

"It cannot be a Pishogue can it father?" He took hold of one of the sticks and tried to pull it from the ground. His hand slipped off the stick which had been covered in unsalted butter.

"It's unsalted butter isn't it Phelm. Isn't it? His father again lashed out at one of the sticks and demanded that his son should confirm his findings.

"It's the pishogue alright father." Phelm tasted the butter.

As he glanced back he saw his father with his head down, doing his best to make tracks with the aid of his blackthorn stick. Phelm ran after him and caught up with him before he had reached the stile.

"Not one word of this are you to mention, do you hear me?"

"I'll not say a word but what are we to do?"

"Do unto others as they do unto you." His father continued across the small field towards the barns.

"Now stop father and think, you are not going for the irons, are you?"

"Am I not? you just watch me." Pat pushed open the barn door with his stick.

"Get the fire going Phelm and bring the slans." He cleared and raked the grate in the fireplace.

"Dad! think on. Is it worth it?"

"If you have no heart for it, I'll understand. You can stay and help or go back to the house."

He knew that there was no arguing with his father once his mind was set. He lit the fire and placed the blades of the two slans on the coals. Soon both were fiery red and glowing.

"Get the bucket son and put the slans in it then cover them with the hot coals."

Phelm ran a bar through the handle. Holding the bar between them they carried it across the fields to where the sharp willow sticks were stuck in the ground.

"Bless yourself son, In God's blessed name bless yourself and pray. Now pass me a slan," He blessed himself and took the Slan from his son. The blade of the slan spat and sizzled as if releasing all its venom. He approached the first willow and scorched it. The willow began to smoke and splutter as the butter caught fire. He repeated the operation on each of the thirteen willows until they were reduced to smoking embers.

"There will be burning flesh in some household in the not too distant future I'll not doubt." Pat stuck the Slan in the ground. Returning to where the second Slan was in the bucket, he removed it and stuck it in the ground. Picking up the bucket, he called on his son to bring the Slans to the stream. There he pitched the coals into the water and quenched the slans in the running stream.

"It is done now son and cannot be undone." He handed the Slans to Phelm. Picking up the bucket they both returned to the house.

(A Pishogue is a curse placed on a person or land. It takes many forms and shapes. In this case the worst Pishogue of all had been put on Pat's beasts and fields. Unsalted butter had been used to increase the power of the curse. Salted butter could not be used as salt is sacred both in the Christian Church and Irish pagan magic. Whatever animal or bird that they put into the field would pine away and die.

There was no cure unless the Pishogue could be found and reversed. Reversing a Pishogue would bring untold agony on the perpetrator. Pat had chosen the ultimate punishment Fire. Soon they would hear news of a house catching fire mysteriously and one of the occupants being slowly burnt to death within its walls. The person burnt would be the guilty party. It was to avoid this cruel punishment that Phelm called on his father not to use the hot irons.)

Desolation on the road to Cloncagh

Phelm was rudely awakened one morning by Shelia nudging and calling to him.

"Listen will you! Your mother and father seem to be arguing about something."

They lay in their bed listening to the argument that was getting more tumultuous.

"Now listen to me Patrick Griffin once and for all, you are not going to Cloncagh and that is final." His mother was not one for mincing her words.

"You had better go and sort matters out before they come to blows," Shelia half laughed.

"Now, what is all the argument about? You're acting like a pair of tinkers at a fair." Phelm entered the kitchen and noted that his father had a letter in his hand. Delivered no doubt that morning on the mail coach from Cork.

"It's my brother Luke. He is at death's door in the family home outside Tullylease, you know on the way to Ballingarry. Here, read Nora's letter for yourself."

"I know where it is, but why are you arguing?"

"It's your mother, she does not understand." He handed the letter to his son.

"Understand! I understand only too well! Your father wants to go to Tullylease and he in no fit state."

"Dad you know well what we heard about Cork. The city has been put in quarantine and the countryside is riddled with plague. Putting all that aside, you are in no fit state for such a journey especially in this appalling weather."

I'll be the judge of that. I'll not be told to abandon my kin in time of need, do you hear? We were always a close knit family and he would do the same for me were the circumstances reversed.

"I'm going and I'll hear no more arguments." Pat stormed out of the kitchen.

Phelm knew that he had little say in the matter, the journey would have to be made. Respect for the family in time of need was paramount.

"What if I went in his place Ma? I'm sure they would understand." Phelm volunteered to go and represent his father.

"I don't want either of you to go, will you just look at the weather. Still if it will bring peace to the house then ask him yourself."

Phelm made his way to his parent's bedroom. His father was staring out of the window, his back to Phelm.

"I've made my mind up and going I am." Phelm could see his father's shoulders stiffen, knowing the situation had already been resolved.

"I suppose that she sent you with some fool proposal."

"Very well then we'll both go, that way I can keep an eye on you. And no, mother had nothing to do with it. If you must know it was my idea."

Phelm watched, as the weight of his father's troubles eased. The stiff, broad frame sagged slightly, Pat's burden would be shared. He left his father watching the blanket of snow whitewash the countryside. It was some time before Pat left the window.

Anne prepared the food for the journey as Shelia selected their warmest clothing and weather proof outside garments. The snow accompanied by a biting cold wind was still falling as they left the cottage early the following morning. They took the midday coach from Limerick to Newcastle West, arriving at their first stop of the journey late that night. They would rest in the local hotel and continue their journey to Dromcolliher next morning. They booked an early call in order to make sure that they would be ready for the morning coach.

The snow was still falling the following morning as they were getting dressed. Both knew that the roads would be impassable except on foot. His father insisted that they continue the journey. There were bound to be drays on the road willing to pick up any stranded passengers he optimistically predicted.

South of the crossroads near to the village of Mahoonagh

they happened upon a number of people shambling aimlessly along the bank of a river. As they watched, three of the wretches collapsed, one landing face down in the shallows. All three began to convulse, their emaciated skeletons acting out the last dance of some insane puppeteer. After a few minutes they lay still. Exhaustion brought on by the pestilence and starvation had staked the final claim on their bodies.

In order to avoid contact with them, they retraced their steps and took the old track leading towards the ruins of St Bartholomew's church.

They could still see the travellers, who had now abandoned their three compatriots shuffling aimlessly along the bank. Phelm walked ahead of his father along the narrow track. Rounding a corner he noticed a child doubled over the hedgerow. He was bald and his back was covered in open bleeding sores. The child stumbled and slipped. Still clinging to the hedge with one hand. He contorted his body in a robot manner to face Phelm and his father. The naked body was bloated to almost three times its normal size. The boy, that much at least they could discern now, stared at them with glazed, unseeing eyes. His stomach convulsed and retched as he disgorged a mass of grass and blood. The child was covered in his own excrement and the putrefying smell coming from his body forced Phelm to cover his nostrils. Turning swiftly he grabbed his father's arm and dragged him away from the horror blocking their path. They watched in repugnance as the boy staggered along the path. He was sweating profusely although the temperature was below freezing. Even at a distance, they could still discern the lice and vermin crawling in and out of the folds of the now useless flesh. He was oblivious of any pain or suffering, a living host for the many parasites that were slowly consuming his body.

Following slowly, they were brought up suddenly as the boy took a spasm. Dropping to the ground he began to roll over and over. Gravel bit deeply into the weeping sores. He began to scratch himself violently and mutter incoherently. Watery blood oozed from the deep wounds. What flesh there was on his body came away in long narrow strips from the violent scratching. Yet he seemed oblivious of any pain. He crawled along the path on his hands and knees in an ape like manner, making long tracks in the snow and slush with his hands and feet.

Rising to his full height he dashed headlong through a gap in the hedge. For a few moments it seemed as if he had heard his Saviour's cry and ran to the river to meet him. Slowly it seemed, almost determinedly, the river rose up and swallowed the boy. A head and shoulders appeared briefly, the arms floundering in the ice cold water before being claimed for a final, dreadful time.

Phelm stood staring at the river. Behind him he heard his father praying. All Phelm could do was watch.

"Perhaps it was for the best son, for this day he will be in paradise, God rest his soul." His father rose to his feet and returned his rosary beads to his pocket.

"Amen to that father."

Phelm removed his cap and looked towards the river as a mark of respect. He recalled a prayer from his own childhood.

"O Most sweet Jesus, through the sweat of your precious blood which you shed in the garden at Gethsemani, have mercy on this poor wretch, have mercy."

Blessing himself he followed the path ahead once more. They had a long journey before them and it was imperative that they complete it before nightfall. Avoiding any further contact they continued on their way towards Tullylease.

By late afternoon, the journey and the intense cold was beginning to tell on Pat though he stubbornly insisted that he was not tired and wanted to press on. His mouth was now half open and his breath came in short gasps.

The cottage of death

Phelm, aware that they couldn't go much further tried to uphold his father's stubborn pride. He began to plead tiredness and suggested that they should stop at the nearest shelter and partake of a meal and rest.

Nearing the village of Feohanagh they came across what they thought was an abandoned cottage. There they would rest and cook their meal.

Phelm lifted the latch and went inside followed by his father. The interior was icy cold but that could be put right with a good fire. Whoever had lived here had left in a hurry for the house was fully furnished. They would take refuge within its walls before continuing their journey the next day.

"Sit yourself down, I'll see if there is any turf in the haggard." Phelm removed the haversack from his shoulder and laid it on the table.

There was plenty of turf and he soon had a welcoming fire lit. He filled the iron kettle with fresh water and putting it on the crane set it over the flames. When it came to the boil he placed two eggs inside. His mother had supplied them well with provisions and he soon had a respectable meal of soda bread and boiled eggs on the table. He brewed the tea in the same water as he had cooked the eggs in.

With the meal inside him and a good roaring fire warming him Pat soon perked up. Taking his mug of tea he crossed the room and sat on the settled bed.

"Don't sit on that dad it may well be infected," Phelm cautioned him. His father quickly rose from the bed and returned to the chair by the table.

As they sat relaxing over their tea, they heard a disturbance coming from the back bedroom. Both men watched apprehensively as the door slowly opened. A young girl her breasts barely formed manifested herself in the doorway. Her skeleton of a frame was as naked as on the day that she was born.

"Merciful Jesus! where did you come from." Phelm gripped the ledge of the table and shielded his eyes.

"It's my mother, she's sick." The girl ignored her nakedness as she pleaded for help.

"Your mother, she's not well you say, what is it?" Phelm took a step back, he had no intention of coming in contact with any sick people.

The girl stood to one side of the doorway and pointed into the interior of the room.

Pat, noting that his son was somewhat reluctant, accepted the challenge. Leaving his tea to one side, he crossed the floor and entered the room.

In the dim light he saw a woman lying on a litter of foul smelling straw in one corner of the room. Her stomach had collapsed and he could clearly see her spine and rib cage.

This emaciated wretch of a woman on seeing him opened and closed her mouth but couldn't produce a sound.

He was distracted by a sudden movement in the far corner where there was another foul smelling make shift bed. Cautiously he moved nearer. Two beady eyes appeared from under a rotting putrid blanket. He stood transfixed as a huge rat disclosed itself. Standing upright on its back legs it looked around the room. Then it began to preen its whiskers. Seeing Pat it made a dart for cover and in doing so, pulled the rotting blanket to one side. Pat was shocked to see the half eaten corpse of a man. His rotting trunk was being eaten by the rats who were now scurrying to safety on hearing intruders.

This he presumed was the girl's father or what was left of him. As he stood there the horror of what was happening within the cottage became clear to him.

The mother and daughter, too weak to move were living in the same room as the putrid corpse on which the rats were feeding. Soon they too would become a mere meal themselves.

Keeping his distance from the girl he slowly left the room, there was nothing that he could do for them.

"God be good to you all, you have our prayers." Tears welled up in his eyes as he looked in pity at the girl.

"What is it father?" Phelm called.

"We must be leaving now, sorry to have disturbed you," he signalled to his son to collect their belongings.

"Good God Phelm, this country must be one mass open graveyard, there were two further corpses in the bed."That girl, God help her, will not last the night."

"Is there nothing we can do, Father? We just cannot abandon them."

"What do you suggest we do ? There is no place to take them and even if that were possible, moving them would kill them."

"If we stay here then we too will contract whatever plague they are dying from. In there lies the body of what was once a man and he half eaten by rats. Will you come away in the name of God son."

There was a blizzard blowing as they left the cottage. Trudging along through the bleak countryside, Phelm began to worry. His father was lagging behind.

"Come on dad let me help you, we must find shelter," Phelm encouraged him.

H was nearing exhaustion from carrying his father and fighting the storm. If he did not find shelter soon then they too would die. He would have to leave him in some sheltered spot and seek sanctuary. He cursed his father for his stubbornness.

Finding a holy well set into the road with a canopy of stone over and several blessed candles glued to the slab he called on his father to take refuge inside. Taking his tinder box he lit the candles and told his father to warm himself and await his return.

"Whatever else Father, try and keep warm and for God's sake don't move from here, I'll be back soon as I find shelter. Pray for us both."

Two miles down the road he came to a signpost. Climbing the stone wall he cleared the snow obliterating the sign.

He cried and prayed his relief as he read and reread the directions; Dromcolliher two miles.

The blizzard held no fear for him now as he retraced his steps back to where he had left his father. Pat was still sitting in the recess with his obligatory rosary beads in his hands.

"Feeling better dad? I've got good news, the town is only two miles ahead." Through sheer will power and the knowledge that there was sanctuary within reach, they forced their tired and freezing bodies to continue.

Never was there any town more welcome than was the town of Dromcolliher that night.

Stopping at the first cottage showing a light, they knocked on the door. It was opened by a young woman of about twenty-six. She stood in the doorway, the light from the kitchen silhouetting her friendly face. Even from here they felt the warmth of the kitchen as they pleaded for sanctuary.

"Come in and welcome," these words were worth more than all the prayers in heaven to them.

"God bless the house and may His peace reign within," Pat invoked his blessing on the house as he crossed the threshold into the kitchen and stood with his back to the fire.

"Where have you two come from in such atrocious weather might I ask?" The woman looked across at Pat who was as near to the comforting heat of the fire as he could safely get.

"We've come from the other side of Limerick and are on our way to Tullylease to see my brother, God help him. This is my son Phelm," Pat informed her as he hugged the fire.

"My name is Anne Kilderry and my husband Tom is confined to his bed with a heavy cold, your welcome to stay but I'm afraid we have no food to offer you."

"You're hospitality is more than generous and for it we invoke the blessing of God on this house." Once again Pat called a blessing on the house and its inhabitants.

"Could we be so bold as to ask for some hot water to make a drop of tea?" Phelm asked as he lay his haversack on the table.

"You're more than welcome, take what you will." Anne pointed to the iron kettle in the corner of the fire belching out steam.

Phelm prepared a meal and invited the young woman to join them. She thanked them for their generosity but declined.

"Did you not hear tell of the problems they are having over in Cork?" asked Anne.

"To tell you the truth Mam I was warned," Pat replied,"It was my stubbornness and family loyalty that brought us here. You see, my brother Luke over in Tullylease is seriously ill. If I had the time over again I would have stayed at home, but it's too late now." He admitted.

"You wouldn't be Luke Griffin's brother now, would you?

"The very same, do you know him then?" He chirped up.

"Well! Not really but you are here now and welcome, I'll not keep you up any longer. The settled bed is more than comfortable. I must take the lamp but there is enough light from the fire." Bidding them"goodnight," Anne left to tend to her husband.

Phelm thought it strange that the woman had asked about his uncle and then shied away from any further discussion. However the puzzle held little relevance as no sooner had they laid their heads on their makeshift pillows than they were fast asleep.

It was late next morning when they were awakened by the crying of a baby.

"Good morning, you must have been really tired." Anne was standing by the table with a baby in her arms.

"If you wish to freshen up there is a basin in the scullery and plenty of hot water."

"We'll be beholding to you Mam," Phelm thanked her as she discreetly left the room.

With their ablution finished and a warm meal taken they thanked her and were once again on the road. At least it had stopped snowing though it would still be difficult going.

Passing the church dedicated to Muire na Sneachta on the final leg of their journey Pat remarked on how ironic it was that there was little if any snow in the old churchyard. Was this not the place where the woman Ui Liatain built her church?

"I've never heard of this place before."

Pat began to tell the story of 'Mary of the Snows'.

"It is said that the woman wanted to build a church to Our lady but was undecided as to where to build it. It was a beautiful summers day as she wandered, searching for a suitable site with little success. Then an out of season snow storm suddenly obliterated the town. All that is except for one field.

Taking this to be a message from the Blessed Virgin she had

the church built in the field. She dedicated her church to 'Our lady of the Snow'."

Phelm stopped, and looked around at the Yew trees overhanging the graveyard. With the thick blanket of snow all around them it wasn't difficult to believe that perhaps the legend was true after all.

Journeys end

About a mile further down the track Pat opened the gate of a long drive leading up to a cottage.

"We're there son, thanks be to God, we made it." Walking up the drive there was a noticeable absence of activity about the house. Lifting the latch Pat walked into the kitchen followed by his son. A woman was bent over the fire stirring the contents of a pot. Hearing the door opening she turned and looked at the two figures silhouetted in the doorway.

"Good God! Are my eyes deceiving me or is it yourself Pat? And you too Phelm? Come in, come in. You got my letter then? I didn't expect that you would make it, especially in this weather." She dropped the spoon into the pot and ran to greet them.

"Ah Nora, Nora. God help you. Sorry for your troubles," Pat closed his arms around his brother's wife.

"Its God's holy will, so it is. Come on, sit yourselves down. I'll make a drop of tea for ourselves," she released herself from her brother-in-law's arms.

"Where is he? resting no doubt, can I see him?" Pat asked question after question.

"Slow down, have your tea and I'll explain all to you both." Nora said no more as she busied herself with setting the table for the meal. When all was ready she joined them and began her story.

"Your brother is dead Pat, God rest his soul. There was nothing that could be done."

"The light of Jesus to his soul. Whatever happened to him"? Both men crossed the kitchen and dipping their hands in the holy water font blessed themselves. They then returned to their seats by the fire.

"Luke and his friends had been called to a gathering at Millford to discuss the rising demand for increased rates and taxes. On the return journey they were caught in a violent snow storm and took shelter in a deserted cottage near to Kilbolaine castle.

There was Luke, Seamus O'Keefe and Pat McCarthy in the company of each other. Like they always were, folk around about called them the three apostles.

All was fine in the cottage and they soon had a good roaring fire going. They saw no sense in leaving the cottage until the storm had abated and settled down as best they could for the night.

Luke removed his boots as did the others and all snuggled close to the fire. Luke, God be good to him, chose a corner away from the draught near to the chimney stack. Well he would, and him with a bad back.

It was well past midnight so he told me, when he heard Seamus O'Keefe call out in agony,"Jesus I've been bitten."

The others thought this hilarious and at the same time annoying, as they had been sleeping or at least dozing.

"Go back to sleep will you, its no more than a wayward flea." Pat McCarthy chided him.

Some minutes later Luke felt something crawling up his leg and reaching down he tried to brush it off. It was then that he too was attacked and bitten.

Then God be merciful to their souls, all three were attacked by vicious hungry rats. They screamed in agony and terror as more rats, smelling the blood and intent on a meal, attacked them.

Luke saw Seamus grappling with a huge rat as it tore at his throat. He scrambled across the floor to help before he was once again attacked himself. Poor Luke fell to the floor unable to dislodge the rats. Two more giant rats joined the frenzy as blood flowed freely down his face and neck. They were fearless in their attack and tore at poor Luke's face and throat.

With God given strength he reached the fireplace and grabbed at a sod of smouldering turf. With this as a weapon he attacked the brutes holding onto his face. The smell from the burning hair entered his nostrils and throat making him choke.

The turf burned his face and hands but he ignoring the pain and continued to burn them with it.

113

For a moment or two longer they continued their attack on him. Then falling to the floor screaming they retreated to the nearest bolt hole.

Luke staggered to his feet and went across to help Seamus who by now was lying unconscious on the floor with rats crawling all over his poor body.

With the aid of the burning turf he was able to drive them back into their bolt holes.

Pat, who had escaped the worst of the attack, was none the less covered in blood and bites. With God given strength he staggered to the fireplace and threw the creel of turf into the fire. The wicker basket soon caught alight.

In the light from the fire they saw that the cottage was swarming with packs of rats of all shapes and sizes. They seemed to be fearless and in a frenzy as they ran up and down their clothing biting at their necks and faces.

It was now a matter of survival. Grabbing several pieces of smouldering turf they made their escape to where Seamus lay. How they got him and themselves out of the cottage was a miracle. Yet suffice to say that they had left their boots and coats behind them.

They staggered from the cottage dragging Seamus between them through the snow and on to the Tullylease Road. They did not stop until they reached the cottage here.

In answer to their insistent banging on the door I came into the kitchen and drew the bolt What a sight greeted my eyes. God in heaven! I pray that he will spare me ever having to witness such again. My Luke was covered in blood from head to toes. Seamus was bitten and cut around the face and arms. I got the impression that he was dead. I could see clearly the bite marks on their faces.

Pat was not that bad, but bad enough, if you know my meaning. I done what I could for them.

I was angry with them because I was under the impression that they had been in a fight. Then Luke told me what had happened in the cottage.

They spent the rest of the night reliving over and over again the horror of that place. Well Pat and Luke did, Seamus as I said, was near to death and not one word did he speak. I let them carry on. It was best that they got it out of their systems.

I could not get Pat to stop talking like a madman, he was delirious, God between us and all harm. I could not leave them alone nor could I go and tell their folk. They were babbling like babies, making no sense whatsoever. Pat kept clinging to me and pleading with me to stay with him. Luke ran into the ashes and began picking up the red coals from the fire and began throwing them around the house.

They were neither coming nor going if you take my meaning. That is all except Seamus, he did not recover consciousness until the next morning. I called on their families next day so I did. They came and somehow or other got them to their homes.

For the next two days or so their wounds seemed to be healing and they were well on the road to recovery, or so we thought.

Then Pat took a sweating fever and was confined to his bed. Seamus collapsed the very next day with the same symptoms. Your brother Luke collapsed that afternoon with the fever. It was put down to the fact that they had got wet and cold after having to abandon their clothes and boots in the cottage.

But the fever was getting worse and they were burning up. Why I could hardly touch Luke's body with the heat and he kept on and on talking what to me was nonsense talk.

Their wounds that we thought were healing erupted, I can use no other words to explain it. Oh God help us all, the smell. Oh the smell! I'll never forget that putrefying smell, for as long as God leaves life in my body.

It was as if the Devil himself had taken over his body.

The doctor from the dispensary came and examined Luke. Then he asked me what happened and I up and told him about the rats. There was no more to say or do for all three were removed from their homes and taken to the isolation hospital.

The bedding was taken from the house and burnt. They gave us new bedding and carbolic soap and told us to scrub every inch of the house. We were told that we would not be allowed to visit them until they began to show signs of recovery. Seamus died that night God rest his soul and Pat went the following day."

Nora, stopped her tale and stared at Pat, tears standing in her eyes.

"My Luke hung on suffering untold agony, so I was told for a couple more days and he calling my name before he too died.

We were not allowed to see them, God be good to them one and all. They died alone. The Priest gave them final absolution from outside the door. They are now lying in sealed coffins side by side in the mortuary attached to the hospital. They would have been buried there and then but for the fact that I insisted that it be delayed until all the relatives had been notified. It was the only concession that they allowed us and that for just three days. You see the burial is to be tomorrow. The family graves have been opened and I am told that when the coffins are interred the graves will be covered in quicklime."

As Phelm watched, his father's expression changed from disbelief to horror and finally to anguish as Nora recounted the story.

"God be good and merciful to them all, what a death to suffer", stammered Pat.

"Where will it all end?" Pat looked up at the picture of the Sacred Heart with the cross of St Bridget below it. The shock was obviously telling on his father. Pat for no apparent reason began to tell of the encounters that they had on their way. His narrative was shambling, half-hearted, his thoughts obviously elsewhere.

"What in God's name brought you two here in the first place I'll never understand?" Nora broke into the tale. A look of bewilderment crossing Pat's face.

"Did you not hear of what happened in the village of Skibbereen? The streets there are littered with dead and dying. Starving rats, cats and dogs are fighting over the corpses. In one cottage they found a whole family. The father was still barely alive. His wife and five children were dead lying on the bed. Their cat had dragged the dead infant from the mother's breast and was eating it. The plague has spread into Cork city itself and is at this very moment creeping towards Limerick. Nobody is making any effort to contain it. God forgive me for saying this, but in some villages the parish Priests are stopping any strangers from seeking within their boundaries. I very much doubt if you would have found a friendly house past here. The roads are patrolled by vigilantes bent on protecting their villages. More likely you would have got an ash plant across your back at the very least and ordered back to where you came from.

They are predicting that the plague will soon reach the ports of Limerick and Cork. There will be no more relief ships from America. Ireland will be left to the mercy of the rats and the plague.

Pat looked very old and tired as he sank into his brother's favourite chair by the fire.

"Surely God and his Blessed mother will not allow such a catastrophe befall on holy Ireland, we must all pray, prayer is powerful." Nora blessed herself and looked up at the sorrowful picture of the Sacred Heart above the fireplace. Pat was by no means as convinced as his sister-in-law.

Next morning, the villagers assembled at the Church to celebrate mass in memory of the three men. The mass had to take place without the presence of the coffins.

On leaving the church, the dray came down the road with the three coffins side by side.

They tried to fall in behind in the traditional procession as was the custom but that too was denied them. They were held back by the peelers until the coffins had been interred in the graves and covered in quick lime. Only then they were allowed to approach the graveside to say a prayer.

Afterwards Phelm remarked on how wise this decision had been and should be followed in all cases where death was caused by plague.

They spent the rest of the week renewing old acquaintances. By the end of the week the weather had improved and the coaches were once again operating. They decided that this would be an opportune time to take advantage of the situation to return to their home in Castlelurgan.

Tady brings sad news

October gave way to November without any respite in the foul weather. The snow continued to fall, this together with a biting cold wind added to the misery of the starving people. Anne having seen to Pat's needs sat in her old rocking chair knitting. The patchwork quilt that she had made with her own hands, covered her legs and lap protecting her against the icy cold draught blowing in under the half door.

She listened to the wind howling in the chimney stack and prayed that her son would return home safe. Snow flakes fell in a flurry onto the blazing fire before they sizzled out in a cloud of steam.

Slowly she succumbed to sleep. She was awakened by the rattling of the latch. Again she heard the latch rattle. Only this time there was an urgency about it. Removing the quilt from her knees she crossed the floor and opened the bolt on the main door. An icy blast of wind followed by drifting snow greeted her as she opened the door. Outside the half door she saw silhouetted in the failing light the outline of a tall gangly man covered in snow. She had to look twice before she recognised him as none other than Tady Quin.

"Good God, it's you Tady. Come in man, come in and welcome." She drew the bolt on the half door and held it open in greeting.

Drifting snow followed Tady through the door as he took advantage of the welcome. Anne closed both doors and locked them before joining Tady.

"It's wild out there Anne, the worst that I have witnessed in my whole life." I wouldn't be troubling you but I got caught on the road between Tipperary and Limerick." Tady was still his old apologetic self.

"Will you take off that wet coat Tady and sit yourself down by the fire. There's no need to apologise in this house," Anne took Tady's coatamore and placed in on a peg in the scullery to dry.

"Now Tady, I expect a mug of hot broth and a slice of scone would not go amiss." Without waiting for his reply she went to the fireplace and taking hold of the crane holding the pot of broth, set it over the fire.

"I'm more than obliged to you Anne, so I am. Tell me how are all the family?"

"Phelm is up in the house of his father-in-law and should be back soon. Pat is not all that good and is resting in the bedroom. I'll not disturb him just yet, have your broth first." She lifted the lid off the pot and stirred the contents.

Tady rose to his feet and turning his back to the fire lifted up the tail of his coat over the heat.

"I'm more than sorry to hear of Pat's illness. Not too serious I hope? And Phelm is married, who is the lucky girl? Would I know her by any chance?.

"You Tady Quin. Sure you must know half the country people. It's none other than Shelia McNulty."

"Little Shelia from the Castle farm? I remember the family well. Generous as the day is long, how the years have gone by."

"The very same family, now sit down and eat you must be famished." She placed a generous plate of sliced buttered scone on the table. Then going into the scullery she returned with a large bowl and filled it with steaming hot broth.

She watched as Tady ravenously consumed the food placed before him. He finished the meal by using the last of the scone to mop up what remained in the dish.

Thanking her, he returned to the warmth of the fire. Tired out by his arduous journey and aided by the welcoming heat from the fire, he soon fell into a deep sleep.

It was dark when he was awakened by someone entering the kitchen. Looking up he saw Phelm dusting snow from his cap against the leg of his trousers.

"You're more than welcome to the Griffin house, Tady Quin." Phelm came forward smiling, his hand outstretched in greeting.

"Thanks Phelm, I'm to understand that congratulations are in order." Both men shook hands warmly.

Anne came from the bedroom carrying a food tray.

"So you are back at last, Phelm"? Everything alright, I hope? There's hot broth in the pot. Pat's awake now Tady, and is anxious to meet you. Don't be expecting too much of him."

Tady entered the bedroom, he could see at once that Pat was indeed a sick man and in great pain.

"Your welcome Tady, I see that the thatch is getting a little thin like my own." Pat stroked his hair and tried to rise from the bed with little success.

"I am sorry indeed to hear that times are not too good to you Pat. I'll not be forgetting you in my prayers."

Tady looked with sympathy at his old friend.

"Sure you know that I'm not the one for complaining. Will you put a few sods on the fire, before you tell me all the news."

"Can I have a drag or two on the pipe, that is if it won't upset the company?" Tady having seen to the fire sat down on a chair opposite Pat.

"Sure I'll join you myself, helps the concentration.""Would you be so good as to light my pipe for me." Pat pointed to his pipe lying beside the bed.

Tady lit both pipes and handed Pat his, before he settled down to relate all the news from the city and county.

"I'll tell you this Pat, you're in the best place," Tady sent a cloud of sweet smelling tobacco smoke towards the ceiling. "The whole of the country is now in the grip of starvation and plague, Pat.

Skibbereen is on the verge of death. Corpses are piling up in the street and in the hedgerows. The rats are no longer frightened and are joining the dogs and cats in eating the bodies.

Luckily, if it could be called luck, the intense cold is preventing the plague from spreading. Cork has made plans to close the city to all outsiders. There is little food and the situation can no longer be contained.

There are many too weak to fight the plague and hunger. They feel that their God has deserted them and can you really blame them? For three long years now, as you and I well know to our cost, they have endured the hunger and placed their fate in the hands of God. He has not listened to their pleas.

Why did he not show any compassion to the children dying in the arms of their mothers? Their poor little innocent gaunt faces and staring eyes showing how they had suffered before death mercifully put an end to their agony.

Did I not see it with my own two eyes. Mother's their empty breasts dripping the green saliva around the nipples. I saw one woman chewing grass and feeding it to her baby, desperate to keep the child alive. The following day both were dead.

I can tell you Pat, I cried unashamedly at the sight and it shook my faith in God. I often wondered if God was so convinced of their love and devotion towards him, Why was he inflicting such crass punishment on them?

Poor innocent babies, who never harmed a soul."

In his frustration Tady gave a kick at a sod of turf that had escaped from the fire. Sparks raced up the chimney.

"Those about to die found a quiet spot preferably beside a church to lay down their lives. They said their last goodbyes to their families and friends and having said their final prayers waited for death. They would not intrude on the sympathy of others. They would accept death freely. Hoping that God in his mercy would understand their plight on this earth and be generous in his punishment to them in purgatory.

I crossed the Slieve Aughty mountains, through the gap at Derrybrien some months ago and came to the village of Bunnaglass.

It was there, that I came across, for the first time the practice of bricking ones family inside the house to die."

"You're not telling me that the landlords are now bricking their tenants up inside their cottages? Jesus in heaven, what next I ask" Pat was shocked.

"No! it's not the landlords Pat. I was told on good authority, that when the family caught the plague, they retired to their homes and make their peace with God. Once inside they brick themselves up in their cottages and secure the door from within. There they die together away from the eyes of their neighbours and the shame of it all.

Sure I saw one of the houses myself. I was assured that the whole family were entombed inside and long dead."

"Now, why in God's holy name would they do such a thing?"

"Don't you realise Pat, there are no coffins. Even the sliding coffins are wearing away. They wish to die with dignity, so they do.
I asked one man why he did not try and fight on? He told me,"It's God's holy will, so be it." Tady paused to rekindle his pipe.
"It was said that from Cratlow through the Burren and on into Donegal little if any life remains. Not that I have been there myself. Others have been and confirmed the rumours.
Those who have not died from the hunger and the plague are being deported to Canada by their landlords.
In Limerick, a ship broker and landlord by the name of Spaight, bought a ship and offered free passage to any of his tenant families willing to demolish their hovels and leave Ireland forever. He claimed that he had found a solution to the Irish problem for the paltry sum of £3 per head."
"Three Pounds for a human being, sad days Tady, sad days indeed." Pat pulled the blanket tighter around his waist.
"Sad or not this is the sum it cost him to supply passage and food on board his ship for each person. Still, I suppose it is a far better offer than some other were given." Tady paused to rekindle his pipe.
"Did you not hear of what Lord Palmerston of Sligo done to his tenants, and him the foreign secretary, if you don't be minding?"
"Sure how would I hear any news lying here. Go on, you'll tell me anyway." Pat shuffled himself in the bed.
"He decided to get rid of as many of his tenants as possible without any fuss.
He acquired nine ships and persuaded 2,000 of his unwanted tenants to accept passage to Quebec in Canada.
He told them that they would have a new life there and that he would provide them with free passage and food on the journey. On their arrival in Canada his agents would be waiting for them with warm clothing and the sum of between two pounds and five pounds for each family. depending on the number of dependants."
"Well that was a generous inducement and better than dying of hunger." Pat interrupted.
"It would have been were it true, but it was nothing but a

charade to get the tenants off his hands." Tady pointed his pipe at Pat, to get the message home.

"Hundreds died on the journey and were buried at sea.

Those who survived were shocked to see the docks covered in freezing snow and ice. The cold ate into their frail bodies."

"I thought you told me that his agents would meet them," Pat interrupted.

"I done no such thing, are you listening at all", Tady chided Pat for his lack of attention.

"There was no sign of any agents. It was all done to get them quietly off his land.

Barefooted and with nothing to cover them but rags they were wearing to cover them. Sure many were naked as the day that they were born. They were dumped on the quayside."

Do you know where Lord Palmerston agents are ?" The poor deluded emigrants questioned the puzzled stevedores.

Many by now had collapsed and others were dying. Mother's lay their children down on the quayside and found on trying to lift them again that they were trapped in the freezing ice where they died.

The French and British Canadians on seeing the plight of the emigrants returned them to the ships.

They ordered the masters to hold them on board until they returned.

Soon on sleigh and on foot they returned with blankets, food and hot drinks.

Then they opened their hearts and houses to them until they could recover and get settled.

On being asked what they thought of Lord Palmerston one spokesman replied.

"To the Devil I give the black heart of Lord Palmerston."

Many of the other English landlords are following suit. You should be at Limerick docks and listen to the stories of horror that they tell. These are mariners who have sailed on these boats so they know what they are talking about.

One mariner told me, and he near to tears, of the mass graves of dead Irish on Gross Island in the St Lawrence river in Canada.

Yet the poor Irish are taking no notice of their warnings.

They would rather risk the passage than starve to death in Ireland.

Mercenary passage brokers are displaying a loaf of bread in their office windows in Liverpool in England. This to lure the emigrants to book passage with them, on the pretence that full board is included in the fare. Nothing is further from the truth. Each Hell ship is filled beyond capacity. What food there is on board is soon eaten.

I tell you Pat, it is little short of murder." Tady paused and took a deep breath.

"The mariners told us that it is illegal to carry passengers below the Plimsoll line. Yet it is in these holds that men women and children are being incarcerated. There are little if any complaints, for every one who refuses to take a berth, two are waiting to take their places.

The vile stench that permeates from the holds when they are opened in the morning and again in the evening to let the emigrants get a little exercise, fresh air, slop out and remove their dead is overpowering."

"Conditions must be appalling for the poor wretches, Tady" Pat tried to adjust his pillow without success.

"Here let me do that for you." Tady lifted Pat's head and settled the pillow.

"Go on Tady, you must think me a proper cripple."

Tady ignored this remark and continued with the news.

"Now the American passenger ships on the other hand are far superior to the British and conditions are acceptable.

I saw the American ships myself, so I did. Tall, slim, graceful and clean. Lady like if you catch my meaning."

"I know what you are trying to say Tady, thoroughbred, aristocratic like."

"Aren't you the one for the fine words Pat Griffin. I could not have put it better if I tried."

"Go on anyway don't let me interrupt the flow." Pat dismissed the compliment.

"The fare on these is higher than that on British ships. That's why the landlords are sending their tenants on the British ships. It is said that even the healthy ones sometimes never get there. Most of the ships the British are providing are rotting from stem to stern.

A sailor told me that he was on board a merchantman, sailing some miles behind one of the coffin ships in the Atlantic ocean. There was a swell, but this was to be expected. The lookout saw her bob up and down on the horizon. Then for no apparent reason she floundered. They made full sail to the spot. On arrival the seas were covered in flotsam and bodies. Not one of the three hundred who were on board were alive to be rescued.

The Americans are now refusing to accept any ship in her ports carrying sick Irish emigrants. The masters are told to take their human cargo north to Canada.

They are British citizens and Canada is British territory, they are their problem. I heard tell of some who tried to get into America by walking ashore to prove that they're healthy. Most collapse on the quayside and are carried back on board the ships that they had tried to escape from.

"You must be parched dry from all the talking," Anne came into the room carrying two mugs of tea.

"Thanks Anne, you're so thoughtful." Tady took the mugs from her.

"Here Pat, can you handle it?"

"Thanks Tady, I'm fine. Pat reached out and took the mug. Tady cupped the mug in his hands and continued his tales.

"Those fit enough, walk across the border from Canada and enter the United States illegally. They do not want to be part of anything British, and honestly Pat, who could blame them."

"Most people I've talked to believe that Ireland is doomed and that only America offers any hope for them. Those who make it to Canada are abandoned without adequate clothing or food. Many are picked up dead, literally encased in ice. Men, women and children, roam the snow covered streets in their bare feet. Many seriously ill with the plague. Bodies are found days, sometimes weeks, later covered by the drifting snow.

The Canadians are more than generous to the masses of half starved naked Irish. They have given them free access to their barns and provided them with food. In many cases where children and mothers are involved they have shared their homes with them.

When they could do no more for them, they cried in sympathy with them. Sure I'm repeating myself now."

The chat was interrupted by Anne entering the room with a tray of refreshments.

Tady stayed in the house for the remainder of the week and his constant chatter and company was a tonic. His stories and yarns had a therapeutical effect on Pat.

Anne was grateful to Tady and was not lacking in her generosity when he finally and reluctantly left the house.

Phelm seeks help and finds a nightmare

Pat's health was deteriorating at an alarming pace and it became obvious that he needed more than the care given by Anne. Gentle and caring though she was. He now needed qualified medical attention. Phelm decided that he would have to get to the city, it being the nearest place where he would find a doctor.

Donning his warmest clothing and taking provisions for the journey he left the house promising that he would return with the doctor. If not, then with medicine. Keeping to the shelter of the woods he made good progress through the appalling weather and soon found himself outside the village of Singland.

Seeking respite and shelter he came upon a dilapidated house. The house, what was left of it, had long been tumbled. No doubt, thought Phelm, on the instructions of the landlord. The roof had been opened to the weather. The walls purposely caved in, the windows smashed. This was one house that would never be occupied again. What there was left of it would give him sanctuary and privacy to partake of his food before the final leg of his journey.

Phelm entered through what was once the front door. As his eyes became accustomed to the darkness, he went deeper into the ruin seeking a sheltered corner. Then he noticed that someone had dug out a scailpeen at the gable end of what was once the kitchen.

Cautiously he approached the entrance. Calling to the occupants to assure them that he was a friend. There was no reply to his pleadings. Perhaps they were huddled inside in mortal fear for their lives. Again he tried to reassure them that they had nothing to fear from him. The silence that greeted him was oppressive. His senses were more alert than they ever had been. There was someone present, he could hear them scuffling about.

Moving closer he pulled some timbers blocking the entrance to one side. Behind which was a length of hessian sacking. He was sure now that there were people inside, for the entrance had been secured from within. Again he called on the occupants, to reveal themselves, they had no reason to fear him. He waited in anticipation for some acknowledgement to his greeting. His blood raced through his ears and his heart beat faster. He waited there was no reply.

With trembling hands he cautiously opened the sacking. The sight that met his eyes was beyond comprehension. Deep inside the ruined cottage next to the gable wall was a makeshift bed. On it lay the emaciated body of a woman with the remains of a naked infant lying across her chest.

Rats of all shapes and sizes were feeding on the two corpses. On seeing Phelm they abandoned their banquet and stared at him. Their beady eyes flashing in the dim light. Slowly they backed away baring their yellow teeth as a warning. Then as one they scurried for the safety of the nearest bolt hole. Phelm felt his stomach retch and retreated to the nearest corner where he was violently sick.

Feeling intimidated and in a state of panic he tried to escape from the scene. In his confused state he ran deeper into the scalpeen. To his utter horror he fell over the body of a man and landed on the earthen floor between the bodies of two young boys.

All were dead, their empty staring eyes looking directly at him, their mouths wide open in silent screams. Inside one he saw a rat backing away deeper inside the corpse. Their stomachs moved and heaved, he knew that there were more rats inside the corpses. Although the bodies were frozen there was still a foul sweetish stench permeating from them. What nation would perpetrate such obscene abomination and pestilence on their own citizens. He wanted to get as far away as possible from the grim spectacle.

Yet as in a spell he found that he could not move. In a blind consternation he finally scrambled from the hovel and ran as far away from the ghastly scene as he possibly could.

Running blindly through the snow he stopped at the welcoming front door of a cottage. He banged the door with both his fists, demanding admittance.

In answer to his insistent challenge, the door was finally opened by a gaunt looking man. His eyes were sunken deep in his head. He had several sacks tied around him from head to toe. As Phelm had sacking tied around his feet to keep him warm, he presumed that the man had done likewise.

The man invited him inside and closed the door behind him. The house was icy cold and in the fire grate was one perhaps two sods of wet turf making a brave effort to stay alight. Snow kept falling down the chimney, forming piles of black slush on the kitchen floor.

In a bed next to the fire lay a young woman, her face drawn and haggard for her young years.

"This is my wife Mary." The man pointed a long bony index finger towards the bed.

Phelm removed his cap and greeted her. The woman made no effort to return his greeting. Ignoring him she pulled the threadbare blanket over her and faced the wall. She shook violently from the intense cold and muttered to herself.

On the table stood a basin filled with dishes and cups. These were covered in a solid mass of filthy ice. From his observations he noted that the cottage had not been cleaned for some considerable time.

Under the circumstances he wondered if it was worth relating what he had witnessed to them. From what he had observed within the house they were in dire straits themselves.

He had to tell someone though or go mad himself. Finally he told of finding the family dead in the scailpeen. The man listened in silence as he related his story. Then he began to walk like a puppeteer, slowly around and around the table, drawing on its ice covered surface with his index finger. Stopping he looked directly at Phelm.

"Dead were they, is that what you say?" The man repeated over and over again. Crossing to the fireplace he knelt down in front of the fire and blew on the wet turf. His eyes became red raw from the smoke and tears streamed down his cheeks. These he wiped away with the sleeve of his ragged coat. The miserable fire sent out a few sparks before it resumed smouldering once again.

"They were dead, I tell you, dead. All of them, and I could do nothing." Phelm was getting hysterical at the indifference being shown.

"Dead you say, that would be the O'Donnells if I'm not mistaken. Friends of the wife's if you must know."

Rising to his feet he wiped his wet nose again on his sleeve. Retracing the marks he had made previously on the table top with his finger. He lifted his feet knee high as he slowly walked round and round the table.

"Suffering from the Yellow Fever they were following the tumbling of their house." He continued walking round and round the room talking to himself. He would stop occasionally and look towards the fireplace.

"Will you stand still man and listen." Phelm was showing his annoyance.

"The O'Donnell's are dead Mary", ignoring Phelm, he went across to the bed and looked down at his wife. A tear fell from his cheek onto the threadbare blanket. His wife ignored this information and pulled the blanket closer around her neck.

"It's the famine fever you know, it will come to us all sooner or later." He pointed at Phelm with his index finger of his skeleton of a hand.

He looked like the Grim Reaper and sent a cold shiver through Phelm.

"Jesus is present now, he has come to take us to his paradise, Praise be to you Lord Jesus." The man opened his hands wide and faced the fireplace. Falling to his knees he prostrated himself in the shape of a cross in the wet slush.

"On your knees man! behold this is Christ, the saviour of the world." The man was obviously delirious. Rising to his feet he blessed himself and approached the bed.

"The time has come Mary! did you see and feel the presence of Jesus. Today we will all be with him in paradise." He tapped his wife on the back but she made no movement whatsoever.

"What fever?, in God's name pull yourself together man," Phelm was getting exasperated with him.

"They returned and built that Scailpeen, not to be meddled

with that Jack O'Donnell, a proud and stubborn man is our Jack, salt of the earth."

"I tell you they are all dead!, dead, you fool, can't you understand." Clenching his hands in frustration he faced the man and banged the table. A cup fell off the table and landed with a crash on the floor.

"I'm sorry about that." Phelm looked contrite at the man.

The man ignored him and crossed to the bed to lay down beside his wife.

"Why don't you get a doctor for your wife?" Phelm moved away from the bed.

"Hospitals, doctors, are you too out of your mind, there are no doctors for us. Rising to his feet he once again returned to the fireplace where he went on his knees and blew on the smouldering wet turf.

"There's not even room in the workhouse in the city." He began to cough and shake uncontrollably.

"It's full I tell you, full of the dead and dying, this land is cursed." He held his fists tightly by his side and seemed to stretch.

"We will spend our last days on earth here together, my Mary and me.

My sons left for the States last year, I heard that the ship floundered. Is this true? You're not one of them are you? Come to take us to the States have you? It is the will of God and his Blessed Mother," The man continued to ask and answer his own questions.

Phelm could hardly believe what he was hearing. The man was delirious, he had capitulated to death.

Yet in some far recess within his mind the man remembered his sons and their promise to return for them both. He knew also that their ship had floundered and that they would not be returning. Yet he still clung to the hope that he was mistaken.

It was not his sons that he was waiting for. It was his God to come and take both himself and his wife to paradise.

"You may go or stay, all we can offer you is our prayers, and a lot of good they done us."

The man rose from the fireplace abandoning the smouldering fire. He crossed the room and raising the thin blanket he once again lay down beside his wife. Phelm crossed the floor and took hold of the latch on the door.

"Close the door when you leave, there won't be any more callers. Pray for our souls whoever you are, Sir." He placed his thin hand around his wife. She placed her hand in his, perhaps for the last time.

Phelm turned and looked at the couple in the bed. They had made their peace with the world and could not be hurt any more.

Phelm looked across at the fire as the last of the turf began to send out a warm glow. This was soon quenched by more snow falling down the chimney. There was no further movement from the couple in the bed. The fire continued to smoulder.

Phelm looked across at the couple their hands were now entwined. As he looked he saw a wedding ring on the finger of the woman. He could see that it was of little value. A shaft of light coming through the window made it sparkle for a moment. Their God would surely welcome this innocent couple into Heaven.

"May God give you peace and with his angels and saints welcome you both into his paradise."

He dipped his hand into the holy water font at the door. His intention was to give a final blessing to the couple. Fate had again struck a cruel blow, the font was empty.

Making the sign of the cross and with a final prayer he lifted the latch. Ice cold snow hit him in the face. He found it refreshing, compared with the smell of death within the house. Slowly and with due respect he closed the door leaving the couple to themselves and their God.

From what he had witnessed and heard he decided that no useful purpose would be served by going to the city.

The place was riddled with plague and yellow fever. He did not know just what these plagues were but he was apprehensive enough to avoid the city and its people.

His whole being cried out for the comfort of his wife and family. He had a strange premonition of fear and anxiety. Why he felt like this he put down to the trauma of his recent experiences.

Although tired and distressed from his exhausting journey

Phelm did not rest until he reached his own home and the comfort of his family. Once there he again related his horrendous experience on the road to Limerick.

He was disappointed that he was unable to obtain any medical attention for his father. It was some comfort however to see that his father was once again able to sit by the fire. He was now so traumatised that he was falling asleep over his supper.

"You had best get some rest now, there is no need to be in any hurry to rise in the morning." Shelia comforted him.

"Do you know I am so tired that I could sleep on the prongs of a hay fork." He rose from the chair and went straight to his bedroom.

In the early hours of the morning Shelia was awakened by her husband screaming. Looking down at him as the sweat poured from his body she could see that he was having a nightmare.

She shook him until he awakened and looked at her confused.

"Jesus help me, Shelia! I was dreaming that I was back in the Scailpeen and the dead people were trying to catch me."

"Go back to sleep, it was just a bad dream, you are overtired."

He tried to sleep. but sleep came only spasmodically, as he tossed and turned all night long.

Medical relief at last

"Come on lazy bones, get this down you." Phelm was awoke to see Shelia standing at the side of the bed.
She reached out a cup of tea to him.
"Did I sleep in, whatever time is it?" He reached up and took the cup.
"You had a good sleep and its no more that you needed,
"It's gone twelve." Shelia drew the curtains.
The snow was still falling and there was a distinct chill in the room.
"There seems little reason for me to rise, but still I'll be up as soon as I finish the tea."
In the afternoon he cleared a path through the snow to the barn, they were lucky in that they had a good supply of sweet hay. The cow would milk well for as long as it lasted. He had previously moved the hens into the barn with the cow, in the hope that they would lay a few more eggs in its heat and comfort.
The few hens that they had left kept themselves warm by scratching around the cow droppings in the straw and jumping up at the sheaf of corn left hanging from a hook on the barn wall by his mother.
What little flour and vegetables that they had they used sparingly.
During the second half of the week the snow abated and the villagers began to clear their roads.
The road to Limerick was also being cleared by men on the relief scheme. These were projects thought up by the government to give work to the needy.
Pat spent his day nursing the fire and cursing his bad luck, in that he was unable to move about.
Soon as the road to the city was passable, Anne asked Shelia if her brother Patrick would be able to take her and Phelm to the city in the trap. Provisions were running low and seeing

that there was a break in the weather they should take advantage of it.

Patrick was only too willing to oblige his sister and no doubt grateful at the same time for the opportunity to get away from the monotony of the farm. It would be a day out for them after the drudgery of the confinement during the bleak weather.

Patrick arrived early next morning with the pony and trap.

Anne heard the trap in the boreen and looked across as the latch was lifted. Patrick entered the kitchen and closed the door behind him.

"Will you have a bite to eat before you go?" Anne asked him, as she fussed over Phelm.

"Will you tell that mother of mine that I don't need all these coats and cravats." Phelm pleaded with Shelia.

"If you do what mother wants we will get away all the sooner." Patrick leaned against the jamb of the door and trailed the horse whip across the floor as if fishing.

"I asked if you wanted a bite to eat." Anne reminded Patrick.

"No thank you Mam! but a cup of tae wouldn't go amiss. Look at me? I'm wrapped up like a Christmas parcel." He pulled at the large scarf tucked inside his coat.

"Now Shelia, here is the shopping list and the money, look after it. Come on, get this down you." She handed Patrick the cup of tae.

"You won't forget my bit of baccy now will you"? Pat reminded Shelia.

"I put it on the list, will you not fret so." Anne reminded him.

Phelm and Patrick left the house followed by Shelia.

As Shelia began to leave Anne took her to one side and spoke to her quietly.

"Now whatever else don't forget to tell the doctor in the city about Pat's pains. I have no doubt but he will give you something to help." She went to the holy water font and sprinkled the blessed water over Shelia.

Anne stood at the door looking after the trap waving until it had left the boreen.

"I hope that they will be alright in the city." Anne remarked as she closed the door.

"There's no need to worry about them, they are no longer

your responsibility. Will you put the latch on the door there is an icy blast hitting me right in the back." Pat grumbled as he pulled the blanket tightly round his shoulders.

"Will you hold your whist Pat Griffin, I know you better than that. The way you mollycoddled Shelia when you heard that she was pregnant. One would think that she was made of glass." Anne took a delight in teasing Pat at every opportunity.

"I did no such thing, if you must know."

"Oh yes you did! you're just an old softy at heart."

He knew that he could never win an argument with Anne. Taking his pipe from under the blanket he lit it and relaxed back against the pillows, smiling to himself.

By late evening Anne heard the trap enter the lane and came out to greet them.

"Got everything then"? she asked as Patrick stepped down from the trap.

"That and a lot more besides, sure I had a job getting the two of them out of Limerick." Patrick rubbed his hands together. "God! let me look at the fire, my fingers are like icicles." He blew on his hands as he made a bee line towards the welcoming heat of the fire.

"Will you show a little manners and not hog the fire" Pat grumbled as Patrick stood before the fire.

Phelm helped Shelia down from the trap and began to unload the groceries. She placed the carrying bag on the table and took two half pint blue bottles from it.

I got the medicine that you wanted." She handed Anne the two bottles.

Anne picked up one of the bottles and removing the cork smelt it.

"You'll love this Pat it's strong enough to strip paint off the cart." She rubbed her nose as the fumes irritated her nostrils. The second bottle contained liniment to rub on his painful joints.

"I didn't forget yourself, if you must know." Shelia went across to Pat and handed him a hand of twist tobacco.

"There, didn't I tell you that she would not forget." He held the tobacco up for Anne to see.

He was more interested in his tobacco than he was in all

their bottles and cures.

Anne visits the Sideog Ri

The potato crop had now completely failed. The hunger grew in intensity. Neighbours became jealous of each other and begrudged them any little comfort. Should anyone show the least sign of prosperity then they became the target for rumour. Rumours grew to resentment, resentment grew to jealously and jealously to hatred. People who were the best of neighbours for untold years became sworn enemies.

There was constant friction of one kind or another. The people of Ireland known for their kindness were fast becoming resentful of the least sign of prosperity by their neighbours. Instead of sharing they now fought each other for a turnip or a crust of bread.

Pat and his family were to be no exception to this jealousy. Anne was the first to notice that some neighbours were ignoring them.

She could not conceive this undeniable hostile treatment and went to see those she suspected. They were filled with compunction that she should even think so little of their loyalty. They denied emphatically that they were involved. Anne knew better she had it out in the open now and was satisfied within herself. She would not be the one to make bad blood.

She never told her husband of this one sided vendetta. He was in no fit state to be burdened with such troubles.

Some days later she was to discover the extent of the resentment.

Going to the barn she was surprised to find that someone had placed a branch from a yew tree across the path leading to the barn. This was the first sign that a pishogue had been put on them and their house.

The Yew tree is regarded as sacred by some and evil by others. Should she inadvertently pick up the yew branch, then she would be cursed. She was aware of the powers of the pishogue and avoided any contact with the branch.

Picking her steps carefully she returned to the house and procured a bottle of holy water.

Opening it she faced to the East and sprinkled the branch with the water. She blessed herself. This ceremony she repeated to the west, to the North and to the South. Only then did she attempt to pick it up and lay it to one side. Secure in the knowledge that she and her family were now safe, she went to the barn where she milked her cow and fed her chickens.

No mention did she make to any of the family about her ordeal. These were matters best taken care of sympathetically. That evening she on her coat and a stout pair of boots and putting a bottle of holy water in her pocket she took herself off to the old graveyard. Seeking out the old pagan yew tree she approached it. Removing the cork from the bottle she blessed it. Only now that the tree was blessed would she dare to approach it. Sure enough someone had cut a branch from it.

Ah! the villainy of it all she thought. So there was evil intent towards her and her family. Her next stop was at the parish church where she opened a novena to St. Benedict.

Saint Benedict was the one saint who could protect her and her family. Finishing her prayers she rose from her knees and crossed the road to the priests house. There she asked the priest to get her six medals of St. Benedict. With no disrespect to his holy office, but to have them specially blessed by none other than the Franciscans monks in the city. The priest knowing that something was worrying her invited her into the parlour. He was well acquainted with the curse of the Pishogue and all its implications.

"Anne tell me truthfully has someone put a curse on your farm."?

Anne explained how she had discovered the branch from the pagan yew tree across the path.

"Sure that could be anything. It does not mean that anyone has put a Pishogue on you. No one would be that foolish knowing who you are"

The priest knew of her reputation and that she was in liaison with the Sideog Ri. Not that he approved of this pagan custom. He was at a cross roads between his strict Catholic upbringing, in not believing in such pagan customs and of his own experiences in the past with the powers of the fairies.

He crossed the room and taking the Sacred Stole from his wardrobe he kissed it and placed it round his shoulders.

Kneeling in front of Anne he place one end of the sacred stole in her right hand. Anne sank to her knees and blessed herself.

The Priest then invoked God to protect her and her family from all evil doers. Prayers finished they both blessed themselves before rising to their feet.

Anne did not feel fully content within herself as she left the priests house. She crossed the road and followed the long forgotten track to the old Fairy Fort. She crossed the stream to the place where the mistletoe grew in the old pagan hawthorn. A secret spot known only to her and the fairies.

There she took several small stones from the stream and made a small Cairn on its bank. Removing another stone she took it to the Cairn Mor. This she added it to the mound out of respect to the fairy King. Only then did she dare disturb the Fairies and give them the message that she, Anne Griffin, was for the calling.

The Sideog Ri would be glad of her presence. He would know that she had good reason for visiting him and would respond to her request.

She explained her predicament to him and called on him to exercise all his powers to protect her and her family. She wished him well and left him a little gift of iron. Contented now she returned to her home.

When she entered the house Shelia was in the process of cooking a meal.

"Where is Pat?" She removed her shawl and looked at the vacant sugan chair.

"He's not feeling himself, what with his pains and all, he took himself off to bed." Shelia told her.

Anne took Pat a bowl of gruel and a strong cup of tea, just the way he liked it. When supper was finished she left Shelia and Phelm sitting comfortable at the fireside.

Going into the scullery she removed the bottle of

Camphorated Oil and the medicine and went into her bedroom.

Phelm and Shelia smiled to each other as they heard Pat moaning about the smell of the oil.

"Will you stop moaning and lift yourself off your shirt." She was about to rub the oil into his bones.

"Will you not worry about me woman, if I were a donkey you'd have me put down."

"You a donkey, more like a stubborn mule, now lift yourself off your shirt."

She removed his shirt and opening the bottle of oil poured some into the palm of her hand and began to rub his back with it.

"The smell from that stuff is enough to kill me on it's own. No doubt you'd be happy then."

"Kill you, are you forgetting that I have to sleep in the bed too?" She poured more oil into her hand and slapped it on his back.

"You take a sadistic delight in doing that, don't you?" Pat winched at the sudden slap.

Finishing her task and replaced the cork in the bottle. He watched in apprehension as she opened the second bottle and poured a generous amount into a large soup spoon.

"Come on open your mouth you old goat," Pat reluctantly half opened his mouth and looked at the evil smelling concoction.

"Will you open your mouth, nobody is trying to poison you", She grabbed his nose and forced the spoon into his mouth.

"Suffering Jesus!, that stuff tastes like turpentine."

"Do you know, that man, bless him would tempt the patience of a saint." Anne continued into the scullery, a contented smile on her face.

"I'll not be joining you for the rosary this night, Pat and I will say our own, Good night to you both." She crossed the floor to her room and closed the door.

Not long after Shelia quenched the lamp and calling to Phelm they too retired for the night.

The weather continued stormy, with heavy falls of snow. Pat was showing no improvement and to add to his problems he developed excruciating pain in his right leg. They were finding it impossible to find a doctor with any time to visit him.

The old owl is worried

It was several days into the second week since Anne found the yew tree branch across her path.

She had all but forgotten the incident of the Pishogue as she entered the barn to milk the family cow. Inside she was confronted by a restless bird in the rafters.

It was the old barn owl who had lived there for many the year. She was surprised that he was wide awake and as nervous as a bag of bees. Usually he would be sleeping at this time of day, and would not move until evening when he took himself off in search of mice and voles.

Anne looked up at the owl and called to it.

"What is troubling you, don't you know that it's me?

The owl tooted and flew from rafter to rafter. Perhaps, she thought there is a hawk hiding somewhere in the dark recesses of the roof timbers. Shading her eyes, she looked long and hard along each nook and cranny, anywhere that a hawk might be hiding.

Then she noticed a hessian bag, hanging from a rafter in the shadows.

"There's no need to be frightened of that, I'll have it moved, you silly old bird."

The owl turned his head round in a complete circle and looked at her.

Anne left the barn and went to the house and called on Phelm to come and remove the sack. Phelm climbed up the raking ladder and crossed the half loft to where the sack was hanging over the hay that they had saved that year. Cutting the string holding the bag, he brought it down. As he reached out the sack to her, she stepped back and refused to accept it.

"What is wrong with you, you're all nerves, Why? It's nothing but an old sack." Laying the sack carefully on the ground he cut the string.

Looking inside the sack he was more than surprised to note that it contained hens eggs.

"Well now that's strange indeed, this bag is filled with eggs."?

"How many are there Phelm?" His mother blessed herself and kept her distance from the sack.

He removed the eggs from the sack one at a time and laid them on the ground, there were thirteen eggs in all.

"These eggs are old Ma, rotten by the sound of them, he shook several of the eggs."

"Thirteen eggs, you know what this means, don't you?" His mother looked at him and together they blessed themselves.

"Jesus help me." Phelm looked at his hands and rubbed them against his trouser legs.

Someone with evil intent towards the family were determined to evoke the power of the Pishogue.

The eggs would be stolen a few at a time by the culprit until he or she had accumulated thirteen. These would then be placed out of view in a barn or outhouse Others would also be buried in the fields. The belief in this case was, that as the eggs putrefied so would the fresh hay in the barn rot. Any beast or crop in the field would also perish. Thus depriving the cow of her winter food and the family of the benefit of her milk. As the family would not be in a position to obtain any alternative feed for the cow, they would be forced to sell up and abandon their home.

"Don't tell me, some blackguard has put a Pishogue on us again." Phelm took one egg from the ground and pelted it against the nearest tree, the rest followed.

"Here we are in the middle of the Great Hunger and some bad bastard has nothing better to do than try and put a Pishogue on us."

The putrefying smell from the broken eggs prevailed over the whole yard making them both cough.

"Did you say again, Phelm Griffin? So this is not the first time, is it?" His mother questioned him.

"It was some time ago now. Dad found the willow sticks in the meadow and they smeared with the unsalted butter"

"Good God! What did he do about it?, he never told me."

"He did not want to worry you. He....," Phelm paused and looked away,"well he called on the irons." He half whispered.

"Blessed Virgin Mary! he must have been really annoyed."
Anne blessed herself.

Whoever is doing this must be very jealous of us for only this past two week I found a yew branch across the path." "Why did you not tell me then"? Phelm was annoyed and concerned.

"Why didn't you tell me what your father did? Still what's done is done and cannot be undone."

"I've been to see the priest and have ordered six St. Benedict medals. I also had the word with the Sideog Ri. Why should I upset the whole family"? His mother defended her action.

"We will need to be extra vigilant now, for they will go after the cow next."

"The cow! Good God, I never looked."

Phelm ran to the barn where he examined the cow, paying particular attention to her tail.

"So far she seems to have been spared the curse." He told his mother on his return.

"Now not a word about this to your father. Should he hear word of this it could kill him." She held on to her sons sleeve.

For several days and nights they took it in turn day and night to keep watch. They especially watched the crisp snow for any tell tale foot marks.

Seeking the Intercession of St Benedict

On the morning of the eighth day Anne took the milk bucket to the barn to milk the cow as was her task now that Pat was incapacitated.

She felt at ease with the world and hummed a lilting tune.

She felt the crunch of the crisp virgin snow under her feet.

Nearing the barn she noticed the tracks of boots in the frozen snow. She stopped and looked towards the cow house door. On it were the frozen traces of splashed milk. She knew instantly that another Pishogue had been put on them. In her shock she dropped the bucket and ran to the house calling on her son to come to her aid.

"Your mother is calling you Phelm. She seems upset?." Shelia ran into the scullery where he was washing his face.

Dropping the towel, he ran from the house and down the lane to be met by his mother.

"Its happened Phelm, God be praised! it has happened." She fell into his arms.

"Calm yourself Mother, what has happened"?

"Come see for yourself." Together they returned to the cow house.

"You're not going to enter there without the blessing." Anne pulled at her sons sleeve and prevented him from entering the barn.

He waited patiently outside as his mother went to the house and returned with the holy water. She blessed them both before Phelm approached the door.

At the door he paused and ran his hand over the frozen milk. Once again calling on his God to protect him he blessed himself. Raising the latch he entered the barn followed by his mother.

They both looked across at the cow but made no effort to approach her.

The cow on seeing them let out a deep roar. No doubt

wondering why Anne was making no effort to milk her.

"Don't touch her yet Phelm for all our sakes." She cautiously approached her cow and sprinkled the blessed water over the beast. He called on his mother to sprinkle him once again with the holy water. Then blessing himself he crossed cautiously over to the cow. He ran his hand nervously along her back until he reached her flank.

Lifting her tail he saw that a lock of hair had been discreetly snipped from it. He held the damaged tail up for his mother to observe.

"Get the bucket mother, and milk the cow. There's no time to waste, we must go and find out if the Priest has got the blessed medals yet."

"What was the matter with mother?" Shelia asked as he entered the house.

"Nothing really, she heard something in the barn and got frightened." He dismissed her question.

"Your father is not all that good this morning, he hardly said a word." She remarked.

"We had best leave him to mother, she knows what is best for him." He sat down at the table.

When Anne finished milking, she dipped her thumb in the bucket of milk and made the sign of the cross on the flank of her cow. This a thanksgiving for the milk.

Tilting the bucket she spilled a few drops of milk on the ground to appease the fairies as custom demanded.

Entering the house she gave Shelia the bucket and asked her to see to the straining of the milk. She had to attend to her husbands needs urgently.

Entering the bedroom she noted that Pat lay rigid looking towards the ceiling.

"Not feeling too good then are we? she crossed the floor and looked down at her husband.

"It pains me to move even one inch Anne, whatever is the matter with me?" He questioned his wife with his eyes making no effort to move his body.

"Sure it's nothing to be worrying yourself about. It's probably the soaking you got on the day you took a stroll along the woods." She tucked the blanket around him. She riddled the fire, sending sparks up the chimney before putting on fresh turf.

She left the room and returned to the kitchen. Shelia had strained the milk and was in the process of making a scone of bread.

"Shelia, there's a good girl, will you ever make a pot of tea." She sat down on the nearest chair exhausted by all the trauma of the morning.

Taking Pat's favourite mug, she filled it with sweet tea and took it to him, before she sat down to her own. As she was finishing her tea Phelm entered the house and asked her if she were now ready.

"Sure I'm ready, as ready as I'll ever be." Slowly she rose to her feet and put on a heavy black shawl which covered her from head to toe.

"You look just like a big black Jackdaw in that." he laughed.

"Laugh you may Phelm, but Shelia will tell you they are a God send." She wrapped it tighter around her as Phelm opened the door where they were met by a blast of ice cold wind accompanied by freshly falling snow.

Together arm in arm they fought their way against the driving snow down the boreen and on to the cross road. They had never known it to be so quiet. There was no sign of any of the neighbours. It was as if the whole place had been deserted. They went firstly towards the church, where they would enter and say a few prayers. As they walked up the gravel drive, she looked across at the old monastery and its ivy covered gable end.

"That's one piece of real estate that belongs to us." She remarked.

Leaving the church they crossed the road and took the long walk to the presbytery. The snow was falling heavier than before as they hurried up the drive. Phelm lifted the big iron knocker with the lions head holding it in his teeth. He banged the knocker hard in his anxiety to escape the bitter cold and snow.

In reply to his insistent knocking the door was answered by the servant girl. For a few moments she looked at them in amazement, then she bid them enter.

She closed the door behind them. The priest entered the hall and looked in amazement at the two people standing before him. They were both encased in snow and looked like two snow men. All he could see was a pair of eyes looking at him from under a cap and next to him what he could only describe as a plump penguin.

"Who have we here? You look like a pair of snow men." He greeted them.

Anne removed her shawl from her head and as she done so snow fell off the top and landed on the hall floor.

"Oh I am sorry Father!, I'll clean it up, we should have shook it off before we came in."

"It's you Anne and you too Phelm. you're more than welcome." The priest dismissed her offer to clean up the hall. The servant girl returned and took Pats coat and the shawl.

"Come into the parlour it's far more comfortable there." He opened the door where they were met by the commodious heat from a roaring peat fire.

"Excuse me a minute will you, I'll get Sally to make us a nice pot of tea."

The priest picked up a small brass bell and ringing it summoned Sally.

"Now what brings you two here on such a foul day, sit down will you, no need to stand on ceremony."

"It's the Pishogue, Father, we need those medals now, did you get them? Anne wrung her hands in her anxiety.

"The medals are here and blessed, I was going to bring them myself but the inclement weather beat me, please accept my apologies"

Anne explained how the barn had been desecrated and a curse put on the family. The priest listened in silence as she told the whole story. She also reminded him of Pat's illness.

"Sure I'm more than aware of poor Pat's illness, God help him, I pray for his speedy recovery at every opportunity."

She continued to explain to the Priest what had taken place in and around the farm. She was interrupted by a knock on the door, it was Sally with the tea.

Anne took charge of pouring the tea without thinking. It was a task that she regularly performed at home. The priest did not interrupt her as she continued to outline all that had happened. Finally she had exhausted all the information and sat back awaiting his advice.

"Well Anne, I can well appreciate your anxiety and worry. However you know how the mother church feels about such matters, it considers them innocuous. They could never harm you."

He looked from Anne to Phelm and could see that they were indeed troubled and far from convinced with his assurances. He would have to do something to embolden them that he had the power, given to him by God to protect them.

"Now that I have heard all the story of the wickedness and stress imposed on you. I am going to intercede personally to St. Benedict on your behalf. In the meantime I want you to bury the medals, one in each of your fields and one in the laneway. At the holy Mass on Sunday, which I am going to offer up for your intentions. I will be bringing to the attention of the congregation the grave sin of tampering with the devils work. I'll not be mentioning any names mind you, but I'll be doing the reading and watching. If the cap fits they will wear it in sorrow.."

"God bless you Father, you have taken a mill stone from my heart and for that I am grateful, God bless and keep you." She took hold of the Priests hand and kissed it. As they prepared to leave the presbytery, he handed Anne the envelope containing the Blessed medals.

It was their successful management of the farm that had brought the Pishogue on them. Someone was jealous of their prudent management of the farm in that they were still able to produce a few eggs daily. There was the also added bonus of their milking cow. This was an enviable situation compared to the problems of some of their neighbours.

The curse that had been imposed on them never came to fruition thanks to the intercession of St Benedict. And in no small measure to the intervention of the Sideog Ri.

The Captain leaves for England

With Christmas rapidly approaching Shelia was praying and hoping that her child would be born on Christmas day. The baby it was predicted would be born about this time. God willing.

Pat's health continued to deteriorate. His continual worry was that he would not live long enough to see his first grandchild. He knew that it was now only a matter of time to his demise. Although his family told him that he was getting better, He had no such delusions.

"Will God spare me long enough to see the baby, Anne?" He would ask periodically.

"Now if I heard that once, I've heard it a thousand times. The way that you are behaving you'll drive yourself to an early grave." This time she was determined to reassure him. She left the room only to return moments later with Shelia in tow.

"Now, tell him will you!, once and for all, he just won't listen to me the old fool."

"Dad you're only upsetting yourself and Mum, talking of death like that. Don't worry you will be one of the first to hold the baby and if it's a boy then we are going to call him Patrick after you."

"Did you hear that Anne, I told you, Oh God bless you Shelia now I know that I'll get better." Forgetting his pains in his excitement he tried to raise himself from the bed but found the effort too painful.

They looked down at him in sympathy, there was little else that they could do. The prospects of a doctor calling to see to his needs was now more remote than ever.

The yellow plague had more or less cut the city off from the surrounding countryside. His complaints were not considered urgent compared with the epidemic.

Captain Singleton was finding that the hunger was having a knock on effect on his resources. There was little income from his tenancies. Many of the small holdings had been deserted or burnt for non-payment of rates and taxes.

As the houses were emptied of occupants he had the roofs removed. Buildings devoid of their roofs were exempt from taxes.

He would leave his Irish estate in the hands of Tom Roche to manage. He and his family would return to their home in England until such time as the country returned to some semblance of normality and prosperity.

"Now the problems and misery that he and his kind inflicted on the Irish are coming home to roost. They say that God moves in mysterious ways, you mark my words this blessed night. The captain will die by the curse of the Fire and Water. Anne reminded her family of the curse on hearing of his imminent departure.

"More like a rat deserting a sinking ship. Getting out like the rest of his kind when there are no more soft pickings." Phelm banged the table in his frustration.

Was it any wonder that the English landlords wanted desperately to distance themselves from this cursed land.

The people spoke openly of the seven plagues of Egypt and the curse of God coming on the land. There were more miracles seen in Ireland during the famine by starving peasants, than for the last two thousand years in Europe. The holy family was seen on church walls, statues of Christ cried or bled in many cases both.

The Blessed Virgin cried for the people and even spoke to some. Like stranded people in the desert they were now hallucinating. Clinging to their faith and hope in God's divine mercy.

There was to be no mercy however and no divine intervention for in the winter of 1846-1847 a new plague visited their land. It was noted that some people were turning black. It was first seen on their arms and legs in the form of black spots and became known as"Black leg." It was believed that this was another contagious disease to add to their misery. Many of the victims were left outside the gates of the workhouses to the mercy of the beadles running the homes.

This would be their final refuge. These families were not apathetic to the needs of their kin. There was nothing that they could do for them under the circumstances. Whatever hope of recovery there was in the workhouse, there was only death outside its sanctuary.

This however was no contagious decease it was Scurvy brought about by the lack of vitamin C. It was abundant in the potato but completely absent in the Indian meal that they were now eating.

Indian corn was an alien diet to the Irish people. They had no idea as to how to cook it.

The British authorities were warned that to make the corn palatable it would have to be ground twice. Ignoring this advice the minister of the day ordered that it be ground just once. Many suffered untold and unnecessary agony in their digestive systems. It was more noticeable in the infants and children who's systems could not cope with the harsh grain. The question was asked over and over again, why?. Why in God's holy name did the minister order that the grain be ground only once.

There was no logical reason for this order except to bring agony and misery on a desperate nation. It tore at the stomach linings of children and adults alike and became known sarcastically as Peel's brimstone. This was because of the agonizing pains suffered after eating it.

Christmas came and went, there was to be none of the traditional merriment and exchanges of presents.

It was now the end of the first week in January and Shelia had gone into labour. Despite the cold and hunger the neighbours rallied round to offer their help and assistance as was the custom.

Her baby was born on the first day of the second week. Pat lying in his bed repeating his rosary over and over again as he waited in anxious anticipation for the birth. Hearing the cries of his first grandchild, he prayed and cried his thanks to God for the safe deliverance of mother and baby.

Letting his beads fall from his fingers he looked and waited for the door to open, It seemed like hours. Perhaps they had forgotten him. He called out but there was no reply. He could hear people moving from the room to the kitchen and talking in whispers. Getting more and more frustrated he called louder and louder.

He stopped calling, they had forgotten their promise. He felt despondent and deserted. If only I could get out of this bed he thought, looking anxiously again and again at the door. The door was finally opened and in came Anne carrying his first grandchild.

"You have a young relative come to see you as promised. Your grandson Patrick, has come to wish you a very happy New Year." She held the baby down to him.

He reached out for the baby, it did not matter that it pained him to do so. This was a moment to relish and remember. With sheer determination he reached up and taking the baby in his arms kissed his forehead and hugged him to his chest. Then with tears of joy he fell back on the pillow holding the infant tightly.

"Pat Griffin, why you old fool, that's the first time that I ever saw you cry." She was nearly in tears herself at the sight of grandfather and grandchild together.

She looked down at Pat, then at the infant. Here were three generations of Griffin's under the family roof. She attempted to retrieve the infant from Pat's grasp.

"Must you always be in such a hurry, I waited a long time for this and I intend to savour every moment of it. Away with you woman."

She retreated from the room and left him holding the baby. "Shelia I think that your son has been kidnapped." She laughed as she entered the room.

"Sure he couldn't be kidnapped by a better granddad." After some time Anne returned and took the baby from his arms. "We're off now, wave good bye to Granddad." She waved the infants right arm in front of Pat where he could see him. Daily the baby was brought to see Pat at his insistence. He would cuddle him and spoil him. After a week of Pat's nursing Anne noticed that it was getting more and more difficult for him to hold the baby and fearing that he may lose his grip on the child she insisted that she remain by his bedside whenever he was given the infant to hold. As the weeks turned into months, the baby spent more and more time in his grandfathers care.

A family celebration

Phelm and Shelia decided that as Patrick was now that much older it was time that he was removed from the bed and into a cradle of his own. Phelm went with Shelia's brother to the nearest river bank and collected as many stacks of supple sally ash that they thought would be required to make a Moses's cradle. That evening Phelm brought his father from his room and sat him down in his sugan chair by the fire.

They brought the stacks of ash into the kitchen and placed them on the floor. She procured two sharp knives from the kitchen and together they sat crossed legged on the floor stripping the bark from the lengths of ash. This bark they piled up ready to be placed at the back of the fire.

As Anne had nothing to occupy her she decided that she would do a bit of spinning. She would prepare some wool to knit a garment or two for the baby.

Pat watched as she dragged the"Tuirne Mor" from the back room. He felt embarrassed and uneasy within himself. There was the time not long since when he would have lifted it with one hand and placed it in front of the fire for her.

The Tuirne Mor was the big spinning wheel so popular in Munster. Anne liked it because it had the platform so low that one could sit on it instead of standing or sitting on a separate stool beside it when carrying out the task of spinning. She started the wheel turning and began to spin the wool.

She began to sing in time with her foot as it kept the wheel in motion. Her singing grew into a crescendo much to the enjoyment of her family.

She sang the songs of Ireland's troubled history. She sang the old lullabies and she lamented the passing of better times. Pat sat back in his sugan chair puffing at his pipe and he with that far off look in his eyes. With the comforting heat from the fire and Anne's singing, he found himself slowly dozing. He was awakened by the noise of his pipe falling to the floor.

"Anne, the blessings of God on you. Were you not always one for the old commallies. He looked with loving admiration at his wife.

"Now listen to who's talking and you the one everyone asks for at the gatherings to sing." She reminded him.

"Come on granddad, let's have one from yourself" Shelia called.

There would be no asking twice of Pat, for no sooner had he been asked than he was singing like the lark himself.

My Mary of the curling hair,
with laughing teeth and bashful air,
Our bridal morning is dawning fair
With blushes in the skies!

chorus..

Shule, Shule, Shule agra,
Shule a Socar agus Shule Aroon!
My love, my pearl, my own dear girl!
My mountain maid, arise.!

For we were known from infancy,
Thy father's hearth was home to me
No selfish love was mine for thee,
Unholy and unwise.

chorus..

I am no stranger proud and gay
To win thee from thy home away
And find thee for a distant day
A theme of wasting sighs.

chorus..

But soon my love shall be my bride,
And happy by our own fireside
My veins shall feel the rosy tide

Which lingering hopes denies.

My Mary of the Curling Hair (Trad.)

As the night wore on the family continued to entertain each other. Forgotten were Pat's pains as was the hunger and the plague. At least for that night. As the night wore on Pat was showing signs of tiredness. Shelia nudged Phelm to take him back to his bed.

Having settled his father comfortably he was about to leave the room when his father called him back.

"Phelm would you make me a"leaba shuidheachain" beside the fire in the kitchen." He looked with pleading eyes at his son.

He explained that grateful as he was to his son, he suffered excruciating pain every time he was lifted from the bed to the chair. It would also save on the turf as they would have no need to light the fire in the bedroom, This would be more than helpful to Phelm who now had the task of cutting the turf alone.

Perhaps he was embarrassed every time he was carried like a babe from his room to his chair by the fireside in the kitchen. Or was it that perhaps that he wanted to spend more time with his grandson. Whatever the reason, Phelm agreed to make him the bed.

When Anne heard what Pat wanted she was secretly overjoyed for she knew that her every twist and turn in the bed brought pangs of excruciating pain to her husband.

She often thought of hinting to him that he might be better in a bed by the fire in the kitchen. Yet she would never suggest openly that he should be removed from his room. He was still the master of the house and as such had the prerogative to make all decisions affecting the household.

The day came when Pat was ceremoniously moved to his new bed. There was not a person in the whole of the land more conceited that day as he snuggled into the pillows.

"So well he should, Shelia burned the midnight oil making a mattress and two large well filled pillows of the finest goose down feathers." Anne remarked.

The potato crop is
in God's hands

February 1st the feast day of St. Bridget when as tradition
would have it marked the beginning of the tilling and
sowing. Phelm would have to plough the land for cultivation
alone now. His father could not participate in the task. He
would guide him and give him of his valuable experience.
Phelm had learned his lessons well and soon had the land
ready.

This year he would grow the corn in the old potato field and
move the potato crop to the oat field, rotating the crop as he
was taught.

They were lucky in that they were able to buy seed potatoes
late in the autumn of '86. Others had little or no seed and
were now trying as a matter of urgency to purchase some.

Anne and Shelia had cut and dressed the seed. There would
be no planting however until lent had passed, God help any
farmer found sowing a crop during lent, not alone would he
be beaten from the field by the Priest. He would have his
name read from the pulpit, bringing shame and ridicule on
his family.

Shrove Tuesday came and the family ate what perishable
food there was in the house.

This was the feast of the Lenten fast when all perishable food
had to be disposed of. There would be no more eggs or meat
eaten during the forty days of lent with the exception of St.
Patrick's day, which falls on the seventeenth of March when
special dispensation is given by the Church to the Irish
people.

Good Friday came and the table was set with dry scones and
well water only. There would be no other food eaten in the
household in deference to the crucifixion and death of Christ
on the cross. This was a solemn day and several visits were

made to the church.

Easter came and although the long winter was still with them. Phelm decided that the ground would now have to be prepared and the seeds sown. Yet his plans were thwarted. The wind howled and the snow continued to fall. This was followed by severe cold. Would there ever come the time when he could put the seed into the ground he thought.

By now he was anxiously counting the days as snow continued to obliterate the countryside. Should the inclement weather continue for much longer then it would be too late to sow the crops.

Phelm could hardly believe his luck when the weather miraculously diverted to the west. With it came the warm westerly winds so generous to the potato crop. Whatever there was outstanding would have to wait. The planting would take precedence over all else. It was now a matter of urgency, there was no alternative. They had to take advantage of the weather. On the morning of the planting Anne and Shelia prepared the breakfast early. They desperately wanted to get as many ridges of potatoes planted as possible before nightfall.

"Pat! I have no doubt but you will be in your glory looking after young Patrick for the morning." Shelia lifted the baby from the cot and put him in his arms.

"Are you ready yet Phelm?" His mother anxiously called as she swung the planting triple dibber in her hand. The dibber would be used to make the holes for the seed potatoes.

Shelia went to the barn and collected the ciscean. Filling it with seeds she and Anne helped to hoist it on Phelm's back. "You have no consideration for this poor ass," he joked as they helped to adjust the shoulder straps.

He went down the ridge trench carrying the ciscean on his back.

As Anne made a hole in the ridge with the dibber, Shelia took the cut seeds and placed them in the holes before covering them with soil. For hour on end they carried out this back breaking task until noon.

Hearing the church bell toll for the saying of the Angelus. They stopped their work and with heads bowed waited for Anne to lead the prayers.

159

"The angel of the Lord declared unto Mary." Anne began the Angelus.

With the prayers finished they returned to the house. Anne prepared the midday meal leaving Shelia to look after the needs of the baby and Pat. Phelm went into the loft and brought out more prepared seed potatoes.

"Am I thinking right or is the weather on the mend?" Pat asked his son as he glanced towards the window.

"Dad! I never saw it so good, Thank God that we have the west wind back again. I feel it in my bones that the potato crop will not fail us this year God willing." Phelm was now chirpy and showing his confidence.

"If you don't sit down and eat we'll be out there till the Lord calls us." Anne placed a plate of food on the table before Phelm.

"Did I tell you that those two are driving me like a donkey all day."

"Don't mock it Phelm, I wish to God that I were in your position." His father chided.

"Come on then, back to the grind stone." Phelm having finished his meal rose from the table and picked up the ciscean.

"Well then! are you going to hoist it on my back or not?" he called to the two women.

"Will you hold your whist for a moment can't you see that Shelia has to see to her baby." his mother chided him.

"Two minutes ago you were bawling me out for dallying, now you tell me that I am too impatient, women!." He laid the ciscean back on the floor.

"Tell you what! I might chance another mug of tea while I am waiting, want one Dad"?.

Without waiting for a reply Phelm filled two mugs and took one to his father.

"I wonder how the people living in the booleys have survived this terrible winter." Pat asked by way of conversation.

"Talking of Booleys reminds me of poor Philomena Carey away in the mountains of Tipperary. I'll go one day this week and find out how she is coping. I could take them a little something."

"You're one caring son and I am proud of you." Pat reached out and touched his sons arm.

"What would you and Mum think of me if I were that selfish, it is no more and no less than my Christian duty." He rose from beside the bed and drinking the last mouthful of tea from his mug he placed it on the table.

"Come on then give me a lift with the ciscean." He called to the two women.

"Come here!, do this!, do that,! isn't he the fine one for giving orders." Anne frivolously remarked.

By dusk the task of planting the potato crop had been completed. What they thought would take two days they had accomplished in one. They were tired and weary when they returned to the house and felt that they had really over done it.

"The blessings of God on the crop. I hope all the labour and hard work was worth it." Phelm remarked as he sat wearily on the nearest chair.

"Amen to that." Pat blessed himself.

"Now there is no need to be such a pessimist. I, for one know that the crop will be a success, you mark my words." His mother replied.

"Tell you what, I'll warm the stirabout and we'll all have a bowl. What about you granddad?" Shelia was already at the fireplace putting the pot on the crane.

"I don't mind but would someone take the baby from me, my arms are going numb."

Anne went and took the baby in her arms and returned him to his cradle in Phelm's room.

"I know now how the poor neddy feels," Phelm rubbed his aching back.

"I've got the right cure for that, haven't I Pat? Anne looked towards him and laughed.

"If you have any sense son, you'll avoid any cures from that quack."

"If he is all that sore now just wait until he starts on the sowing of the corn."

"Did you say he starts on the corn, don't you really mean 'We'." Anne remarked.

"Whatever you are doing I'm off to my bed, thanks for the

stirabout." Phelm rose from his chair and went to his room.
"If to morrow is going to be another back breaking day like to day then I'll join you." Shelia collected the bowls and took them to the scullery and washed them before she too retired for the night.

Anne having seen to her husbands medication, left him comfortably in his bed beside the fire.

Next morning Phelm was up early and showing his impatience at the delay in starting on the sowing.

"Will you tell the other's that I have gone down to mark out the field for sowing. Don't forget and call me when breakfast is ready." he told his father.

Phelm was still marking out the field when he heard Shelia calling from the house.

Leaving the markers in the field he returned to the kitchen. As he entered Anne and Shelia were already sitting at the table.

"I hope that you left me something." He looked towards Shelia.

His mother rose from her seat and fetched his breakfast from the front of the hob.

"Here! do you know you must be the most pampered child in the house." She laid a well laden plate of food before him.

"Is this all I get." He laughed as he decapitated one of the three eggs.

"It's more than, you deserve for the cunning trick you played last night."

"What cunning trick?, I don't know what you are talking about."

"Don't talk with your mouth full. The way you sneaked off to bed early so as to get us up at the crack of dawn."

"How is the marking going, is the field ready yet." Anne rose from the table.

"I've marked out the field with the sticks ten feet apart as usual."

(This was the area that he was capable of covering with the sowing fiddle.)

His father always used the ten foot mark for sometimes a noticeable gap would be left between the sowing at twelve feet. Pat's father always called it 'Over-stretching the mark', others called it 'The hungry gap'.

Having finished breakfast he returned to the task of marking out the field leaving the women to wash the dishes. By the time he had finished Anne and Shelia were on the scene.

Anne had already put on her large heavy skirt and scooped up the corners, into an envelope.

"We're ready whenever you are", his mother displayed her skirt.

Phelm came up the field and filled a bucket with corn and tipped it into her apron.

Picking up the sowing fiddle he placed the strap over his shoulder and went down the field between the markers working the bow as he went. Corn seed scattered left and right of him.

Anne walked on the outside of the markers and broadcast extra seed to ensure as even a sowing as possible.

Shelia was busy making the wooden crosses into scare crows with old clothing and straw. These she would place in strategic positions throughout the field to deter the crows and other birds. With the crop sown they returned to the house for a midday break.

"How is it looking to day?" His father asked.

"Thank God that it is drying, the harrowing should not be too much work." Phelm told him.

In the afternoon they again returned to the field where Phelm donned the harness. Anne attached it to the harrow and as Phelm dragged it up and down the field she kept it on as straight a course as possible. This action would roughen the ground and bury most of the seed. Finally having finished the harrowing they returned it to the side of the field and attached the Levelling Box to the harness.

Once again Phelm put the harness over his shoulders and with Anne guiding it he smoothed the ground. Thus anchoring the seed in the soil below. Although the field was no more than an acre or so they were more than glad when the task was completed.

Shelia took the scare crows into the field where he set them firmly into the ground using a large home made wooden mallet.

Pat did have a good horse once, for ploughing and heavy

work around the farm. The finest in Castlelurgan it was said. The captain wanted him. He offered to buy the horse. Pat saw no sense in selling a good horse that he needed and refused the offer. No matter how often the captain offered to buy, the answer was always the same, no sale.

One morning Pat went down the meadow to collect the horse and found him missing. He reported the matter to the local constabulary. They told him that his horse was found wandering on the captains land.

He was keeping him until Pat compensated him for the damage caused. Pat went to the manor and asked what were the damages. He was willing to make good any damage at his own expense. He did however need his horse for the many heavy tasks around the farm. He was told that the horse had trampled a valuable field of oats and played havoc with the young saplings in the wood. Then there was cost of replacing the fencing that was damaged.

Pat found all this reported damage as incredible.

"Are you telling me that my horse done all this damage overnight? I would like to inspect the damage for myself."

"There is no doubting the damage and we have witnesses." The agent informed him.

"I'd still like to see it for myself if you don't mind."

"We do mind, the damages we have assessed at twenty four sovereigns."

"Twenty four sovereigns, that's ridiculous and you know it."

"We have your horse, when you come with the money you can have him back."

"The captain wanted that horse and has used this as an excuse to get him."

"Be very careful what you say, my man."

"You may keep the horse for all the good it will do you or the captain."

That was all along time ago and Pat never purchased a horse since.

The Nation starves

Although the Griffin family were able to purchase seeds there were those who could not even afford to purchase a quarter stone of peas at two shillings and six pence a stone or oats at the same price. With wages of one shilling per day to keep a wife and an average family of eight children what prospects had they.

The British government of the day voted that they would give a grant of £50,000 to the landlord's enabling them to purchase seed for distribution to their needy tenants. Many landlord's withheld the distribution of the miserable sum allocated in order to drive the tenants from the land.

They watched with indifference as their tenants buried their loved ones who had died from starvation in the fields and ditches. In many cases they were made to dislodge the bodies from their lands. This added to their misery and distress.

As they refused to distribute the free seed the plight of their tenants became unbearable. They sold or tried to sell every piece of furniture, and anything else that they could to raise enough money to buy seed.

The Quaker's went from hovel to hovel offering what little seed that they could afford to give.

The granaries on the dock side of Limerick and in other coastal cities were bursting to capacity with Indian corn.

Prices for the corn began to collapse as more and more ships brought in supplies. Yet although these supplies were more than adequate to meet the needs of the country, the people of Ireland were condemned to starve. What food was distributed to the starving was through the soup kitchens and they were few and far between.

In desperation the people began to talk once again of insurrection against the Crown.

As rumour spread of insurrection in Ireland soldiers were despatched to guard the grain stores. The people could not afford to buy the grain and the government refused to let them have it free.

Food riots began to spread from town to town. What angered the Irish more than any hardship, and God knows they were suffering, was the exporting of Irish grain. Ships were loaded with Irish wheat, cattle, pigs and cheese at the costal ports of Limerick, Galway and Cork for export to England. The dock gates were guarded by mounted soldiers, infantry and field guns. Outside the Irish were huddled in masses awaiting inevitable death from starvation.

The great hunger was taking it's toll on a down trodden nation..

They could buy Maize from the mill at two pence per pound. To keep a family for one day they would require eight pounds of maize. Those fortunate enough to obtain work were paid eight pence a day. What were the parents to do, decide who would live and who would die within the family. In the Skibbereen area of Cork the Irish were dying at the rate of 60 each day.

It was estimated that the Irish population was depleting by a million every year.

This rapid depletion did not seem to worry the government. They were now encouraging the landlords to deport their tenants.

No account was taken of the thousands who had found watery graves in the Atlantic nor of those who froze to death on the streets of Quebec and other foreign cities. Many having survived the trauma of the coffin Ships were to find watery graves in the St Lawrence river. There were so many deaths that thousands were buried in mass graves on Grosse Island in Canada. Yet the landlords on the whole were indifferent to their plight. There were one or two exceptions but you could count them on one hand.

England was now getting exasperated with the starving Irish. She was now being to asked sustain a nation whose only assets were starving and rebellious peasants. She did not consider herself responsible for the people of Ireland. The Irish would have to look to themselves from now on. There would be no more free hand outs to the starving and there would be no money for the work houses. Ireland would have to survive on the rates and taxes collected by the landlords. If ever there was a travesty of justice and a renege on ones duty and responsibility then surely this was it.

England drew up a bill called"The Irish Poor Law extension Bill" It paid no attention to the starving Irish. What it did was to transfer responsibility for the Starving Irish from the English to the Irish rate payers of which there were few. This was a strange anomaly for a country that claimed jurisdiction over the island of Ireland and her people.

The starving and plague ridden people of Ireland were now abandoned to their fate. England had created the problem and now she was reneging on her responsibility. Landlords would now have to shoulder responsibility for the people?. Was England being very naïve or very cunning. The latter was more to the truth.

Daniel O'Connell that great Irish orator and liberator, suffering from chronic ill health at the time, stood before the honourable members of the House of Commons shortly before his death and pleaded Ireland's cause.

"Ireland is in your hands and in your power, if you fail to save her, then she cannot be expected to save herself. I call on you in God's name to recollect. I predict with sincere conviction that one quarter of our population will die unless you come to our relief." He resumed his seat with tears streaming down his face.

Disraeli was asked what he thought of the heart rendering speech.

"Who was that feeble old man I saw muttering." He joked as he wiped his nose in his cravat.

This was to be Daniel O'Connell's last appearance in the house. Shortly after he died at Genoa regretting that he could do no more for Ireland.

As the weather continued to improve and the wind continued to blow from the west, what crop of potatoes had been planted continued to make excellent progress. England took this as a sign that the famine was now past and that she could forget it.

As Charles Wood, the chancellor of the exchequer said at the time.

"They have been hardly decent whilst they have their bellies filled with our corn and their pockets stuffed with our money."

Did England not realise that the potato crop was still under the ground, there was no food in the country.

There may have been ripening corn in the fields but that was ear marked to pay the rates and taxes to the landlords. This they would export as they had always done. They saw no reason as to why they should not maintain their comfortable life style. What potatoes there were growing in the country were insignificant compared with the demand. There was no certainty that they would crop. The grain stored in the warehouses of Limerick, Cork and elsewhere was sold off to the highest bidder and any that remained unsold was shipped back to England. This although part of the stock had been donated freely by the United States and other countries.

Phelm finds a holocaust

There would now be four weeks respite before the first lanu or earthning of the potatoes and all the other crops had been set. Phelm would have little work to do about the house that could not be managed by Shelia and his mother.

Sitting around the fire one evening the conversation turned once again to the plight of the evicted and especially to the plight of Philomena Carey and her children.

"It's often that I wonder how the poor creatures managed over the terrible winter. I pray God for their deliverance constantly." Anne sympathetically remarked.

"'Tis no more than a few nights ago when passing the captains drive that my thoughts returned to the calamitous day that Tom Carey went to see him.

If that bastard had not been such a damn liar then Tom would be alive this night, God be good to him. Will you tell me in God's name how can he live with himself?" Pat remarked.

"Talking will do no good for the living, Phelm, you promised that you would go and find out how they are keeping, and now is as good a time as any."

"So I did as you rightly reminded me." He looked up at the clock and rose to his feet.

"Very well then, to morrow God willing, I'll pack what food we can spare and see if they are still in the booley. That is if Shelia does not mind."

"If I don't mind! why were it not for the baby I would join you. Was not Philomena a good friend of mine. Away you go Phelm and may God guide your feet."

Early next morning Phelm rose silently from his bed to make preparations for the journey. He was more than surprised to find that his mother was already in the kitchen. He noticed that the scone oven was hanging on its crane over the roaring turf fire and with red hot coals on the lid. Whatever was his mother doing baking scones at the crack of dawn, he thought.

"What are you up to at this hour of the morning?."

"So you're up and ready, keep your voice down your father is trying to sleep." She ignored his question and continued putting coals on the lid of the scone oven.

"I'm far from sleep, that woman has me pestered this last hour with her banging the pots and raking the fire." Pat complained from under the blankets.

"Alright then, if you both must know I'm making a few scones and hard boiling a few eggs for Philomena and her children, satisfied?"

"Oh Mum! you're all heart and I am really proud of you" going across to the fireplace he hugged his mother.

"Will you just look at yourself, you have covered your best clothes in flour now."

Phelm brushed the flour from his clothes and filling his shaving mug with hot water from the kettle went across to the scullery where he lathered his face and began to shave.

"Whenever you are ready Phelm, your breakfast is on the table."

"I'm just about ready, be with you in two shakes of a lambs tail."

Shelia came out from the bedroom holding the baby, in her arms.

"Don't tell me that he has gone without as much as a good bye."

"You won't get rid of me that easy." Phelm came out from the scullery and teased her.

"Here granddad, hold the baby while I deal with this husband of mine." Pat reached out and took the baby from Shelia.

Shelia ran at Phelm but as she approached he caught her round the waist and planted a kiss on her lips.

"Are you going to eat this breakfast or not, it's getting colder by the minute." Anne took the plate of food from top of the oven and placed it on the table.

"Here I'm only going across to Tipperary, not to the other end of the country." Phelm looked down at the over laden plate.

"You had best eat it, for I have no doubt it is about all you will have until night fall." Shelia picked up the pot and filled his mug with tea.

In the meantime his mother filled his shoulder pack with the food for the Carey family.

"Now whatever else you do, be careful. The roads are filled with highway robbers."

"Don't worry too much about me, I'll be alright." He finished the meal and picked up his shoulder pack.

"Wish me luck and don't stay up waiting if I'm late home." He kissed his wife and son goodbye and leaving the house wended his way across the meadow towards the hills.

Reaching the wood he skirted round it towards the spot where he had previously found the Carey children at play. As he followed the path round the periphery of the wood he noticed that it had slipped in places down the mountain side. This made him extra cautious, he did not want to suffer any injury to himself in such an isolated place. His progress was getting slower as the pathway became more dangerous.

As he rounded a bend where the path ran parallel with the mountain stream he saw that the road had been washed away completely. He cursed his luck, this would mean that he had to retrace his steps and find an alternative route. This called for strategic planning on his part. He would sit down on the hillside and have some refreshments and perhaps a drag on his pipe to help his concentration.

Deep in thought he looked at the high ground above the wood This was beyond his capability. He could not go forward nor could he go back the only route was down. This would add several miles to his hazardous journey and bring him in contact with the people wandering the roads many of them plague ridden. No disrespect to their plight, he thought to himself. He did not want to become a victim and unknowingly infect his family.

Climbing down the side of the hill he joined the Tipperary road. He would have to keep the wood in his sights as this was unfamiliar territory to him. Should he lose sight of his bearings then he would not be able to find the place where he had first seen the children.

The road was thronged with displaced people wandering aimlessly. Others were lying along the hedge rows. There was no doubt in his mind but that many of these people were long dead.

He was sorry for the children who approached him begging in the name of God for a crust. He dare not open his pack and let them have any of the food. The adults in the groups would surely rob him of the food and perhaps leave him for dead. Cruel and heartless though it seemed he had no choice. "I have no food, like you I'm on the road." He lied.

Seeing a boreen to his left in the direction of the woods he prudently decided to leave the main highway. On reaching the end of the boreen he came to open ground and before him he again saw the old path on the hill side. This was indeed a lucky find. He quickened his step and joined it. This was now familiar territory to him and soon he would be near to the concealed opening leading to the home of Philomena Carey.

By now it was getting late and long shadows of twilight came from the tall trees. The dew was beginning to form on the grassy mounds. There was no sign of life not even the mocking cry of the nightjar. He longed for the company of a fellow human if only to shorten the boring journey.

There was nothing but the moonlight slowly rising above the trees. It followed him like a beacon bringing him nearer to the Booley. Then he was upon it. He took a deep breath and thanked God for a safe journey. As he walked cautiously deeper into the woods he began to call Philomena by name. His calling disturbed a resident owl who flew past his face on silent wings.

In the shadows he saw the outline of the booley and approached it cautiously. He did not want to frighten Philomena nor the children. She would be happy to know that he had not forgotten his promise.

He was surprised that there were none of the children about. He hoped that they had not moved away.

He called her by name once again to reassure her. There was no reply. Nothing but the mocking moonlight and the silence of the night. The owl returned and curiously watched him from the safety of a high branch.

He was within touching distance of the booley. Should he take a bold step and enter ? He was left with little choice.

Opening the covering that served as a door he entered and saw on the bed of rushes the outline of an adult.

Again he softly called her name. There was still no response. Becoming bolder he approached the bedside and gently shook the occupant. There was no need for him to remain silent and cautious any longer, he now knew that Philomena Carey was no more. He did not pull the covers back, he let her be, and crossed to the children's bed.

He found the children where she had tucked them into what she must have thought was a warm sheltered bed. They too were dead. Had he come a day sooner perhaps they would be alive now. He sat on the old log that Philomena used as a chair and reminisced on the conversation that they had and of the baby that he bounced on his knee. He looked across at their peaceful faces and cried as he never cried before.

If only I had come sooner, he thought, perhaps I could have averted this catastrophe.

Philomena Carey and her children had gone to join their father in a better land.

Phelm spent the night in the shelter of the booley. Next morning he took the slan and went to a green sward where he dug a long grave. When it was to his satisfaction he returned to the booley and removed the body of Philomena from the rushes. He did not uncover her face but wrapped the blanket completely round her. He would respect her modesty she would have appreciated that. He took her in his arms and gently placed her at the head of the grave. Collecting each child in turn he placed them gently beside their mother.

Phelm filled in the grave and tamped it down with the slan. Returning to the booley he collected some of the rushes on which Philomena had died and wove them into the cross of Saint Bridget. St. Bridget was her favourite saint in life. It was to her she turned for help in the many crises in her young life. He made a cross from two pieces wood and this he stuck in the ground at the head of the grave and hung the cross of St. Bridget on it.

In her little garden outside the booley he saw that she had made two circular flower beds. In them grew the wild flowers of the woods, no doubt collected by her and her children.

There were cowslips and primroses in profusion and dotted here and there the occasional forget me not.

The beds were surrounded by pieces of marble no doubt foraged from the near by quarry by her children.

On each side of the path leading into the booley she had planted bluebells. These were now sending up their long leaves with their clusters of flowers about to burst forth.

They would never see the bluebells in full bloom, nor would her children shake the bell shaped flowers to call the fairies.

Phelm was calm as he went about his sad task. Yet boiling up inside him was resentment of the English landlords and their lackeys who had perpetrated this carnage.

He would like to think that their spirits had left the booley on the night that they died and were guided to a better land by Diana the moon goddess. Her light reflecting on the yellow flowers.

He carefully dug the flowers from the garden and replanted them on the grave. He dug up each and every bluebell and planted them around the grave.

The forget-me-nots he planted down the full length of the grave and across the head in the shape of a cross.

He watched a cheeky robin dig in the fresh soil seeking any grubs that may have been disturbed.

"Philomena Carey! may God be merciful to you and your children. I swear! as God is my judge that as I mark your grave with flowers, I will return one day and mark your grave with a permanent stone of granite. Emblazoned on it will be your name, the names of your children and that of your husband Tom. This I swear."

The robin cocked its head to one side but made no effort to fly away. Perhaps it was the pet of the Carey family and used to being disturbed.

Rising to his feet he returned to the booley and began to dismantle it methodically. Then slowly like a spring uncoiling he released all his pent up emotions and began to tear at the sticks supporting the structure, screaming as he did so.

"You English bastards! you robbed us of our culture, you destroyed our language, you stole our lands. This bloody murder of innocent women and children calls to the God almighty for vengeance."

His curse rang through the silent woods mocking him with their echo. He was all alone with nothing to vent his anger on but the few remaining sticks of the shelter that Philomena Carey built with her own hands. When there was nothing left of the booley he sat on the old log and buried his head in his hands and cried to his God to avenge their deaths.

Rising to his feet he took one last look across at the grave. It was well hidden, there was little chance of anyone finding it. What if they did? Were there not thousands of such graves the length and breadth of the land.

An encounter on the
road to Tipperary

Collecting his pack he placed it across his shoulder and came down from the woods and joined the boreen.

Once again he was back on the Tipperary road heading for the county of Limerick.

On the road he passed a woman in her bare feet and she with five children trailing behind her. They reminded him of goslings in the stream swimming behind their mother.

"Good day Mam! Fine day thanks be to God." He raised his caubeen in salutation.

The woman ignored him and passed on her way, she neither looked right nor left. The children passed in line behind her. They too were bare footed and what clothing they wore was in tatters.

He could not but notice their emaciated bodies and their stick like legs, and the tell tale green slime trickling from their mouths. They must have found some grass along the way. The youngest of the family looked at him and smiled.

"What has he to smile about"? He thought to himself.

Then he remembered the food in his shoulder bag. "Missus!, please stop, I've got some food here." Again the woman ignored his generous offer. There was little doubt that she distrusted this stranger and walked on slowly.

Running back up the road he stopped in front of her. Both she and her children were so disorientated that they walked into each other before they stopped. Taking the pack from his back he opened it and took out one of the scones and placed it in the hands of the woman.

"Is this for us? Or are you too being cruel?" she looked deep into his eyes, as her lower lip quivered in pent up emotion. The children on seeing the scone gathered around their mother, yet they made no effort to reach out for the bread.

"It's for you and your children, please take it." He closed her hands round the scone.

Going to the side of the road the woman sat down and was soon joined by her children.

"Do you mind if I take the liberty and sit awhile with you?" Phelm asked as he too sat down.

"Sit where you will it matters not. Soon there will be more than enough room for those of us that are left, if any." She began to break the scone into pieces and hand them to her children.

"Where have you come from, you look weary." He watched as the woman slowly broke a pieces from the portion of cake she retained for her own consumption and placed it in her mouth.

"Me! I came from the other side of the Burren some days ago. My husband died from the hunger. I suppose he could really have saved himself but he sacrificed all for me and the children."

"The Burren in Clare? Good God." he looked from her to the children."That's a very long journey indeed."

"There is only one Burren and that has been laid bare, it is all but empty of people. I come from Mullaghmore, but I doubt very much if anyone on God's earth ever heard of the place. But then Cromwell's General Ludlow found us in 1651 and he was far from impressed, I can tell you. Not mind you that we were for the asking. Do you know what he had the audacity to say of it ?,

Well I'll be telling you anyway. He said that there was not enough water to drown a man, not enough wood to hang him, and not enough earth to bury him. That is the place that I come from now that you ask.

But there was enough to bury my Joseph, so there was. I know for did I not dig his grave and bury him with my own hands." She opened her hands and in so doing the scone fell to the ground.

"But why did you not stay in Limerick or Ennis. Where do you think you are going to?." He ignored the assessment of the Burren as he retrieved the scone and returned it to her.

"We got some soup from the Quaker's and a scone of bread there. I think that was yesterday or the day before, in

Limerick I mean."

"But where are you going to now.? There is nothing beyond here."

"I hear that one can get passage to Liverpool and then to America. I'm told that this is the right road.
If God should take me then at least they will have a chance." She looked pitifully at her children.

"But have you any money? The nearest port is at Limerick. I doubt if any of the ships masters will take you and five children without payment."

"All we have left is hope in God Almighty. If they don't show us Christian charity and take us, then God will, won't he"?, was her philosophical response.

"Come on I'll go as far as possible with you and see if I can be of some assistance."

"That is most generous of you, but why should you help us nobody else has."

"Well it is a long story but I suppose it was for the better that I met you." He had no intention of adding to her misery by telling her what happened in the wood.

Taking the hands of the two youngest children he led them back towards Limerick.

"What is your name if I may be so bold as to ask?" Phelm looked over his shoulder and noticed that the others were lagging behind. He stopped and waited for them to catch up and repeated the question.

"Did you say something Sir?, or were you talking to the children." the woman asked.

"I would like to know your name, if I'm not asking too much."

"My name is Alice Devine."

"You won't mind if I call you Alice for the rest of the journey. I don't want to appear too familiar but it's so much easier to hold a conversation that way don't you think"?

"Call me Alice and welcome, I've never been one to stand on ceremony." She seemed to have cheered up somewhat.

"My name is Phelm Griffin and I come from the village of Castlelurgan, not too far from Limerick city. You can call me Phil, everyone else does."

"Did you ever notice that the road is that much shorter when there is someone else to talk to." Phelm tried to make conversation.

"Is it not the long road then that has not a turning for some soul. Before I met you I was at my tethers end and that's for sure."

From the way the woman was now talking she was sure that Phelm was her guardian and would help her to get out of Ireland.

"There is no guarantee that you will get passage, paying or otherwise in Limerick. Don't build up your hopes just yet."

Should he go all the way to Limerick and try helping her and her family or leave them at the cross road leading to his village and home, his mind was in turmoil. On reaching the cross roads he stopped and waited until all the family had caught up with him.

"This is where we must part company." he held his hand out to Alice.

"I thought that you were going to come as far as Limerick with us? Thanks anyhow! 'twas nice to meet you, we'll manage." It was manifest that she was disappointed,

"Good bye now and thanks again for the scone, it was more than welcome I can assure you." Reaching out she shook his hand warmly.

As they walked down the road once again in single file the children looked back at him and waved their goodbyes. The youngest once again smiled at him with his large blue saucer eyes.

He waved to them for some time then turned left into the road leading to Castlelurgan.

He had walked a mile or so when he felt the pangs of hunger. Sitting down next to a clear running stream he opened his shoulder pack and took out one of the last of the scones and broke a section off. Rising to his feet he took his tin mug to the stream where he filled it with crystal clear water.

Sitting by the side of the boreen eating his food his mind wandered back to the recent events in his life. Soon now he would be home to his wife and family. There would be no good news for them regarding Philomena Carey and her family, God be good to them.

Then he thought of Alice Devine and her children walking all the way to Limerick in the hope of getting to America. The more he thought of them the more his conscience became disturbed. He was finding it hard to swallow the food. Then the picture of the youngest with the laughing blue eyes haunted his memory.

"Oh mise! mise," he sighed as he threw the piece of scone he was eating into the stream. Rising to his feet he slung his bag over his shoulder and retraced his steps down the road and on to the cross roads. He turned into the Limerick road and with a spring in his step headed towards the city.

He was not surprised to see in the distance the line of children with Alice at their head. They had made little progress. Alice was now carrying the youngest child in her arms.

"You didn't get too far then." he called to Alice.

"What are you doing here?, I thought that you were going home to your own people." She set the child down on the ground.

"To be nothing but honest, I couldn't abandon you and your children. If I can get you settled in the city then I can still make it home by nightfall."

Alice looked at him for a moment, then tears welled up in her sad eyes and she began to cry.

"Oh come on! it's not that bad really. I was being selfish. My conscience was bothering me if you must know." Phelm picked up the child and held him close.

"How can you be so kind? Why Limerick must be filled with Alice Devine's and their children."

"I'm not promising you anything but at least we can try, come on or else well lose the light." Phelm went to the head of the line and transferred the child from his arms to his shoulders.

"You look like St Christopher crossing the stream with the infant Jesus on his shoulders." Alice remarked as she looked at her child gurgling in contentment perched on his shoulder. By the time that they reached the city it was night fall, He took them past the hotel where he and Shelia had stayed and on to the quay side.

The Shannon river was in full flood and several ships were preparing to leave on the tide. He walked round the quays seeking passage to the new land for Alice and her children without success. One look at her and her five children was enough to put the master of any vessel from even considering them.

At the far end of Arthur's quay he saw a smaller ship secreted in an insignificant berthing. It was not a passenger ship but it was his last hope. He told Alice to stay where she was and pray for his success. Then he ran along the quay side to the ship as the crew were taking the holding ropes off the bollards. He noticed the name on the side and remembered that it was an American ship. His mind raced back to the board on the dock side. It was indeed the S.S. Sara-Anne-Jane.

This is a good omen, he thought as running up the gang plank he approached the captain. He related the tragic story as briefly as he could as he anxiously watched the crew preparing to sail.

"Why come to me, what can I do for her and her children?" The captain continued to instruct his crew and treated Phelm as a third party.

"If you cannot help her, then she and her children will be dead within the next day or two."

"Those are hard words indeed Mister, you wouldn't be trying to bribe me now would you,? This is not a passenger ship. We occasionally take a few fare paying emigrants but not on this trip. We are shipping out to Pittsburgh and are running light. Who is this woman anyway and has she got any money. It is one thing taking her to the States, but how will she support herself if she does get there? Have you thought of what you are doing to her ?"

"Money!, she has nothing but what she stands up in, but God will reward you. She has managed to survive so far and where there is life there is hope. Will you, if not for my sake then for God's sake show her pity and take her and her children away from this cursed land.

"You people seem to have a great belief in this God of yours and look at you, starving to death."

"You will take her, won't you please?" Phelm held on to the masters arm.

"Is she and her family clean, what I mean is there is any

plague among them."

Phelm's hopes rose when he saw that the captain was showing interest in their welfare. He was sure now that he would take them.

"Clean as the driven snow, Sir, In God's name I ask you please give them this last chance of life."

"Go tell her to come here and let me look at them but no promises."

Phelm raced down the gang plank and on to the far end of the quays. Alice and her children were sitting around a blazing brazier taking advantage of its heat.

"Come on! come on; quick as you can, I found a ship willing to take you to America." In his excitement he had forgotten his promise to the master.

The captain watched as Alice and her children came up the gang plank. As he looked at them he was having second thoughts. Whatever possessed him to make such rash promises. It was doubtful if they had the energy to withstand the hazardous journey to America. Alice and her children lined up on the deck before him.

The master looked into the gaunt faces of the emaciated family. He looked at their mother, then at the children huddled around her. His eyes filled, he just could not refuse them.

"Will you be coming with them ?" he looked at Phelm as he swallowed the lump building up in his throat.

"Oh no Sir! I have to go home to my wife and family."

"Can the woman cook and clean, I never had a woman work her passage before." He half laughed.

"Does she realise that we are shipping out to Pittsburgh and not New York. If we don't hurry we'll miss the tide."

"In God's name Sir! if you cannot take me then take my children." Alice fell to her knees on the deck and held on to his feet much to his embarrassment.

Phelm went forward and helped her to her feet. Opening his back pack he took out the remainder of the scone and handed it to Alice.

"God bless you and your family, Alice Devine, and may your God go with you." Phelm intoned as he patted the children's heads.

"Here you take the bread, we have plenty provisions on board." The captain took the scone of bread and returned it to him.

Alice stood on the deck as the ship slipped her moorings and sailed slowly down the Shannon, the ships horn sounding melancholy. Round her clinging to her skirt were her children, was this to be her last glimpse of Ireland. What destiny lay before them, she wondered.

She thought of the man who had taken her from the depths of despair to a life of hope and prayed that God would reward him.

He waited on the quay side and watched the Sara- Anne - Jane sail down the Shannon and out of view. He too wondered what would become of them. Had he done the right thing by them? He turned his back on the city and retraced his steps back to the bosom of his family.

He reached his home in the early hours of the morning. Carefully he lifted the latch so as not to disturb his father. He had forgotten that the old door creaked no matter how much grease was put on it.

"Good God! it's yourself back again are you alright Son?" It was the voice of his father."

"Keep your voice down, I'm well but tired." He slumped down into the sugan chair and added a few sods of turf to the banked up fire to give it some life.

"How did matters go then?" His father whispered but there was no response. Tired out from his traumatic experiences and long journey he had succumbed to sleep.

It was next morning that he was awakened by the creaking noise from the idle back. His mother was putting the kettle on to boil.

"Did I awaken you and you sleeping so soundly?" she looked with sympathy and admiration at her son.

"No it's alright, I'll take a nap after breakfast." He rose from the chair and stretched himself. Then he went to the scullery to shave and wash.

"Good heavens I look a mess." He scratched the heavy growth of beard on his face.

"Did you say something?" His mother called.

"Not really, but where is that sharp scissors, I'll never get all this beard off with the razor."

He was still washing himself when Shelia came into the kitchen.

"And when did you get back to the land of the living." She chided him.

He winched at these words as he remembered Philomena and her family.

"I got back in the early hours, don't anyone ask me to do anything. After breakfast I'm off bed."

"Tell us how is Philomena and her family, did you see them, had she any news." Shelia was anxious to know how he had got on.

"Yes I saw them, but it's not good news I'm afraid. Poor Philomena and her family are no longer of this world. I found them alright and I wish to God that I hadn't."

He told in vivid detail his agony of finding the Carey family dead in their booley and of his encounter with Alice Devine. There was shocked silence in the household for some time before his mother spoke.

"The light of heaven to them all, we know how you must feel. " Laying her hand gently on his shoulder she patted him affectionately.

"Do you know you're just like your father, he would give the shirt off his back to a beggar." His mother remarked."Well now that you know all the news I'm off to my bed." with these words he left the kitchen.

Phelm kept a wary and captive watch on the potato ridges. He counted the shoots of green growth as they slowly emerged from the earth.

For the first few days of spring the shoots burst forth haphazardly. Then as the spring sunshine warmed the soil there was an urgent growth across the length and breath of the field. It appeared as if the shoots were jockeying for space along the ridges. The family watched in trepidation as the growth became thicker. The potato crop was in a healthy state. No longer was there the doom and gloom of the past. Like children they told each other over and over again that God had heard their prayers. The famine they hopefully predicted was a curse from the past.

Now was the time for the first"lanu" or earthning up of the

potato crop. Phelm went to the outhouse where the old soot was kept dry.

He mixed slack lime in equal measure to make a fertilizer. The purpose of which was to kill the potato beetles and wire worms. Both pests were calamitous to the delicate tubers.

Next morning before the cock had time to finish his heralding of the day with his raucous crowing. Anne was down the field spreading the fertiliser between the ridges.

"Good God! was it you who called that rooster." Phelm remarked as he and Shelia came over the brow of the field with two slans.

"You're not going to do any earthning surely.?" Anne looked shocked at Shelia.

"And why not? I was handling the slan long before I made your son an honest man." She laughed.

As she continued to sprinkle the mixture along the ridges Phelm and Shelia followed with the slans and covered up the delicate green shoots. This would protect them from any ground frost. It took two days of back breaking work before all the drills were covered and protected.

Spring was a hectic time on the farm for no sooner had they finished earthning up the potatoes than they turned their attention to thinning and weeding the swedes which were growing in long rows the length of the field. These would be used to supplement the winter vegetable store and give variety to their diet. Not mind you that Phelm needed any help in supplementing his diet for if it were edible, then he ate it. They would also be added to the feed for their cow.

This year the crops were showing all the signs of a heavy harvest. This was indeed a very busy time for the Griffin family now that Father was so ill.

Yet being humble folk they found time to express their thanks to God not alone for his blessings but for the calamities of the past two years. It was his holy will that they should suffer and who were they to question.

A month had passed since Phelm returned from his calamitous visit to the booley of Philomena Carey. Although the memory of it would never be obliterated from his mind. There were now more pressing worries as the potatoes were now shooting above the .ridges once more. They were now ready for their final Lanu. Once again they took their slans and covered the crop.

It seemed that the worry of the hunger and the plague had now eased and the people of the village became more cheerful. The cottages were freshly painted and ochre wash was applied to the walls. Attention was paid to the thatch from where the blackbirds had stolen rushes for their own nests.

It was as if they were trying to obliterate the horrors of recent years from their minds.

Yes! the spring of that year was a blessing from God.

Pat is found dead

On the morning of the third day of June, Anne came from her bedroom to prepare breakfast. This was the day that Phelm and Shelia had planned to do a days cutting and stacking in the bog if the weather permitted it. On opening the curtains she was delighted to see the twinkle of the gentle dew on the grass a sure sign of a fine day."The morning sum will soon burn up the fog." She said to herself.

It was late in the season for the cutting but they were trying to keep on top of the many tasks that required their attention. When Pat was in charge everything went like clock works. His leadership was badly missed, but God was good and they would manage somehow.

Crossing the kitchen floor she noticed that her husband appeared to be sleeping soundly. This was indeed exceptional, for Pat was always an early bird. Did she not say that he was like an Irish sergeant Major sleeping with one eye open. Why if a spider crossed the floor he would hear it.

Not wishing to disturb him she began preparing breakfast. Shelia entered the room carrying the baby in her arms.

"Dad is ever so quiet this morning, he must have had a restless night." Anne put her finger to her lips.

"Let him rest on, I'll put the baby back in the cot for now." Shelia prepared the baby and placed him in his cot before calling her husband.

Pat appeared to be still sleeping soundly as they prepared to leave the house. They consulted as to whether they should awaken him or let him be.

"He must have had a restless night. I'll make a fresh pot of tea after you're gone, then I'll call him." Anne dismissed their concern.

Shelia finished buttering the scones. She filled the tin can with sweet tea and covered it with an old woollen sock to keep the contents warm.

"Now there is no need for you to come up to the bog. We can manage. You have enough on your hands with dad and the baby."

Together they left the house and crossed the hillock that led to the communal bog.

Reaching their steppings, Phelm wasted no time in discarding his coat. Spitting on his hands he was soon slicing the turf at a steady pace..

Shelia collected the sods as they landed on the bank and began to stack them into small piles to dry.

"Is that yourself down there." Phelm looked up on hearing the familiar voice.

"Why bless my soul if it isn't Tady Quin himself. How are you then?" leaning his slan against the side of the trench Phelm came out of the cutting to greet him.

"Do you know I mistook you for your father, Didn't I forget that he was still poorly, no disrespect now."

"None taken Tady, indeed times are not too good to him, only this morning we had to leave him sleeping after a restless night no doubt."

"God bless and protect him that's unusual for Pat. Why he was always the first into the church for early morning Mass. I have little doubt that you'll miss him this day. No finer man swung a blade in this bog and I'll vouch for that."

"You're a fine upstanding friend, so you are Tady Quin." Phelm slapped him on the back in appreciation.

"Now look here Phelm, no disrespect to you, but I'm only up here hoping to cadge a few sods of Fum.

"Why don't I put my back into it and help you."? He had his coat off before Phelm could reply.

"Do you mean that now, that's decent of you I must say."

"Decent you say, sure I'll never be given a days cutting and anyhow the practice will do me good."

"Right you are then, but first we'll have the sup of tae and the scone."

With the tea finished Phelm returned to the cutting, Tady was now helping Shelia to stack the sods.

"Hey slow down there, we can't stack them that quick.""Will you stop your whining and get on with it, we haven't got all day." Phelm spat on his hands and continued cutting at a steady pace.

"Leave him be, if you don't he'll only get upset." Shelia warned Tady.

"Sure I'm only joking and 'Tis well he knows it."

"Come on Phelm let me have a go at the slan." Tady jumped into the cutting.

"Did she send you down here to annoy me, I'll show her how to foot turf."

Phelm continued stacking the turf as Tady tossed the sods onto the bank. Occasionally a sod hit Phelm only to be pelted back. It was all in good fun and helped to pass the time spent at the arduous and boring task.

Shelia noticed a neighbour running towards her waving her hands, she waved back in acknowledgement.

"Come home, in God's holy name come home! something terrible has happened." She was in a state of agitation and tried to pull Phelm out of the bog.

"What has happened, in the name of Jesus, control yourself now." Phelm dropped the turf he was stacking.

"Is it our baby, what has happened to him?" Shelia clung to the woman's arm and shook her.

"No nothing has happened to you baby. It's your father Phelm, he's dead God rest his soul."

Phelm on hearing this news raced across the bog like a hare on the moor. He did not stop until he reached his own home. The door was wide open and several of the neighbours were entering and leaving.

He noticed that the mirror over the mantle piece was covered and the clock had been stopped. There was no mistake, his father had passed away.

His mother was sitting on a stool beside the bed holding his fathers hand a vacant look in her eyes. She seemed completely oblivious as to what was happening around her. "Mom! are you alright",? Phelm stroked her face and spoke to her. It was some time before she responded.

"Phelm!, Oh Phelm!" She let go of her husband's hand and rising to her feet approached her son.

"It's all over son, he will suffer no more." Then she collapsed sobbing into his arms.

Phelm consoled his mother for some time before he called on

one of the neighbours to come forward and take her from the bedside.

His father was still lying on his side in the bed. No effort had been made to cover the body.

Laying his hand on his father's head he knelt down beside the bed and whispered the act of Contrition into his ear. The gathering seeing Phelm praying knelt on the stone floor and joined in the prayers. Pat Griffin would not go to Heaven hungry for a prayer.

Prayers finished he rose to his feet settled his father in the centre of the bed and drew the sheet completely over his face.

Shortly afterwards Shelia and the neighbour arrived at the house.

"Will you take the baby to the bedroom, there are things that must be done." Phelm asked, Shelia understood.

She would not be asked to participate in any of the preparations nor would Anne, although she would supervise the wake and funeral.

The body of Pat was removed from the bed by the crooners and laid on the kitchen table which had been covered in a linen sheet beforehand.

The settled bed was then prepared for the reception of the corpse.

When all was ready Pat's body was taken gently from the table and placed on the bed. A linen cloth was passed under his chin and over the back of his head to obscure it from view. The family bible was placed under his chin. Two pennies were place over his closed eyes. Finally his hands were joined and his rosary beads intertwined in them. All was now ready for the three day wake.

Patrick Griffin was now ready to receive callers for the last time under his own roof. The door would remain open day and night.

Phelm and Patrick went to Limerick to purchase the clay pipes, tobacco, snuff and a barrel of porter for the mourners as custom demanded.

Morbid though it may seem, Anne had prepared for this day. Her Pat would have a funeral befitting him and a wake to be proud of.

Tradition demanded that the mourners should be treated with the esteem and dignity due to them. A poor wake would bring disrespect on the house.

As the light faded that evening she went to the dresser and removed the blessed Coinneal Mor. Taking it from its linen cloth she kissed it and put it inside a jar containing blessed earth from the graveyard and placed it in the window recess. "The light of Heaven to my Pat and all the Holy Souls this blessed night." She prayed as she lit the candle.

The blessed Coinneal Mor would guide the steps of the many mourners to the home of Patrick Griffin.

For two days the corpse was laid out in the bed and there was never a moment but some mourners were crooning or saying the rosary round the corpse.

The morning of the third day the coffin arrived from the city and the body was removed from the bed and placed inside it. It was taken to rest on two backless chairs in the kitchen for one more day.

That day Phelm and Shelia's brother Patrick went to the old monastery church accompanied by his mother to open the grave. She wanted things done proper by her Pat, the spacing had to be just right.

With the grave opened to her satisfaction, she sprinkled holy water over it. The two men placed their spades in the form of a cross on the open grave as tradition demanded and returned to the house. No evil spirit would be able to hide within the confines of the open grave.

Only then did Anne go to see that the priest was aware of his Christian duties.

"Anne! Will you not be worrying yourself, sure I know what is required of me."

"Father, not being disrespectful to the cloth. It's my Pat that you are burying and only I and God know what's best for him." She told the startled Priest in no uncertain terms.

It was daylight when they sealed the coffin and awaited the gathering of the neighbours, the Priest and the Acolytes.

Anne heard in the distance the church bell toll the death knell. She knew now that the Priest was on his way to the house to escort her Pat to his Heavenly home.

Phelm went to the door and looked down the boreen, He

saw the large procession of neighbours led by an acolyte carrying a large brass crucifix and behind him the priest flanked by two more acolytes.

As the procession came to the door Phelm, his cousin Patrick and two others lifted the coffin and placed it on their shoulders.

As the door was opened the mourners threw the chairs across the room. The men began to shout and clap and the women began a crescendo of wailing. This would confuse any evil spirit lurking outside the door hoping to steal Pat's soul.

Pat Griffin could now be removed from the threshold of his house for the last time.

A gap was now made in the sad cortège, between the Priest and the congregation for the pall bearers.

Turning the priest blessed the coffin before leading the procession down the boreen to Pat's last resting place.

That evening unknown to anyone, Anne took herself off to the Cairn Mor of the Sideog Ri.

"Sideog Ri, its myself that has come to you seeking comfort" She looked across at the Cairn Mor upon which decades of moss was growing.

A wayward frog jumped onto the cairn in pursuit of a juicy dragon fly who was drying her wings. With a croak of victory he stretched out his hind legs and leaped. This time he was out of luck, the dragon fly was away on her lace wings.

"Sideog Ri, I have little doubt but you are aware that I buried my Pat this day and that my heart is heavy." She paused and took a deep breath to prevent her crying.

"Times are not that good in old Ireland. God forbid, but I feel that soon we will be holding the American wake for my son and his family. There is little to keep them here and the America's are beckoning for the sons of Eireann. Would you be telling me when the hunger will pass"?

Rising stiffly to her feet she adjourned to the babbling stream and retrieved a pebble and placed it on the top of the cairn.

"Slan leat Sideog Ri. You'll not be forgetting me now, will you?. She looked again at the cairn and at the stones of generations past placed within its structure.

She remembered the times her mother and her grandmother before her, took her as a young girl to pay her respects to the

Sideog Ri. Were these not some of the very stones that they placed on the cairn and they now covered in moss.

"Ah yes! Sideog Ri I owe a lot to you, for was it not you that put the charm on my Pat and assured him to me."

She retreated along the secret path and returned to her home.

Draconian demands for payment

Captain Singleton accompanied by his wife and family arrived at his mansion unannounced one fine afternoon of that year. "Come back to collect his blood money has he." Phelm remarked on hearing the news.

His prophesy came true all too soon. Within days his rate collectors came knocking on Phelm's door.

"What brings you here? it is not time to pay the rates as yet."

"We've come to assess the new rates on your home and lands."

"What new rates are you talking about. You know well that my father has died and that we have little income."

"We know that your father is dead and we are sorry for you. The captain has been advised that the income from his estate does not justify his investment. All rates are to be doubled with effect from this season."

"We cannot meet this Draconian demand, we had no crop last season, if you take all our crop this year then we will starve."

"Starve you might. England has stopped all relief to Ireland. Have you not heard of the Gregory Clause. The captain has to see to his needs from his estate. He too has to pay taxes to the crown, or have you conveniently forgotten."

The Whig Poor law had an amendment inserted on the insistence of William Gregory, member of parliament for Dublin. It stated that any peasant owning or occupying more than one quarter acre of land would not be considered as destitute. There would be no relief for these people. They would not be allowed to seek sanctuary within the walls of the workhouses.

If however, they were willing to abandon their piece of land and cottage then and only then would they receive any food.

The enforcement of this Draconian law was left in the hands of the landlords. As the landlords wanted the Irish off the land it served their interests to increase the rates. It became known as the Gregory Clause.

The captain's agents went from cottage to cottage informing the occupants of the Gregory Clause and the new tax. It took many weeks before the realisation of what was about to happen to them and their families became a reality.

"He wants us off the land and to that end he is determined to starve us out. He has taken a page from the book of Oliver Cromwell when he told the Irish to"Go to hell or to Connaught." Anne remarked as she sat in the sugan chair that evening.

First there were verbal protests against the taxes. As these protests proved fruitless more drastic action was called for. His bailiffs were now physically assaulted. The inevitable happened when one of his bailiffs was murdered.

Soon the message got to the Captain that he was a marked man. Should he show his face outside his estate then he too would be killed.

This frightened him so much that he hurriedly despatched his wife and family back to England.

He stayed behind in his mansion and turned it into a fortress. In desperation he sent a messenger to the police inspector in Limerick. He demanded a detachment of troops to protect his life and estate.

The reply he got was not what he had expected. He was informed that there was no man power available to mount a full scale defence of his estate. They would however send one police officer to the village. One policeman to cover the whole village and the surrounding country side, this was a derisive offer.

More urgent despatches followed demanding protection, all to no avail. Finally in desperation he went in person to plead his case before the superintendent, only to be told bluntly that several landlords had fled the country and others had been shot. He should as a matter of urgency look to his own security and employ more agents, the state could do no more.

In the fall of the year he sent his agents to collect the new taxes. The people were by now despondent. They had little to support themselves, let alone to meet Draconian payments. At each door the heavily armed agents were met by a large gathering of the neighbours all refusing to pay. Realising that this was an organised rent strike and that the law of England was being flouted, he again sent an urgent despatch to Limerick. The tenants were in revolt and refusing to obey the law.

This news brought an immediate response, for next day a platoon of troops came into the village accompanied by the Captain's agents. Leading the platoon, mounted on a chestnut hunter rode the captain in full military uniform. He was flanked on both sides by heavily armed mounted dragoons They would not tolerate any gathering of the people. They lined up, two abreast, each side of the street with muskets and fixed bayonets. Their very presence intimidating. The captain removed a scroll from his pannier.

Clearing his throat he read the proclamation forbidding any gathering of more than two persons in the village. Forbidding any singing that would incite. Forbidding any act whatsoever that could be construed as incitement against the crown. Finally he read out the penalties for any violation of the order. Disobedience by any person or persons would be punishable by a lashing, imprisonment or deportation.

He called on the bailiffs to do their duty. Knocking on the first door the agents demanded the rates and taxes. The occupants replied that they had no money and no crop to pay them with. The response was swift and cruel. The parents and their children were hurled from the house. Then the Crowbar gang entered and threw everything belonging to them into the street and put the house to the torch.

This savage treatment continued all afternoon until ten families were homeless. Their humble homes burning before their very eyes. This would be a warning to the rest of his tenants.

To add to their miserable plight the evicted families were driven like cattle before the mounted troops out of the village and on into the country side. There would be no refuge and no provisions for the women and children.

The harvest is decimated
by stealth

Anne decided that it was now time to go and see her old
school friend Tom Roche. If anyone could appease the
situation then it would be Tom.

Approaching the drive to the manor she was surprised to see
armed soldiers posted along the road and on into the
driveway. The nearer to the home farm she came the more
soldiers there were. The captain had surrounded himself with
a wall of steel.

She knocked on the door of the estate office and turning the
big brass handle entered. At the desk sat a stranger reading
one of the many ledgers before him.

"Yes! What can I do for you?" He looked over his half
spectacles at her.

"I'm looking for Tom Roche, would you tell him that I wish
to speak to him."

"Tom Roche was dismissed by the captain on his return from
England, can I be of help.?"

"No! no not really it was Tom that I was looking for."

"Oh very well then." He returned to studying the ledgers.

She had no intention of disclosing any of her business to this
stranger.

Thanking him, she returned to her home disappointed.

"Whatever happened to Tom Roche?" she thought.

"Did I tell you that Tom Roche was dismissed by the captain."
She informed Shelia on her return to the house.

"What did you say." Phelm came out of the scullery.

"Oh! I didn't know that you were home, I was telling
Shelia..."

"I know what you said, but how did you know this?"

"I went to the manor looking for Tom to settle the rates and
taxes but it seems that he has been dismissed."

"You went to the manor, What brought you there? You should know from experience that you'd get little satisfaction from them."

"Well I thought that if Tom was there he would help."

"What's done is done. We have better things to do. We must start on the harvest this week, come what may."

"I was in the village this afternoon and most of the troops have gone. there were just two guarding the bridge." he added.

"They are not gone that far for I saw dozens of them guarding the captains estate."

"I'm not at all surprised, for I hear that a man by the name of Fintan Lalor from the Queens county has rallied the people to call a rent strike."

"A rent strike indeed! you tell that to the unfortunates roaming the country this evening homeless."

"Mark my words, there will be trouble in the country yet, the English have gone too far." Phelm predicted.

"Now Phelm you leave all that to the agitators and get on with your own affairs, you have a wife and child to look to." His mother warned him.

"I suppose you're right, I'll sharpen the scythe and make it ready for the morning."

It was early morning when they entered the field of oats, Shelia crossed into the meadow and with the mowing sickle cut several swaths of long meadow hay. Then with the rope maker she began to make hay ropes. These would be used to bind the swaths of corn. Having completed her task, she returned to the field and gathering up the freshly cut corn. she bound them into swaths and stood them upright counting six bundles to a stack.

Phelm had to stop periodically to sharpen the blade with the strickle. All morning they worked harvesting the corn. By midday they were feeling the strain and were relieved when his mother came to the brow of the field and called them for a meal.

"The yield from the corn looks good this year, doesn't it Shelia? It must have been that late spring."

"That crop will be the death of me. No sooner have I placed one swath against the other than they collapse" Shelia flopped into the nearest chair.

"Why don't you get Mum to show you how to really do it."
Phelm laughed.

All too soon they were back in the field hoping to save at least a quarter of the harvest by night fall.

It was late afternoon when his mother again came into the field. This time she was carrying a can of welcoming tea and buttered scones.

"You don't intend to let us stop then, do you." Phelm joked.

"Let you stop, you don't seem too keen to stop yourselves."

"What are you doing with that? you know that I prefer this one", Phelm remarked on seeing his mother with the corn scythe."

"Don't fret yourself I have little intention of doing any cutting. I just want to cut a few swaths to hang in the barn for the hens."

With just over quarter of the field harvested and the light fading fast they decided to call it a day.

"To morrow with God's help and fair weather we could about finish." Phelm was being really optimistic.

It took three long days before they finally cut the last swath of corn.

The following two days were devoted to saving the hay which would be needed to feed their one cow.

Finally the potato crop was harvested and taken to the frost free barn and covered in a thick layer of rushes. It was in this barn that his mother's two she cats slept.

Should any mouse or rat be brave enough to run the gauntlet of them then invariably they wound up as a tasty morsel.

Now that the harvest was safely gathered in and the hay rick tied down with stout ropes they could relax.

The corn would be taken to the miller to be ground in due course.

With the fields emptied of crops, the villagers could now relax and enjoy themselves. There would be the cross road dances and of course there was the calling of the match maker but not to their home.

It was always a time of great mystery as to who had been chosen and by whom.

Ireland was by now a festering cauldron of rebellion.

Insurgents roamed the countryside calling on the people to take up arms against the crown. There were calls for the Act of Union to be repealed and for Ireland to find her own destiny. They talked openly of rebellion and of throwing the English into the Irish sea.

Proudly they reminded the people of the siege of Limerick. When valorous Irishmen challenged the might of the combined English, Dutch, German and Prussian forces, together with their long ranged guns and fought them to a standstill. When near to defeat the women of Limerick joined the fray and beat the foe off the city walls in the year 1691.

They boasted of the Boys of Wexford who fought with pikes against the English armies in 1798.

It was all patriotic jargon, a few dedicated Irishmen calling on the people to purchase arms at their own expense. The intention was to challenge the might of the most powerful nation of the time with the aim of freeing mother Ireland.

The people weak with hunger and too demoralised from years of oppression from State, church and landlord were trying to vent their anger on an indifferent foreign power,

In the second week of September a platoon of soldiers accompanied the agents of Captain Singleton came to the Griffin house.

Phelm was in the upper meadow trying to snare a few rabbits for the pot. On hearing the hoof beats he returned to the house and was immediately confronted by the agents.

"We've come to collect the rates and taxes, have you got them ready."

"Yes you'll find them in the first barn over here." He led the way across the yard and opened the door. Inside was stored one half of his harvest as payment.

"Is this it then"?. One of the agents asked looking with derision at the sacks of corn, the potatoes and the hay stacked up awaiting collection.

"This won't do you know, you were warned that the taxes were to be doubled this year."

"I know this and that is why I set aside half of my harvest in payment. I might tell you that it is more than a fair half considering the state of the country."

"This cannot be half of your harvest. It is only about the same as you gave in past seasons."

"We've had two years of hunger as if you had not noticed. We could not get any seeds to buy, so the harvest is that much smaller."

"Smaller is it, let's look in your other barns." Accompanied by armed soldiers the agents went and opened the family storage barn.

"Now that is what I call a harvest to be proud of" the agent looked at the their sacks of oats and potatoes retained for their own consumption.

"Bring that dray over here." He called on the driver to bring the large four wheeled dray drawn by two shire horses forward.

"You cannot do this to us, we have given you half of our crops as agreed."

Phelm stepped forward between the barn and the agent but was quickly pushed to one side by a soldier.

"Take warning lad, any opposition could earn you a long spell in Van Deimen's land." He was warned.

"We'll not be too hard on you this time, although you tried to cheat us. We'll take half of this together with the other lot."

There was little use protesting when looking down the barrel of a musket. They watched as their share of the harvest that they had sweated to grow and save was depleted by half. The captain was determined that he would not be the loser because England refused to give help to the starving Irish.

He was now finding it difficult to maintain his life style. What with half his tenants evicted and the others in a state of turmoil, there was little income from his estate.

"Now mother do you see why the Irish are in revolt?, we sweat and toil on our own soil to keep an English bastard in the lap of luxury."

"What can we do about it? If we don't pay, then he will evict us from the farm."

"He may as well evict us as starve us out."

We'll manage son, you will see God is good." his mother tried to calm him.

"God is good, God is good indeed, good to that parasite." Phelm pointed towards the dark walls of the manor.

"I hear that there is to be a meeting in Limerick to morrow

night and I'll be there have no fear." Phelm left the house and went down the boreen.

"Leave him be, he'll calm down, give him time." Anne told Shelia who was about to stop him.

But he did not calm down, he spent the day cursing the captain and all belonging to him. That evening his mother watched anxiously as he took his caubeen from the peg and left the house without as much as blessing himself.

"I'm off to find out what this meeting is all about, wish me luck"

Shelia ran forward and clung to his neck,"Please stay home, there may be trouble."

"Don't worry yourself I have no intention of getting into trouble, I promise."

Felons of our land

Limerick was indeed speaking revolution, it was like a huge cauldron slowly coming to the boil. All it needed was just that one spark to start the revolution. There were meetings at every street corner denouncing England for her indifference to the plight of the people.

Phelm joined the milling throngs and listened as the followers of Tom Mitchell and Fintan Lalor called for recruits to the Young Ireland movement.

The island of Ireland belonged to the Irish people they declared and with the help of the Divine Trinity and her people they would repeal the Act of Union. They would break free of the fetters and chains holding them slaves. The green flag of Ireland would fly in freedom over their land.

There would be no more famine nor plague in the land. They were promising a Utopia, a new horizon. The emphasis was put on the land and the right of the people to self determination. This was the language of revolution that the people wanted to hear. The crowds holding blazing torches in their hands cheered at every word of insurrection uttered from the platform.

They were oblivious to the sound of galloping horses coming from the direction of the castle. Their iron shod hoofs beating a noisy tattoo on the cobbled stones. They assembly fell silent for a moment and listened to the quickly approaching horses. Ignoring the forewarning of an impending assault they once again faced the platform. They stood spell bound as they listened to the accomplished oratory of the speakers. The noise from the horses hoofs grew louder. Their echo vibrated across the River Shannon drowning the prattle of the waters flowing over the Curragower falls.

All too late they heard the order to... Charge!. The cavalry drawing their swords charged headlong into the assembly scattering the people to the four winds.

There was pandemonium as people were crushed and trodden on by the horses. Others suffered cuts and bruises from the impact of the sabres as the soldiers charged again and again into the fleeing people.

Phelm not being a native of the city did not know which way to run and found himself hemmed in against a wall by two horses of the mounted soldiers. He could smell the rancid breath coming from their foaming mouths and saw the terror in the whites of their eyes. Soon foot soldiers came on the scene and dragged him through the streets to king John's castle.

There he was incarcerated, beaten, questioned and detained until early dawn. As he knew nothing of the pervaders nor their whereabouts and was a stranger they released him with a stern warning to stay away from the city.

Next day he returned to the bosom of his family. Battered and sore from the beatings and his arduous journey. He was still as defiant as before.

"I told you not once, but time and time again to stay away from the city, but would you listen. Oh no! you had to go and be chastised by the English." His mother chided him.

"Mum will you shut up for once. I'm tired out and in no mood for any discussion. No foreign power can ever chastise a Griffin." Phelm went across to the bedroom.

"Are you alright? would you like something to eat." Shelia asked.

"No I'm fine just let me rest for a little while."

"Have you no regard for your wife and child, galavanting around that city. Looking for trouble if you ask me." His mother continued to reprimand him.

But Phelm was indifferent to her scolding and went to his room closing the door behind him.

They let him sleep on for the better part of the day and did not disturb him. That evening he related to them what had happened in the city.

"I'm telling you that something is going to happen, everyone is on tender hooks."

Days passed into weeks and the talk of rebellion subsided. The people had other more pressing problems. Where to find enough food to alleviate their hunger.

The weather after a short respite again deteriorated. The snows came early bringing with it the biting cold east winds from Siberia.

However bad the situation had been in 1847 it was far worse now. The soup kitchens had been disbanded and the people thrown on the non-existent charity of their respective landlords.

Then came the news that the Priest's were backing the call for a revolution. This was greeted with hope and joy by the down trodden people. At last their church was aware and listening to their plight. With the blessing of the mother church they would surely succeed.

Phelm told his doubting mother the news. She would now have to be supportive of their struggle to break from the English yoke. Their cause was blessed by the Holy Father himself. This was of course an exaggeration of the true story. The jails of the country he told her were filling up with Irish rebels. In part this may have been true but the majority committed crimes hoping to be sent to prison. Once incarcerated within the grim walls of the prison, they would obtain a daily meal.

The rumour that the Pope himself was supporting the rebellious Irish soon got to the notice of the Roman Catholic Hierarchy. Although the Church made strenuous attempts to disassociate itself from the rumours they still persisted.

England worried that the Irish Catholic clergy were supporting insurrection within the country sent one of their diplomats, Lord Minto hurrying to the Vatican State on a secret mission.

His assignment was to plead with the hierarchy of Pope Pious IX to admonish the Irish Clergy. The English knew that this was a calculated risk. It was a crime of treason in England for any member of the government to communicate with the Holy See of Rome. Had the synod of the Church of England known of this secret mission, not alone would there be a revolution in Ireland but in England as well.

The Protestant church would never condone nor tolerate any communication whatsoever with a Papist cleric. It would be considered profanity for a minister of the crown to step inside the papal state. England had no diplomatic relations with the Vatican State. This would be blasphemous and an act of heresy against the established Church. It would be an affront to Queen Victoria who was head of the Church of England.

It had to be a very delicate mission to be undertaken in secrecy by a chosen few. Had the Catholic countries of Europe, more especially France and Spain heard of this mission it could have repercussions throughout the whole Christian Churches.

There was no mention of this clandestine meeting to the outside world.

At the meeting the plight of the Irish nation was ignored. Not that there was any need to mention it, for the Vatican was well aware of the suffering and death in Ireland.

There no mention of the thousands of troops on to the streets of Dublin, Limerick, Cork and Belfast. Their duty was to harass and intimidate the starving Irish. Much to the shame of the Holy See they never questioned England's disgraceful treatment of the Irish. They and England would use subterfuge to avoid any embarrassment to their offices.

The Holy See decreed, much to England's satisfaction, that no insurrection would be tolerated by the Irish against the English.

Anyone taking part in such an act would be guilty of murder in the eyes of the Church and excommunicated.

Catholic leaders in Ireland were incensed at this betrayal by their mother church. They were bound by their oath of obedience to reluctantly condone it. Millions of Irish Catholics were dying, yet the Vatican did little to alleviate their plight. Their deaths were partly on the consciences of their clergy.

England won the day and at Sunday Masses in February of that year, the priests unwillingly on instructions from their bishops read out the letter. It condemned

anyone talking of, supporting or condoning rebellion against the English crown.

Ireland and her people would once again be betrayed and left broken and bleeding, only this time by her own mother church.

A night of the Sean Sceal

The evening was clear and crisp as Phelm wended his way home from a meeting where the present crisis within the Church was the topic. Without thinking and day dreaming at the same time. He inadvertently crossed the hillock where the Hungry grass grew. This area got its name from the day in 1846 when hordes of starving men women and children, many riddled with typhus, scurvy, typhoid and galloping dysentery ascended on the hill and devoured every blade of grass and shrub growing on it. Then left as quickly as they came leaving nothing behind them but the naked earth and their unburied dead and they with the green grass still sticking out of their mouths.

Hearing enchanting, melancholic music echoing from the bewitched water fall at the foot of the hillock, he fell to his knees and blessed himself.

He knew of the dead on the hill, for had he not helped to bury them in their lonely mass grave.

Were these he thought the fairies who dwelt in the hill fort coming to cleanse their mountain. Whatever possessed me, to be on that hill at such an hour, he thought. He knew that he was intruding and that there would be no escape until daybreak. A fog slowly encompassed the hill and obliterated the surrounding country side. He was now trapped. He dare not move, for should the fairies become aware of his presence then they would do him great harm. He prostrated himself on the ground and remained motionless.

This was the Cloone Sidhbair and Phelm should have known better than to trespass on their domain. He was now trapped within it's confines and any mistake on his part would have disastrous consequences for him.

He saw a band of fairies tripping up the hill, where they formed themselves into a circle and joined hands. From the gathering came a fairy girl who took her place in the centre

of the circle. Phelm glanced across at her as she began an intricate dance. Round and round the circle she twirled and began to shower silver dust within it's confines.
He was shocked to hear the others start singing....

Phelm Griffin, we know you are here
Of the Tuatha De Danann have no fear
Come into the circle and find your queen
And death no more will cause you fear.

The fairies continued to dance and sing, calling repeatedly on him to come and join their band. He knew that they would continue to sing and dance until they had hypothesized him. When no longer able to resist he would be forced to rise and disclose himself. He would then be lured into the circle. Once inside it's confines, the circle would close around him, there would be no escape. He would be married to the fairy girl and never be allowed to leave the fairy world.
They could not see him nor could they capture him for as long as he stayed where he was. He stuck his fingers in his ears to drown the crescendo of the enchanting music and song.
He remained glued to the earth like a hare hiding from a hawk. His body completely numbed with cold and fear. It was early morning when he dared to rise up and look all around him.
One unfortunate who made his presence be known was given two humps on his back to carry for the rest of his natural life.
There was no more music from the water fall and no mist. He took himself away from the hill as fast as his legs could carry him. On reaching the house he related his adventure on the hillock to his mother and his wife.
"Whatever possessed you to cross that hill. This is an ill omen for all of us, the Priest should be told of this. He will know what to do." Shelia predicted
Be it Irish superstition, imagination or any explanation one cares to think of, but there are many stories of unequalled encounters on the Hungry Grass Hill.
"It will be all to the good, never you fret, leave it in my

hands." His mother enlightened them.

They knew that she would be going to see the Sideog Ri.

That afternoon Josie O'Brien, a distant cousin, from far beyond the bridge over the river Avondale at the Long Pavement arrived at their home.

"God bless all here." He tapped on the half door and entered the cottage.

"Good God, if it isn't yourself Josie O'Brien as I live and breath." Anne came from the scullery to greet him.

"Sit down!, sit down man aren't you the sight for sore eyes now."

"It's not too often that I come this way as you well know. I'd never be one to pass the door of Patrick Griffin." Josie was a rare one with the compliments.

"Sit yourself down! Phelm shouldn't be too long away. You'll have a sup of tae in your hand while you wait no doubt." Anne pushed the idle back holding the big iron kettle over the coals.

"I suppose Phelm and himself are busy in the fields, did I call at an inconvenient time.?"

"You wouldn't know of course, but I buried my husband some time ago." Anne threw a sod of turf on the fire sending sparks up the chimney.

"Ah no! you couldn't have, poor Pat, God be good to his soul."

He rose to his feet and going to the holy water font dipped his finger in and blessed himself.

"Now that is sad news indeed, so it is." He shook his head from side to side in sympathy, as he crossed the stone flagged floor.

"It's the will of God and there is nothing that we can do about it." Anne retired to the dresser and fetched two cups and saucers and laid them on the table.

"With bad news there is always good news to follow." Anne took the muslin cloth form a scone and cut it into slices, these she placed in a large china dish.

"Our Phelm got married to a fine girl and they have a son so there you are." She picked up the butter knife and began to spread butter liberally on the sliced scone.

"He is at this moment sleeping soundly in the back room.

Soon as Shelia returns you can see him for yourself. Pat, God rest his soul was ever so proud of his grandson, as well you can imagine. God spared him in this life to see him born, so he did." She glanced at the leaba shuidheachain and uttered a deep sigh.

Taking two eggs she placed them in a ladle and opening the kettle put them inside.

"Don't you miss him about the place, Heaven help you?."

"No! not really, although I must confess, when I am alone at night, perhaps. Then I have his grandson to comfort me, God bless him. Not forgetting or belittling Phelm and Shelia who are the salt of the earth."

"Excuse me for asking Anne! but where is Pat buried?

"Pat is buried with the monks below the high altar in the old monastery." Anne rose to her full height in pride.

"A fitting spot for a saint of a man, and I have no doubt but you had a hand in it Anne, knowing the good charitable woman that you are."

"Ah come on now, sit yourself down and less of the chatter. Sure you can call and visit his grave on your way home, Pat would appreciate that."

"I'll say this for you Anne, you were always the one to set a good table."

As he went to the table, he heard the half door opening and saw Phelm entering.

"Sorry to hear of your fathers death, a fine saintly man and a great loss to the community." Josie reached out his hand. and at the same time he offered his condolences.

"Thanks Josie, you're more than welcome, sit yourself down, I'll join you if I'm not bothering the company."

"Hasn't changed a bit, has he Josie? where there is food you will find him."

"You wouldn't be begrudging me a sup of tae to take my thirst away, now would you?" Phelm teased his mother.

There was the sound of buckets being deposited outside the door and again the door opened.

"This I have no doubt is the blushing bride, I'm Joseph O'Brien, a harmless cousin from county Clare." He rose from his chair and went forward to greet Shelia.

"Well now, seeing as I have you all together I may as well

feed you all at once."

"Let them get on with their chatter, they must have plenty of man's talk to get on with, I'll help you." Shelia follow Anne in to the scullery.

That evening when sitting by the fire gossiping, Phelm once again related his experience on the hill of the hungry grass.

"Now what person with an ounce of sense would come home through a fairy fort, will you tell me?" she chided.

The Ferryman meets the Devil

You should heed your mother, you know that she has the gift. You were indeed the lucky man, Phelm!, Someone must have been praying for you. Fairy forts should be avoided at your peril as you well know.

But who am I to talk? for not alone have we the Fairies. We have the devil himself to contend with, so we have." Josie blessed himself and looked all around the room.

"God be praised, you don't mean it." Anne stopped raking the fire and she too blessed herself..

"I mean every word of it. Far be it for me to tell tales about such a matter. Ah yes! true as I'm sitting it this chair. God bless the mark."

"I don't suppose you would remember the old bridge at the Long pavement, the one past the haunted glens of Killeely? Well! it matters not for it's an insignificant bridge to the stranger. To the local people it brings terror and foreboding after the stroke of midnight."

They realised now that this was to be a ghost story and could take some time to relate.

"Hold it now until I fetch a creel of turf in, I don't want to miss a word of this." Phelm grabbed the creel and went to the haggard where he filled it with dry sods and returned to the house.

"You can start now whenever you like." He placed the creel next to the fire.

There are several stories told of the happenings at the crossing between the counties of Limerick and Clare but none more true than the story of Quinpool, where the woods of Cratlow meet the river Shannon."Josie had started his story.........

"Quinpool was a very important crossing point between the

two counties in days past, still is come to think of it.

It was Christmas Eve night, the year being 1633, the gates of the city of Limerick had been locked and secured for the night. Far beyond the citadel and the city gates at a place named Quinpool on the river Avondale the ferryman sat awaiting any stragglers wishing to cross into Clare."...

Josie reached into his pocket and withdrew his pipe, stuck it in his mouth and blew into the stem to clear any obstacles before he filled it with tobacco and lit it.

"Now where was I"? he handed his tobacco pouch to Phelm.. "Ah yes! as I was saying."..He continued his story

The ferryman idled his time away listening to the night noises and in between saying the odd prayer or two, it being Christmas if you take my meaning. He listened to his faithful dog as he barked and chased the wild life in the woods of Cratlow. Finally tired of his hunting the dog returned to his usual spot in the prow of the ferry where he soon succumbed to sleep.

The ferry rocked gently in the water. He began humming a Christmas carol to himself. There was an unmistakable icy chill in the air, the like of which he had never experienced before. Pulling his heavy coatamore tighter around him he cursed the weather. Then looking across the river to the Limerick side, he saw what he described later, as a cloud of dense fog approaching. He watched fascinated as the cloud moved nearer to the river bank and stopped. There would be no more customers, the descending fog would deter any travellers. He was about to anchor the ferry and retire for the night when the fog began to disperse ever so slowly and from it stepped a tall man wearing a black cloak with red lining and on his head he wore a cocked hat. A gentleman of some repute no doubt thought the ferryman. Taking the oars in his hands he was about to row across to collect him when a prognostication came over him. There was something evil about this man.

The man saw him hesitate and again called on him to take him across the river at once. The ferryman who under normal circumstances would be more than grateful to accept the fare was now sitting petrified in his boat in fear and trepidation of this intimidating passenger.

"I demand to be taken across the river." Again the gentleman's authoritative voice boomed out across the still waters.

"It was a kind of echoing hollow voice if you can imagine it, like speaking into a bucket."

He feared that this stranger was none other than the devil himself.

"God between us and all harm, this night." Anne interrupted the story and invoked a blessing on the gathering on hearing the Devil being mentioned.

"Amen to that." They answered and blessed themselves.

Josie took this opportunity to replenish his pipe before continuing.

"Now I seem to have lost my thoughts, Ah yes!." He continued...

"He took comfort in the fact that the devil would not be able to walk across water and so he felt reasonably secure. Blessing himself he called on his God to protect him. He could not and would not take his ferry across the river this night.

The dog was awakened by the insistent demanding voice of the stranger. Alert and curious as to know who had disturbed his sleep he stood up in the prow of the boat and looked across to where the man stood on the far bank..

On seeing the tall man his hair stood on end and he cocked his ears. Looking straight at the stranger he began to shake uncontrollably yet no sound came from him. He continued to stare at the man. Saliva gathered at the sides of his mouth as he stood hypnotized staring blankly at the stranger and he in an uncontrollable fit.

"Jesus have mercy on us all this night." Shelia whispered and blessed herself.

He prayed as he looked towards his dog. The dog was now transfigured into a cowering whelp. His eyes rolled around in his head as he took a last pleading look at his master. Then with a parting sigh he fell dead into the bottom of the boat. The ferryman looked shocked and frightened at the body of his faithful dog lying in the boat. Alone now he prayed aloud to his God. He prayed louder to reassure himself.

"Jesus all merciful and compassionate forgive me my sins and deliver me from this evil."

His prayers were interrupted by the booming voice of the stranger. Again insisted that he be taken across the river.

With strength beyond comprehension, he took the oars in his hands and rowed, not to the Limerick side but to the safety of the banks on the Clare shore.

Leaving the boat as fast as his leaded legs would carry him, he ran from the shore never casting a glance behind him. His heart ready to burst was now beating like that of a cornered hare. Where he was running to he did not know nor did he care. He wanted to distance himself as much as possible from this repulsive force.

On reaching the cottage of a labourer he thumped on the door until his knuckles bled. He demanded sanctuary. He banged on the door repeatedly demanding that it be opened in the name of God. Finally in what seemed like hours to him the door was opened by the master of the house.

"What in God's name is the matter with you.?" He looked at the ferryman holding tightly to the jamb of the door muttering incoherently. Removing one hand from the door he pointed towards the shore before he collapsed in a dead faint on the threshold.

The master of the house carried him into the kitchen and put him into the Leaba shuidheachain. There with the help of his wife he revived him.

"Whatever ails him, Sean? he looks frightened to death." The masters wife pulled her cloak around her and looked towards the door in fear.

Frothing at the mouth and holding his hands to his chest he related what had taken place that night on the banks of the river Avondown. The story that he told was incredible and was that of a demented man. The master asked him to repeat his incredible story over and over again. Was he sure of his facts.

"Perhaps you were sleeping and hallucinated when you were suddenly awakened by the man calling, it does happen you know."

"If all that you say is true, then what of my dog?, explain that. I'll not return to that ferry this blessed night."

"You can spend the night here and welcome. To morrow we

will go and see if your dog is alright." The master assured him.

"Sean think again, should we be keeping him in our home." His wife objected.

"What did you say Kate? This is our ferryman, Jack Quinlan. Sure there's no harm in him, have you no Christian charity woman"?

"It's not that Sean! it's who is outside that worries me."

"Kate! don't worry about that now, take the Holy water and sprinkle in on the door, Jack can bed down in the Leaba Shuidheachain." To morrow morning with the help of God I'll go back to the ferry crossing with him myself."

There was little if any sleep in the house that night as they waited in apprehension for the dawn.

Next morning they both returned to the ferry crossing. Jack was reluctant to approach the landing and had to be persuaded to come to the boat by Sean. There they saw the body of the dead dog in the bottom of the boat.

"Now will you believe me, there is the proof." He pointed to the body of his dog.

Sean removed the body and placed it on the bank of the river.

He enticed Jack into the boat and taking the oars in his hands he rowed across to the Limerick side. Leaving the boat they walked along the bank to where the stranger had stood the night before.

Then horror of horrors, looking down at the spot where he had stood, they noticed that the grass had been burnt

black. To them this was a sure sign that the Devil was out and about in the country side.

"The story did not end there though!, No by God!, it did not." Josie sucked on his pipe, Then once again replenished the bowl with fresh tobacco before lighting it and returning to the story.

Like all such stories the warning soon spread throughout the countryside that the Devil was out looking for souls.

It was claimed that he had visited the old burial grounds at Killeely to steal the body of a vagrant who never believed in God nor man. The man had been interred that night but the devil had been thwarted in his efforts.

You see the old graveyard is built in a circle with a long entrance to the east. Now we all know that the devil will never go to the east. So he must have wasted a long time looking in vain for the entrance. Whatever happened that night at the ferry crossing it put the fear of Christ into the people.

The ferry crossing remained unmanned for several weeks much to the detriment of the people. Finally the service was acquired by a man from Dublin City who dismissed the story as an old wives tale. He did however demand and got extra large payments for his services. He became more and more audacious in his demands.

One morning as the local people approached the ferry, there was no sign of him. The heavy coatamore that he wore to protect him from the night air was lying in the bottom of the boat.

For several weeks they searched the countryside for him but with no success. He was never seen or heard of again. It was sworn to by many that he was seen walking along the long pavement at midnight. He was accompanied by a tall man wearing a black cloak and a tall hat.

It was in that same year of 1634 that the matter came to the urgent attention of the mayor and corporation of Limerick. The loss of the ferry was affecting the revenue coming into the city. It's loss was also causing great hardship to the citizens of both counties. They decided that the only alternative was for part of the bog at Monabraher to be drained and a new road and bridge be built on the site at the expense of the city of Limerick.

Today that bridge still stands and on its foundation stone one can read in Latin......

HUNG PONTEN AC-VIALMSTR
ATAM- FIERIFECTIT PETRUS
CREAGH-FILIVUS-ANDRE MAIP
CIVITATIS- LIMERICENSIS
SUMPTIBUS ELSDEMCIVITATIS
 ANNO DNI 1635.

PETER CRAIG, SON OF ANDREW CRAIG-MAYOR OF LIMERICK CITY HAD THIS BRIDGE CONSTRUCTED IN THE YEAR OF OUR LORD AD 1635.

There was silence for a time after he finished the story.
"Is this really a true story or just a ghost story." Shelia asked.

"There is no doubting the truth of this story. Whenever you are in Killeely go out the long pavement towards the village of Parteen. There will see the bridge and the inscribed stone. It is as plain as a pike staff for all to see and read. It's a little insignificant bridge now, compared with the grand bridges of the city and would hardly be noticed by strangers. It is still the cause of a lot of controversy in the neighbourhood."

"God bless the house and all within"

"Amen and welcome" The gathering looked up to see who was calling.

"We came for the craic and the news." Two of the neighbours took their seats by the fire.

"You missed the best story of the night, so you did" Anne remarked.

" I'm sure there are plenty more stories to be told before the cock crows. Tell us one Anne? Josie took his pipe and rekindled it from the fire.

"There are indeed and I'll not be insulting the company by refusing." Anne volunteered.

The Black Castle
at Lough Gur

"Now you all know that here in the east of Limerick on the shores of Lough Gur is where the fairies come from.

My story began on the banks of the river Camog which feeds into the black lake at Lough Gur.

One day as the Earl of Desmond who owned the now ruined black castle was out riding. In the still air he heard singing. It was so mellifluous that the wind in the rushes had stopped to listen. Not wishing to frighten the singer he urged his horse forward on cautious reins. Halting behind a bush he parted a branch and looked. There before his eyes sat Aine the fairy goddess.

The Earl stood up in his stirrups enraptured by her charm. He watched her as she brushed her silken hair. Gold sparkles entered the water each time she stroked her hair with the brush.

The Earl became a captive of her charms there and then. This was his lucky evening, if only he could capture her then she would have to marry him. Nobody had ever caught a fairy less alone a fairy princess.

There was only one chance, he would have to steal a garment from her before he could make her his bride.

Dismounting from the saddle he cautiously approached the rock where she sat. He had good reason to be cautious for she was guarded by fairies who could and would put a powerful spell on him.

He saw her cloak draped over a rock some distance from where she was sitting. Dismounting he crept forward, crawling on his hands and knees. The cloak was now within his reach. He pulled the cloak towards him and gathered it up in his arms. Then joyfully he held it aloft for all to see.

"This night you will promise to be the wife of the Earl of

Desmond." He called to her in triumph. Showing her the cloak.

There were grand wedding in the black castle on the day that they were wed.

A year and a day following the wedding a son was born to Aine. They named their son Geroid Iarla, the enchanted one. Aine then put a spell on the Earl. He would never show any surprise at any magic performed by his son.

As Geroid grew into manhood the spell was forgotten. Then one evening at a great banquet given by the Earl. Gerald fell in love with one of the princesses present.

In order to impress her he rose from the table and jumped into a leather wine bottle and out again.

At that moment the spell was broken and he had to return to the lake shore. There he pondered for some time on his stupid mistake. There was to be no second chance, no reprieve. Geroid dipped his right hand into the lake and was immediately turned into a swan.

He lives to this day on the lake awaiting his time to return to land. He can be seen once each year swimming from his castle on Gerroid Island. Nobody would harm a swan from Lough Gur. To do so would bring the wrath of the Sideog Ri upon their household.

Once every seven years on Saint John's night, the night of a full moon the earl and Aine comes down from her hill at Knockainey mounted on two white stallions. Halting at the shore of Lough Gur they call on their son to come forth and bring his army of fairies. On their signal Geroid rises from the centre of the lake and flapping his huge white wings rises gracefully from the lake leading his army. From there the family travel the length and breath of Ireland calling on other fairy princes and princesses.

"Is it true Anne that the Banshee lives in the lake"? One of the callers asked.

"The stories of the Banshee are true enough. What one does not know is that at the keening for a child she brings the Buachailleen along with her."

"The Buachailleen is it Anne. I heard tell of him."

"The Buachailleen or the little boy is used as a decoy. When a fairy child is born deformed they send the Banshee with the deformed fairy to the house where a healthy human baby has been born. There they swop the babies leaving the poor mother with the deformed Buachailleen.

Mothers have to be very careful and make sure that they light the Connail Mor as soon as the baby sees the light. Should she hear mellifluous melancholy music she shut her ears, place the iron poker over the crib and sprinkle salt across the threshold."

"Why iron, and why salt?

You may well ask, for no fairy can lift Iron. Salt is a blessed commodity and the fairies are forbidden to cross over it.

"Are you not a Seeress (a wise woman) to know all these things." Anne ignored this compliment and continued.

"You'll often see a mother crying through the woods and she, poor thing calling on the fairies to restore her baby child."

"I'm going to make up some stirabout." Anne rose from her chair.

"That was one good story, I doubt if Shelia will sleep this night." Phelm laughed.

"Good heavens is that the time.?" Josie looked up at the clock.

"Now don't be worrying about the time, you are to stay here for the night and no arguments." Anne told him as she placed a bowl of stirabout before him.

"Well that's more than decent of you, I doubt if I could make it home without some rest."

"Well that's settled then, you can now relax."

"Did I mention that there have been several revolutions in Europe." Josie changed the conversation.

"Revolutions!, what kind of revolutions?" Phelm was all ears on hearing this information.

"Did you not hear then? Why the throne of France has fallen and they have declared a Republic. In Sicily the king was forced to abdicate and the Austrians have been pushed out of Italy.

"You should have been in Limerick, they are now calling on the French to return and avenge the broken treaty."

"I told you that it would happen, but no! you would not believe me. The French will be on the Shannon and in the streets of the city. They will come to Ireland to help us regain

our freedom" Phelm was getting more and more excited.
"Will you stop all your shannagin, and talk of revolution. Did
you not listen to one word that the Priest spoke, Come on
Josie, forget it and tell us another story, His mother had no
time for such revolutionary gossip.

The Greedy Old Crone
from Herbertstown

"Tell us one about the fairies Anne" A neighbour requested "Alright then, but this one will frighten nobody. It too happened not too far from here at Lough Gur. You know where the Black Prince is seen on midsummer eve riding his horse with the silver horse shoes.

"Just beyond Lough Gur on the road to Hospital town lived a greedy old crone. Why she was so greedy that she would deny a traveller of the road one of the cippins that fell from the crows nests to kindle their fire.

It was on a moon lit Halloween night that she heard the knocking on her door. Now who would be calling at her door she thought. This was the first time that anyone was so bold as to cross her threshold. Rising from the ashes she looked across at the door and scolded the caller.

"Away from my door before I put my ash plant across your back." she warned.

Yet the caller was persistent and continued to knock at the door much to her annoyance. Taking her ash plant, she opened the door with the intention of giving the intruder a sound trashing.

She hesitated when she was confronted by the smallest man she had ever encountered. Behind him on the road side stood a golden coach driven by four hares.

"Come with me, your services are needed. Your coach is waiting."

"Services! What services? Get away from my door you mischievous whelp" She raised her stick to hit the man.

He looked straight at the stick and before her very eyes he turned it into a blade of grass. Before she could say Cock Robin she was inside the coach and it being driven at high speed across the moors towards the glen of Aherlow. As they entered the glen the coach slowed to a halt and the man insisted on blindfolding her. Although she resisted, she had little choice in the matter. The man for his size had the strength of an ox.

The coach moved deeper into the woods and then stopped. "This is our destination, you are required to deliver our new king and for this you will be amply rewarded." The driver told her as he removed the blindfold.

He returned to the driving seat and drove the coach into a clearing. She saw that they were approaching a miniature castle. The nearer to the castle they came the larger it grew until by the time they reached the portcullis it was large enough to allow them entrance.

As the coach was driven deeper into the castle compound she noted that it was occupied by none other than Irish fairies. Her luck was in, she thought, for there were good pickings from the fairies.

"You are the midwife from Lough Gur, are you not?" One of the fairy ladies in waiting asked her.

"Yes I am indeed." she lied as she rubbed her hands together. Was it not common knowledge that they had a crock of gold buried in every field. She intended to get her greedy hands on one.

"Very well then, come follow me." She escorted her to a very silent room where the fairy queen lay sleeping on a gold bed. Somehow she managed to deliver the baby that night. He was the most beautiful and tiniest baby that she had ever set eyes on.

Returning to the palace chambers following the delivery of the baby King she asked for her payment. She would have to remain in the castle for a period of ten days.

"But what of my cattle and my hens? they will starve."

"Your animals will be well looked after as will your home."

"You will have all you need to eat here and of your choosing."

"If I agreed to all that you ask, then I must have food from the outside world and not fairy food."

(She knew that anyone who ate fairy food would be kept a prisoner indefinitely by them)

With her request granted she was compelled to stay.

On the eight day she was given a sweet smelling oil to anoint the head of the baby with instructions not to let it spill on the eyes of the child, nor was she to steal any of it.

This she took to be a magic potion and secreted some in her flask.

On the tenth day she was blindfolded and returned to her village and released.

Looking around her she cursed herself for not getting her promised reward before she left.

Reaching her home she opened the flask and rubbed the contents on her face. She remembered the Fairies warning and tried to avoid her eyes. A drop got into her left eye and she tried to remove it without success.

Closing her right eye she looked through her left eye.

Immediately her hovel was transformed into a grand mansion. She soon discovered that her every wish would be granted by looking through her left eye.

The fairies had certainly kept their promise. Then she realised that they tried to be more than clever by cheating her out of her reward. It was only by stealing the magic oil that she was rewarded, no thanks to the fairies.

In the days and weeks that followed the old crone took full advantage of her gift and greedily wished for more and more wealth and power much to the detriment of the people of the village.

With her new found power she put a curse on anyone who dared to cross her path.

One day as she walked through the vast estate she had by now acquired. She entered a fairy fort. Showing her contempt for the fairies she arrogantly broke a branch from a fairy thorn tree. Immediately a little man came out from the centre of the bush and began to scold her.

"Why did you steal from my tree. don't you think that you have enough of your own." the Little man chided her.

"Don't you dare talk to me in that tone of voice, I can put a curse on you and I think that I will." The old crone reacted immediately.

"Are you able to put the curse on me with your right eye closed?" he asked.

"I am that." Closing her right eye she looked at him with her left eye and turned him into a warted toad but the fairy immediately turned back into himself.

"Can you curse me with your right eye." He again teased her and laughed."

"Yes I can." Closing her left eye she looked at him with her right eye and tried to turn him into a pig but the fairy never changed. With his hands on his hips he laughed and tormented her. She tried again and again without any success. In her annoyance and frustration she threw the fairy branch on the ground.

Immediately the fairy picked it up and whacked her across the left eye blinding her in that eye. As the fairy ran across the fields laughing she heard him call to her.

"When the blind eye sees again, your wealth will be found in the waters of Lough Gur."

When the old crone opened her one good eye she found that all her wealth had gone and she was once again back in her old hovel. She closed the other eye and tried to retrieve her wealth, but without success. Its the wise one that can outwit the fairies.

It is said that the gold is still in the waters of Lough Gur awaiting for a woman with a blind left eye to find it.

Neighbours hearing that a visitor had arrived at the Griffin home came to the cottage seeking news. They stayed and joined in the story telling and the singing of the old lullabies and songs.

This was the way it always had been in the Irish homestead, there was always a cead mile failte. There were no strangers only neighbours.

Whenever asked why they did not ask who the stranger was, the reply was always the same.

"Sure if they weren't good neighbours then why would they come through my half door?" This was the philosophy of a simple people.

It was day break when the neighbours began to disperse to their own homes.

Josie was happy when he got the leaba shuidheachain to himself.

He was awakened next morning by Shelia shaking him. In her hand she held a welcoming cup of hot tea.

"Now was that not a night to remember or was it?" He scratched his head as he rose from the bed.

Shelia retired from the room and left Josie to dress.

Hearing a baby gurgling he looked across to a crib in the corner.

"And who have we here"? He crossed to where Shelia's son was gurgling and kicking his toes into the air."

Leaving the cup to one side, he picked the infant up from its cradle.

"Now will you come here and let me see you.?

Shelia came back into the kitchen."What is your verdict Joe"?

"Sure he has the eyes of his grandfather and your nose Shelia." He bounced the child up and down on his knee.

"Are you not the glutton for punishment, where in heavens name do you get all the energy from." Phelm came from the bedroom.

Anne came into the kitchen with the bucket of milk from their cow and took it to the scullery.

"Do you know Josie you kept the neighbours up so late that they all seem to have slept in."

"Go on now blame me, any excuse for a good lie in." He laughed.

It was midday before Josie decided to return to his home in County Clare.

"Do you know it always makes my day to come to the house of the Griffins and that's no lie. Now where is that child?"

Josie crossed to the cradle and placing a half sovereign on the babes pillow made the sign of the cross over him.

"When you're talking to the angels to night don't forget to mention your friend Josie O'Brien." The baby held onto his finger and was reluctant to let go.

"Sure there was no need for that", Shelia picked up the silver coin from the pillow.

(A silver coin was always presented to a new born baby to bring it wealth in later life).

"I'll be walking with you part of the way if you don't be minding." Phelm was already putting his coat on.

"Glad of the company Phelm, sure the road is long enough as it is."

"Slan lib go leir is go n-eirig an talab lib. (Good bye and may the road rise with you.) I won't leave it so long next time! oh yes! would you ever tell Shamey Quirk that I'll send him the words of that song that he liked so much." Josie raised his ash plant in salutation.

On the road towards the city Phelm told Josie that he was going into Limerick to find out for himself if it were true that the country was about to rise in rebellion against the crown. "Now what would the likes of you be interested in a rising for, what could you do.? Do you know something, that mother of yours is right. You're like a bull at a gate."

"I see what is happening to our country, The English intend to annihilate the Irish."

"Phelm! in the name of God have some sense and turn round and go home, nothing good can come from this."

No matter how Josie tried to persuade him Phelm would have none of it. He was going to Limerick and fight old Ireland's cause. As they reached the suburbs of the city they saw field after field with troops encamped in them. The nearer to the city they came the more troop movements there were.

"Tell me in the name of Jesus, what a few hundred Gob Shites armed with a few hay forks could do against that lot." Josie pointed to the rows and rows of bivouacs occupied by troops with fast moving horses ready for any disturbances in the county.

There are always the French you know! they will come with arms and men."

"Phelm Griffin! I doubt if you listened to one word that I said last night. You're living in cloud cuckoo land man. There is now a civil war raging in Paris, the streets are barricaded. Ireland is the least of their worries. Go home man!, go home and use your God given sense and attend to the needs of your wife and child."

When they entered the city Phelm was surprised to find it calm with no signs of any insurrection.

"I'm leaving you here now Phelm Griffin. Please return to the bosom of your family like I am. Give me your hand on that." He reached out his open hand to Phelm.

"Oh alright then Josie, do give our regards to Delia and all the family." Both men shook hands and went their separate ways.

Phelm commits blasphemy

With Josie now safely back in his home in County Clare, Phelm was anxious to set about the preparation of the land for the sowing. There was little prospect of this as the snow continued to obliterate the fields. Like a mariner riding out a storm he watched the skies for a sign of good weather to come. He was worried that the bitter cold and the persistent snow would put an end to any prospects of a bountiful harvest.

As April gave way to May he became more and more frustrated. There was an anxious urgency about him as he looked with foreboding at the ciscean of seed potatoes awaiting his attention. Their green sprouting shoots denoting the urgency to plant them.

"Don't worry about the early snow son, sure it can only prevent the blight coming over the land. There will be plenty of time for the planting. His mother noticing the deep furrows on his brow comforted her son.

How true his mother's forecast was to be.

By mid May there came a long mild break in the weather. By the end of the month the potato crop had been set. The worries of the past months were now a fast fading memory. There was that air of confidence in the people as they performed their daily tasks.

People who would normally set aside a few roods for the planting of cabbages, carrots and turnips now devoted every scrap of their land to the production of the potato.

Phelm was of the same mind, but his mother insisted that he should continue with the old ways.

"We will not rely on the potato alone and put all our eggs in one basket. Why your father, God rest him would turn in his grave." His mother had her way and he was compelled to adhere to her wishes of setting some land aside for the cabbages and root crops.

From one end of the country to the other it appeared to be one mass crop of potatoes. There was not a spare patch of land that did not have some potatoes growing in it.

On into June and early July the crop continued to thrive. There was of course the odd case of blight but nothing to cause alarm. It was common for a few cases to be reported even in the best of times.

As the crop continued to flourish, so did the spirits of the people. Castlelurgan, was no exception. A cross road dance was planned on a grand scale.

Neighbours came from far and wide to enjoy a night of, dancing singing and match making. Spinsters and bachelors came in their best finery strutting around like Peacocks and they seeking a match.

Even the parish Priest made his appearance. No doubt to watch proceedings and to ensure that there was no undue familiarity between the unmarried couples..

The Uisge Baugh flowed freely as did the odd bottle of Poteen change hands. This even though they were under the ever watchful eye of the parish Priest. Not mind you that the P.P. himself was not too adverse to the odd glass on the sly.

As the fiddlers and accordion players were plied with more and more drink the music got wilder and wilder. It was proper mêlée as to who could outdo the other.

The"walls of Limerick, the"siege of Ennis","The Pig at the door." Jigs, reels and sets were all played and danced to with gusto. Paddy Quinlan tried to dance a hornpipe with Anne only to land on his rump in front of the parish Priest.

He staggered to his feet and in his embarrassment claimed that he slipped.

"It's not the drink father! I'm a moderate man myself." He excused himself as he retrieved his caubeen from the road and dusted it against his trouser leg.

Girls danced the sets and reels singly and in groups and shyly looked at the boys who took their fancy.

The odd brazen one showing her ankle only to be chastised by a frown from her parents or a wagging finger from his reverence. There would be no familiarity however for not only was the parish Priest cold sober and on his toes watching proceedings but their respective parents and the match makers also.

By early morning most, if not all had "danced the buckles off their shoes", as the saying went. The gathering dispersed to their respective homes.

It was late next morning when the village awoke. What a contrast it was from the night before. Gone was the fine weather of the past weeks. A cold miserable sleet was falling over the land.

By evening the wind rose driving the sleet and rain before it making it most uncomfortable for the people.

It was not until the third day of continual rain and sleet that the people began to worry, were they about to witness once again a repeat of the great hunger of 1845/46.

They did not use the word hunger when speaking to each other. It was as if mentioning the word would bring disaster upon them.

Again they turned to their God in supplication. Most had sold all they possessed that spring in a gamble on a heavy crop to meet their outstanding rates and taxes and to having enough over to feed themselves and their children. For the crop to fail now would be a catastrophe beyond comprehension.

There would be no income to alleviate their sufferings. The soup kitchens had been abandoned and England had sold off or removed all the grain from the granaries.

(the peasants being a derogative name for the poor Irish who rightly owned the land until it was stolen from them after the ignominious signing of the treaty of Limerick.) They could now claim relief for their family if they owned a quarter acre of land or less. Whereas before this magnanimous gesture by the occupying English, owning any land no matter how small the acreage they were excluded. They claimed that by their generosity they had saved many the life. One would have to be an imbecile to believe such blatant propaganda.

There was no mistaking the stench that prevailed over the countryside. The blight was back with a vengeance.

The people of Ireland knew what this meant as did the landlords.

More and more men women and children would die from hunger and related plagues. The wasteful carnage it was felt would surpass that of previous years.

Matters would be even worse now, were that possible, than 1845. For few people had grown root crops to supplement the potato.

Phelm surveyed the rotting potato crop. Was this the abomination that they had sweated and toiled for?

With the persistent rains the meadow was submerged and the hay rotting.

They had to prepare themselves for a calamity of unknown proportions. If they lost the meadow hay there would be little if any fodder for their cow. She would have to be slaughtered in due course. The fowl would no longer lay and they too would have to be disposed of. Phelm could hardly comprehend the magnitude of the catastrophe that was about to befall them.

There was little use in trying to hide the urgency of the situation. He would have to confide his feelings with the whole family.

That evening as Shelia nursed the baby on her lap he related his fears for the coming winter to them.

"Don't worry son, God is good he will provide." Anne once again placed her faith in her God.

"Mom! don't keep telling us that God will provide, God has done nothing for us for as long as I can remember. Nothing, do you hear me nothing! So let's talk some sense. I'm sorry if I upset you but the facts are staring us in the face."

"May God and his Blessed Mother forgive you, Phelm Griffin, I never thought that I would hear such blasphemous words from a son of mine." Anne was distressed at the lack of Faith in God's mercy by her son.

"Calm down Phelm! blaming God won't help our situation." Shelia gave the baby to Anne and went to console her husband.

"There is no solution, is there? we must face the facts."

"Your father would have looked for a solution and found one" his mother intoned.

"Father is dead, and if something is not done soon then we will all be dead." Phelm buried his head in his hands and wept.

"This land is cursed and make no mistake." He rose angrily from his seat and went across and opened the front door. As if to confirm his findings sleet driven by high winds swept into the kitchen drenching the floor and table.

The wind blew smoke from the fire around the room.

"There look for yourselves, this is holy Ireland. A land of Saints and Scholars, is that not what you always tell us. Well look for yourself, it's a land full of rotting corpses."

"Phelm! what in God's name has got into you? Come in at once and close that door." His mother rose quickly from her seat, startling the baby, who began to cry. Then crossing the kitchen she took hold of the door and closed it herself.

"Go on that's it, close the door and all will be well. Why don't you tell that God of yours to make the rain stop. Tell him how the people are suffering. Go on! go on I dare you, when you are at it tell your Sideog Ri" as well."

"Leave him be Mum, cannot you see that he is worried for all of us."

A terrible revenge

The country waited in trepidation for the cataclysm that was about to engulf them. If ever there was a despondent people then the people of Ireland were. Despair gave way to acceptance as once again the inevitable crucifixion of the people took its toll. Whole families lay down and awaited death. To the stranger it must have appeared obnoxious to see babies suckling the breasts of their dead mothers. Parents wrapped their dead ones in straw out of respect and where possible secretly deposited them in the tombs of past generations.

Yet the landed gentry or landlords still insisted on their rates and taxes.

It became common for whole families, the victims of the plague, to brick themselves up inside their cottages and await death with dignity.

Even then the landlords would not wait to gain possession. They sent their agents with the Crowbar gangs to the hovels of dying families. Once there they battered down the door and dragged the occupants into the street where they left them to die in shame.

Yet the shame was not on the dying Irish but on the callous landlords and the inept government of the day.

Never had any nation suffered such humiliation as did the Irish at the hands of an occupying power.

The agents of Captain Singleton were finding it harder now to collect any taxes at all. In their exasperation they resorted to beatings and murder.

"Where do you expect these people to find money from. You cannot get blood from a stone." The captain was told by the commander of the troops when he called for more rigid enforcement of the law.

The people of England were appalled by the indifference being shown to the starving Irish by their government and the landlords.

The Quakers rallied once again and gave the Irish what help they could afford. They asked nothing in return but gratitude. Their efforts they hoped would give the people the chance of survival.

They would not die from hunger and with God's blessed help the American people would send them food ships in time.

Yet as they waited huddled together for warmth, their doors were smashed open. They were whipped out into the cataclysm.

The landlords had ordered their agents to set an example and evict the tenants into the continuous cataract where most died of hypothermia and hunger.

It was now rumoured that the captain was once again about to return to his family estate in England. He had enough of the Irish and their constant whining for free hand outs.

The estate was being run down and would be sold when better times came, to the highest bidder.

Knowing that he would not be able to sell the estate with tenants on it, he began the systematic destruction of the houses. It did not matter if they had paid their rates or not they would all be evicted.

As the momentum of the evictions increased the people became more resentful and stubborn.

They attacked his barns at night and set them alight. This did not worry him unduly. He wanted the estate derelict, that way he would not have to pay taxes to the crown.

The people evicted from their homes in the Golden vale of Limerick moved north into county Clare and settled in Bog Dens throughout the burren and northwards.

Bog Dens were to be found in the bogs throughout Co Clare and on into Galway. In the bog where the turf had been removed they roofed the cutting with timbers and rushes.

The irony of it was that if the home the landlord had demolished was in the vicinity of the bog, then they used the building materials from it to erect their"Bog Dens." This was not always available for in most evictions the house would be put to the torch.

The bog holes were to prove a greater disaster than the

booleys for they were constantly wet and airless, a breathing ground for plague, bronchitis, pneumonia and pleurisy.

Under these circumstances the suffers died in excruciating pain as their lungs unable to function starved their bodies of oxygen.

With no creditable roads into the bogs, those concerned for the welfare of the bog dwellers, mainly the Quakers. were in too many cases unable to locate them. Many families were annihilated completely. Their bodies preserved as a testament to the agonizing death that they suffered.

On August the tenth of that year the Captain accompanied by his bailiffs evicted six families and tumbled their houses.

Rumour was rife in the cities that the treasury under Lord Trevelyan was refusing to come to the assistance of the starving Irish.

"They had their hands for far too long in the purse of the British treasury." He is quoted as saying.

The Irish were no longer to be treated as British subjects when help was urgently needed. England was content to lord over the land at the expense of the indigenous population.

That evening there were riots in Limerick, Clonmel and many other towns and cities. All available troops were called upon to quell these uprisings.

This left the captain unguarded in his mansion, with the exception of his few agents.

Now was an opportunity long overdue for his tenants to extract revenge. Taking advantage of the situation that night, a band of hooded men forced open the large iron gates and entered the grounds. They intended to vent their anger on the captain and his staff.

What the captain had done that day was of such a barbaric nature that it was unforgivable.

A bed chamber maid saw the attackers in the drive and alerted her master.

"Light the beacon at once." He called to one of the servants.

The blaze from the kindling and pitch lit up the night sky.

Any troops in the vicinity on seeing the blaze would know that his manor was being attacked and come to his immediate assistance.

The attackers hesitated for a moment on seeing the blaze.

"Forward men, we owe it to old Ireland." One stalwart holding his cudgel encouraged the others to resume the attack.

Charging up the drive they smashed the large windows in the ballroom and entered the house.

As they ran across the floor the doors were flung open. They were confronted by the captain with a naked sword in his hand. Behind him were his bodyguards armed with guns, cudgels, knives and a ceremonial sword.

"Your time has come Captain! there are no soldiers now to protect you," he was warned.

"You had best leave my house at once, the troops will be back shortly." He defiantly challenged the trespassers. Raising his sword he ordered his agents to expel the intruders.

"We're not leaving this house Captain, not until you promise to give assistance to your tenants."

"I'll see you all in Hell first." The captain raised his sword and charged into the intruders.

He hoped to contain the fight until the troops arrived.

A vicious and bloody skirmish followed, in which no quarter was given. Across the ballroom and out into the marble floored hall they fought.

The fire from the beacon grew larger as more and more kindling was added. It lit up the night sky. The outline of the great mansion was silhouetted in its glow.

The sentinel kept looking towards the long drive, what was delaying the troops he wondered.

The captain and his agents were now nearing exhaustion. Although they had put up a valiant struggle, they were overpowered by the sheer strength of numbers and the determination of the attackers. As they pressed home their attack the agents scattered.

Two of the assailants grabbed the captain and frog marched him from the house. Other's followed screaming insults and goading the unfortunate captain.

Defiantly he called on his agents to come to his aid. Did he not know that many of them had by now been killed or had fled.

He was alone and at the mercy of the intruders.

Struggling and screaming he was dragged into the walled

garden where the well supplying the estate was situated.

Removing the large round oak cover from the well,they took the rope from the bucket and tied it around his waist and lifted him bodily on to the rim.

The captain looked down the deep shaft, with terror in his eyes.

Now that he was alone with his captors he changed his defiant stand to one of pleading.

"Good God, this is inhuman, I'll die down there, let me go please. I'll do anything you ask, I swear." By now he was willing to participate in any agreement asked of him.

"This is how you left our people to die, now your time has come."

Struggle as he may there was to be no escape and he was lowered deep inside the bowels of the well.

The rope end was tied to the cross bar and he was left dangling a few feet above the water.

They replaced the cover and retreated from the garden.

His cries for mercy echoed round and round the interior of the deep shaft. He shouted to his staff to come to his aid. There was nobody left to rescue him.

Slowly he swung to and fro, in his delirium he called on his troops to rally to his side. He pleaded with God to show him mercy and he called to his family. His echoing voice mocked him.

He listened to the insistent drip, drip of water from the toes of his boots entering the well water below him. Like a pendulum he swung backwards and forwards, he no longer struggled, he was resigned to his fate.

He was awakened by the cry of his favourite Peacock, it was now early morning. With renewed hope he prayed that his strength would sustain him until help arrived.

Anxiously he waited as he heard the chimes of the clock on the tower ring out the hours. As the silence continued he realised that there would be no rescue party.

Mercifully he lapsed into unconsciousness and succumbed to death.

It was late that afternoon before they found him, he had been dead for several hours.

There was the usual rounding up of suspects and their

subsequent torture and questioning.

The perpetrators of the crime were never apprehended and brought to trial. England had more pressing problems than the murder of yet another landlord.

Now that the estate was deserted there was no means of collecting any rates and taxes nor could any more evictions be carried out. It did not take too long for the abandoned manor to be denuded of its furnishings and valuables.

It was soon turned into a squatters paradise. It was a cruel irony that many of the people he had so cruelly evicted from their homes were now living in his manor.

Nobody it seemed was willing to come forward and claim the estate.

England wanted the small estates to be consolidated into large conglomerates as they were doing on the mainland. There were no buyers interested in investing any money in impoverished estates in Ireland.

The policy of cleansing the land of the Irish continued throughout the terrible hanger of 1848.

With the help of the Sheriff and hired thugs protected by the army, the pathetic skeletons were dragged screaming from their hovels. Children without enough clothing to cover their emaciated bodies were torn from the protective arms of their mothers and thrown into fast moving streams. Fathers who tried to rescue them were driven back by the soldiers. Although drowning by asphyxiation was a cruel death it was merciful when compared with the agonizing deaths suffered by the members of the families left behind. Like zombies they roamed the country side, riddled with plague and starving. Their attenuated bodies acting as hosts to the vermin spreading the plague. Yet like the parasite it is, having devoured one body it readily found another host. Parents had little alternative but to look in anguish, as their children died slowly.

Many of the landlords offered an agreement to their tenants. Should they demolish their hovels voluntary then they would be allowed to keep their chattels and furniture. They would also be allowed to take with them any part of their hovels. This generous offer they claimed would allow the dispossessed to rebuild elsewhere.

Ireland cried and begged for help from the international communities but her cries went unheeded. England was her master and no nation was willing to challenge it's authority. The dejected and disorientated people in their ignorance were accelerating the death rate by removing the clothing from the corpses and giving them to the living.

Throughout all this misery and hunger the debilitated people were humbled further. Having to watch as ship after ship was loaded with Irish cereals, bacon, lard etc; in the ports of Limerick, Cork and Galway bound for England.

Next to them perhaps one lone American ship unloading Indian Corn. This to be sold at a handsome profit.

In was noted that the starving people were in contention with the birds at the dockside. There they squabbled with each other for the smallest grain of corn. More often than not the birds were the winners.

The farm is returned to the family, or is it?

It was in early September of that year that a letter arrived at the door of the Griffin family offering them the sale of the farm should they wish to purchase the freehold.

Anne read and reread the letter over and over again. She found it hard to comprehend what she was reading.

"Phelm come here quickly, the farm is ours once again." She held the letter out to him as he entered the kitchen.

He flopped down in the nearest chair and read the official looking document.

"If we can raise the sum of £400, then we can have the farm lock stock and barrel."

"Just think, if only father, rest his soul, were alive to witness this day."

"That is all very well mother, but where are we to find that kind of money"?

"Perhaps we could borrow the money, my brother might oblige" Shelia looked towards Phelm.

"Father always maintained that we should never be borrowers nor lenders it only makes for bad blood, thanks anyway." He dismissed the offer.

"I suppose now is as good a time as any to let you into my little secret." Anne crossed the floor and entered the scullery and opened her secret hiding place under the old salting barrel. Taking out her deed box she placed it on the kitchen table.

"In there are 140 sovereigns, some were my savings and the rest are the savings left for you by your father after I die. You may as well use them now as later, I'm sure that Pat would understand."

"You know what this will mean, we will have nearly enough to buy the farm back into the family."

Phelm opened the box and took the document relating to the

burial plot from it.

"Is this a will of some kind then"? He opened the document relating to the purchase of the burial plot and read it.

Tears welled up in his eyes he looked nostalgically towards his mother.

"What's wrong Phelm." Shelia looked at him with a worried frown.

"Nothing! nothing at all, I just got something in my eye." He made his excuse and wiped his eyes. Composing himself he returned the document to the box.

"Do you know Shelia, what with my savings and your dowry we will put together enough to buy the place."

"Now let's not be too hasty, you should write and tell them that you would be in a position to raise £300 for the property and that should include the wood and the bog."

"The wood and the bog, now that would be something to get our hands on." Phelm crossed the floor and looked across at the woods of the late captain.

"To morrow I'll go to the city and get a solicitor to answer them and to make the offer together with proposal that the wood and bog be included."

It was several weeks before they received a reply from the solicitors in Limerick asking him to call at their offices.

"Did they mention anything of your offer"? his mother asked.

"Nothing! read it for yourself. I am to call at their offices as soon as possible, nothing more."

"We must all pray to God and his Blessed mother for a successful outcome, are you going now Phelm.?"

"Going now! How long do you think it would take me to get to the city? We've waited a long time for this. Another day will make no difference."

It was doubtful if anyone slept in the Griffin household that night. No sooner had the dawn crossed the sky than the family were up and about.

Phelm was given the lions share of the breakfast. Shelia kept going to the door and opening it.

"Shelia are you expecting someone.?" He asked.

"No! not really, just looking." She left the main door open and closed the half door.

"Well that's all we need in this weather, fine fresh air." Phelm sarcastically remarked as he looked towards the open half door.

Having finished his breakfast he went to his room to prepare for his journey to the city. He heard the distinct clip clop of hooves outside the window.

"Did I hear a horse" he called.

"It's alright, Patrick has come to take you to the city."

"Patrick!, who sent for him at this ungodly hour?

Oh I see, you cannot wait to hear the news can you, I don't blame you."Phelm laughed as he entered the kitchen.

"Are you ready then, I hope it is worth it." Patrick entered the kitchen.

"Be with you in a jiffy."

"Come on Phelm, hurry up the quicker that you get there the better."

"Look do you think that the solicitors will be waiting for me."

"Come on Phelm, if we don't get out of the house now then someone is bound to have a heart attack." Patrick returned to the trap.

They entered the solicitor's premises through the magnificent Georgian doors of number 121 George Street.

The receptionist cordially invited them in and offered them tea whilst they waited for their appointment.

At ten o'clock precisely the outer door opened and a pompous gentleman entered the office.

"Good morning Mr Nicholas." The clerk came to her feet and took the top coat offered to her by the gentleman before putting it on a wooden coat hanger. She then took his outstretched hat and hung them both on the hall stand. Carefully he placed his silver topped walking cane in the receptacle attached to the hall stand.

He ignored both Phelm and Patrick as he entered his office and closed the door.

"Who is he when he is at home?" Phelm asked.

"Sir! that is Mr Nicholas our senior partner in the firm. He will send for you when he is good and ready."

After a short period of time a bell rang out in the inner office and the receptionist rose from her seat and entered.

Returning she held the door open and called to them both.

"Mr Nicholas will see you now." She ushered them into the

inner office and closed the door.

The pompous solicitor ignored them for some time as he studied a large pile of papers with a plan attached. Adjusting his half glasses he looked at Phelm and Patrick.

"And which of you is Mr Phelm Griffin?" Taking a handkerchief from his pocket at the same time he removed his glasses and polished them.

"That's me, I'm Phelm and this is my brother in law Patrick McNulty."

"I see, now Mr Griffin you are aware of the asking price for the valuable title are you not?"

"Yes, but you see we don't think that it's worth all they are asking."

"Precisely, that is my next point, the freeholders are willing to accept your offer on condition that you will not be seeking a loan on the property. Can you meet this obligation"?

"You mean that they are willing to sell here and now." Phelm rose from his seat and spitting on his hand held it out to the solicitor.

Ignoring such uncouth methods of dealing and bartering, the solicitor continued.

"You may if you so wish consult a solicitor of your choice to conduct this transaction. The matter is entirely in your hands."

"I'm satisfied if you are, a deal is a deal, isn't that so Patrick."

"I'm sorry Mr Griffin but this is not a cattle fair. Whatever you sign here is binding on both parties in a court of law."

He rang the brass bell sitting on his desk. The receptionist entered promptly.

"Now if all parties are satisfied, the transaction will be witnessed by my receptionist and by you Mr McNulty, do we all agree." Taking his glasses in his hand he looked to each party for their agreement.

The plans of the farm were laid out on the table for all to study as the solicitor droned on about areas coloured red, blue and green and of the amended clauses to include the bog and the woodland.

When all were satisfied that this was indeed the farm, the woodlands and the bog, they signed the deeds and the plans.

"Now Mr Griffin all that is required is for you to pay me the sum of £300 as agreed plus the duty.

Phelm took the bag of money from his inside pocket and laid it on the desk.

Opening the bag the solicitor counted out the three hundred pounds.

"There is the fee and duty which amounts to ten shillings and four pence over and above the agreed price."

Phelm reached into the pocket of his breeches and took out a handful of money. He counted out the requested sum and placed it on the table.

Opening a large safe resting against the back wall the solicitor took out a cash box opened it and deposited the three hundred pounds inside before closing the safe once again.

Then writing a receipt for the money he handed it to him. He picked up the fee money and placed it in a drawer of his desk.

"What about the deeds and my luck penny." Phelm held his hand out.

The solicitor looked at Phelm's outstretched palm but had no intention in desecrating his position by accepting it.

"The deeds will be lodged with the court house and you will get them back within the week. I'm afraid we don't issue luck pennies." This man was showing all his arrogance and contempt.

Phelm was not too worried about the luck penny. The farm plus a large slice of the captains land were now in his family once again and that was all that mattered to him.

"Well Patrick, I'm now one of the landed gentry. Not alone with my own freehold farm but with land and woodland formally owned by the late captain.

"Good luck with it Phelm. Tell you what we'll do, we'll go and have just the one drink to celebrate." Together both men adjourned to the nearest alehouse.

There was celebration in the Griffin household that evening on the acquisition of the farm.

"Wasn't it strange that they let us have all that extra land and the bog without asking for more money." His mother remarked.

"Stranger still was the way that they so readily accepted our lower offer, thanks to you Mum." Phelm went across and hugged his mother.

He spent most of the afternoon and evening in pegging out and fencing his newly acquired farm of land.

Gone now was the despondency of the past months, he now had renewed faith. Soon he predicted, the hunger and hardship in Ireland would pass and that his farm would be worth treble what he had paid for it..

Anne looked up from her baking some days later to see a stranger at her door. He was leading a horse and had two leather pannier bags over his right shoulder.

"Is Mr Phelm Griffin at home?" He asked.

"Phelm, there is a man at the door to see you," she called back into the kitchen.

"I'm Phelm Griffin, what can I do for you." he studied the stranger up and down.

"This is for you, would you mind signing here." He handed Phelm a long envelope the flap of which was sealed with sealing wax and a purple ribbon.

Signing for the document he bid the stranger good morning and closed the door.

"Well what is it? open it and let's see." His mother rubbed the flour from her hands.

Phelm broke the seal on the envelope and took out the contents.

"It's the deeds to our new farm, look at the size of it now." He spread the plan of the farm across the table.

"Bring out the old deed of dad's and lets see how much we have gained." Like children with a new toy they read and re-read the deed.

"Do you know we could be making history this day." Phelm remarked as he held up both deeds.

"Its not all that long ago that we, as Catholics were forbidden to buy any land, nor to be a gamekeeper or to be educated. They even forbid us to leave Ireland to be educated. We were forbidden to bequest our land to our sons unless they became a Protestant. Here am I Phelm Griffin, no doubt the first Catholic to own his own farm."

"Not only that but if we owned a good horse and a Protestant offered us £5, for it we would have to accept no matter what it's real value was.

Lucky for you Phelm that you were not a Roman Catholic teacher some years ago. There was an offer of £10 bounty on your head. More if they heard the sedition you are now espousing against the Queen.

"Shure Phelm Allanah! aren't you the clever one. Was it not myself that read to you The Articles of old Limerick many years ago. It is those articles that are to this day a disgrace to the English governments. You left out one very important article and that was that no Irishman would every be allowed to sit in parliament nor to rule over his own people. Sure one day who knows you may be the king of Ireland. Remember Limerick and the broken treaty always."

The family were behaving as if they had freed old Ireland.

"You'll have your work cut out now Phelm. Young Pat will have to grow up fast to help." Shelia looked across at the infant.

"I was looking at the trees in the wood yonder, they must be worth a lot. I could sell them to Spaights the timber merchants in the city and make a tidy sum." He was already ahead of the rest of the family in his plans for the future.

The hunger and plague still retained its heinous grip on the country, particularly in the South West. The workhouses were inundated with emaciated and plague ridden people seeking food and shelter. With no sanitation within the homes the unfortunate inhabitants were soon covered with fleas and lice thus spreading the epidemic further afield.

Starving men women and children screamed and fought each other to gain access and shelter within their stone walls.

Little did they realise that they were hastening their own demise. Discipline was abandoned as the sheer weight of numbers overpowered the staff.

The management of the workhouses was in shambles, there was little food. What clothing there was had been salvaged from the corpses and passed on without any laundering. This careless act spreading the plague further. Whole families walked round and round its court yard seeking a vacant place to lie down.

The landlords were now finding that by their crass action in evicting the smallholders, they were being left with hundreds of vacant farms and no income. Middle class farmers the cream of the farming community,began to abandon the land and emigrate to America and Canada. Large tracts of lands were for the asking, free of any restrictive laws.

The problem was exacerbated further as now there were no poor rates being paid by the tenants. Yet any outstanding rates due on the farms were their liability.

As the bankrupt landlords left Ireland vast estates were abandoned and left derelict.

This land became the property of the crown and anyone settling on it would be liable for all past rates and debts.

Ireland was becoming one large workhouse as the country was slowly being denuded of its people.

Estates in the most fertile lands of Limerick and Kildare were being offered at knock down prices to anyone willing to take on the debt and the tenants, but there were no takers.

On a wet morning early in September the bailiffs came to the village of Castlelurgan and to the home of the Griffin family "What brings you here? This house and lands are ours now we bought the freehold." Phelm indignantly approached the bailiffs.

"That is why we are here, for in buying the farm and part of Captain Singletons estate, you also bought part of his debt to the crown."

"What debt? We always paid our rates and taxes it's entered in the ledger at the manor."

"As you well know the manor is derelict and all records destroyed. We have no record of any rates being paid on the Captain's property this quarter. We are now giving you notice that a debt is to be levied on this farm. It will be your responsibility to meet this debt in full." With this stern warning they departed.

"Now we know why that crafty bastard let us have the farm and land so cheap. We have inherited the captains debt to the crown." Phelm banged the table in his frustration.

"Do you know how much the debt is, did they not tell you?. Perhaps it's not as bad as you think." His mother tried to calm the situation.

"Don't you see! they have ruined us on purpose, by selling us the farm. A farm that we could have had for nothing if we accepted the poor rate debt on it. How could I have been so stupid, stupid! really stupid."

"Are you telling us that along with being robbed of all our savings that now we are obliged to meet the debts of the late captain"?. Shelia asked as she instinctively picked up her son and held him close to her breast as if to protect him.

"That it seems is the law, for once we bought over the land we also bought the debt or at least part of it."

"Law or no law, you take yourself off to that fine city to morrow and have words with that smart alec of a lawyer. Two can play that game." His mother was of the opinion that they would obtain some redress.

Phelm went next morning to have words with the learned gentlemen in the hope of putting this unjust matter to rights. Not being a diplomat, he did not mix his words. He was soon embroiled in a heated argument with the solicitor and called him a liar, a crook and a scoundrel.

"Look here Mr Griffin! nobody forced you to buy that farm. It was your decision and yours alone, so don't make the excuse of blaming others."

"You are nothing but a fraudster. You knew that there were debts on that land and that is why you were so nice. Giving us the sweeteners of the woods and the bog. You knew full well what you were doing for your fat fee, didn't you"? He rose to his feet and stood over the terrified lawyer.

The lawyer fearing for his safety from this boorish farmer nervously picked up the brass bell from his desk and rang it vigorously. Immediately the receptionist entered. By the speed of her entry there was little doubt but that she had been listening at the door.

"Call the Peelers at once and have them remove this creature." He retreated to the farthest corner of the office and nervously waved his hand.

"There is no need, I wouldn't dirty my hands on you, you Judas sheep. I have trod on cleaner scum than you." Phelm turned on his heels and left knowing that there was no satisfaction to be gained by pursuing the matter further. Too late Phelm took the time to visit the land agents and find out what prices farms in the country were fetching. There were vacant farms and estates by the score from Cork to Donegal for the taking. Anyone willing to pay the rates and taxes due were offered the farms without any other outlay whatsoever. "You could walk the miles from Limerick to Galway and not find a single farm occupied." He was told.

Who cares that they starve?

It seemed that the whole population was now on the move. Those with the means to do so were booking their passage on the first ship in the harbour.

All that were left in Ireland it seemed were the very poor and the occupying army.

It was known that a great calamity was waiting to happen. As winter rapidly approached there was little food in the country and no effort was being made to secure any. The people were in the depths of despair. England it seemed had decided to let nature take its course in Ireland.

Those who could not survive were to be let die from what was called natural causes namely"Starvation and Disease."

What was Ireland's loss in man power and farming knowledge was America's gain. The country was systematically drained of its best farmers. They were leaving Ireland in their thousands to buy cheap farm land in the United Sates and Canada.

If the best farmers left Ireland now then who would be left to do the planting for the next season.

Phelm was in a despondent mood as he returned home that evening. It was now that he needed his father's advice more than ever. What would he tell his wife and mother waiting anxiously for his return. They had very little money left and inflation was rising daily. He would have to find the money to pay the rates due or he would be evicted from his farm. They waited anxiously for the news of the rate but it never came.

"Strange that we have not been notified yet about the debts due?" Anne remarked some weeks later.

"You don't think that they have forgotten about them, do you"? Shelia asked more in desperation than hope.

"Forgotten! that lot, why every debt is engraved on granite stones with Irish blood, never to be erased." Phelm informed them sarcastically.

"Well whatever is stopping them from enforcing the law it must be important, that's for sure." His mother remarked.

How true his mothers words were for the dreadful news was soon relayed from county to county that another plague had befallen the cursed land. Cholera had broken out in the north of the country and was spreading out of control towards the south.

The government made no contingency plans to contain the plague. Their negligence and indifference encouraged its spreading. Victims wandered aimlessly south without any restrictions whatsoever on their movements.

They came seeking non-existent relief. All they succeeded in doing was to deplete the already weakened population further.

The cries for the troops to be called in to stop the movement of people fell on deaf ears.

"How can we feel compassion for these hopeless people" one English politician remarked,"If is not famine then it is plague. It is about time that they sorted out their own problems and not keep putting them on our shoulders."

In desperation and unquestioning faith the people once again sought solace from their God. He was now their only hope of salvation.

They prayed earnestly before the crucified dead Christ for compassion and mercy. Had they not suffered enough. What more sacrifices did he want?. They gave him their babies, their youth and their parents.

"God of mercy and compassion let us not implore in vain they prayed."

What! many thought was the use in praying to a dead Christ who himself had been crucified. They too were being systematically crucified.

The year 1848 gave way to the year 1849 without any sign of the Cholera epidemic abating, far from abating it was now raging all over Ireland. It was carried from person to person in the overcrowded workhouses and by the vermin infested victims. Then came yet another plague to torment the weakened and destitute people in the form of a flu.

Commonly known as the Black Flu it quickly decimated the

young, the weak and the old who had managed to survive the plague and hunger.

Dublin the capital city was now no more than a ghost town its once elegant streets littered with beggars suffering from fever, cholera and typhus. All commerce was at a standstill. Not only had the people suffered the seven plagues but it seemed that new ones were being added weekly.

Corpses littered the country side with little effort being made to bury them.

England had destroyed the ancient Irish Breton laws. Laws that were far older and more honourable than the laws created by their so called mother of parliament. Not content with this they were now systematically destroying the last vestige of Irish pride. English justice was again being exposed as the charade it was. The Irish culture was forbidden to be practised and her language muted. Yet the Irish nation somehow even in all its adversities rose to reclaim her island home time and time again. This year would be no exception, A few volunteers attempted an insurrection of sorts. Half starved and with little if any arms capable of even one skirmish. They challenged the might of the British Empire. The result was a forgone conclusion, the leaders would be hanged and their followers transported to Van Deimen Land and other British penal colonies.

This pitiable insurrection did nothing to alleviate the hunger in Ireland. All it achieved was the denying of any help to the people. Ireland would be left broken, bleeding and starving by her masters. They would be taught a lesson that they would not easily forget. This punishment the English hoped would ostracize the rebels from the people.

English diplomats were now being questioned as to what was happening in Ireland. Emigrants arriving in America brought the news of the wholesale destruction of towns and villages. they told of the bodies of the unburied dead piling up on the beaches and in the countryside.

England could no longer ignore these horrific stories. Nor could she ignore the fact that the Irish emigrants were bringing plague to their countries. The proof was exposed on every coffin ship that docked.

Emigrants arriving from central Europe were fit and ready to take their places in the infrastructure of the state.

The majority of the Irish had to be hospitalised cared for fed and clothed and in too many cases buried.

Questions were being asked as to what England's role and intentions were towards the Irish. Answers were required not platitudes.

A diplomatic solution was concocted in Whitehall.

The Queen of Ireland, Victoria, together with Prince Albert, and their children would visit Ireland. This would show the world that she was concerned and felt dearly for the welfare of her loyal Irish subjects.

Little if any attention was paid to the need to set new season crops in Ireland. The government was preoccupied with the plans to welcome the Queen. The visit of her Majesty and her consort took precedence over the needs of the people.

Money was now arriving daily from relatives in the United States and Canada. They wanted to take their families away from the barbarity of the English landlords. The Queens visit was of no concern to them.

There was work, land and opportunity in the new countries of America and Canada. There was no need to suffer any more in Ireland.

It was pathetic to see whole families crowded on the decks of the American ships taking one last sorrowful glimpse of their native land. They knew that they would never be able to return. Yet they were to form themselves into societies and for generations were to be more Irish than those left behind. If they would never see the shores of Ireland again, then by the grace of God their children would. They would be taught to remember the Black Hunger and the suffering of the Irish nation. English justice would find itself in the dock by generations yet unborn.

The Griffin family had now planted what acreage they could afford to buy seed for. Once again they hoped and prayed with that Irish dogmatic optimistic outlook mingled with superstition so prevalent amongst the Irish that God would bless this crop.

Such faith and perseverance was the envy of the British. What nation would go on year after year suffering one disaster after another. Yet continue to believe their omnipotent God would secure the next seasons crop. To accept without question that the deaths of millions of her people was the will of God.

A message arrives from over the seas

Anne's day dreaming was interrupted one afternoon by the appearance of a stranger leaning over her half door. He was carrying a large sea kit bag on his shoulder.

"Good day Mam." The stranger called in a long drawl of an accent.

"Good day to yourself." Anne looked up startled by the presence of a gangly man dressed in the clothes of a seafarer.

"Would I be right in saying that this is the home of the Griffin's Mam?"

"I'm Mrs Griffin, is there something you want?" He could see by her expression that she was puzzled.

"Actually it's your son, Phelm that I wish to speak to, I'm an old friend of his." He wished to put her mind at ease.

"Phelm is over beside the wood. I'll go and fetch him. Come in and take the weight off your feet, who will I say wants him?"

"Well now Mam,he'll know me well enough when he sees me." The stranger smiled.

Anne put her knitting to one side. Leaving him sitting in the sugan chair and went to fetch Phelm.

Hearing Phelm and his mother coming up the path he rose to his feet. Phelm entered the kitchen and stood studying the stranger for some moments.

"Well bless my soul, Whatever brings you here? This mother is captain Grey. You know the one who took pity on Alice Devine and her children."

"Phelm told me so much about you. 'Tis proud I am to meet the likes as you." Anne wiped her hands on her apron and took the captain's outstretched palm.

"My wife and child will be home, soon, would you like to sit down and share a pipe." Phelm reached above the mantle and took down his pipe and pouch.

"I'll wet a pot of tae, I'm sure that you must be thirsty."

Anne lifted the lid off the iron kettle to see if there was sufficient boiling water inside.

"I brought some provisions Mam, I hope that you won't be offended." The captain placed the haversack on the table.

"There was no need for that, sure we can manage. Thanks all the same, it is appreciated." She looked as he proceeded to empty the food onto the table.

"We're all grateful to you, now sit down here and tell us all the news, do you know where Alice is now"?.

"You'll be glad to know that she is doing very well in the States. You'll think me awful for an old sea dog but I married Alice in Pittsburgh, and I can tell you that I have no regrets. The children are settled down and going to fine schools. I doubt if you would recognise them now."

"Congratulations, that is indeed good news, but how did you find me?"

"Find you! I never lost you. Alice reminded me over and over again. Telling me what a fine Christian you are and should I ever dock in Limerick again I was to make sure and find you, so here I am." The captain slapped his thigh.

"I never told her where I lived, now did I."?

"You may have well forgotten but not Alice, bless her. You left her once at the cross roads outside the city, remember? You said that you were going home to Castlelurgan,"

Shelia came through the door, holding their son by the hand. The captain once again rose to his feet out of respect.

"This is my wife Shelia and my first born son Patrick. This is captain Grey, Shelia, the gentleman who was so good to Alice, the woman that I met on the road, remember?"

"So you are the mystery sailor who became my husbands hero. How is the woman and her children?."

Once Again he repeated the story of how he was now married to Alice.

"Look here Shelia, the captain brought all this food for us from the States."

Anne got up from her chair and began to cry, then she ran into the scullery.

"I am sorry is something wrong.?" The captain was startled

and embarrassed.

"Sit down man, my mother is a proud woman and rather sentimental. She is taken aback by your generosity as we all are. Thanks!!."

Shelia let go of the child's hand and immediately he ran to the side of the captain. Taking his cap from his knee he placed it on the child's head.

"Now, let's see what we have here." Reaching into the pocket of his breeches he withdrew a leather purse that was folded in two and held closed with a press stud.

Curiosity getting the better of the child, he tried to take the purse from the captain.

"Now Patrick behave yourself." Shelia wagged her finger at him. The child retreated to his mothers side.

"Oh, he's alright just like all children over excited." He opened the purse and called the child to his side.

"What do you think this is"? He held a silver dollar coin out to the child.

"This is a silver American dollar and it's all for you. You'll be staying the night, won't you? There's little reason in you rushing off." Shelia invited him to stay.

"I'd like to, thanks. That is if I'm not putting you out."

Shelia took young Patrick to the bedroom and settled him down for the night.

Long into the evening they sat talking and exchanging gossip.

"I hear that matters are no better in Ireland, how are times treating you?." The captain queried.

"Times are far from good if one asks, we would manage but we were robbed by a blackguard of a solicitor, so we were" Anne informed him.

"Will you not be annoying the captain with our problems." Phelm scolded her.

"Well someone has to say something don't they."

"I'd like to know what happened, really I would that is if you don't mind."

"Well you heard half the story so I see no harm in telling you the rest." Phelm sat back and related how they were tricked into buying the land.

"How ever will you be able to pay them back, it could take years."

"Oh God is good, we'll manage somehow, we have for the past five years.

"Now that gives me the chance to tell you all just why I am here." He took his pipe from his mouth.

"Over in the States in a town called Pittsburgh where I live, they have opened a new smelting foundry. They are crying out for workers. It's hard dirty work but by God the pay is the best in the country."

"You're asking us to emigrate to America." Shelia looked shocked.

"No! not exactly, Phelm could come with me and see if he liked it there, and at the same time earn enough to pay off the debt on the farm. Then if he wished he could send for you or if not return home."

"That's more than a decent offer and we are most obliged to you. We would need time to consider it." Phelm looked towards Shelia.

"There is no hurry and I didn't mean for you to come with me on this voyage. Take your time and talk it over. From what I have seen and heard so far you have nothing to lose."

"It's getting late and you must be tired out, I'll make the settled bed up for you." Anne rose from her chair and went across to the bed by the fire.

"What's wrong with this comfortable chair, it's better than the hammock that I sleep in on board." he snuggled deeper into the sugan chair.

"I'll not hear of it in my house. What do you think the neighbours would say?" She continued making the bed.

"You have quaint customs in this country, but real nice ones."

"We'll leave you to it now, the lamp is beside the bed. You can quench it in your own good time. Come on all of you off to bed." Anne crossed the floor to her room.

She paused and looked across at the stranger."Good night and God bless you." Slowly she closed the door to her room.

"What do you think of the captains offer." Phelm whispered to Shelia.

"It's tempting, but before we make up our minds we had better sleep on it."

The captain was up and about long before the family rose, Anne saw him through the half door crossing the meadow as she entered the kitchen.

"Out for an early stroll were you then.?"

"Do you know this is indeed a lovely land, I was enchanted by the species of different birds singing in the bushes."

"I must say that I never really noticed, I suppose living here makes one complacent. Now what would you like for breakfast?"

"There's no need to be too fussy with me, whatever you are having."

Phelm and Shelia entered the kitchen, Shelia carrying the child.

"And how is the young skipper this morning.?" The child began to cry and clung to his mother.

"Oh alright then, you know your own." The captain retreated to the fireplace.

"Come on then, you sit here, Sir." Anne took hold of the back of a chair.

When breakfast was finished Phelm said that he would accompany him as far as the city.

"Why don't you call on Patrick, he will take you in the jaunting car." Shelia suggested.

"There's no need, the walk will do us both good, and we have a lot to talk about."

"I'll say good bye for now and give your regards to Alice." The captain shook hands with the women of the house.

Phelm's mother went to the half door and waved them good bye as they went down the boreen.

Anne remembers the O'Flattery family

Anne opened the half door and crossed the yard to where the potato crop was growing.

"So you are the cause of Ireland's troubles." She looked down at the stalks wafting in the morning breeze.

The flowers were beginning to show and there was no sign of any blight that she could see. The air smelt fresh with the aroma of hawthorn.

The smell of putrefying vegetation of the previous season was now a fading memory.

Sitting down on the nearest flat stone she surveyed her farm and let her mind wander back to the days when she and Pat turned the first sod together.

Would she now be forced after all the sacrifice that they had made to abandon the land.

What of granddad and grandma buried under the old yew tree. Who would be left to say a prayer over them when their anniversary came around.

Worse still what if she did go to the America's and die there. She would be buried in foreign soil far away from her Pat. It did not bear thinking about.

There never had been an American wake in the Griffin household.

If circumstances forced her to leave the homestead she would feel that she had Sold the pass.

Rising to her feet she walked along the boreen. Reminders of Ireland's sad past were all too close to be ignored. She looked up at the dead gable wall of the home of the O'Flattery's. She noted the dark brown patch where the chimney once sent its scented turf smoke spiralling to the sky. Slowly being obliterated by the wild wallflowers growing in the crevices. The fields where the children played. Where

Mary and her husband Jimmy had worked the accursed potato crop were all now covered in thistles.

Where had all the daisies and buttercups gone to? There were plenty when the children made daisy chains and stuck the buttercups to their chins. Who's ever stayed on the longest would be married first. How they laughed and nudged each other as the flowers fell off one by one. They were the flowers now, they would never know married life nor would they know sorrow. Like the Children of Lir they would never grow old. Their innocence was taken away from them by a brutal and callous landlord.

Perhaps in the stillness of the evening they still played their innocent games in the spinney. Far away from the cruel landlord and his agents. They would freely dance and sing with the fairies of old Ireland. Perhaps! Anne thought letting her mind in fancy wander as she was prone to.

"Anne Griffin, you sentimental old fool." She spoke out loud to herself and wiped a tear from her eye before taking a deep breath.

The O'Flattery's were not so lucky. The captain had demolished their home around them one week before the quarter day.

It was at this time that he also demanded rack rent. It was on that same day that the constabulary came to evict the family with the help of the red coats. It was a day to remember in sorrow and shame.

Jimmy O'Flattery had vowed that they would not be driven from their home without a fight and had barricaded himself and his family inside.

The neighbours including herself and Pat, rest his soul had gathered outside in a vain effort to show their solidarity and opposition.

Their defiance was no more than symbolic. The officer in command, ignoring their protestations ordered his mounted troops to withdraw some one hundred yards down the boreen. Then drawing his sword he ordered the charge.

Snorting horses with foaming lather coming from their mouths thundered towards the house scattering the protestors like chaff in the wind. Anne could still hear their ghostly screams of agony in the quiet of the evening.

The Crowbar gang helped by the constabulary erected the battering ram in front of the door and attached a stout oak beam to the rope. They swung it to and fro all eight of them, four each side there were.

Above the din of the ram the people heard Jimmy begin to sing Bold Robert Emmett.

I can still hear them singing, that is Jimmy, Mary and the children bless them all. Anne spoke out loudly to herself.

Jimmy could still be heard singing his defiance as the old door stubbornly refused to capitulate before the onslaught of the ram.

Defiantly he continued to sing ably stimulated by his family. In his frustration and annoyance the captain ordered his troops to loudly shout out each stroke of the ram. This he believed would mute the defiant singing.

How mistaken he was, for up stood every man, woman and child present and joined in the singing.

They cried as they sang......

No rising column marks this spot,
Where many a victim lies;
But oh! the blood which here has streamed,
To Heaven for justice cries.

It claims it on the oppressor's head
Who joys in human woe,
Who drinks in tears by misery shed,
And mocks them as they flow.

It claims it on the callous Judge,
Whose hands in blood are dyed,
Who arms injustice with the sword,
The balance throws aside.

It claims it for his ruined isle,
Her wretched children's grave;
Where withered Freedom droops her head,
And man exists a slave.

O Sacred Justice! free this land

From tyranny abhorred;
Resume thy balance and thy seat-
Resume- but sheath thy sword.

No retribution should we seek-
Too long has horror reigned;
By mercy marked may freedom rise,
By cruelty unstained.

Nor shall a tyrant's ashes mix
With those our martyred dead;
This is the place where Erin's sons
In Erin's cause have bled.

And those who here are laid at rest,
Oh! hallowed be each name;
Their memories are for ever blest-
Consigned to endless fame.

Unconsecrated is this ground,
Unblessed by holy hands;
No bell here tolls its solemn sound,
No monument here stands.

But here the patriot's tears are shed,
The poor man's blessing given;
These consecrate the virtuous dead,
These waft their fame to Heaven.

Robert Emmett

Did he have a premonition as he and his family sung this patriotic song, written by Robert Emmett on the burial ground of Arbour Hill, in Dublin? On the spot where the men of the 1798 uprising against the British Crown were interred. Did he not realise that he too and his family would soon be buried,"Where no rising column would mark the spot."
Bang! Swing, bang! they swung that cursed battering ram back and forth, back and forth. The sweat glistened on their brows. Irishmen betraying their kin for a paultry English

shilling. Their tempers fraying as Jimmy continued singing defiantly encouraged by the villagers.

"That was our own Robert Emmett, the darling of Ireland." She began to hum the song and to recall the memory of the day that the village defied the landlords.

She remembered too the momentary hush as Jimmy finished his song. The silence did not last too long. Once again the noise of the ram echoed across the valley. Its relentless battering heralding the death knell for the old house.

Then through the din came the melodious voices of Mary and her eldest daughter Noreen, as they sang in unison.

> There is not in this wild world a valley so sweet
> As that vale in who's bosom the bright waters meet
> Oh! the last rays of feeling and life must depart
> Ere the bloom of that valley shall fade from my heart
>
> Yet it was not that nature had shed oe'r the scene
> Her purest of crystals and brightest of green;
> 'Twas not her soft magic of streamlet and hill,
> Oh! no-, it was something more exquisite still.
>
> 'Twas that friends, the beloved of my bosom, were near
> Who made every dear scene of enchantment more dear,
> And who felt how the best charms of nature improved
> When we see them reflected from looks that we love.
>
> Sweet vale of Avoca! how calm could I rest
> In thy bosom of shade, with the friends I love best,
> Where the storms that we feel in this cold world should cease,
> And our hearts like thy waters be mingled in peace.

The Meeting of the Waters

This was Mary's message of peace to her neighbours in the valley. She relayed it to them from within the walls of her cottage.

Did not a white dove land on the old castle wall as they sang. Sent no doubt by the great Master himself with a message of hope. No dove ever since has been seen there about. There was many the sad eye when the last notes died away."And our hearts like thy waters be mingled in peace."

As in a dream the banging continued. Shock waves from the ram shook the glass in the windows. The crows and magpies in the chestnuts were by now getting annoyed and agitated. They cawed their annoyance at the indefatigable perpetrators of their territory. The sweeps of the ram were getting longer and longer. But that old door was made of finest Irish oak and had withstood many the storm. It would no more surrender without a fight than would Jimmy and his family.

Bang! crash! Bang! crash! the rhythm and discipline of each stroke strictly in tempo hit the door.

"Remember Limerick" came the defiant shout from Jimmy within. This was a famous battle cry throughout Europe in respect for the people of the city who had defied the might of the finest armies of England and Europe in defending their city in 1691.

The people cheered loudly in support and cried out "Remember Sarsfield." (The Irish general in command of the garrison at the time).

The villagers began to throw sods at the crowbar gang and soldiers.

The soldiers drew their swords and charged up the hill scattered the gathering.

The rhythm of the ram grew softer as the old door slowly succumbed to the onslaught.

Finally with a crashing sound it gave way. The crowbar gang charged into the house with their ash plants and cudgels at the ready.

Jimmy was the first to be dragged from the house with blood flowing freely from a gaping wound in his head. Inflicted no doubt by one of the weapons. Mary and two of her children followed and they trying to hide in the folds of her skirt.

When all were evicted from the hovel, the Crowbar gang threw their cursed English spleen into the thatch setting it alight.

Flames lit up the country side for miles around as the roof collapsed in on itself.

With the carnage completed to his satisfaction the officer

called his men to order and made preparations to leave.

It was at this point that Jimmy sprang free from his captors. Then like a deer at a leap he attacked the officer, trying to dislodge him from his horse.

Drawing his sword the officer brought it down on Jimmy's head, splitting it as easy as a turnip, God be praised,

Jimmy lay dying on the ground chocking in his own blood. Did she not encompass Mary and her children in her arms to protect and shield them from seeing the mortal wound inflicted on Jimmy.

Was it not her Pat that took his life into his hands. He hastened to Jimmy's side before his life blood ebbed and flowed and said the act of contrition into his ear. Was it not her Pat's quick thinking that sent his soul deathless to his heavenly home. Were they not both this very day together in Paradise, her Pat and Jimmy.

We buried Jimmy that evening in the spinney down by the stream. His last resting place remained a secret. That was with the exception of his God, his family and the villagers. It was in the ruins of the house that we discovered the bodies of Mary and the children some two weeks later. They must have returned unknown to anyone, perhaps seeking out the grave of Jimmy. Who knows?. They died there every last one of them from cold and hunger. They could have sought the help of charitable neighbours but they did not wish to bring the wrath of the system upon the village. The cruel landlords had a lot to answer for before God.

Tears welled up once again in her eyes as she relived the horrors of that morning.

She crossed the old stile and walked up the path to the ruin. The remains of the burnt out roof lay rotting within its walls. The bird's had taken their share of what was left to build their own homes. They may as well for the family would have no use for it now. Rounding the back of the house she entered the haggard. It was still as dry and solid as the day that Jimmy and her Pat put their backs into the building of it. Leaving the haggard she went down the field past the fairy fort and into the spinney. Before her eyes stood the simple cross marking the final resting place of the O'Flattery family. Jimmy, Mary and the three children. She knelt on the green sward and try as she might she found it impossible to pray, her thoughts were on her own precarious circumstances.

She rose to her feet and left Jimmy and his family to rest in peace.

On hearing the latch being lifted, Shelia saw the door opening and Anne entering.

"Where have you been? I made the tea ages ago."

"I took a stroll to give myself time to think about the captain's proposal. What do you think of it all?"

"To be honest my mind is in a quandary, I don't know what to think."

"Well we cannot put it out of our minds. We will need to reach a decision and that's for sure."

"Wait until Phelm returns and we'll discuss it then, in the meantime let's sit down and have a cup of tea."

Phelm returned long before night fall to the bosom of his family.

"Did the captain have any other news then." Shelia asked.

"He had little more to say, except that the invitation stands. I can stay with him and Alice until I settle down."

"it would appear that you intend to go then, come what may." His mother returned to the fire.

"No! It's not settled as yet, but you must admit that it is a tempting offer. He will be back in Limerick in twelve weeks time, that gives us ample time to reach a final decision."

"Far be it for me to stop you improving yourself son, but this farm of land was always in the family. Granddad and grandma are buried down by the stream. Not to mention your father, God rest him in the old church yard. Remember you can count the pips in an apple, but you cannot count the apples in a pip." His mother continued to poke the fire as she spoke.

"Mum will you sit down and stop riddling the fire. There won't be a spark left in it if you don't stop." He crossed the floor and guided his mother to the nearest chair.

"This farm will always be a Griffin farm for as long as God spares me and that goes for my son too." He put his arm around his mother.

"Don't worry yourself so,if Phelm has to go then it will only be to pay off the debt. What is there to worry about?" Shelia comforted her mother in law.

Will the Queen
visit Limerick?

The spring of 1849 came with the hope of better times ahead.
The weather was mild and the air smelt sweet.

There was also a strong supposition that Queen Victoria was
about to make her promised tour of Ireland and that Limerick
was to be included.

"You never know Ma! She may even come and visit you."
Phelm laughed.

"Coming to Ireland indeed, she'd do far better by sending
food over to the starving people." Anne was showing little
interest in the visit.

"Sure it's common knowledge that she is coming, but I doubt
if Limerick will be included in her chronicle."

"Well wherever she is to visit, she will not get a reciprocal
reception, I can assure you." Phelm promised.

The advice given to the government of the day, by the
landed gentry as to the merits of such a visit by an English
monarch to Ireland in the middle of plague and hunger, was
ignored by Dublin Castle.

She would not however visit Limerick nor was there ever any
intention of inviting her to a city filled with Fenian rebels. She
would visit Cork and Dublin in that order.

The main thoroughfares would be cleared of all beggars and
the houses along the route would have their façades spruced.
Curtains would be put on the windows of the abandoned
houses and flower boxes on the cills. All broken window
panes would be repaired. This charade of a peaceful orderly
society was for the benefit of foreign dignitaries and
journalists.

The irony of her visit was that the cost would be levied on
the Irish purse. This depleting the meagre resources destined
for the starving. This provocative megalomania fuelled further

the already boiling cauldron of hatred within Ireland towards the crown.

She, her prince and the children would be shielded from the ordinary citizens. What they were suffering was no concern of hers.

As the preparations for the visit of the royal family continued, the potato crop failed once again.

It was believed that although the people were dying from the hunger, they would respond to her visit and give her an illustrious welcome.

This waste of public money caused resentment within the gentry. Whereas some welcomed the visit of Her Majesty others thought it obscene and felt that the money would be far better spent on the welfare of the starving nation.

Yet whatever the world and the people of Ireland felt and thought the visit went ahead as scheduled and England claimed that it was a great success.

Had the mayors, the high lieutenants, the viscounts and the Whigs taken her to the many workhouses or to the hedge rows and booleys. Had she seen the dead the dying and starving would she still have enjoyed the many banquets held in her honour in Dublin castle and the grand mansions?.

She did however give the sum of £300 towards the relief of the famine in one year. A magnanimous gesture on her part for which the Irish did not show their gratitude.

Phelm is arrested

Phelm could no longer overlook the captains generous offer. His mind was in a quandary. The situation was made no better by the worrying remarks from his mother.

One night as he tossed and turned in his sleep, Shelia decided that he would have to speak to someone about it.

At breakfast she suggested that he should go over to his cousin Josie O'Brien in Clare and seek his advice.

"Do you know Shelia, you're a little darling, you can read me like a book." She at least appreciated his predicament.

"I'll go and ask Patrick to loan you the mare and saddle."

"That would be a great help. If he loans me the mare I can make it over and back in a couple of days."

All was arranged for the journey. Patrick brought the mare and saddle that night.

"She's not all that fast Phelm, but she is reliable. There is no hurry back, let her have her head you'll get on much better that way." Patrick stroked the old mares neck in affection.

It was pitch dark when Phelm arose next morning and slipped quietly into the kitchen and lit the lamp.

Going to the fire he picked up the tongs and placed fresh turf on the embers. Looking up at the wall clock he noticed the time, twenty past five.

A bit early he thought, but then that gave him time to make some breakfast.

He put the griddle pan on the crane and went to the scullery to get some dripping. When he came out Shelia was beside the fire.

"What are you doing up at this God forsaken hour." He whispered.

"Go and get and yourself ready, and saddle the mare, I'll see to your breakfast."

He went to the barn and saddled the mare. Leading her into the yard, he tethered her to a tree growing near to the kitchen door.

"It's not a good morning out there for travelling along unknown roads, there is no moon out." he rubbed his hands together as he closed the door behind him.

"Not frightened of the dark are you, do you want me to accompany you.?" Shelia laughed as she placed his breakfast on the table.

"I'll be back as soon as I can, and don't worry I may stay a few nights." He rose from his chair and taking his coatamore from beside the fire, where his mother had placed it the night before to keep it warm he put it on.

Her concern for his welfare pleased him as he felt the warmth of it hugging his body. Phelm blessed himself as Shelia sprinkled him with the holy water and placed a heavy scarf over his head and round his neck.

Kissing his wife good bye he opened the door cautiously. He did not wish to disturb his mother nor the baby.

Mounting the mare, he slung the pannier bags containing his supply of food over the back of the saddle and set out on his journey into Clare.

He waved his good byes all the way down the boreen, but doubted if Shelia saw him in the dark.

As he rode along the road towards the city he stroked the mares neck and talked gently to her.

He awoke from a drowsy slumber to see the dawn breaking over the city. In the distance he saw someone waving a lantern in the centre of the road. As he came nearer to the light he heard a voice call out.

"Halt in the Queens name."

Before him stood a platoon of soldiers. One challenged him as the others removed their carbines from their shoulders.

"Whoa, Whoa!" Phelm called to the mare and pulled on the reins. The mare neighed in reply and stopped in front of the soldiers.

"Dismount at once." The corporal challenged as he jerked his rifle up and down to indicate what he wanted.

He dismounted as ordered and approached the soldiers.

"What are you doing on the roads at this early hour?" One of the soldiers went across to the horse and removed the panniers.

"I'm Phelm Griffin from Castlelurgan and I'm going to Clare to visit my cousin.

"Visit your cousin is it, and what is his name and address."?

"Joseph O'Brien better known as"Josie" and he lives outside the village of Dunneen."

"Why do you have to visit him at this time of the morning?" The soldier searching through the panniers asked.

""I won't get there all that early, this is not a race horse." He stroked the old mares neck in affection.

"I asked you a question and can do without your smart answers." After a night in the cold the soldier was in a foul mood.

Then closing the panniers he threw them back over the saddle, this made the old mare jump.

"Whoa! there, steady now." Phelm took the reins and comforted the animal.

"Come on! get a move on if you are in all that much of a hurry." The corporal dismissed him..

Continuing his journey he entered the city. The streets were as deserted as the countryside. That is with the exception of soldiers posted at all strategic crossings and bridges.

On through the city he rode. Past St. Mary's Cathedral and on towards King John's castle where he was once again challenged by one of the sentries on the bridge at Thomondgate.

Without waiting to be asked he dismounted and leading his horse approached the sentry.

"Halt where you are." Came the command stopping him abruptly in his stride.

The sentry aimed his rifle at him and called for the guard commander. What a nervous lot, he thought as he heard footsteps behind him. Looking around he saw what he took to be an officer coming towards him holding the scabbard of his sword.

"What's the trouble soldier?" He challenged.

"Stranger approaching the bridge on horseback, Sir, dismounted in a threatening manner, Sir." The soldier replied still keeping his rifle and bayonet pointed at Phelm's chest.

"Is this the man, soldier?" The officer looked at Phelm.

"Yes Sir."

Now seeing that there was no other traveller on the bridge and none leading a horse Phelm smiled at this qualification. "What is there to smile about, and why are you leaving the city so early?" The officer was so close to him that the tip of his scabbard was rubbing against his leg.

"I'm not leaving the city, I'm just passing through on my way to Clare."

"Nobody is allowed to enter or leave the city until eight o' clock, now how did you get into the city."

"Me! I came in on my horse through the Black Battery and down John Street."

"Were you not challenged by the sentries there then.?"

"I was indeed and searched, then they told me to be on my way."

"Whatever you were told was wrong, you will be detained in the Castle until that patrol returns to confirm your story."

"What about my horse ?"

"Call that a horse? You can leave her in the Island field with the others."

With that the officer escorted him back towards the castle.

Phelm looked back at the old mare, she looked at him and shook her head. Perhaps, he thought, she is as perplexed as I am with the whole proceedings.

Entering the castle ahead of the officer he looked along the blackness of the foreboding walls before him. Then he looked up at the portcullis and felt that the soldiers in the rooms above had him under constant observation.

A melancholy wind sent its disagreeable echo through the castle as the lights from the tallow candles threw long ghostly shadows on the floor and walls.

"Will I ever get out of this place, and what will become of the mare", he though.

Abruptly his thoughts were interrupted by the officer calling him to a halt in front of a door.

Opening the door the officer pushed him inside and closed it behind them.

The room was sparsely furnished, it had a camp bed, a desk and chair. On the desk stood a large oil lamp which was lit. From its blackened globe came a constant cloud of foul smelling oil that perpetuated the room.

"Someone hasn't trimmed the wick properly or not at all. Trim the wick and clean the globe, that way you'll see better." Phelm pointed to the offending lamp.

The officer ignored this advice. He unbuckled his sword and scabbard from its leather belt and sat down on the chair behind the desk.

"Now Mister, let's have some details as to who you are." He opened a bottle of ink and taking a pen from the desk dipped it in the bottle.

Phelm was looking up at a painting over the desk of a fat lady looking stern with a ball in one hand and what looked like a fancy stick in the other.

"Is that your wife up there?" Phelm tried to make conversation.

"She, you ignorant lout, is Queen Victoria, Queen of England."

"You don't say? Do you know I often heard tell of her but never knew what she looked like. Has she got a husband?"

"Never you mind, just answer the questions."

He gave the officer what information he could regarding himself.

Finally the officer looked up at the clock and rose from the desk.

"Come follow me", picking up his sword he again attached it to the leather holder.

Phelm followed the officer once again along the hall and out the castle gate.

"Collect your horse and be on your way, I see no reason to detain you further." The officer pointed in the direction of the island field.

Phelm went to where his mare had been tied and led her out of the field and on to the bridge.

By now several farmers and merchants were crossing the toll bridge into the city.

Leaving the bridge on the Clare end, he made mental notes of the route that he would take.

First though he would have some breakfast and feed and water the horse.

Entering a field at St. Munchin's cross in Thomondgate he removed the saddle. The mare kicked her heels in the air in relief and cantered into the middle of the field. Soon she was chewing her cud in the lush meadow grass.

Settling down under a large sweet chestnut tree he opened his pannier and took out some food.

Shelia had done him proud. There were three hard boiled eggs with a pinch of salt in a twisted piece of paper, there were two scones of bread and a generous portion of salted bacon. He would not go hungry on the road. He collected several bunches of water cress from the banks of the river Shannon.

Relaxing he settled down to his well deserved meal and rest. As the morning sun began to fill the Irish sky, he lay back on the green sward and watched the deep red glow of the early morning sky change to a mellow blue as feathery clouds raced and crashed into each other.

"Poor Ireland, isn't it grand you look as I bid you top of the morning," he greeted his native land.

Placing his hands under his head, he continued to watch the billowing clouds. Slowly he became mesmerized by them and succumbed to sleep.

He was awakened by gentle drops of rain falling on his face. Rising he wiped his face and went down the meadow to where his mare was grazing.

"Come on old girl, I don't expect that you know the time."

Wiping the mare with a clump of dry grass he threw the blanket over her back and fixed the saddle on top.

"Now that we've had our rest, let's get a move on." He held on to the saddle and mounted the mare.

Setting his sights on the old graveyard at Killeely he nudged the mare into a gentle canter.

Passing the grave yard he removed his cap out of respect for the holy souls and said a prayer for all those buried within its walls and for those victims of the Great Hunger buried outside. He would not be one to let the holy souls go hungry for a prayer.

As he entered the village of Parteen he became the focal point of attention by the local Royal Irish Constabulary. They watched him with suspicion but made no attempt to stop him.

Phelm sat up straight and proud in the saddle ignoring their questioning glances.

Once more he found himself out in the open country side. There was neither man nor beast to be seen. Where he thought had all the people got to. Soon his question was answered when he came across a number of cottages that had recently been tumbled.

Dismounting from the mare he removed the branch that had been set across the driveway into one of the cottages and walked up the path. The old door was still in the same place where it had fallen in surrender. The marks from the battering it took from the ram showing clearly on its surface. Kneeling down he fingered through the deep marks and wondered what had become of the occupants.

They were evicted of that he was sure, but were they then hanged, transported or imprisoned?

Was this the Ireland that he was so concerned about. A nation where whole families could vanish from the face of the earth. Where wives and children were made homeless their fathers left strangling on the gibbet. Their few possessions stolen but worst of all the raping of the mothers. This was Ireland's darkest hour, her destiny in the hands of usurpers. He rose to his feet and looked into the blue sky and cried out.

"If there is a God in heaven, then why does he let my country haemorrhage when her tormentors prosper?"

His words echoed around the walls of the cottage and disturbed a family of rooks sitting on the chimney stack.

"The sooner the revolution comes to Ireland the better." He thought as he left the driveway and continued on his journey. There was no more time now to dilly and dally he had to make the village of Dunneen by midday if at all possible.

Soon he heard the waves crashing against the rocks and smelt the kelp as it dried on the shore. He was now within striking distance of the village.

Passing it on the land side he went up the Moher road and saw the reek from the chimney of Josie's house.

"Get up there now, can't you see we're nearly there." he tapped the mares sides with his heels.

The mare stuck her ears forward and cantered up the hillock.

"Ah! God help you old girl, it's doubtful if you were ever

taught the art of galloping." He again slapped the Mare on the neck. Dismounting, and let her to walk on at her own pace.

Empty pride exposed

Josie was standing by the five barred gate when Phelm approached.

"Well, bless my soul, it is you is it not, Phelm Griffin as I live and die." He removed his cap as he spoke and scratched his head.

"Yes! it's me alright. Like the bad penny I've shown up."

"Brendan come out here and take the mare from your cousin." Josie called to his son.

"Come on up to the house and tell us what brings you here? Not bad news I hope."

Sitting beside the fire Phelm noticed how Josie had developed a stoop. He that much thinner since they last met.

"You'll have a drop of the crathur, Delia should not be that long away." Josie rose slowly from his chair and went to the dresser.

Removing the bottle of poteen, he poured out two over generous helpings.

"Is that what I think it is?" Phelm looked apprehensively across at the crystal clear drink.

"Will you not be asking such daft questions, you know very well what it is."

"A drop of water wouldn't go amiss in it, now would it." He held his glass up to Josie.

"Slainte leat" Josie held up his glass in salutation.

Josie returned with the jug of water and sat down in his chair. Phelm could not but notice once again how old he looked. His hands were now as thin as rushes and his eyes were sunken back into his head.

What age was Josie now he thought, was he fifty,? if that." He looked like a man of sixty five or more. This was not the same fit Josie who visited him not that too long ago.

Yet his mind was as sharp as ever. Whenever Phelm raised any question he was always thinking that one step ahead.

The latch was lifted on the door. Both men looked up and saw that it was none other than Delia.

"Well look who's here," she came forward and reached out her hand.

"You're looking well yourself Delia, getting younger by the day." He rose from his seat and took her hand.

As yet he had not explained why he had come to see them. He had a premonition that all was not well in the household. Brendan their only son who would normally be the life and soul of the company sat silently in the corner with not as much as"How do you do" out of him.

He was surprised that she had not made the customary offer of a bite to eat.

"Delia my throat is parched dry from the"Poteen" any chance of wetting the kettle."

"We're more than ashamed to have to admit it, but there is not an ounce of tea in the house,. Nor for that matter a cake of bread."

"I'm right sorry you had to find us under such circumstances, but times will improve." Josie twirled the glass round in his hands.

"There is nothing to be ashamed of, are we not just keeping our heads above water ourselves. Bring in my panniers will you. Shelia gave me more than enough to keep me going."

"We wouldn't hear the like of it, not on your life." Delia folded her arms, resisting the generous offer.

"Hear of it or not, family are family and in it comes." As the others were reluctant to take advantage of his offer, he rose from his chair and collected them himself.

What there was they shared. From the ravenous way Josie ate it was a long day since he had his last meal.

"Do you know it's just like the story in the bible, us sharing the loaves and fishes, only this time it is bacon and soda cake." Phelm laughed.

With the tense atmosphere now broken they could get down to serious talking. From what he had seen and heard he was now determined more than ever to leave Ireland and go to America.

He told the story of his meeting with Alice Devine and the subsequent encounter with captain Grey. He also related how they were tricked into buying the farm and land of the late captain Singleton.

"I'm not at all surprised, does not the devil make his Satanic pies with lawyer's tongues and their clerks fingers." Josie always had an answer.

"There is always good that comes out of evil, Phelm Griffin. You take the God given opportunity and leave this God forsaken land." Delia told him.

"I wish to Heaven that we could go with you. God but I'd jump at the chance so I would. But you know now how we are situated. Right now we are awaiting the knock on the door" (the knock on the door was the calling of the agents and the sheriff to evict a family)

"There will be no need for them to knock on your door Josie. I'm taking all three of you back to Castlelurgan with me."

"What would we do there, we'd only be a burden on Anne and Shelia." Delia looked at Josie, yet there was hope in her voice.

"Now come off it man, use your God given sense, generous as it is of you to offer. We could not put the cross on your backs now could we?." Josie replied choking on the words with the emotion building up in his craw.

"Look it's a sound idea Josie! We could go to America and make some money. Brendan is a fine strapping lad and could help around the farm. Sure there is more than enough land there to feed all of you."

"Jesus! Phelm what can we say, what indeed can we say." Delia repeated over and over again, then took on a fit of crying that embarrassed him.

"Will you not take on so, sure now you are making me upset." Josie rose from his chair took a swig of poteen that made him cough and went towards the door.

"Why must I stay at home? I want to go to America too" Brendan protested.

"Now look here, Brendan your parents have enough on their minds without you putting in your half penny worth." Phelm chided him.

The whole of the conversation that evening was about their future prospects.

"Do you know if we liked the states we could all settle down there." Delia cheered up somewhat.

"Yet it's a crying shame that we are forced into this situation in our own land. I suppose you could call it ethnic cleansing." Josie remarked.

"Ethnic cleansing in our own land, don't talk silly, England has been trying that for the last four hundred years. Remember Cromwell and his policy of 'To hell or to Connaught.' He failed then and so will this lot" Phelm was always a great believer in that Ireland's right is Ireland's might.

"If we do decide to go then at least we will be taking our religion with us, they cannot suppress that." Josie remarked.

"I wouldn't read too much into that if I were you. Did not the bishops give strict instructions to the clergy that no Irish person was to be given absolution if they supported the Fenian cause. Was there not a clandestine meeting in the Vatican itself between the English and the Popes representatives. The sole aim was to suppress Ireland's call for justice. Did you ever hear the church condemn the landlord?. Did the Vatican with all its wealth send us any relief?

They would condemn us to Hell fire for defending our homes and families. There is a higher authority than they. I wonder what he will have to say to our fine bishops. What of Josie O'Flattery and the others who were condemned to hell fire for their part in protecting their homes and families? Denied the rights of the church they were. There was to be no Christian burial for them. What will God have to say about that I wonder?"

"If what you say is true Phelm, and I'm not doubting your word, let there be no mistake about it, then they will have to answer to God."

"Oh come on now the two of you, never argue religion nor politics, it only makes for bad blood. We should all get a good nights sleep." Delia took a candle lit it and left the room.

Early the following morning Phelm left the house without disturbing the others.

In the village of"Dunneen" he bought several mackerel and a bag of flour. Not the best but good enough to make a scone of bread, some tea and a portion of butter. Delia saw him approaching the house, a mischievous smile on his face like that of an errant school boy. He was carrying several mackerel attached by their mouths to a long reed.

"Been fishing then, have we?."

"No finer fisherman than myself ever fished the sea." He laughed as he held up the fish for her to see.

"Breakfast will be a little late this morning, I want to see how good a scone maker you are." He placed the fish and the groceries on the table.

"You shouldn't have gone to so much trouble. How did you get all this." Delia opened the bag and began to remove the groceries.

"Well you should know, money does not talk, it screams. I showed them the money and miraculously all these appeared." He spread his hands across the table.

After their meal they returned to the topic of their planned move from Clare.

"I'll be leaving early to day for home. In the meantime you should store what you intend to take with you in the haggard, Have you still got the horse and cart?"

"The cart is out back but the horse had to be sold, still no doubt I'll be able to swop some of my furniture for one."

"Very well then that settles it. Leave the damn place to the landlord and his cronies." Phelm mounted the mare and set off back to his own home.

Phelm springs a surprise

To say that his mother was glad and surprised to see him was one thing. To be told that he was planning to bring another family into the home was a bomb shell.

He outlined his plan of how he and Josie intended to go to the States and make some money and return home rich.

"The times that I heard that story over and over again, one would think that dollars were there for the picking." His mother was far from impressed with her sons plan.

"Now you heard what the captain said, the money is there to be made and I intend to get my hands on my share."

"It's always I with you, did you not think to ask what Shelia wants, well did you.?" His mother insisted on an answer.

"Think of Shelia! Mother they are hard words and hurtful and well you know it. I would work my fingers to the bone for her, our son and you. Will you, listen to me for once, you know what the situation is. We slave on this farm year in year out and have in the past had to give two thirds of our produce to the landlord.

Now although we own the farm we are still in his debt. Even in death he is like a parasite slowly gnawing away at our very souls."

"I know son and I am sorry for my harsh words, will you forgive an old fool." She was conciliatory, as she looked with tears in her eyes at her only son.

"Mother Mo Cree,(mother of my heart) come here. You're as soft as butter and a lashing from your tongue is as gentle as a cloud." He hugged his mother to him.

"Well now what have we got here, is there something going on that I should know about." Shelia came through the door holding her son by the hand.

"Did you have a long walk then?" He bent down and held his arms open. The child ran forward giggling and they both embraced.

285

"So much for a loving husband, he never done any such thing for me." Shelia laughed

He gave the baby to his mother and swung Shelia around the kitchen.

"Now that was a fine way to treat an expectant mother."

"What did you say, did you hear that mother? When?" Phelm held her from him at arms length.

"It could be right now from the ways you swung me. No really it will not be for a long time yet, please God."

"Everything is happening at once, sometimes I think that the world has gone mad, now explain yourself to your wife." Anne remarked as she returned to the scullery.

Shelia accepted the situation, what else could they do under the circumstances.

Attached to the main house was a long room that was seldom in use. This they decided would be the home of their cousins until they could get matters sorted. Phelm and his brother in law, Patrick, divided the room into two and broke through the outside wall and erected a stout door. This would give them privacy and the freedom to come and go as they pleased without feeling obliged to the family.

"When do you intend to go over to Clare and let them know?" Anne asked.

"If all goes well I'll go in the next couple of days, that is if I can have the mare again."

"Is it my mare that you are talking about? I don't know about that now!." Patrick interrupted

"What do you mean, you won't let Phelm have the mare?" Shelia was annoyed.

"No I won't, the last time I lent him my mare he got her arrested and locked up. Why she is so embarrassed that she hardly ever leaves the field."

"Patrick McNulty, I'll swing for you one day." Shelia ran after her brother.

"Mind the baby now will you." Phelm called after them as they both ran up the hill away from the house.

"Baby, what baby? Now don't tell me I'm going to be an uncle again."

"That's good I must say, I'm having a baby and he gets the congratulations"

"All right then, we will congratulate you, Mother come out here." Patrick called his mother in law from the kitchen.

"Now mother let us sit here. Shelia, you over there on the threshold."

"What's all this about anyway?" Anne came forward and sat between the two men.

"Now mother lets begin."Patrick began to sing one of the romantic songs from the pen of one of our romantic writers. As the first notes echoed across the valley, the family picked up the tune and joined in the singing. Shelia could not restrain herself and tapping her foot in time with the singing she too joined in the melody.

> The violets were scenting the woods, Maggie,
> Displaying their charm to the bees;
> When I first said I loved only you, Maggie
> And you said you loved only me.
>
> The chestnut bloom gleamed in the glade, Maggie
> A robin sang loud from a tree;
> When I first said I loved only you,Maggie
> And you said you loved only me.
>
> The golden robed daffodils shone, Maggie
> And danced in the breeze on the Lea;
> When I first said I loved only you, Maggie,
> And you said you loved only me.
>
> The birds in the trees sang a song, Maggie
> Of happier transports to be;
> When I first said I loved only you, Maggie,
> And you said you loved only me.
>
> Our hopes have never come true, Maggie,
> Our dreams were never to be;
> Since I first said I loved only you, Maggie
> And you said you loved only me.

Maggie (Trad.)

"Your going daft, the lot of you and dragging me along with you" Anne laughed

"That deserves a mug of tea at the least, and I am grateful for the song, sad though it was."

"It was instantaneous you must appreciate, I hadn't got my thinking cap on"

"Never mind, it's the thought that counts, come in and have your tea."

The Crowbar Gang are
in Dunneen

Phelm watched and waited impatiently for the weather to mend before setting out to collect his cousins.

When the weather did improve he took advantage of the situation and saddling the mare took himself off to the home of the O'Brien's.

He was surprised to see that the road leading from the village of Dunneen was crowded with"Red Coats." They were to-ing and fro-ing up and down the road carrying long poles and ropes. He knew that evictions were taking place.

Seeking permission from one of the villagers he left his mare in the field and went on foot across the hill to the home of his cousin.

Skirting the whin bushes he came within sight of the house. Outside the front door several agents of the landlord were erecting a tripod. He had arrived just in time. He watched as they fitted a stout rope through a steel hook at the top of the tripod and attached the rope to the eye hooks at each end of the ram. He heard the familiar sound as the Crowbar gang swung it backwards and forwards, backwards and forwards. Gaining in momentum as the ram seemed to move into perpetual motion. They adjusted it periodically, to gain maximum efficiency.

There was no sign of the family and he began to worry for their safety. Surely Josie had better sense than to resist the bailiffs.

He moved nearer to the scene of the eviction where several of the villagers were sitting on the high ground watching the proceedings with interest.

"Are the family inside still?" He asked a neighbour.

"Will you hold your whist." (keep quiet) Sure Josie and his family are sitting over there."

Phelm saw the family sitting some distance away and went to join them.

"What is going on, it looks as if I got here just in time, who's in the house"?

"Sure there's nobody in the house, last night several Fenians came and told me that the house was to be tumbled and that we should get out. We spent the night in a safe house whilst the Fenians barricaded our house from the inside. Then they left by the chimney stack."

"Are you telling me seriously that there is nobody in the house?"

"Course I am, but they don't know that, The Fenians swear that they'll never break the door down however much they try."

"This is something that I must see."

"See and hear if you wait long enough", Delia laughed

"You lot are up to something, I can feel it in my bones."

Delia looked at Josie and hugging her son Brendan and began to laugh.

"For folk about to lose their home and possessions you seem cheerful."

Soon the ram was in the right position and the crowbar gang lined up on either side. The officer came forward and called on the occupiers to surrender for the last time in the name of the Queen.

"Right men! do your duty." The officer reined his horse back and retreated from the ram.

"One, two, three, four" the ram was slowly swung forward and backwards gaining momentum at every stroke.

Soon it was hammering on the door, crash, swing, crash, swing, the ram hit the door time after time. Each time the ram hit the door, it jumped back a few feet, as this happened the people cheered much to the irritation of the landlord.

"There! this shows what savages the Irish are, no regard for their fellow country men." He sarcastically remarked.

Then like a colossus, a tall man stood up and climbed the kissing rock. Stretched his arms as if about to address an army he opened his mouth and shouted above the din of the ram,

"Remember Limerick and Garryowen." Then he shook his

huge fist at the troops.

A strange silence prevailed and enveloped the scene, the ram was stopped. All eyes were cast on the big man.

Like the wail of the Banshee (the spirit that announces a death) the people found their voices. In unison they began to sing.

> Let no Bacchus's sons be not dismayed,
> But join with me each jovial blade;
> Come booze and sing, and lend your aid
> To help me with the chorus:-
>
> (Chorus)
> Instead of Spa we'll drink brown ale,
> And pay the reckoning on the nail;
> No man for debt shall go to gaol
> From Garryowen in glory!
>
> We are the boys who take delight
> In smashing Limerick lamps at night
> Through the streets like sporters fight
> And tearing all before us.
>
> (Chorus)
>
> We'll break the windows, we'll break the doors,
> The watch knock down by threes and fours;
> Then let the doctors work their cures,
> And tinker up their bruises.
>
> (Chorus)
>
> We'll beat the bailiffs out of fun,
> We'll make the mayor and sheriffs run
> We are the boys no man dare dun,
> If he regards a whole skin.
>
> (Chorus)
>
> Our hearts so stout, have got us fame,

For soon 'tis known from whence we came;
Where'er we go they dread the name
Of Garryowen in glory.

(Chorus)

Johnny Connell's tall and straight,
And in his limbs he is complete;
He'll pitch a bar of any weight,
From Garryowen to Thomond gate.

(Chorus)

Garryowen is gone to wrack
Since Johnny Connell went to Cork
Though Darby O'Brien leapt over the dock
In spite of all your soldiers.

(Chorus)

Garryowen (Trad.)

The ram was once again set in motion on the orders of the captain.

This did not deter the people of the village. Defiantly more Irish rebel songs followed. The crowbar gang sweated and swore in their frustration. Try as they may that door would not yield.

The Irish could do nothing to stop the evictions but they could at least sing their defiance.

The landlord sat on his horse some distance from the mêlée as was the usual case.

Finally exasperated with the singing and the resistance of the door, he called for the task to be abandoned.

"Get the Spleen ready, we'll burn them out, like the rats that they are." The captain called in frustration.

Again he came forward and called on the occupiers to give up the fight. He was greeted by the eerie silence from within.

"Stand clear." Came the shout as several agents rushed forward with the torches and set the thatch alight.

Flames and smoke bellowed from the blazing thatch. The

awesome sight brought the villagers to their feet.

Had there been anyone in the cottage they would have been burnt to death.

In defiant mood the handful of stubborn villagers challenged the power of the greatest empire on earth.

Once again the tall man rose to his feet. Then he challenged them with one of the most hated and banned national and patriotic songs. A song that is full of patriotic fervour. It called defiantly in the face of oppression and tyranny. Through the tears of the nation and the blood of its dead people, to free themselves from foreign despotism.

The villagers rose to their feet as one, this was a proud day in Ireland's troubled history.

He was joined almost immediately by the whole village and Phelm was to be no exception.

They would sing the song for as long as the green grass of Ireland grew.

Tears of pride filled their eyes as they proudly and defiantly sang.

> Oh, Paddy dear, and did you hear
> The news that's going round
> The shamrock is forbid by law
> To grow on Irish ground;

> Ah! St. Patrick's day no more we'll keep
> our colours can't be seen
> For they've made a cruel law against
> The wearing of the green.

> Now I met with Napper Tandy
> And he took me by the hand-
> Saying;"How is poor old Ireland,
> And how does she stand?

> She's the most distressful country
> That ever yet was seen;
> Sure they're hanging men and women there,
> For the wearing of the green.

Then if the colours we should wear
Be England's cruel Red,
Let it remind us of the blood
That Irishmen have shed;

You may take the shamrock from your cap
And throw it on the sod,
But never fear,'twill flourish there
Though under foot it's trod.

When laws can stop the blades of grass
From growing as they grow,
And when the leaves in summer time
Their verdure dare not show,

Then I will change the colour too,
That I wear in my caubeen
But 'til that day, Please God, I'll stick
To the wearing of the green

And if, at last, our colours
Should be torn from Ireland's heart,
her sons in shame and sorrow
from the dear old land must part;

I've heard whispers of a country
That lies far beyond the sea
Where rich and poor stand equal
In the light of freedom's day

Oh! Ireland, must we leave you,
Driven by the tyrants hand:
Must we ask a mother's welcome
from a far but happier land?

Where the cruel cross of England's
thraldom never shall be seen,
But where please God, we'll live and die
Still wearing of the green.
The Wearing of the Green (Trad.)

Strong men, women and children sang and wept as they remembered those who died for Ireland in the hills and glens. England could forbid the wearing of the Shamrock but she could not stop it growing on Irish soil.

The assembled crowd cheered defiance at the soldiers from their vantage point. The roof of the cottage collapsed in on itself sending flames and sparks sky high. Had there been any mortal soul inside the cottage then they would most certainly be long dead by now. The ram was moved to the gable end of the cottage and again swung into action. The incessant banging continued for some time against the stout walls.

Bang!, crash! bang! crash! The heavy ram was swung with gusto to and fro, to and fro. Slowly the old wall began to surrender to the attack and was breached.

As the wall collapsed in a cloud of dust the agents rushed forward. They were annoyed when they saw that the door had been jammed solid with boulders from the inside.

Having satisfied himself that the cottage was now uninhabitable, the landlord together with his henchmen prepared to leave the carnage. They were to be given a rousing farewell as the villagers once again broke into song.

> When on Ramillies battle field,
> The baffled French were forced to yield,
> The victor Saxon backward reeled
> before the charge of Clares' dragoons
> The flag we conquered in the fray,
> look lone in Ypres choir they say,
> We'll win them company to-day,
> Or bravely did like Clares' dragoons.
> Viva la! for Ireland's wrong
> Viva la! for Ireland's right
> Viva la! in a battle throng,
> For a Spanish steed and a sabre bright.
>
> The brave old lord died in the fight,
> But for each drop he lost that night,
> A Saxon cavalier shall bite
> The dust before Lord Clares' dragoons.

For never when our spurs were set,
And never when our sabres met,
Could we the Saxon soldiers get
To stand the shock of Clares' dragoons.
Viva La! the new brigade!
Viva La! the old one too!
Viva La! the rose shall fade,
And the shamrock shine forever more.

Another Clare is here to lead,
The worthy son of such a breed;
The French expect some famous deed,
When Clare leads on his bold dragoons.
Our colonel comes from Brian's race,
His wounds are in his breast and face,
The Bearna Beal is still his place,
The foremost of his brave dragoons.
Viva La!, the new brigade!
Viva la! the old one too!
Viva la! the rose shall fade,
And the shamrock shine forever new.

There's not a man in squadron here
Was ever known to flinch or fear:
Though first in charge and last in rear,
Have ever been Lord Clares' dragoons;
But see! we soon have work to do,
To shame our boasts or prove them true,
For hither comes the English crew
To sweep away Lord Clares' dragoons.
Viva la! for Ireland's wrong
Viva La! for Ireland's right
Viva la! in battle throng,
For a Spanish steed and a sabre bright.

Oh! comrades think how Ireland pines,
Her exiled lords, her rifled shrines,
Her dearest hope, the ordered lines
And bursting charge of Clares' dragoons.
Then fling your green flag to the sky,

Let Limerick be your battle cry,
And charge till blood flows fetlock high
Around the track of Clares' dragoons.
Viva la! the new brigade!
Viva la! the old one too!
Viva la! the rose shall fade,
And the Shamrock shine forever new.

Clare's Dragoons - Thomas Davis

The assembled villagers clenched their fists and raised their cudgels in defiance. The landlord and his lackeys left the scene protected by rows of Red Coats.

It was passive resistance for there was no way that they could or would have attempted an assault.

"I don't know why you were singing and cheering so loudly Josie. Did you not lose all you possessions in the fire?."

"Tell you the truth I was worried that they might search the haggard. Remember you told me on your last visit to store it in the haggard." Josie laughed.

"So all the landlord got for his trouble was the destruction of his own property. If ever he finds out what you done, then God help you."

"Find out as much as he likes, we'll be far away by then, won't we"?

"Come on, there is a good neighbour who will give us a meal before we get on our way."

Phelm and his cousins left the cottage and crossed over the hill. Having spent that night in the safe house of their neighbour, they rose early next morning. Cautiously they returned to the ruins of the cottage. With the help of Mark Douglas and the neighbours, they loaded their few remaining possessions on the cart.

Mark was one decent friend and at great risk to the security of himself and his family had loaned them his mare.

"There is one thing for certain Mark Douglas, should with God's blessed help, fortune come my way in the States, then I'll be beholden to you." Josie held tightly to the hand of his neighbour as he made this vow.

"Yarrah! will you away with that, you'd do the very same for me would you not." Mark slapped him on the back in affection.

"We'll not take the road through the city. You never know just what may be waiting for us. We'll cross the Shannon at the Lax weir and then go as far as the Abbey river and cross the ford above Annacotty"

"You know best, Phelm, you go on ahead with your mare and we will follow."

"There is no doubt about it, but it will add many the mile to our journey. It will take all of two whole days to make the journey all going well."

"God is good Phelm, we feel safe in your hands." Delia encouraged him. Then tightening her shawl around her she took hold of the shaft of the cart.

Slowly the sad cortège left the village by the back road. They had put sacking around the wheels to muffle any sound coming from the iron rims of the wheels.

This to prevent the agents and red coats from knowing that they were leaving the village.

No audible words of good bye were to send them on their way and no words of sorrow. Just the knowing wave from their neighbours and friends as they bid their last good bye to the village of Doolin.

The local Sagart stood on the brow of the hillock and blessed the sad cortège.It was a long and arduous journey through mud tracks and across river fords before they had skirted the city and were on the highway to Castlelurgan.

A joyous reunion

Hungry wet and dishevelled they finally arrived at Anne's door.

"Mhuise!, will you look at them, God help them." She called as tears of joy and sorrow filled her eyes.

Like a waggon train in the mid west of America they came down the boreen, Phelm walking beside the old mare, and she with her head bowed in exhaustion.

"Will you look at yourselves, what in God's name kept you so long? We were so worried.

You're all safe and more than welcome, praise be to God."

"Before you go on with the questions mother, will you let me catch my breath." Phelm Wearily dropped the reins.

"Well Brendan!, you have grown, haven't you, come in. Come in! all of you and don't just stand on ceremony at the threshold."

"Will someone ever go and fill the creel, I'll poke a bit of life into the fire, sure you must be wall fallen with the hunger."

Anne rushed from task to task, getting nowhere in her hurry to make them comfortable.

Phelm rose from his chair and taking the creel from beside the fire left the room.

Returning he dropped the creel at the fire place and taking some of the dry sods, he screwed them into the centre of the fire. Taking the handle of the bellows he began to turn the wheel slowly. Sparks from the revitalised fire began to race up the chimney and across the floor.

"I think you can stop now Phelm, the fire has got the message." His mother remarked as she saw the flames dance higher into the chimney.

He let go of the handle, and taking hold of the crane pulled it forward and placed the iron kettle on the crook.

"Now that I have set the fire and put the kettle on, perhaps one of you would wet the tae."?

299

"Sit yourself down, You look jaded. I'll make something to eat." Anne rose from her chair and went into the scullery.

"Thank you Jesus! Praise be Jesus and his blessed mother, they're safe." Anne kept repeating as she busied herself in the scullery.

She came back into the kitchen wiping the tears from her eyes on her apron.

"Mother will you sit yourself down, we're home now and that is all that matters." Phelm tapped the sugan chair, inviting her to rest.

"Where's that son of mine"?

"He'll be back soon, he's down at the well with his mother." Shelia came to the door with the bucket of water in her hand , Their son holding on to the leather handle.

Mother and son ran into the kitchen, water spilled from the bucket across the floor.

"Thank God, Thank God you're home." Shelia dropped the bucket on the floor and ran to greet her husband.

Later that evening, Phelm and Josie related their adventure in Doolin. Ably abetted by Delia.

"I'll tell you this now and I mean it. For as long as the hammer strikes the anvil, I'll not rest until I can avenge what the landlords have done to us." Phelm was in his old rebellious mood again.

"What is done is done, can we forget it for one night at least." Shelia came from the kitchen carrying a cake of bread.

"Sure and why not, lets have something to eat, I'm starving." Phelm went to the table and sat down.

"Will you look at him, always one to be the first at the table." When the meal was eaten, Anne invited Delia to come and inspect their temporary home.

"It's not a palace but you have most of the things that you will need. Brendan will be as comfortable as a bug in a rug in the leaba Shuidheachain" Anne patted the sofa bed by the fire side.

"Don't be fussing so over us Anne Griffin, you are more than generous. May the devil not know you are dead until you are in heaven."

"There's no need to write me off so soon Delia, if you don't be minding. I'm not all that much older than yourself." Anne laughed.

Anne went across to the door and closed it. Patting the sofa she called on Delia to sit down.

"I wanted to talk to you alone, Delia, away from prying ears if you know what I mean. Now! what do you make of their plans to go to America of all places."

"Anne Griffin, I heard all about you worrying yourself sick about this, now what do you want? For them to stay here and finish up on the highway like the rest or to take their chances in America?"

"I don't know what to think. That is why I am asking you."

"Are you seriously asking me for my opinion. I have just had my home set on fire with the spleen and been forced to leave my village and neighbours. God Anne Griffin but you are very naïve."

"I suppose I should not have asked, but I had to get it off my conscience."

"Off your conscience indeed. What you need is a pair of worry beads. Let them go to America. There is many the one would give their eye teeth for such a generous offer."

"You're right Delia as usual, let them go then and may God go with them. Come on they'll think that we have got lost." Anne rose from the seat.

"Come here a minute, now before you go are you satisfied in your own mind?" Delia insisted.

"I'm content now that we had our little chat, sure won't Josie be there to keep an eye on him."

"Good, now lets us go and warm the cockles of our hearts with a drop of the cratur."

Several weeks passed, Josie and Phelm were kept occupied repairing fences and looking after the crops.

Brendan was being initiated into the running of the farm in anticipation of their forthcoming departure for America.

Not that Brendan took too kindly to being left behind to look after the farm. Although as was pointed out to him, he was to become master of the farm in their absence.

He considered that looking after the farm and three women was the job for a sissy and not a suitable occupation for an Irishman.

Looking after the farm was one thing but three women as

well, that was asking the ultimate sacrifice.

As the weeks turned into a new month Phelm was wondering if the captain would be as good as his words. Would he return or was he giving them the blarney.

The American wake

On the morning of the first day of the month they received a letter from Captain Grey. The S.S. Sara-Anne-Jane would set anchor in Limerick docks within a matter of days. He would call on them within the week.

True to his word he arrived early on the morning of the second week, bringing with him more provisions for the table.

Phelm introduced Josie and Delia to him and related what had happened to them and how they too would like to emigrate to America.

"There is plenty room on my ship. I can assure you, we will be travelling light. Ever worked a ship?" He looked at Josie.

"I'm a good hand at the fishing boats. Been doing it all my life"

"Well! That's a start anyway, you'll not get sea sick." Captain Tom laughed.

"Come to the table all of you and keep the chat for later." Anne smiled in contentment at the well laden table.

"Now don't be leaving any of the food. When you say grace don't forget to ask God to reward the good captain.

"Will you not call me Tom, I get called captain all too often."

"Very well then Tom!, but we are not ones to take familiarity too easy." Anne replied to his request.

That evening sitting round the turf fire the plans were made for their departure within the week for America.

Their excitement knew no bounds nor did their sorrow. They knew now that an American wake would be held in the house within the week.

Anne left the house late that evening and wended her way across the hill to the fairy fort and the cairn of the Sideog Ri. Crossing the stream not once but twice as tradition would have it, she closed her eyes and reaching into the running water. She picked up the nearest stone to her hand, and holding it carefully, continued on her journey. Should she drop the stone, there would be tragedy within the family.

As she reached the highest spot where the large fairy Kings stone cairn stood she knelt down and placed the stone from the stream on the cairn. She watched with trepidation to see if her stone would be rejected. To her relief the stone remained on the cairn.

The fairy King would not put a curse on her. He would give her one wish that night. She thanked him by building a small stone Leactha beneath the fairy thorn where the mistletoe lurked hidden in its branches. She did not look at the mistletoe. She was not supposed to know that it was there, yet she knew.

She promised that she would place a stone each May day on the King's cairn if her children were spared from death and misfortune in the new world.

"Sideog Ri, its myself, Anne Griffin, who has come calling." She paused as she waited for a sign of his presence. A gentle zephyr shook the old hawthorn, she knew then that he was present.

"I suppose there is no need of me doing the telling of why I'm here, but I'll tell you anyway." Anne told the Sideog Ri of the imminent departure of her only son to the America's. She told him of her worries and asked him to send his spirits to protect him. The old hawthorn swayed in the gentle breeze. Anne looked at it and smiled.

"I'll be beholden to you Sideog Ri. You can be assured of my thanks."

Satisfied that her mission was successful and that her family would be protected, she retraced her steps to the house.

She would not tell the priest of her sacrifice to the fairy king. He would only make her promise not to believe in such pagan sacrifices, and forbid her from ever returning to the fairy kings cairn. No! she would keep her promise. There was no reason why she should tempt faith.

Failing to keep her word to the fairy would result in her having a curse put on her or worse still on the village. Then the neighbours would find out that she had called down the wrath of the fairies. What would she do then, what indeed?. The lights were burning brightly in the house as she wended

her way up the boreen. They must still be about, no doubt still making plans for their imminent departure, she thought.
"Where have you been, we thought that you had gone to bed." Phelm looked up surprised as she entered the house.
"Don't worry yourself about me, I just went out to gather my thoughts." Anne removed her black shawl and placed it over the chair.
"Will you try some of this, it will warm you" Tom held out a bottle to her.
"That's decent of you and I won't insult the company by refusing."
"I'll get you a glass, sit into the fire you must be frozen." Shelia went into the scullery.
"Here we are then, now sip this slowly it's pretty strong."
"Strong it might be, but we make a brew here that would scrape the very cockles off your heart." Anne took the drink and sipped from the glass.
That week was spent in preparing for the long goodbye and the American wake. Mind you this would be no real American wake. They would be returning as soon as they saved enough money.
There was one hooley of a gathering a few days before the leaving. Captain Tom came with several of the crew members. Paddy Fay who was a fair hand at the fiddle, Young Byrne who played the tin whistle as good as any leprechaun and what with Donovan belting the Bodhran as if chastising the wife. The neighbours came one and all to the gathering and more than welcome they were made.
There was to be no stopping them as the poteen and the Uisge beata flowed like butter milk. Not forgetting Tady McGuire, who could sing the very Blackbirds out of the trees. Sure one had only to sing the first notes of any song and Tady was sure to know the rest. He had the gift for sure. He was called to the fore with a place reserved for him before the fire, he belted out song after song.
A space was made in the centre of the flag stone floor for the dances and reels. They danced to the four hand reels, jigs, sets, The Walls of Limerick, The Siege of Ennis, The Fox at the gate. Was there to be no stopping them, as couple after couple took to the floor and tried to outdance each other.

Paddy Fay put more chalk on the bow to make it slip over the cat gut that much faster. Donovan stepped up the tempo as he tapped out the time with his right foot. The sight of the young ones hopping and skipping to the tunes was a sight for sore eyes.

Anne rose to her feet and without shame lifted her long skirt to show a neat ankle.

"Do any of you know, 'The Wind that shook the Barley'?" she asked.

Paddy Fay tickled his fiddle and let the bow fly across the strings, young Byrne joined in with his flute and Donovan chastised the bodran.

The floor was cleared for her as she called on the musicians to play. Anne put one foot before the other and was soon hopping from one foot to the other like a leprechaun hopping across toad stools.Her golden red hair flashed and sparkled as she twirled and danced across the floor. The duration of her dance was discretely curtailed for the years were taking their toll.

Would there be any stopping them at all. All night long without interruption the songs and music told the stories of old Ireland. The tears rolled down the faces of many the singers, some unable to continue owing to the sensitive nature of the song had to be helped by the others.

"Go on Nora you're doing fine, God love you." Would come the encouraging calls.

The reminders of the hunger was never too far from their thoughts, as many of the songs they sung and the sad stories told that night were witness to.

There were also the satirical ones and the jovial ones. Where the singers would stop singing and hide behind their hands as the gathering laughed. Many exhausted by all the dancing and singing and no doubt by the poteen and the liberal helpings from the many bottles presented by the American crew, sat sleeping or dozing in their chairs.

It was early morning before the gathering broke up and the neighbours returned to their respective homes.

It was agreed that this was indeed the best craic ever held in Castlelurgan.

Tom and several of his crew lay sprawled across the leaba

Shuidheachain, snoring to their hearts content. Shelia went about revitalising the fire.

"This is one gathering that they will not want to forget in a month of Sundays." Anne proudly remarked.

"Is Phelm awake yet, he must be jaded." Shelia looked around the room.

"Are you telling me that you don't know where your own husband is woman?."

"Sure I haven't seen him since we broke up, he could be anywhere."

"Anywhere is it, and who is that half in and half out of the turf creel."

Shelia looked across the room where Phelm was stretched out asleep with his head resting on a dozen sods of turf.

"Oh! let him sleep on, he's entitled to enjoy his last few days in holy Ireland, God love him."

The women set about making the tea and cutting the scones for those who had stayed the night.

Captain Tom awoke and rose from the bed, looking for all the world like a scare crow.

"What's the time, better still what day is it, God but I'm dying with the thirst." He rose to his feet only to flop back on the bed much to the annoyance of one of the other sleepers.

Again he made the effort and this time succeeded in making the front door.

Outside the door was a large wooden rain water barrel, to which the captain was attracted like a rabid dog.

Time after time he ducked his head into the ice cold water. Cupping his hands he scooping up the water. He began to drink copious amounts. By the way he drank he must have had a skin full of Poteen.

"Mum will you go and tell Tom not to drink the rain water, it might not be that good."

"Ah sure the devil a bit of harm it will do him. Let him be for now, go and wake that husband of yours."

"Damn and blast it, what the blazes were we drinking last night." Tom shook his head as he entered the kitchen.

"Had a belly full then, did we, how do you feel?" Anne smiled knowing full well the answer.

"Sorry for swearing mam!. It's the water, there is something in the water here, I'm sure of that. The more water I drink the more drunk I become."

"There's nothing the matter with our water, apart that is from the fact that it was rain water that you were drinking. Were you never enlightened as to the powerful effect of a drop of the cratur."

"What would you like for your breakfast this fine morning."

"Breakfast!, forget it thanks, what I need is a good stiff drink."

"The breakfast is made now, what there is of it, would you like to call your men."

Slowly the house returned to some semblance of normality as captain Tom and his crew prepared to return to Limerick.

"Thanks for everything, we must return to the ship, but I will be back in a few days time to collect those of you wanting to emigrate."

"We'll be all packed and ready, have no fear on that score." Josie came to the door to see them off.

"You are getting up some time to day, are you not?" Josie kicked at Phelm's foot.

"What the blazes is this.?" Phelm awoke and took a sod of turf from under his head.

"Come on the party is over and your American friends are gone."

"Did we have a good night or not?" Phelm smacked his lips and rising from the creel and began to scratch himself.

"You're like a old shaggy dog coming out of the barn, get washed and cleaned up." Shelia told him.

"Where is young Patrick then?."

"From the way you swung him around last night with your boasting it's a wonder he's here at all."

"Ah! sure it was only a bit of fun, was it not." Phelm was full of remorse.

Shelia springs a surprise

In the days that followed, Phelm and Josie spent their time checking that the farm would be manageable in their absence. They briefed Brendan on the more intricate duties.

"Phelm are you sleeping yet." Shelia called as she lay in the bed a few nights before departure.

"Just about if you would shut up and let me."

"I've decided that we are going to America with you."

"What do you mean by 'We' are going to America?' You cannot do that, what with you pregnant. Mother would not hear of it in a month of Sundays."

"Whatever mother might or might not say Patrick and I are going with you and that is that."

"Go to sleep we'll discuss this in the morning." Phelm snuggled into the pillow.

"There's nothing to discuss, I told captain Tom that we were going as a family and he approves."

"He does! does he, well I'll have something to say about it to morrow."

"Good night love, pleasant dreams." Shelia smiled to herself as she settled down to sleep.

Shelia was humming to herself as she prepared the breakfast early the next morning. Anne came into the kitchen with the pail of milk.

"You're bright and sprightly this morning any special reason."

"What would you say if I told you that I am going to America with the child and Phelm."

"It's no more and no less than I expected of you, a wife's place is beside her husband."

"You're not annoyed then, you don't mind." Shelia looked surprised.

"You know Shelia, what the good Lord has joined together should stay together, you go to America and return with an Irish American grandchild to me with God's blessed help."

Phelm entered the kitchen shortly afterwards and disclosed to his mother, Shelia's intentions.

"Phelm before you go any further I must tell you that I fully agree with Shelia, where else should she be but by your side."

"Thanks mum, you are a great help. Here am I trying to persuade her to stay at home and you encouraging her to leave."

"I'm doing no such thing. Should she stay here she would only worry and get under my feet. The experience will do you both good."

"So it's settled then? There is little for me to say."

"Oh come on old sour puss, you know in your heart and soul that you were wishing for this." His mother ran her hand through his hair tossing it.

Josie returned from the city in the afternoon and went straight to the house of the Griffins.

"Did you hear the latest news."?

"What latest news, don't tell us that the captain cannot take us."

"No it's nothing like that,"

"What is it then, that's so important?"

"The Irish, its no longer to be taught in the schools and all Irish writings and poetry is banned." They are dismissing any teacher who will not comply with the new directive."

"Sure they were not teaching Irish in the first place, so what's so different."

"The difference is that it is now official. Any child learning the Irish or speaking any word of it will be chastised with a good caning."

"Now if that is not encouragement to leave Ireland then what is."?

"I'll tell you this Josie O'Brien, if one of them teacher's set about my son for speaking the Irish, I'd swing for them."

"Well it's a good job then that you and I are on our way to the States."

"You know talking about the States, did I tell you that Shelia and young Patrick are coming too."

"Brendan will have something to say about that, I have no doubt, still it's for the best."

"What you too, what's got into everyone, am I the odd Bob here." Phelm confronted Josie.

"Oh I see! your mother thinks it a good idea too, leave me out of this."

"There's great talk in the city of a Fenian rising against Queen Victoria and her German Prince.

"Well good luck to them, it wont affect us, we will be on the high seas."

"It's only talk, and you know talk is cheap. Yet I admire them for speaking out, it cannot be too easy for them."

"England has done her worst, she has destroyed the fullness of our lives, forced us to abandon our native tongue. Condemned our people to live in the ground like vermin while they built grand mansions on our land that they stole from us. Now my own flesh and blood has to emigrate."

Anne left the kitchen and went to her room, no doubt for a good cry.

"We know all that and now the ultimate insult to be deprived of the right to live in peace in our own native land. For me and my family there is little left now, this is indeed Ireland's holocaust."

"Will you two talk about something cheerful, you are putting years on us." Shelia came into the kitchen holding Patrick by the hand.

"Alright then, give me the child, you can wet the tae for us."

"Thank you very much, a woman's work is never done so they say."

"We have completed all the packing, so there is little to do now but wait for the return of captain Tom."

"I expect that he will be calling any day now? I wish he would hurry, for the excitement is about killing me." Shelia told them.

At about midday of the next day that the captain came to the farm and he sitting on the drivers seat of a long dray drawn by two horses.

"Here I am then, I hired this to convey your luggage to my ship." He jumped down from the dray.

"It's big enough, that's for sure, what do you think we are taking with us anyway?."

"Well it's all that was available at the quay side, so let's make the best of it."

"I've set the table, will you not come and join us." Anne invited Tom to partake of the meal.

"Come on Phelm, get Shelia and Patrick, I'll get my luggage from the house." Josie rose from the table.

As Phelm and Josie were loading the dray, the neighbours came down the boreen to their door, some carrying small gifts. The Parish Priest came and wishing them good luck he then blessed them.

"This is it then, I suppose, parting is such sweet sorrow." Phelm took his mother in his outstretched arms.

"Don't worry Mum, we'll be back with our pockets full of American dollars."

"Forget the dollars, you come back safe and sound, and you too Shelia. Oh good God in heaven! Let me hold my grandson." Anne took the child from Shelia and held him close to her breast.

"God! It will be a lonely fire side awaiting your return."

She handed the baby back to Shelia and taking up the hem of her apron held it to her eyes.

"Now Mum, remember you promised, there would be no tears." Still holding the child she fell into Anne's arms where she too began to cry.

Up the boreen came Shelia's brother Patrick on the back of the mare.

"Going without saying good bye to me were you?" Patrick dismounted.

"Now how could we do that, we would have stopped at the house have no fear." Shelia embraced her brother.

"He could have come with us but he had to take his mare, didn't you." his mother chided him.

Josie embraced Delia and went to embrace Brendan but he would have none of it. Holding out his hand he said his good byes as all men do.

"I hate to break up a party but remember that time and tide for no man waits." The captain took his place on the drivers seat.

The families and neighbours watched as the dray wended its way down the boreen.

As the dray took them farther and farther away from their

home, Phelm looked up at the chestnut trees, their leaves were now a russet brown, their horned seed casings splitting open displaying the mahogany coloured seed inside.

His thoughts returned to his days when as a boy he challenged his friends to try and break his seasoned conker. Would his son ever return to his native shore and play as he had.

Along the lake side in the mirror waters of the lake the occasional trout leaped in pursuit of a tasty fly. Then landing with a belly flop back into the water.

Phelm held Shelia's hand tightly reluctant to let it go, she looked round at him and smiled.

"A penny for your thoughts Phelm Griffin." He heard her say as if in a dream.

"Sorry Shelia I was day dreaming as usual, I was wondering if there are any chestnuts in America."

"You'll find the same trees there as here and many more." The captain interrupted.

Soon they were in the city and felt the gentle breeze coming off the Shannon on their cheeks.

"The weather is settling in, is it not?" Shelia tightened the blanket around her son.

"Here we are then, this will be our home for the next five weeks depending on the weather. Before we go on board, call me captain from now on, it's the way it's done. It maintains discipline within the crew and makes for greater harmony."

Soon they were settled in their respective quarters, Captain Tom and his carpenters had done them proud. Part of the ship had been partitioned off as their private quarters. With special attention being paid to the cabin occupied by Phelm, Shelia and their son Patrick.

"You can go up on deck if you wish, but keep to starboard, we'll be sailing on the tide." Captain Tom told them.

Phelm and Josie went to the prow of the ship and stood looking towards the open sea.

"There is little use in turning back now Josie, is there"?

"It's sorry I am to say this, but I have no intention of ever returning to Ireland. What with the starvation, the evictions and the burning of my home, can you blame me."

"I knew Josie before you ever told me, that you were intent on a new home in America; you need feel no shame."

Shelia came on to the deck of the ship and joined them.

There was a lot of shouting of orders as slowly the ship slipped the ropes holding her to the quay.

Soon the Sara-Anne-Jane had her prow pointing towards the swivel bridge, which stood open as if welcoming her into the Atlantic ocean.

They watched as she was slowly manoeuvred through the narrow opening and on into the broad majestic Shannon estuary.

With Josie one side of him and Shelia on the other Phelm placed his arms around their shoulders. No words were spoken. They watched in silence, several larger ships berthing at the new docks.

"What is the old adage, It's the last glimpse of Eireann with sorrow I see." Phelm looked from one to the other.

The Shannon estuary grew wider and wider as the little ship sailed farther and farther away from the shores of their native land.

"That's Loop Head over there and Kerry Head there," Captain Tom came and joined them on the prow of the ship.

"There isn't much of them to be seen if any at all." Shelia looked into the distance.

"Do you know seeing you standing there with your hair blowing in the breeze reminds me of a picture I once saw, it was of the Maid of Eireann standing proud on the prow of a French ship coming to relieve Limerick in 1691." Phelm looked nostalgically out to sea.

"Look there is another ship over there." Shelia pointed to another ship appearing on the horizon.

"We'll meet several of the bigger ships, as they make fast passage to America." Captain Tom informed them.

"All with emigrants no doubt" Phelm remarked.

"There are not alone Irish emigrants, there are Germans and Eastern Europeans as well."

"I suppose there will be no mistaking the Irish they will all be on the coffin ships from England."

As the little ship tossed and rocked in the Atlantic swell, Shelia went below to attend to her child. Phelm and Josie stayed on deck talking, reminiscing and planning their future in Pittsburgh.

The shores of America

Five weeks and two days they had spent at sea and were beginning to wonder if they would ever reach the shores of America.

Then early one morning there was a knock at their cabin door.

"Will you come on deck, Mr Griffin, we have entered the river." The caller informed them.

Phelm and Shelia came on deck to be greeted by the captain and Josie.

"I know that it was a long journey but we are here now." Captain Tom more or less apologised for the slow passage of his tiny ship..

"We are where, I see nothing." Phelm looked to the right and left but all he could see was the ocean.

"This believe it or not is the confluence of the rivers Allegheny and Monongahela. Here they form the great Ohio river. Much wider than your Shannon" Tom spread his hands before him.

"You mean that we are in America." Shelia ignored the fancy river names.

"You sure are lady, and this is good old Pennsylvania."

"Pencil what,! we were under the impression that we were going to Pittsburgh." Josie looked worried.

"Oh I see!, sorry, I should have explained, Pennsylvania is the state and Pittsburgh is our second city. We'll soon reach it. See all those ships coming and going from it."

Captain Tom pointed to several ships of all shapes and sizes in the estuary.

They stayed on deck as the ship moved slowly up the river to its berth.

The pilot manoeuvred the ship gently against the quayside. There was a grinding sound as the ship came to a shuddering stop against the knotted ropes hanging from the sea wall to protect the vessels.

Excited wives and sweethearts waved to their loved ones as the crew came on the deck.

The captain was delayed for some time sorting out docking procedures with the harbour master.

He returned to the ship with the harbour master. There they exchanged documents and shook hands.

Saluting Tom, he went down the gantry.

"Now that is settled we will have to go and see the emigration officials, just a formality." He guided them to a small office on the quayside. With Tom vouching for the new emigrants they had no problems completing the formalities required.

"Welcome to the United States of America. The officer handed them each their documents.

"Come on! I'll organise transport to my house. Alice and the children will be delighted to see you Phelm, and you too." He looked from Shelia to Josie.

Alice and her children were waiting in the driveway as the buggy came up to the front of the house.

"Is it not yourself Alice Devine, as I live and breath?" Phelm jumped from the buggy before it had stopped.

"If you don't be minding now Phelm Griffin, Mrs Grey to you." she ran forward into his arms.

"God bless you Alice but it's a lot of water that has passed under the old bridge since I last set eyes on you."

"Well! You see me now, so what is your verdict."

"Sure I must have been blind that day on the Tipperary road not to have noticed a lady when I saw one."

"Now Phelm you are an Irishman through and through, quick with the wit and a glint in your eye."

"Now sure what am I thinking, I'm being carried away with the change in yourself. This is my wife Shelia,my young son Patrick and my cousin Josie O'Brien.

"You're more than welcome to our home." Alice reached out and took their hands.

She picked up Patrick and held him close to her breast,"Just like your dad, aren't you"?

Phelm looked from one of the children to the other and then to their attire."I would recognise you any place, God be good to you all, a credit to old Ireland, come here and let me hug you."

The children ran forward and clung to his legs and arms.

"What can I say Alice, what can I say at all, I'm choked so I am. The very craw is rising in my throat." Phelm turned his back and wiped his moist eyes.

"Soft as butter is my Phelm, come here allanah." Shelia came forward and hugged her husband.

"Children! take Patrick and show him your den and toys." The children ran to the rear of the house with Patrick in tow.

"They'll get on just real fine, I can tell." Alice looked after the children as they giggled and raced across the green sward.

"Come on in, it's all getting too emotional out here." Tom ushered his guests into the house.

After supper they retired to the study where Alice provided them with refreshments in the form of drinks and cookies (Biscuits).

"Did I tell you what they done to me back in Ireland Alice? They plied me and my crew with what they called The Cratur, I was drunk after it for the rest of the week."

"Little if any harm it would do you, with all you drink, now." Josie you will be staying at the house of Mrs Flynn, two blocks down the street. You don't have to worry too much about the rent at present, you can settle up when you get you're pay."

"Will I be able to find the house alright, it's all very strange to me."

"Don't worry about it, Tom will run you down later in the buggy. Phelm, Shelia and Patrick will stay here until they find an apartment of their own, now that's settled. Tomorrow I'll take you both to the new rolling mills. Have no doubt about it, it's hard dirty work but the pay is very good."

Later that evening Tom took Josie to the home of Mrs Flynn, Patrick settled into one of the boys rooms. Phelm and Shelia were given a room to themselves.

After breakfast on the following day Tom took Phelm and Josie down town to the rolling mills.

They looked aghast at the miles and miles of foundries belching out acrid smoke and steam.

"Whatever do they manufacture in those places?" Phelm

asked.

"I guess if you name it and its made of steel then it is made here in Pittsburgh. Rails for the railways, girders for the building trade, plating for the ships, machinery, tools, the list goes on and on. We can claim to be the biggest foundry in the world and still growing. Now you see why we need more and more labour."

Tom turned the buggy through one of the gates within the complex. Stopping outside a large office block he invited them both to step out of the buggy.

"This is where they recruit the labour for the mill. Remember the greater the wage the harder the work."

Inside several men were sitting on a series of long wooden benches.

Tom went to the office and introduced them to the employment officer.

"Take this form and fill it in, return them to me and sit over there with the rest." Tom helped with the filling in of the forms and told them to sit down as he returned the two forms.

They listened as several of the men were speaking to each other. There was little English spoken from what they could gather of the conversations.

"Who are they when they are at home?" Phelm asked Tom.

"Some are German, more Polish, Italians, Ukrainian, Russian, English and Irish but to name a few."

"Where are the Irish then? I don't see any." Phelm looked around at the faces.

"There are two sitting right next to me just now." Tom laughed.

"Come on you men follow me and be careful, we don't want any accidents." The clerk came from the office carrying the applications.

They found the heat within the foundry oppressively hot. Cranes ran to and fro along the gantry above them carrying loads of steel. From a huge ladle a stream of molten steel began to flow as it was slowly tipped towards a trench.

"Good God Josie, it's like being in the jaws of Hell." Phelm shouted to Josie above the constant noise and boom of the foundry.

After the tour of the works they returned to the recruiting office.

"Now that you have seen the works, you have a chance to decide if you wish to work here or not."

There was a lot of conversation between the men but none rose from their seats.

"Very well then! to morrow morning, I expect to see you all here at seven o'clock sharp, when your duties will be allocated. Bring strong boots and a leather apron, Oh yes! and don't forget your mess tins, lunch boxes or whatever you call them." With that he returned to his office."

It was at six o'clock the next morning when Phelm left the house and walked the two blocks to the Flynn house. There he was met by Josie and together they took a street car to the foundry.

All day long they dragged, hauled and pushed heavy iron wheeled carts along the tracks within the foundry. Tom was right, it was hard dirty work with little respite.

"I suppose we will get used to it in time, Josie." Phelm remarked during the lunch break.

"We had better for we have little if any choice."

Within a period of two weeks they had settled in to their new occupation and were as experienced as any of the others.

A tale from Botany Bay

Arriving home one evening, Shelia was at the door to greet him waving a letter in her hand.

"It's from Limerick and it's for you." She thrust it into his hand.

"All right, don't have a heart attack, it's from my mother." He looked at the envelope and his mothers scrawl.

"Open it! open it please," Shelia waved her hands in the air and jumped up and down.

"Can't a man get inside the door and wash first?" Phelm brushed past her and went on into the dining room.

"Good evening all, and where is my son?" Patrick came running in from the garden on hearing his fathers voice.

"Know what father, I went to school today and I got this." He held out a book of verse.

"To school is it now, and what brought this about?" He asked Shelia.

"It was my idea if you must know, I thought that it would be good for him to be with the younger children. Alice interrupted.

"Good for you Alice, education is no load to carry, is it son?" He picked Patrick up and landed him on his knee.

"Will you look at you, black as the hob, are you going to wash. Hurry, then you can open mother's letter.""

"Very well then, you open the letter, I'll go and wash, what's for dinner?" Phelm handed the letter to Shelia.

"Well what did it say? Good news I hope." Phelm came down the stairs from the bathroom.

"I didn't open it, it's addressed to you, you should read it first." Shelia handed the letter back to him.

"Now we'll get all the news from the Emerald Isle." Phelm tore the envelope open.

"Dear Son, blah, blah, blah," Phelm nodded his head from side to side.

"Oh stop it! read the letter properly will you." Shelia stamped her foot.

"Right then, here goes." Mother says that everything is fine at home and to tell Josie that Delia and Brendan have moved into the house with her for company.

The blight is as bad as ever with little signs of improvement, but God is good. She would say that wouldn't she",

"What's this she says?" Phelm turned the page and read it to himself.

"Shelia they are deporting six men from the village to Van Diemens land by way of Queenstown in Cork. There's the Quigley brothers Stephen and Joe, Pashy McGlinchy, you know Pashy who's not right in the head, Billy Duggan and his cousin Bobby and old Tady who plays the squeeze box."

"Why are they deporting them, sure they are as harmless as children."

"Well! it seems that they were all found guilty of being members of the Fenians. She has enclosed a copy of the secret oath for membership and says that we should destroy it having read it."

Phelm turned the pages until he found the oath.

It read.....

I,.....in the presence of Almighty God, do solemnly swear allegiance to the Irish Republic, and will do my very utmost, whilst life lasts, to defend its' independence and integrity.

I will yield implicit obedience in all things, not contrary to the law of God, to the commands of my superior officers. So help me God."

"Sure them poor Amadans could not read one word of that not alone understand it. It would be a different matter if it had been written in IRISH."

"Pashy got ten lashes with the knotted Cat o' nine tails in Limerick jail for insulting the magistrates.

There are a lot from the city and county being sent there in chains and to Botany bay as well." Phelm continued reading from the letter.

They left the Jail in Limerick on drays drawn by four horses with two tiers of prisoners one above the other."

"Well if it is of any relief to them they will be joining the leaders of The United Irishmen, They were sent there some years ago.

"There's not a lot of good news, if any, is there? She still loves and misses us all especially Patrick. She still insists on calling him the baby. She's looking forward to our news. Oh yes!, she says that Delia will be sending her letters to Josie here until he gets his new place, if that is alright by Tom.

"There is still a lot of trouble with the pishogues. Last week Larry Devine went to the barn to collect his one rhone cow. It was dark morning so it was and he not looking took up his ash plant or so he thought. Driving the cow from the barn he thought that there was something strange about his stick and looking at it, he found that it had been changed for an elder. What a cruel thing to do, now he worries that his cow will die."

(It was believed in Munster (Ireland) that it was wood from the elder that was used for Christs Cross and so is sacred. Using it on animals would mean death to the animal and misfortune to the user. People would not sit under the elder nor touch the fruit from it)

I told him that I would take it to the fairy fort and leave it next to the Leactha An Ri. I pray that the fairy King will be good to our Larry."

There's no more except that she had a mass said for us by the Franciscans."

"Did you say your folks were being sent to Van Diemens land? Tom interrupted.

"Not our folks, mother wrote and told us that the English are once again deporting the Irish to Van Diemens land and Botany Bay.

I've been there and heard of the treatment meted out to your folk. I never appreciated the way they transported your people until I saw it for myself.

I saw some of the old coffin ships rotting in the bay. The berths were only six feet square and six men and women had to share that one berth, sleeping in their own excrement and that of the others. If any of the wretches wanted to move then all the others had to move too as they were all chained together. Their food such as it was consisted of the waste peelings from the crews mess together with hard tack biscuit. It's hard to believe in this age that any so called civilized country, especially one that claims such moral values as England does, could perpetrate such cruelty on a defenceless nation.

God help them, the girls were mostly young virgins in their teens, they were taken and gang raped by the crew members. The death rate on those English ships was unbelievable. It was the weak and the children who died first and were thrown overboard without as much as a Christian prayer over them.

I heard one story from an ex convict. He has now settled on his own farm of land, would you like to hear it.?"

Tom did not wait to be invited to tell the story. Like most sea captains he took his pipe from his pocket and settling down into a chair began to relate the story.

Phelm placed the letter from his mother to one side and awaited the story.

Tom slowly took some tobacco from his pouch and crushed it in the palm of his hand before stuffing it into the bowl of his pipe.

"This pipe too has a story, but that will wait." He held up his pipe for all to see. The pipe was made from ivory, the bowl of which had been carved into the shape of a dragon. The stem took the place of the dragons tail. It was indeed the work of a first class craftsman. Tom had purchased it in Hong Kong in China.

Slowly he lit the pipe sucking in the flame through the bowl and puffing out the sweet smelling tobacco smoke. Removing his pipe from his mouth he began the story.

I suppose you could say that I met him in a tavern at the quay side or was it a prelude to meeting you good Limerick people. Whatever it was here is the story he told me for what it is worth.

He told me that he came from the village of Doonkerdeen near the town of Foynes owned by a Lord whose name escapes me. Perhaps you know the place, his name was Stephen Downey he told me.

Well he admitted that he was young and foolish and went poaching on his Lordships estate and procured a fine hare. As he was leaving the estate he was confronted by two gamekeeper.

I was caught fair and square and what excuse could I offer, he told me, I told them that my wife and children were starving and were at that moment awaiting my return with the food, which was the gospel truth. Sure I thought it would soften their hard hearts. After all who owned the hare in the first place, only me. I caught it fair and square. Sure all my pleadings fell on deaf ears. The devil a bit of notice they took of the situation. They were hard hearted, they took my hare. I was in bared feet,not having the price of a meal not alone a pair of boots. They bound me in chains and beat me all the way to the barracks. The beatings were bad enough but the soles of my feet were so raw that they looked like sliced meat, after being me forced to run behind the cart. Not mind you that we ever saw much meat to know.

Next day I was taken still in the chains to the court. I was sentenced to four years transportation to Van Diemens land. I thought that his Lordship would forgive me. He was sitting in the well of the court looking smug with himself.

I asked to see my wife and three children. God help me that was my biggest mistake. For did not the magistrate order that they too should accompany me, innocent though they were. He ruled that by asking me to get the food they had inadvertently or words to that effect condoned the theft. Not mind you that I knew just what he was talking about.

It was the policy you see to get rid of as many Irish as possible and this was as good an excuse as any. I was taken chained to six other Limerick men on a cart to Queenstown harbour in the county of Cork. I was put on the coffin ship to here, where you see me now. No I tell a lie it was further up there and me as thin as a rush. He pointed to a deserted and rotting wooden wharf.

On the journey we were chained to a berth some six feet square. My wife and children were in a separate berth without chains. Go down any time you like to that wharf and you will see several of them rotting away. I have no doubt with the ghosts of the murdered Irish crying for revenge among the barnacles.

At sea, we were let out once each day to clean up our own excrement. A barrel of water was placed on the deck and we were allowed to shuffle along in a line and take one drink from the ladle each.

The chains were never removed at any time except when on one occasion one of us died. We were two weeks out when a young lad of sixteen died.

I never knew his name, I'm ashamed to say, not that it matters, no disrespect to his soul. We didn't let him go to his maker starved for a prayer I tell you. God rest him.

He had been dying for several days but they still would not remove him from the chains. We were left dragging the corpse between us it was all so pitiful.

The smell coming from his corpse on the fourth day was unbearable, God be good to his soul.

The Red Coats thought it funny, God but they have no hearts. Now I'm getting ahead of myself forgive me.

It was on the second day following that I heard that my wife had been taken to the crew quarters with the other women and repeatedly raped. Several of the women jumped over board on the journey including my wife. You see Sir, although they knew that they were condemning their very souls to Hell fire, they could not stand any more abuse. They were never to see God's earth again. My three children died some days later, I don't know if they died all at once, but then it was far better that I never knew. They were unceremoniously dumped into the ocean, or so I was told, either ways I never saw them again.

I was not aware of the truth of this until I arrived in Van Diemens land. I worked for three years on the road gangs, I've still got my clothing you know.

It was made of rough cotton cloth with large yellow arrows all over, the purpose being that, if we ever escaped we would be easily identified. To add insult to injury they had the barracks name impregnated on them also. There would be a reward to any person bringing us back dead or alive.

Lying in my bunk I could hear the blood hounds howling in the bush, searching for some poor soul trying to make it to one of your American ships.

Sure many the poor soul was dragged back more dead than alive having been attacked by the devil sharks. I tell you in all sincerity, it would have been far more charitable for the sharks to have eaten them, may God forgive me.

In the beginning I dreamed and planned of escaping to the docks and seeking sanctuary on one of them American brigantines. I had heard it said from reliable sources that the American flag would protect me. If the English dared to try and board or fire on the American ship, it would be declaring war on the American flag and that they would not tolerate.

It all came to nought, I tried it once only and was caught and flogged within an inch of my life. I was chained in a dungeon below the ground for six weeks on bread and water with no bedding and no one to speak to. I tell you, Sir, I saw many the good Fenian break under those harsh conditions, and then to have my sentence extended by a further three years. It was often that I lay in my hard bunk and cursed every hare in Ireland. In the end I had a bad accident when lifting a cart to replace a wheel, the whole cart collapsed on my back. I was of no further use to them so they shipped me out and gave me to this Protestant gentleman to work on his land near to Botany bay.

For a Papist and a Protestant we struck it out from the start, a right saint he was although a staunch bible puncher. I wonder do they become saints? Protestants I mean.

Well to cut a long story short didn't the poor bugger up and die. Before he died he took pen to paper and wrote to the Governor, so he did, and obtained for me a pardon and a Ticket-of-Leave. Then he up and signed the farm of land over to me. All legal and above board if you must know. Shure he had neither kith nor kin to leave it to but he was a real gentleman to me. I'm sure that God will be good to him although he was a Protestant. I pray the God will listen to me and take testimony of what I say for the poor Souper. Do you think that God will make an exception in his case?.

You may think that my story ends here, but it does no such thing, no Sir. Do you believe in faith or God?. Well true as I'm sitting here with your good self did not news come that the English were sending young Irish girls here to balance up the population of men and women.

As I was by now a free man I was invited to apply for one to be my wife. They would be arriving on the next ship from Ireland, so they told me.

That was in the spring of the year 1847, and who do you

think was sending out the brides but none other than my brave Lordship.

The very same gentleman who had me deported here.

Well I put my stake in for a wife straight away and being a landowner I got priority. Sure I waited in trepidation for that ship to land and land it did.

I was called forward and without any more ado I was handed. Yes Sir! I deliberately said handed, this young girl. She was no more than sixteen years of age and she dressed in a rag of a shawl. She looked at me and I at her, neither of us knew what to say or make of each other. She was bereft of any foot ware and her clothing, such as it was, was in shreds.

Without shame, I can confess I was taken in by her large blue eyes. Why Sir, the innocence and mystery in her eyes were enough to captivate me.

But she was so emaciated that I could literally look through her. How she made it here I never understood, but suffice to say, made it she did. I had my doubts if the truth be known if I would be marrying her or burying her. Had she been a beast at the mart no man would waste fodder on her. Now there is no disrespect meant in what I say. I'm making a comparison if you must know.

I tell you Sir, I'm no saint and not having been in the company of a woman for many the long year, I found it very hard to control myself, if you know what I mean. I took her to the nearest drapers and purchased her some clothes and shoes, now what else could a decent man do.

Then I invited her to join me on my wagon and we set out for my farm.

She was aware of the terms of her being sent to Botany Bay, or at least I thought that she was. I told her that I was a widower and that if she liked me then we would be wed proper.

Being a sensible girl and knowing that I was a decent Irishman and she an Irish girl,she up and agrees.

We were wed proper within the next day or so, and I'm glad to say that we make as fine a couple as ever sailed into Botany bay.

We have two sons and a daughter, you must come home and

meet them, indeed you must if only to verify my story."

I did go that evening to his farm and stayed for two whole days and I tell you truly that the glowing love I found in that house will live with me for many the day.

"Well! That is the story as related to me and I have no reason to disbelieve one word of it"

There was silence in the room for a time, then Josie spoke up.

"And what about myself and my kin, did I not have the roof burned off my house for little reason. Am I not an exile now thanks to the English."

"Come to think of it, there is my wife Alice and our children, can you picture what they suffered."

"Is there not one Irish family that has not been touched by the brutal laws of England.

"If it is any consolation, they treat their own in England and Scotland little better than the Irish, or so I'm told." Phelm rose from the seat.

"Now you see what comes from opening letters from Ireland, and I still have not had my dinner."

"There is little fear that you will go to bed on an empty stomach."

Castlelurgan house, Pittsburgh

Phelm did not wish to impose on the generosity of Tom and Alice for too long. Not that Tom ever hinted that they should be moving on.

A golden opportunity came their way, when a large tract of real estate down near the hazlewood came up for sale. It had been used as a melon farm and on it was a wooden house. It was in good repair and Phelm could see its potential. The asking price was reasonable and Phelm believed that with it being in the immediate vicinity of the city it was a secure investment.

Shelia was more than surprised to see Phelm come down to breakfast one morning dressed in his best clothes.

"Where are you off to this morning? Not to work I have no doubt."

"Don't ask me please, wish me luck, if I succeed, I'll come home with a pleasant surprise for you."

Leaving the house he took a car to the city and made a bid on the property and land. Sitting in the office his mind wandered back to the day he purchased the farm in Castlelurgan..

This time he would not be fooled, he had asked all the right questions and employed a good lawyer to act on his behalf. It cost him money but he considered it well spent.

Phelm came from the office and walked down the side walk singing and laughing to himself like a child or was it an amadan. He had purchased the land and the house. There would be no turning back now. He boarded the next street car back to the home of the Grey's.

"Shelia!, Shelia are you home, Shelia!" Phelm shouted across the hall way.

"Will you stop roaring like a bull on heat, Sure half Pittsburgh can hear you." Shelia came down the stairs.

"I'm entitled to shout. What did I say this blessed morning

about a surprise? well!."

"I don't know what you say half the time, you're like Jack O' Lantern."

"Well now Shelia Griffin, put on your coat girl and come with me. Have I a surprise to gladden your heart or have I not."?

"What is it, why all the mystery, can't you tell me now"?

"Tell you!, I'll do better than tell you allanah, I'll show you, come on."

"Oh very well then have it your way. I hope that you are not wasting my time or woe betide you, if you are,you'll go hungry this day."

"They took a street car to the centre of the city. Once there he hired a buggy to take them to the hazlewood estate.

"Close you eyes now Shelia and no peeping." Shelia covered her eyes just to please him.

"Turn in here driver please", Phelm pointed out the turning into the house.

"You can open them now Mrs Griffin."

"What are we doing in this place? It looks deserted" Shelia looked out the car window at the rambling wooden house.

"This is to be our new home, I just bought it and all the surrounding lands. Phelm crossed his hands and awaited her remarks.

"You bought this?" She pointed with contempt at the wooden house," how much land is there anyway."

"I'm told that there are about 600 acres or thereabouts."

"600 hundred acres and a wooden house, I suppose all our savings went on it."

"Every penny Shelia, but worth a lot more, you'll see. Come on now, don't be sulking come into the house it has great potential." He guided her to the door.

"Do you want me to wait Mister, it will cost you."

"You may as well wait, I doubt if even I could walk that distance."

Shelia looked around the large sitting room and wandered on into the other rooms, it was far bigger than she at first thought and was surprised at how well preserved it really was.

"Do you know Phelm Griffin, I think that you are right for once, I think that it is grand, real grand." Shelia folded her arms and nodded her head in agreement with her husband. "Just think of it Shelia, a home of our own in the United States Of America. No landlord to harass us and no Red coats banging on the door, God bless America."

"Amen Phelm, but have you forgotten that you have a farm of land in Ireland and a mother."

"I've not forgotten my roots Shelia and well you know it. We'll go back there have no fear of that, but for now we need a home of our own."

"How does Josie fit into all this, have you told him yet."

"I've thought of that too, you know he wants to settle here. I'm going to offer him a few acres free to build a home on, so that he can bring Delia and Brendan out."

"You think of everything, do you know you're too soft for this world, but I would not be without you." Shelia reached up and kissed him firmly on the lips.

"Ah come on now, stop your shannangan, what do you really think of it." Phelm gently eased Shelia away.

"I've already told you that I really do like it. Together we'll make this the finest house in Pittsburgh. I'm going to call it Castlelurgan House She swung round and round in the large empty room.

"Castlelurgan, it is then, may God bless it and us. We had best be getting back. Go and lock up your castle Lady and let's be off." Phelm handed her the keys to the house.

Phelm related to Tom and Alice the fact that they had purchased a house of their own and would be leaving as soon as they got the house in order.

"There's no need for you to do any work in the house, not in your condition anyway, Tom and I will start to morrow."Alice volunteered for them both.

"Will we now, trust you to speak on my behalf, seriously though, Alice is right, you should be taking it easy. Shelia. To morrow we will start putting your home ship shape under your supervision of course."

Late that evening Josie came to the house to enquire as to why Phelm had not shown up for his shift.

"Are you feeling alright Phelm, they were asking about you."

"Me! I'm as right as rain, sit yourself down I have some good news for you."

"Before you start, I could murder a hot sup of tae. There must be enough iron inside me to open my own foundry.

"I'll make a fresh pot, you just tell Josie the good news" Alice retired to the kitchen.

"Now Josie it's like this, I found a house and farm down near the hazlewood. Not the best of places I admit before you ask. It was going cheap and I couldn't resist the temptation so, I up and bought it."

"You mean the old melon farm, sure I looked at that myself and if I could have raised the money I would have bought it, is that the good news."

"No not at all, it's like this I want to give you twenty acres lying at the end of the farm for free. I heard that the land the other side of it will be coming on the market in the near future. Sure, I know that you have not got the money as yet, but you will. Then you could make an offer on it and living next to it, you would, in all probabilities, get first refusal."

"Well now that is more than decent of you Phelm, but I just cannot up and put my hand in a decent man's pocket. No! no way Phelm Griffin could I accept. No disrespect to you and Shelia I assure you." Josie rose from the chair and waved the palm of his hand in protest.

"I suppose you're right Josie and I do apologise. That's me all over again, surmising as usual. Tell you what though, will you give me a luck penny for it."

"I will at that bejabbers, and I'll give you my hand as well." Josie went across and spitting on his hand held it out to Phelm.

"Come on give me that hand of yours and may you never find yourself wanting." Phelm in return spat on his hand and both men shook hands warmly.

"I suppose I'll have to think about building a house of sorts on it. Trouble is I'm no dab hand at building."

"Let the building wait, first you will have to help get the house of Phelm's in order for Shelia and her new baby" Alice told him.

"New baby, what the hell is wrong with me, and me not thinking straight." Josie slapped himself gently on the forehead as if in chastisement.

Several weeks were spent repairing, painting and furnishing

the house before it came up to Shelia's expectations.

Josie not being adept at any house repairs, was confined to clearing the garden and driveway.

Tom took it upon himself to convert a room for Patrick, it had everything that a boy ever dreamed of. He had built a bed in the shape of a boat on hangers. It could be rocked to and fro or backwards and forward just like a ship at sea, he told Patrick. The walls, much to Shelia's disapproval, he decorated with life belts and paraphernalia from the sea, Phelm said that he was trying to relive his childhood. Yet Patrick loved it, and that it seemed was all that mattered.

Shelia by now had acquired a buggy of her own and spent a lot of time in Philadelphia, buying nick knacks for the house.

Shelia conceives a daughter

It was on one of her forages into the city that she became ill in one of the stores. She had fainted and when she came round found herself sitting on a chair and looking into the face of a woman whom she thought at first glance was a nun of sorts.

The woman was dressed in a plain one piece dress down to her ankles with long sleeves to her wrists. The dress continued in one piece up to her neck where it was tied. Around her shoulders she wore a shawl of the same colour as her dress and over the front of her dress an apron of the same colour. Her hair was straight and two plain pony tails hung limply down her back. On her head she wore a black bonnet with a deep scoop. Shelia thought it drab and was meant to distract anyone from admiring her just like a nun.

"What happened? thank you." She pushed the glass that was being held to her lips to one side.

"You went outen" or words to that effect replied the woman in guttural English. Shelia found it hard to understand just what she was saying. Yet she found a warmth in the woman with the kindly face.

From the conversation that followed she learnt that the woman's name was Hannah and that she was a member of the Amish community.

When Shelia felt better the woman insisted on taking her home.

She tied Shelia's buggy to the back of her own, it was different from Shelia's buggy in that it looked more like a carriage with a canopy over it with large wooden wheels and roller blinds on the windows.

Shelia was invited inside. Taking her place beside her the woman guided the horse from inside the carriage.

Shelia found it very comfortable compared with hers.

Soon they were at Shelia's house where the woman untied

the carriage and prepared to leave.

Shelia insisted on her sharing a cup of tea and in the process learnt a lot about Amish community life.

Everything in the Amish household is basic, she was told. The household centres around the bible as does the whole community.

Every child had to learn the bible by heart and know it's meaning before they would be considered for baptism in their teens.

She was fascinated by all she was learning about the Amish people but time was getting on. Making her excuses Hannah left the house promising to come again at a future date.

That evening She related how she fainted in the store and was revived by the Amish woman. Phelm was more concerned for her safety and that of his unborn child than her story about the Amish woman.

"Shelia promise me that you will not go out again alone, I think that you should stay with Alice during the day","How do you expect me to work, and me worrying about you."

"Look if it makes you feel any better then I'll go and annoy Alice all day, satisfied."

It was for the better that she did stay with Alice. On the second day when supping tea and chatting she went into labour.

There was no time to seek the help of a doctor, so Alice had to act as the midwife.

"Now Shelia don't panic whatever you do. Remember I delivered many the cratur back in the old country."

"I have no time to check your credentials." Shelia laughed. Together we'll see this one into the world."

It was late into the afternoon when the baby arrived. Alice swore that she was the prettiest girl that was ever born outside the Emerald Isle.

"So you now have pigeon pair Shelia, I'll get you a cup of tea, you deserve it."

Shelia relaxed in the bed and looked down with pride at her new daughter.

"Listen to me girl, as granny said before we left old Ireland, bring me back an Irish- American baby and here you are God bless you. Ah you may well smile." She tickled the infant

336

under the chin.

"Have you decided on a name for the baby as yet, or is it too soon." Alice entered with a tray of refreshments.

"I have that and now that you are present will you fetch the holy water and we will administer lay baptism."

"Here's the water Shelia, and I'm your witness, now for the name."

"I baptise thee, Anne Alice Griffin, in the name of the Father and of the Son and of the Holy Ghost Amen." Shelia made the sign of the cross on the forehead eyes,lips and forehead of her infant.

"Did you call her Alice for me"? Taking the bottle from Shelia Alice wiped a tear from her eye.

"Not alone did we intend to call the baby after you were it a girl, but you are going to be her God parents. Mind you if it was a boy we were going to call him Thomas. Do you think that Tom will be disappointed?"

"Oh Shelia that is the best present that anyone could give us, Tom will be over the moon, so he will."

"For better or worse it was your Tom that encouraged us to come to the United States and has stood by us ever since. No finer family we could ever wish for friends. Now if you don't mind I am going to have a long sleep with my daughter, before Patrick comes from school and the men come home from work."

"You have a good rest and leave the others to me and Tom." She was persuaded to stay in bed for the next five days, she was waited on hand and foot by Alice and Tom.

The day came when Shelia decided that she had imposed on the Grey family enough. It was time that she returned to her own home.

"Look here Alice you have spoiled me and Anne this last week and been more than good to me and Phelm. For that we are more than grateful. Now it is time that I took up my own responsibilities. Anyway Tom will be returning to sea shortly and we have to have the baby christened properly before he goes." That it would seem settled the matter.

With the christening over the time came when Tom had to rejoin his ship on its return journey to Limerick.

The day before his departure Phelm called at the house with

several letters for his mother, Delia and Shelia's family.

"Now don't forget to give them all the news, and tell them how well we are doing here. You won't forget will you to tell Mother that we called the baby after her."

"For heaven sake! you spent the last week writing letter after letter. What can I tell them that you have not already told them in your letters." Tom held up the bulky parcel of letters. "I regret that we won't be there to see you off Tom. Good luck and may you be in Limerick before the devil knows that you have left." both men shook hands warmly.

"Phelm, if I lived to be a hundred years I could never fully understand your sayings, but I know that you mean well."

"Keep the wind to your back and the sun on your face." Phelm called back as he boarded the buggy and headed for home.

Shelia resumed her shopping trips to the city and once again met up with Hannah.

"Why hallo Hannah, it's many the long day since we met." Shelia called out on seeing her.

Hannah was wearing the same clothes that she wore when first they met. Standing by her side was a young man with breeches that had no flies and were held up by a pair of braces that seemed to be home made. His shirt was as plain as his breeches, the only difference being that it had buttons . There was significant growth of beard on his face and on his head he sported a straw hat that was creased at the top.

"This is Papas eldest one" Hannah introduced the young man standing next to her.

Shelia reached out her hand but the young man ignored her outstretched hand. He lifted his straw hat and smiled at her politely.

"This is my daughter Anne, she was born shortly after we met." She proudly presented her baby to Hannah.

Hannah invited Shelia to visit her home.

Hannah proved herself an encyclopedia of knowledge when it came to explaining the Amish customs.

Firstly she explained that when they returned home the family removed their shoes and went barefooted.

Shelia explained that the people of Ireland had to go barefooted for want of shoes and not by custom.

After Hannah's daughter was born, a white organdie prayer cap was placed on her head and when she reached the age of twelve it was changed to a black one for church. When she weds she will wear the same style white cap that her mother wears.

The mens status was recognised by the hats they wore, in winter the children all wore black felt broad rimmed hats and changed them to straw hats in the summer time. These hats have a three inch rim.

The eldest boys wear hats with creases around the crown when they marry. They also sports a beard but not a moustache! that is forbidden.

Her husband wears a higher hat than his sons and the grandfathers hat is higher again than that of the father and the brim is four inches wide.

All the men sport beards, its our way of life she explained.

Shelia noted how plain Hannah's house was compared with hers, which was cluttered with ornaments and carpets.

Hannah explained that it was their custom not to have curtains on their windows and no upholstery or carpets. Shelia remarked how practical the whole system was. Hannah explained to her it was not done for practical reasons. It was because the holy bible told them so.

Shelia was impressed by their unquestioning faith in the bible.

She began to tell Hannah about the fairy tales that the children in Ireland learn and of the legends and stories of Ireland. As Roman Catholics were forbidden to have their children taught by English laws. They had to educate them through songs and stories.

Hannah looked shocked, no Amish child would ever be allowed to listen to fairy tales or the fantasised stories as told in Ireland.

The children are taught mostly in the German tongue and the German bible. Strict discipline is observed in the home, in the school, and in the church.

Joseph, Hannah's husband came into the house from the field and sat on a wooden stool and removed his boots.

Hannah introduced her to Joseph and received the same response as she did from his son.

As the conversation continued Joseph sat on the stool taking no part what so ever in the conversation, that was until Shelia mentioned that Josie had no house for his wife and family and was no craftsman.

"Did she say he had no house"? Joseph asked his wife ignoring Shelia. Hannah explained to her husband what Shelia had said.

"Tell her that we will construct the house for him within the week."

Shelia wanted to thank Joseph but he rose from his stool and ignoring her he left the room.

She was not offended by his action for she respected their customs. She had found them friendly and hospitable.

Their way of life might appear unique to others but not to Shelia. She had a husband who was so steeped in Irish tradition and sayings that he could baffle the Irish themselves.

Phelm becomes an
entrepreneur

The land which had been neglected by the previous owner was to prove a challenge to Phelm. Yet compared with the damp unyielding soil of Ireland it was not beyond his capability.

Hiring ground clearing equipment he set about reclaiming the land and bringing it back into cultivation.

"You never lost it, did you Phelm? Burning the midnight oil on the land." He heard a familiar voice as he wended his way home in the twilight after his hard days work.

"It's yourself Josie, and what brings you out here?"

"I called at the house and Shelia told me that you were about here. Sure your tea is over ages ago, away home man."

"Was I not on my way when I heard you, is She upset?" He wiped his hand across his brow.

"Upset! what are you talking about, you'll lose that girl if you don't take care, this land will bury you yet."

"Taking it badly then, is she?"

"Do yourself a favour man, take it nice and steady, sure Rome was not built in a day."

Together both men returned in the twilight of the evening to the house.

"So you found my wanderer at last did you, come in both of you sit down and have a bite to eat."

"Josie says that you are mad at me, is that right Shelia"?

"Josie says more than his prayers, but I am annoyed that you are not looking after yourself, now eat up and shut up."

In spite of protestations from Shelia he continued to devote more and more time to the land. It had become an obsession with him. Finally she too decided that it was best to let him work it out of his system.

Joseph, his Armenian friend came and taught him how to

cultivate cucumbers, tomatoes, peppers and many other exotic crops.

He became so proficient that his crops were the envy of the community.

His melon beds were his pride and joy and he nursed them with great diligence to maturity. Shelia complained that he spent more time nursing his precious melons than he did his own son and daughter.

One afternoon a large dray loaded with trees, covered in hessian sacking to protect their delicate roots, came up the driveway to the house. Shelia came to the door and stood looking at the approaching dray.

"Is this the home of Phelm Griffin?" The drayman asked.

"Yes it is, what have you got there"? Shelia pointed to the trees.

"This is part of the order of fruit trees, there are one hundred here and more to follow. Where would you like them put?"

"Would you take them round the back? My husband is not home, what are they anyway?"

"I told you, they are fruit trees, you know, apples,pears, plums, oranges, you name them and your husband has bought them."

Shelia did not know if the drayman was being sarcastic or not so she decided to ignore him.

"Is that you Phelm? you're early." Shelia called out when she heard the key turn in the lock.

"It's none other, were you expecting someone else by any chance?"

"No, it's just that you are that much early, your dinner is not ready yet."

Don't worry about it, I'll go and have a quick wash." He took off his cap and coat and hung them on the hall stand.

"The house is unusually quiet, where are the children"? He missed the usual stampede of tiny feet to greet him.

"They went to town with Alice, they are due back soon."

After dinner, he retired to the study to read the daily newspaper. Leaving Shelia to tidy up the kitchen.

"By the way did you notice all the trees out back? A dray delivered them this afternoon, I thought the drayman was being sarcastic when he told me that they were fruit trees."

342

Shelia called around the kitchen door.

"Damn it to hell! I've been waiting for them." He laid the paper to one side and entered the hall.

"I wish that you wouldn't swear like that, now where are you off to?" Shelia folded her arms to show her annoyance.

"Sorry love! I'm going to see if I can get hold of Josie and Joseph before they make other plans."

"What do you want them for now?" She came into the hall.

"You don't honestly believe that I can plant all them on my own, do you?" He opened the door and was gone.

Shelia came down to the orchard later that evening with a bag of sandwiches in one hand and a flask of tea tucked under her arm. Holding tightly to her daughter with the other and with young Patrick in tow she made her way to where the men were busy planting the trees.

Joseph was busy staking and tying one that he had just planted.

"This is like the cutting of the turf in the old country, is it not? Here I brought you some tea and sandwiches.""Shelia your one treasure from heaven and that's a fact. We don't know how we'd manage without you. Will you look at them don't they look real grand." Phelm pointed to the rows of trees set out in straight rows ten feet apart, no more no less as Joseph had instructed.

"I cannot see you returning to Ireland, not at the rate you are carrying on." Shelia looked at the neat rows and had to appreciate the diligence and effort going into the planting.

"Come on say Good Night to your dad, you two, God only knows when they will finish."

By weekend they had completed the task of planting the orchard and wasted little time in preparing more land for the vineyard.

It was not too long before they had added several large green houses. There seemed to be little time now for relaxation as they spent more and more time on improving the farm. Shelia wondered if the long hours spent on the farm were not detrimental to his health.

Returning home one evening Phelm was more than surprised to see a notice at the end of the drive. Written on it in large block lettering he read:

People in drays and on foot were coming and going to and from the house.

He stopped where Shelia and Alice had rigged up a makeshift stall and were selling the produce from the land.

"What's going on here then? It looks like a market place."

"That's exactly what it is. We grow more than we could ever possibly eat. What better than sell the surplus and plough the money back into the farm." Shelia informed him as young Patrick came into view with a barrow filled with some of his prime cabbages.

"Come on, let's go up to the house and I'll show you." Shelia took his hand and leaving Alice in charge they entered the house.

"Look this is what we've made so far." She opened a tin box filled with shining silver dollars.

Phelm looked at the contents then reaching his hand into the box he withdrew a handful of coins and let them trickle slowly through his fingers.

"Now Shelia that's a grand idea, why didn't I think of that?"

"Because you're too busy thinking of what else to do with the farm."

"Do you know, we could employ a retired man or two part time. That way we could grow and sell that much more. Then I could devote more time to you and the children."

"Why don't you do it full time yourself? There is more than enough work here for you without you killing yourself at the foundry."

"Do you really think that we would make enough to live on and pay back the money we owe in Ireland?"

"Will you take a page from Joseph's book, and the other Amish families. They have no more that sixty acres or less each to support them and their families and you don't see them wanting."

"You're right Shelia, I'll ask Josie to come and work with me." He was getting all excited at the prospects.

"You'll leave Josie alone. Let him continue to help you part time, but don't crowd him."

He resigned his position in the foundry and devoted himself

full time to his gardens.

As his business flourished, he soon learnt that he could not cope alone. He began to recruit a part time workforce. Within a short period of time he had, five full time workers and ten seasonal workers. God had indeed been good to them in the new land.

As demand for their produce grew, they devoted themselves more and more to their market garden and nursery. Soon he had a workforce of some ten workers both full time and part time. God had been good to him and his family in the new land.

His mother wrote to him and told him of his country being slowly bled to death in her frequent letters. More and more penal laws were being passed to suppress the people into subjugation.

The Canting system she wrote was being used more and more to legally evict the Irish tenant farmer from the land.

The landlords knew that they could outbid the tenant. Whole families would be evicted and what crops were standing in the fields would become the property of the new lease holder. This cruel act was a source of great distress and hardship to the Irish peasant.

Not alone, his mother wrote, were they using the canting to evict the Irish but also the Gavelkind. All real and imaginary laws were being used to evict the legal tenants from the land. The people were still suffering from the cruel stomach disorders from trying to digest Peels brimstone It was being offered to the Irish at a price beyond their means. This as their native corn crops, taken so cruelly from them in rent and taxes, were being exported down the Shannon. All too often passing the cursed ships bringing in the Indian corn.

Still the people, many no more than walking time bombs of plague roamed the country side. Like Zombies they ate what nourishment they could find, berries, roots, nettles and grass. Their bodies so emaciated that they were unable to reach the few berries hanging temptingly from the high branches. The Irish had their own names for the plagues and these related in many cases to the state of the dying.

Spotted or Black fever was Typhus
Relapsing fever was yellow fever

Dysentery was famine dropsy
Black Leg was scurvy
Red Eyes was Ophthalmia
The cruellest death of all, was diphtheria. It struck down the very young. His mother wrote telling him of the children being wrapped in straw and left outside the fever hospitals. There they lay gasping for breath their mouths slowly being clogged up with mucus. It would have been more charitable to smother them there and then, she wrote, than let them slowly choke to death.

From his mother's letters and letters received by other Irish emigrants there seemed to be no end to the sufferings of the people.

The Irish societies in America, Canada and elsewhere sent what they could to alleviate the distress at home.

There was a now a scarcity of coffins due in kind to the increasing numbers dying from the great Hunger. The people resorted to using sliding coffins. The coffin containing the body would be placed over the grave. The bottom would be drawn out and the corpse would fall into the open grave. The coffin perhaps riddled with germs would then be taken away to await the next death. All dignity and respect was now stripped of the people.

In many cases Catholics begging for a bowl of soup from a soup kitchen run by the Protestants, had firstly to renounce their religion and become Protestants before they were fed. The Catholics who renounced their religion became known as Soupers Jumpers or perverts. Many of the Protestants refused to participate in this offensive and obscene trade of food for religion. Some like the Earl of Dunraven in Adare in Limerick were more than generous in their giving.

This situation never occurred in the many soup kitchens run by the Society of Friends or Quaker's as they are better known.

Daily reports came to the attention of the various Irish organisations in the United States and Canada of the atrocities being inflicted on the Irish people. Copies of these reports were sent to the office of the president of the United States of America. From there they were relayed to the British embassy demanding an explanation. This demand which

Britain could not defend or explain away was causing much embarrassment.

Phelm planned time and time again to return to Ireland and assess the situation for himself but as always there was an intervention of one kind or another.

Anne confides in the Sideog Ri

Anne was now showing her years and was finding that her once daily visit to the Sideog Ri, had to be curtailed to once each week. No longer could she reach down into the babbling stream to retrieve a stone to make a Crann beag. "You'll understand, no doubt, Sideog Ri, that I am no longer as young as I was. The years, if you must know,have caught up with me." Anne sat beside the Crann Mor and addressed the phantom fairy king.

"I came this day, although crippled with the pains, to ask you to protect the soul of young Martin O'Grady, as it leaves its earthly abode. I'll be away down to the stream to collect the primroses to place across the threshold. It's his mother Kathleen you know, worried she is at his sudden departure, so she is."

Anne rose wearily from her stone seat with the support of her walking stick, only to fall back again on the rock.

"Ah you see, Sideog Ri, the years are telling and of that have no doubt." She laughed as she once again rose from her seat, this time successfully.

"Slan leat, Sideog Ri," Anne lifted her walking stick in Salutation to the fairy king and returned to the home of the O'Grady family.

Martin had died mysteriously and this was causing distress to his parents. They believed that the fairies had taken their Martin and replaced him with a sick fairy.

Anne Griffin was the only one who could put their minds at rest.

She crossed the threshold and entered the cottage. The body of young Martin was laid out in a crude coffin.

"It's yourself, is it not, Anne Griffin, come in and take the weight off your feet, sure you must be jaded", Kathleen,

Martin's mother, came to the half door and assisted Anne to a comfortable chair by the fire.

"Will you place the irons across the coffin, Kathleen, in God's holy name." Anne pointed to the fireplace.

"My mind is in a dodder Anne, will he be safe" She rushed to the fireplace and grabbing the poker and tongs, placed them in the shape of a cross at the foot of the coffin.

"Don't worry Kathleen. I'm here now to assure you. Let me catch my breath for a minute."

She sat down for a few moments to rest and recover her composure before she rose to her feet and approached the open coffin. She placed several of the primroses in the dead hands of young Martin. Then going to the threshold she laid the remainder of the flowers on the stone with their blossoms facing to the north, to the south, to the east and to the west. Content with her arrangements she took the holy water and blessed herself before resuming her seat.

"Will you take this Anne? Good God! but you must be frozen." Anne reached out and gratefully accepted the procured hot drink.

"How are you bearing up,Kathleen, seeing as little Martin has been called away." They both looked across at the face of Martin lying in his coffin. The primroses were now prominent for all to see. There would be no mistake but Anne Griffin had done the calling.

"I'd like to be sure that he is safe with Jesus. He was called away so suddenly. Do you think that the fairies had anything to do with it? You know these things."

"Kate! you can take my word on it, the fairies did not steal Martin. I have the word on that, of that be assured.

"Did you say that you had the Word Anne? Thank God for that Anne Griffin. Sure wouldn't I be the worrying mother, thinking that my son was wandering in the wild woods, I'm now content in my mind."

"You can let him rest in peace now, Kate, so you can.

I must warn you before I leave, do not let any strangers next or near this cottage so long as Martin is under the roof.

I must be off, for Bridget will be wetting the tae. You know what a fuss pot she is, if I'm late home." With these words of warning she left the house and hobbled up the boreen.

"Are you away just now then?" She looked around on hearing her name being called. It was Kathleen's husband Dermott, coming over the style.

She retreated to the hedgerow and sitting down on a flat capping stone awaited his arrival.

"Thanks for waiting Anne, I want to know if you will be in a position to attend the closing of the coffin to morrow night. Kathleen would appreciate your presence. Tell me truly Anne Griffin, did you ever happen to have the word for our Michael." Dermott twirled his caubeen in his hands.

"Have no fear of that Dermott O'Grady, I just left Kathleen and before that I spoke to the Sideog Ri. I'll be there should the good Lord spare me." Placing both hands on her lap, she rose wearily from her seat.

"Just where have you been? Don't you know the time, it's gone Seven and I was worried to death for you." Bridget, a long standing friend of the family ran forward as Anne made her appearance at the half door.

"Will you not be fretting for me, Bridget Byrne, Thanks all the same. Sorry I'm late home, but you know about young Martin.

"Of course I do, and how is Kathleen taking it?" Bridget poked life into the fire. She laid the poker to one side and placing her hand on the bellows wheel sent glowing sparks into the dark recess of the chimney before she subdued them by placing the black iron kettle over the coals.

Returning to the scullery, she took a scone of bread from the linen cloth and cut several slices from it, these she covered in salted butter. Taking two blue duck eggs from the clean straw basket, she entered the kitchen and removed the lid from the kettle. She placed the two eggs inside with the aid of a spoon.

"Delia and Brendan are gone go Limerick. Your supper won't be that long now Anne! Look why don't I remove your shoes and allow your feet to breath." she replaced the lid on the kettle and approached Anne.

Anne was fast asleep, her grey locks covering her face.

Bridget took a cushion from another chair and gently placed it under her head.

"That's more comfortable, is it not" she spoke to herself.

Kneeling in front of Anne, she opened the buttons of her bootees and removed them before placing her feet on the little stooleen.

"Ah Anne Griffin, God be good to you, you poor soul." Rising to her feet she took a blanket and covered her.

Anne's assurance is badly needed

It was dark night when Anne awakened from her slumber and looked questioningly around the room. The kitchen was now silent. The table had been set and the food covered in a clean linen cloth.

Putting the blanket to one side she rose from her seat. She felt the cold of the stone slab floor rising through her feet. She smiled to herself. Bridget had seen that she was comfortable in her sleep. She invoked God's blessing on her for her charity. Replacing her bootees, she sat down at the table and removed the linen cloth.

The blue duck egg covered in a cloth was still warm as was the tea. It could not have been that long since Bridget left.

Finishing her supper, she retired to the settled bed, where she removed her beads from under the pillow and began the rosary. There was nobody now to respond to the prayers. Was not her Pat long dead and her children far away in America. Delia and Brendan had their own problems. Slowly she prayed until her rosary fell from her fingers, Anne Griffin had succumbed to sleep.

Most of the next day she spent in the confinement of her bed, assuring all who called that she was fit and was just having one of her lazy days. Yet in her heart she knew that the time was now near, if it had not already overtaken her, when she would no longer be able to leave the house.

She knew that she would have to attend the closing of Martin's coffin that evening. She had promised and it was expected. Anne Griffin was not one to renege on a promise especially one so dear. Come what may, she would keep that promise.

Rising from her bed, she washed and dressed wearily. Although she would not admit it, she was pleased when

Delia came and prepared the meal. She would need all of what energy she had left to make the journey to the home of the O'Grady family. Not mind you that it was that long a journey. It was that one foot was that much more reluctant to pass the other now.

She did not disclose to Delia nor Bridget that she was going to the closing of the coffin that night.

They were, if nothing but full of good intentions, yet fuss pots all the same. They would have insisted on her staying at home or at least waited for someone to call with a pony and trap to take her.

She encouraged them to leave the house. Then she put her heavy shawl over her shoulders picked up the ash plant, took the holy water and blessed herself before wending her way up the boreen.

The cold night air attacked every bone and muscle in her body as she tucked her shawl closer for warmth and comfort. She could see the beckoning light coming from the cottage as she leaned heavily on her ash plant for support.

The light from the coinneal mor in the window of the O'Grady home beckoned to her. It was so near and yet so far away.

Soon she was joined by other neighbours bent on the same task. What with the chat and the gossip, the journey was that much shorter and for that she was grateful.

Reaching the cottage, she soon realised that Bridget, in her wisdom, had been right after all. Her feet felt like lumps of lead and her heart was pounding like that of a cornered hare. Her breath came in short gasps as she held her hands close to her heart. She did not disclose her discomfort but was thankful to cross the threshold of the home of the O'Grady's.

Delia and Bridget sitting by the coffin were surprised to see Anne hobble into the kitchen. So this was the reason for her getting them out of the house.

Anne slipped gratefully into a chair by the fireside and sat looking into the fire, unable to utter one word of thanks.

"Are you alright Anne, what sort of an Amadan at all are you? Taking to the road on such a night." Bridget was looking into her face and stroking her brow, yet she could not reply.

Bridget left her and returned shortly with a hot cup of tea

and held it out to her.

"Is that for me, just what I wanted, give me the chance to get my breath back. Sure I'll soon be as right as rain." She took hold of the saucer in her hand. The cup rattled and swayed as her hand shook. Reaching out her other hand she steadied the cup.

They left her to herself, for Anne was not one to take too kindly to fussing. Yet they kept a discreet watch on her every movement.

She took no part in the prayers nor the gossip. The rest would do her good and she would come round in her own good time.

It was some time later that they awakened her for the sealing of the coffin.

She rose to her feet and hobbled across the floor and looked in at the dead face of young Martin. She rearranged the primroses. Calling for a chair she took hold of the side of the coffin and sat down.

She swayed backwards and forwards and slowly began crooning. The neighbours took to joining the crooning as Anne opened her eyes and began to sing an old Celtic lullaby out of respect for young Martin and his family.

Sleep little child,
Dream of my own
Winds may be wild
Thou'nt not alone.

Mother and sire
Watch oy'er thy dreams
Soft burns the fire
out of its gleam

Back comes the eyes
Dead long ago
Back comes the sighs
Laughter and woe

Round thy small bed

Gathers a host
Drawn from the dead
Each a dear ghost

All of thy race
Watch oy'er thy sleep
Bennisons Deep
Sleep little child

Dream o my own
Winds may be wild
Thou'nt not alone
My own baby child

Lullaby of a Celtic Child

Finishing the lullaby, the meaning of which she alone knew, she lay back in the chair. Why she thought am I so very, very tired?

Once again she took hold of the side of the coffin and rose to her feet. Then she called on the Sideog Ri to protect the soul of Martin as it left from his earthly abode. She called for the coffin to be nailed down.

Rising to her feet she took the chair in her hands. She threw it across the room together with the irons. This to confuse any evil spirit trying to steal Martin's soul. The crooners began to wail and many ran to the fireplace and covered their faces in ashes. The men began banging tins and pots. The din within the house continued until the last nail had been secured on the coffin lid.

Martin's father blessed every corner of the room with the holy water. The assembled mourners began to pray.

This custom was frowned upon by the Church. It was a mixture of Celtic pagan ritual and Christian belief.

Although Anne stubbornly resisted, saying that she would be alright, her protestations were ignored. She was lifted gently from her chair and taken back to her home in a pony and trap driven by Patrick. She was accompanied by her constant companion, Bridget and her cousin Delia.

A letter of some urgency

Phelm received a letter from his mother that demanded his immediate return. His heart was sad as he read the scrawl of a letter rambling from Irish to English,it read..

Dear Son,

Your letter came on the morning delivery and from the post date it must have come on one of them coffin ships. It took the best part of ten weeks, but I was more than glad I can tell you to hold it in my hand.

I am pleased to know that you are doing so well in America. I pray daily that God and his Blessed Mother will continue to shower their blessings on you all.

Was I not sad indeed when I read that you were thinking of settling down over there. I thought that my poor lamps were deceiving me.

Did I not cling to you and on my bended knee pray to the Dia Uilechumhachtact to protect all of you and to send you safely back to old Ireland.

Did I not against all the warnings not to, go to the fainne Sideog agus titim mise ar an talabh call on the Sideog Ri to let me cut just one wee branch from his Crann and it with the magical Druabus secretly growing in its crown. All of this I done for you so that you could take it to the new land of America to bring you luck. Tell me son, do you still use it to this day to encircle the ground to protect your family or have you planted it in the new land?

Clare Johnson the Tally woman to the late captain Singleton died this past week, bennact De air an ainm.

It was tragic, for did not Sean find her dead beside him in the bed.

More young men than ever before from Munster are being deported to Van Diemens land and Australia. They are bound in chains and sentenced to fourteen years to life and all because they joined the young Ireland movement. They have now made a new law called the Treason Felony Act or so they tell us. John Mitchell the leader has been deported as has most of his followers. Last week in Limerick there was a man speaking on their behalf agus mhaire se ag scarthedth to rab piachanam before he was plucked from the street and dragged away by the soldiers. Och Phelm a lanab is it not glad I am that you are in America at this time.

The Molly McGuires are still up to their shannagins with the landlords. They are getting more and more brazen by the day. It is said that they have taken it upon themselves to murder several of the landed gentry.

Now, Gra geal mo croic I must tell you that it was I who was the agile one long before you were a twinkle in your fathers eye, Bennact De air an ainm.

Och Ochone! nil aon tintean mar do tintean fein remember that the speed of the beast will not stay with one forever. Is there not many the once strong man, and yes! woman for that matter bennact De lib go leir that are stretched on their broad backs. They that bore many the burden are now in the churchyard of St John. Them with the sods of green grass growing above them as they await judgement day.

I tell you all this Phelm for now I am a Sean Bean Boct who is now a child twice over with no kit nor kin to bury her. Do for my sake return to Eireann agus Conndae Luimneac it may be the last time that our eyes will meet. I want you, my only son, to lay me down beside my Pat. You'll not let me go hungry to my grave for want of the family prayers.

God willing but do come and bring Shelia and the children. I must see my grandchildren before God in his infinite mercy calls me into his kingdom.

Ah Phelm remember that 'The clock in it's tower lives on, but the hand that placed it there does not."

I know that God will spare me until you come, may the angels speed you back to me and to Castlelurgan.

The letter concluded with a shaky scrawl of a signature. There was little doubt but mother had written all her emotions and predictions into her letter.

Phelm was deeply upset as he read the rambling letter to Shelia.

Young Patrick and Anne did not understand the Gaelic [Irish] nor the sayings of their grandmother but Phelm and Shelia explained in vivid detail all that the letter entailed.

"Shelia, there is no excuse for us not going now. We have planned year after year to return to mother and always cancelled it for one reason or another. Read her letter there is little doubt but that she fears the worst. We will just have to return to Ireland and mother on the next available passage." She watched as he held the letter tightly in his hand. The anguish of its contents showing on his face.

"Don't worry love, I'll ask Alice to look after the business and Tom will be home from sea soon. Your grandmother will be fed up with us after a few weeks no doubt and regretting her letter."

"Your right as usual love, anyhow we could do with a long holiday."

Alice on hearing the news assured them that she was more than capable of looking after the business. They could leave for Ireland whenever it suited them.

When Phelm disclosed to Josie that he was going back to Ireland on the next available passage, he decided that he too would return to Ireland and bring his wife and son back to live in America.

This news did not please Phelm, he had hoped that Josie would stay behind and look after their interests. Shelia wasted no time in telling him how selfish he was.

He had been separated from his family for some years now and it was right and proper that they be reunited.

Arrangements were completed for their passage from Philadelphia on the next available steamer berthing at Queenstown in Cork.

They would dearly have liked to comfort Anne by informing her in advance of their impending arrival. That was not possible, they would be in Ireland long before the letter.

Alice took them in the buggy to the quayside and reassured them once again that all would be well before she waved her good byes to them.

Phelm spent every available hour of daylight and many more into the night on the deck of the ship. Anxiously looking across the vast expanse of ocean.

It was four weeks to the day since they embarked at the port of Philadelphia. He became a prominent figure as he stood sentry on the deck daily.

He watched a school of Dolphins as they played around the ship. He was returning below decks to inform the children to come and watch their buffooning. His attention was diverted to a growing haze in the distance. He studied this for some considerable time and it appeared to be getting nearer and nearer. Thinking that it might be an impending storm he went and asked the lookout on the prow of the ship as to when the storm would break.

"There is no foul weather about that we know of." He was told in nautical terms.

"Then would you mind telling me just what that is over there"? He pointed to the haze which by now had greatly increased in size.

"That Sir, is what you have been looking for this last four weeks. Yes Sir! that is the good old Emerald Isle, if I'm not mistaken."

"You don't mean, it cannot be, you mean to tell me that we are there at last." He stuttered out the words.

Thanking the lookout and ran along the deck towards his cabin.

"There's no hurry Sir, we won't be there for many hours yet, it won't go away." The look out shouted after him.

"Come on! come up on deck quick all of you, we are in Ireland." He ran into the cabin and ran out as quickly having given the news. Then racing along the corridor he banged on the door of the cabin occupied by Josie.

"Come on Josie we are here at last." He did not wait for them to acknowledge to his call. Again, he raced up on deck where he leant on the rail and watched the haze give way to the outline of land.

His shouting aroused the curiosity of the other passengers and by now the deck railings were jammed with anxious Irish Americans, all wanting to be the first to see the Emerald Isle. Unashamedly many wept with joy as slowly the green hills of their native land came into full view.

Phelm watched with growing impatience as the ship sailed nearer and nearer to the island of Ireland. It would be a further three hours before the ship could berth and discharge its passengers and cargo.

Leaving Shelia to see to the children and baggage, he went on the quayside to make arrangements for transport.

Much to his disappointment he was informed that there would be no transport to Limerick until noon next day. They would have to find accommodation in the nearest hotel for the night.

Phelm was up and ready at cock crow next morning, it was doubtful if he had slept a wink.

"Will you sit down and eat your meal like a civil human being." Shelia chided him at the breakfast table.

"She's right if you must know, the coach will not leave any sooner for you. Get a substantial meal under your belt." Josie told him.

A joyous reunion

Early morning saw the coach loaded and on it's way to Limerick much to Shelia's relief. Phelm had spent most of the morning castigating the porters and drivers. Perhaps now he would relax.

H counted every stop and canter as the coach left County Cork and entered County Limerick at Drumcollier.

He reminded Shelia that it was here that he and his father had battled against the snow on the way to the home of his uncle.

There after a short respite they travelled on to Newcastle West. Once again the coach stopped to allow passengers to alight and board, this much to Phelm's frustration.

"Why don't they get on with it, are all these stops necessary?"

"You know that the coach must stop to let the passengers off and on, stop worrying will you." Josie lay back on the head rest and began to nod off.

"For a man who was so anxious to see his family you seem cool." Phelm looked across at Josie who by now was fast asleep.

There would be one more short break before the coach turned into the Rathkeale road. Rathkeale would be their last stop before they entered the lands of lord Dunraven and his village of Adare. There the horses would be changed for the last time before the final run into the city of Limerick.

Phelm had no intention of spending valuable time there. As the coach stopped outside Cruises Royal Hotel in the city, he was out of the coach and calling on a porter to hire two jaunting cars to take them and their baggage to Castlelurgan. Anne heard the noise from the horses hoofs as she lay half asleep in the settled bed.

"Delia!, Delia come quickly, there's a jarvey in the boreen." She called as loud as she could.

"What's the matter now? Why are you shouting the house

down?." Delia came hurrying from the scullery.

"There's a jarvey in the boreen, are you deaf woman, go and see what they want."

It was then that the door was opened from outside and two noisy children ran into the kitchen.

"O Christ in heaven be good to me, let it be my son and grandchildren." She made strenuous efforts to rise from the bed as tears streamed down her cheeks.

The two children stopped in fright at the sight of the old woman trying desperately to raise herself off the bed and at the same time calling for their father.

Phelm was surprised when he entered the kitchen and saw his mother lying incapacitated on the old settled bed.

Dropping his portmanteau he rushed to the bedside and taking his mother in his arms hugged her.

"It is us sure enough, we're home at last." Mother and son fell into each others arms and openly cried unashamed.

"Thank you God, Oh thank you God! Anne cried as she hugged and kissed her son.

"Come here and meet your granny." Phelm called to the children who had stood back looking at the performance of Phelm and his mother.

"Phelm rise me from the bed, I want to see and cuddle my very own grandchildren. She raised both her arms out to her son.

Phelm went into the bedroom and returned with several pillows and placed them behind his mother's back.

"Ah look at yourself young Patrick, how you have grown. You don't remember your old granny now do you? Come to me you lovely creatures." Tears rolled down her eyes blurring her vision as the two children came cautiously forward not knowing what to expect from this strange lady.

"Would one of you fetch me my lamps (Glasses), I cannot believe how they have grown. Will you look at that colleen, a spitting image of the O'Grady's. Will you look at that head of red hair. Golden as the setting sun, as my Pat would say, God be good to him.

Pity your granddad is dead love, he would appreciate this moment, so he would."

It did not take them too long to become familiar with their

grandmother. Soon both were sitting, one each side of their granny and she hugging and holding them for dear life.

"Mother whatever happened to you, you never told us about this." His concern for his mother was showing on his brow.

"Will you not be fretting over me. Sure seeing you all here this blessed day is more than a tonic to my old eyes. Shelia Allanah would you ever wet a sup of tae."

"Of course mother, it's many the long year since I heard that one." Shelia crossed the floor and putting the kettle on the crane she drew it over the hot coals just as if she had never left the old house.

"'Tis easy I can rest now, what with you all home in dear old Ireland again. God has indeed been good to all of us, you mark my words Phelm Griffin." His mother seemed to have found new life with their arrival.

"Well talk of the devil, look who has arrived." Delia pointed to the half door where Patrick was dismounting from his horse.

"Well now Phelm aren't you the Yankee boy, that's a fancy suit if ever I saw one." Patrick held out his hand in greeting. "Good to see yourself, keeping well I hope, and where is that wayward sister of mine?"

"I'm making the tea and you keep your grubby paws off me." She came forward to greet her brother.

"God you don't look a day older and you the mother of two children or is it more, where are they?" Patrick looked across at the bed where the children were playing with Anne's rosary beads.

"Ah will you just look at them, Irish to the core would you say and just like our side of the family." Patrick called the children to him.

"Just like your side of the family indeed, that's cheek for you if ever I heard it and on my own threshold. Will you just look at the pair of them, that one is a Griffin and no mistake. But will you look at little Anne, are you blind or something, look at that head of hair. That is an O'Grady through and through. Anne folded her arms and looked across at Patrick.

"Okay granny, you win but little angels all the same."

"Now Patrick stop teasing granny, take this tea across to her and tell her your sorry.

"He's not teasing me, are you Patrick, come on give me my tea." Anne laughed.

Shelia returns to America

The following afternoon Patrick and Phelm took a walk across the fields towards the woods to discuss how matters were progressing. Phelm did not want his mother upset by discussing business in the house.

"Phelm, there's little for you to worry about. Every penny you sent I paid into the account in Limerick, it's all in the book." Patrick assured him.

"I know all that. Didn't Delia tell me all about it, but is there any money still due do you know.?"

"I wouldn't have thought so, but I never asked. It being none of my business. Perhaps on second thoughts I should have."

"Never mind Pat, will you take me to the city to morrow and I'll find out how the land lies."

"No problem Phelm, will you be taking the family."

"Not unless Shelia wants to go, I'll have more than enough on my hands without two excited children."

The two men on reaching the woods turned around and returned to the house.

When Shelia heard that Phelm intended to go to Limerick the next day, she too insisted that she should come with the children.

Delia was anxious to purchase new clothes for herself and Brendan prior to their departure to America, so she too would come along.

Patrick arrived next morning in the trap and tied behind it was another horse and trap.

"I hope that you can still drive a trap Phelm?" Patrick laughed.

"Where did that come from may I ask.?" Phelm went forward and stroked the horses nose.

"Ask no questions out of school and I'll tell you no lies."

"If he cannot handle the trap then I can." It was Josie coming round the gable of the house.

"No Josie you lot are coming with me, this trap is reserved for the Griffin family.

Anne, too ill to travel, was left at home in the capable hands of their good neighbour, Bridget Byrne.

Soon Anne and Bridget were alone in the house once more and Anne began to feel nostalgic.

"Ah Bridie love, I see it all now, the green grass will very soon cover the Griffin boreen."

"Will you not be talking like that. They have only gone to Limerick, not a thousand miles away. They'll be home for supper, would you like a sup of broth."

"Gone to Limerick you say! gone for what? To buy new clothes for their return to America." Anne was empathic in her assessment of the situation as she saw it.

"Here get this down you, you should be thanking God that they have done so well, so you should." Bridget held out the mug of broth.

"Would you not be holding the wool over the eyes of an old woman Bridget Byrne, and you a good Catholic. May God and his blessed Mother forgive you for trying to bamboozle an old lady. Come on pass me that soup before it's stone cold."

"Ah! You are the quare one indeed Anne Griffin. There is no mistaking that."

"Talk away Bridget, but talk is cheap. If only God in his mercy would give me a last chance to put my feet on the Talab na H-Eireann. I would go and have words with the Sideog Ri so I would. He'd listen to me."

"Away with you and your fairies, did not the sagart aroon caution you about the fairies and their evil intent?"

"Evil is it indeed? Were it not for the intervention of the Sideog Ri when the pishogue was put on Pats' long meadow and they dragging the cloth with the May dew on it to destroy our precious grass crop. It was the Sideog Ri who dried the grass and put a stop to their evil intent. Go on now deny that if you can." Anne paused and took a swig from the mug.

She knew that trying to convince Anne that there were no such things as fairies was a waste of time. The parish Priest did not help the situation by telling the parishioners that fairies were evil spirits.

Shelia was aware of the concern that Phelm was now showing towards the welfare of his mother. They were due to return shortly to Philadelphia.

The nearer the day of departure came the deeper the worry lines on his brow grew. There was little doubt but that his mother would not be too long for this world.

Shelia unable to cope with his restless nights and bouts of depression, decided to resolve the matter herself.

It was on a night some few days before their imminent departure that she sprang her surprisingly liberal solution to the problem.

"Phelm you know as well as I do that your mother is not too long for this world. As you are her only son you have no option but to stay."

"Shelia, I'm torn between the devil and the deep blue sea so I am. I want to stay and I know what you say is right, but how would you manage."?

"I'll be alright, and the children will be at school. Stay Phelm for if you don't then I'm afraid you will live to regret it. It must be said Phelm, how would you feel at home in Philadelphia, knowing that your mother's coffin was being carried by strangers down the old boreen."

"Your right love, you and the children can go back with Josie and his family. Then when mother gets better I'll come out and join you." He tried to delude himself into believing that his mother would get better.

"Well what use would you be in America? Worrying about your mother, and rightly so. No! it is best that you stay, I can see to matters in the States." Shelia held him close and patted his back.

"You know Shelia, I really do appreciate your concern and I do love you. Let us not delude ourselves. Mother is not going to get better, now is she."?

Together they clung to each other. They were resigned to the fact that soon they would have to part for the first time.

He travelled to Queenstown in county Cork with his family. There they embarked on their return journey to Philadelphia. As the ships horn wailed out its imminent departure he hugged his wife and children to him.

"Don't worry Phelm I'll take good care of them for you." Josie took Phelm's hand in his and shook it in affection.

"All ashore who's going ashore." Phelm heard a crew member call out from a megaphone.

"Well I guess that's it then." He let go of Josie's hand. Then kissing his wife and children goodbye he returned to the quayside.

He watched as the ropes holding the ship to the quay were released fore and aft.

The ship, its horn wailing like the Banshee herself moved slowly out into the Atlantic. He watched and waved until it was out of sight.

Then wiping a tear from his eye he returned to the home of his mother.

Anne is reunited with the Tuatha De Danann

Free from the constraints of his family he devoted all his energy to his mother's welfare.

He watched in sorrow as her health slowly deteriorated. Gone was the excitement of the presence of her grand children. She had little delusions but that she would never see her grand children again on God's green earth. Yet she wasted no time giving him thanks and praise for sparing her long enough to see them.

Bridget came to the house daily to see to her needs and to cook what meals were required.

Phelm walked round the empty farm, now denuded of all it's live stock. The fields once fertile were now deserted and covered in benweed and nettles.

As he rested one evening on the ledge of the half door. He listened to the eerie silence of the now empty farm. He let his mind ramble back nostalgically to the day that the potato crop first failed and to the curses that were put on the farm. He never did find out who were the perpetrators of these evil deeds. He remembered the neighbours and friends who had fallen victims to the famine and the brutal treatment meted out to them by the arrogant landlords.

In fancy dreams he saw his father come down the old boreen. His trusty spade slung over his shoulder. His long gangling frame casting it's shadow in the setting sun.

He prayed for the repose of their souls. Suddenly the silence was broken,

"Penny for your thoughts Phelm Griffin." Bridget came down the boreen.

"Will you look at it Bridget? There was a time when a blade of grass would not have a chance to grow on the boreen before a hen or goose pounced on it. Now the grass is growing up to the threshold, sad times indeed Bridget."

"Phelm in the name of God keep that voice of your down, that is what your mother said. Hearing you talking like that will only upset her."

"Sorry Bridget, but I have to tell someone. I'm in a quandary as what to do for the best."

"Take the advice of an old fool, Phelm Griffin. When the time comes, and it must come to all of us. Take you away from this cursed land for the sake of your family and return to America." She looked across at the settled bed where Anne lay dozing.

His mother was getting weaker by the day. Her mind was beginning to ramble back to the days of her youth in the village. Yet in some far recess of her mind she remembered her Pat and spoke rationally about their meetings and the coming to her parents house of the matchmaker..

One evening she called her son to her and told him a secret that she had kept to herself all those long years.

It happened, she told him, that last Sunday before lent which was known as Chalk Sunday. She had watched Pat Griffin her future husband and his father, arrive at the church with the two chalk marks on the back of his coat. She paused and smiled to herself as once again she saw him in her minds eye walking down the church aisle together with the other bachelors to the men's side of the church.

"Ah Pat Griffin weren't you the broth of a boy and a fine catch." At that she reached her hand out towards the foot of the bed. Perhaps her Pat had come once again to claim his childhood bride.

Ah Pat!, I'm only telling you this secret now because there is little time left to me in this world." She took a deep breath and looked vacantly at the foot of the bed.

"Now Mom!, rest yourself and don't be talking like that." With a lump in his throat and his eyes filling up Phelm took both her hands and held them in his.

"Pat! it's many the long day since you held me like that. If anything should become of me, you should remove my wedding ring and keep it to yourself." She tried to remove the gold band from her finger without success.

He looked at his mother and became more and more

distressed before he once again composed himself.

"I suppose I can tell you my secrets now." Phelm choked back the tears as he listened to his mothers stories.

"Did I not go on the May eve with the two plates to the Fainne Sideog. It was there that I collected the May dew by the beam from the full moon. Then collecting a branch from the rowan tree. I then tied my thumbs in the form of a cross with the bark and went in search for the third largest snail. That was an easy task what with they being so abundant." Phelm could not help but smile to himself as he studied his mothers face.

"I then took the bark from my thumbs and together with three ivy leaves covered in May dew, I placed them under the plates together with the snail.

I placed the plates under my bed that night, next morning I opened the plates and sure enough there in the slime left by the snail were the initials PEG. I never told you this before Pat because you would only laugh."

"No I would not have laughed, it's common knowledge in the village that you are the Fairy Kings messenger.

"Did I not tell you of the time, perhaps not." Phelm stopped as his mother began to cough.

"Go on Pat I'm all ears." His mother squeezed his hand.

Well,! I myself about that time wrote the alphabet on a piece of cardboard before cutting them up and placing them in a basin of water. I swirled them around and around until one stopped in the centre, that letter

was A, so once again I swirled the water and the next letter in the entre was an M right next to the A so I too knew that you were for me." Phelm was well aware of this custom and used it to please his dying mother.

His mother never spoke another word after that neither in the Gaelic, [Irish] of which she was so proud nor in the English. She lapsed into a deep coma. Perhaps she had slipped away that night. Tripping through the dew by the light of the waning moon, to the abode of the Fairy King. Perhaps to keep a long overdue reunion with her Pat.

Phelm would have liked to have thought so, as he held his mothers limp hand in his.

Phelm and Bridget took it in turn to sit by her bedside day

and night keeping a constant vigil.

It was a week later on the stroke of midnight that she opened her eyes and called, not to her God or Son, but to the fairy king. She asked his permission to approach his cairn. Phelm rubbed her hand and called on her, telling her of his presence. Without looking at him she breathed her last breath and joined her Pat.

The only sound within the house was the ticking of the clock. The crickets in the chimney had fallen silent.

He waited for the inevitable call.

Then came the three knocks on the door. The banshee had arrived. Should he inadvertently open the door then his mothers soul would escape and be left wandering through the wild woods.

Apprehensively he watched and prayed as the knocking and the plaintive crying continued outside the door.

Then in a crescendo of wailing she left the house.

He waited until he heard her cries diminish as she returned to the land of the dead, deep in the glens of Aherlow.

He closed his mothers eyes and going to her side whispered the act of contrition into her ear.

He swore on her death bed that he would observe her beliefs, her customs and traditions. She would be waked and buried in the old traditional ways, as her mother and father were before her.

Rising from his knees he went across to the eight day clock, Opening the glass door he stopped the pendulum. He quenched the fire and covered all the mirrors with sheeting. Returning to the fire place he relit the new fire.

"A new fire I light this night
And pray to God to keep us right."

He repeated this old Irish prayer and blessed himself. Looking around the room he made sure that he had observed all the traditions so far.

Now that she was dead her soul was most vulnerable and would need protecting from evil wandering spirits. They would seek revenge on her for depriving them of souls when she was alive.

Phelm, her son and only kin would have to carry out the rituals necessary to protect the soul of his mother. Her soul was trapped within the house. Any mistake on his part now would condemn her soul to wander through the wild woods seeking her Pat. It would he chased from place to place by the evil ones.

He rose quickly to his feet and went to the scullery. There he filled a bag with salt and throwing a chair across the floor he screamed and shouted. Any evil spirits outside the door would be now confused.

Quickly he opened the main door and left the house. Securely locking the door behind him.

Quietly he walked around the house, so as not to let the evil ones know of his presence. As he done so he sprinkled salt in an unbroken circle all around the house.

He could now leave the house unguarded in the secure knowledge that his mothers soul was safe. So long as the circle remained intact no demon would dare try to enter the house.

He then crossed the yard and entered the haggard.

Looking along the rafters he sought out the wise owl. This one was an offspring of his mothers pet. Hearing the owl Hooting he approached her.

"I've come to bring you the sad news that your friend and my mother has passed away." The owl opened her eyes wide and looked down at him.

Then on silent wings she went deeper into the haggard and sat alone hooting mournfully.

He paused for a moment and listened to the owl. He could not delay for time was of the essence.

His next call was on the old wild bees nest. There he stopped and whispered into it.

"Go tell the others that Anne Griffin has passed away."

They would now assist in protecting the soul of his mother. The Evil spirits would use all their cunning to try and steal her soul as it awaited its final destination.

The corpse would not be touched or disturbed for one full hour as custom demanded.

That afternoon the coffin was delivered to the house. Four kitchen chairs were placed in the centre of the floor and the coffin placed on them.

Anne's body was lifted from the bed and placed inside. The

family bible was placed under her chin and her well worn beads entwined in her hands as they were joined as if in prayer.

Instead of coins, two silver medals were placed on her eyes as a mark of genuine respect.

"You forgot to remove your mothers wedding ring." Bridget pointed to the wedding ring on Anne's finger.

"No Bridget I hadn't forgotten. Father put that ring on her finger when they wed. It has never been removed, let it go with her."

No child would be allowed into the house when the coffin was open unless they had firstly been blessed with the holy water.

Phelm went to the Church and procured six large brass candle sticks and six large brown candles. These he placed around the coffin and lit. Now nothing harmful would be able to pass through the circle of fire.

The Celtic Gods and the Sideog Ri would be her guardians on her journey to the next world.

Taking the conneal Mor from its linen cloth for the last time he kissed it. Placing it in a container of earth. He lit it and placed it in the window of the cottage.

Anne Griffin was now ready to receive callers for the last time.

looking through the window towards the fairy fort he whispered.

"Mother has passed on Sideog Ri."

A shooting star crossed the night sky, Phelm smiled.

No tears passed his eyes, for to cry would be frowned upon, his emotions would have to wait until he was alone.

Aine arrives from Lough Gur
as Anne is waked

Later the Keeners came to the house, these were women who would wail and pray in sympathy with the bereaved all night long.

On entering the house the mourners went to the side of the coffin and kneeling prayed for the repose of Anne's soul. They partook of what refreshments were on offer including the clay pipes and the pinch of snuff.

As the night wore on Phelm called on Bridget to set a meal outside the house. There would be many the lonely spirit calling that night to visit the soul of his mother.

As the news of Anne's death spread mourners came from the surrounding villages to the house. Soon one voice was heard to start singing an old lullaby which was taken up by the gathering. It was not long before individuals were being called upon to sing. There was no disrespect intended and none taken for this was a traditional Irish country wake. Tales that told of the fairy army waiting to come fight to free old Ireland were told.

"If Anne Griffin, God be good to her this night, were able, then she would be doing the calling."

"Did she not at many the wake put the fear on us, I can tell you." All looked across at the open coffin.

"It would be the brave and foolish one who would cross our Anne Griffin with the rough words. Shure had she not the ear of the Sideog Ri himself."

"Amen to that, and no mistake I'm sure" An old man replied as he spat into the fire.

"Was it not myself that she gave the cure for the pains to and me crippled, bless her, and where did she get the cure from?. I'll tell you here and now, from the fairy king of that have no doubt."

"True!, true! Never a bad turn did she do, as she well might have, and she with the gift.

"Shure!,I'm shure, you are all aware of the plight of young Donovan over there. He was at deaths door with Diphtheria this year past. There was never a doctor from the fine city that could offer any hope. Who was it who took him in her shawl and away with him? None other than Anne, God be good to her.

Did she not return with him two hours later and hand him to his mother and he breathing better than you and I. I'll say no more."

"No! God be good to her this night, she never did anything but good on this earth."

"Will you hold your whist, sure we could spend all night Praising poor Anne. Taken for granted she was and that's no mistake."

"Tell you what, why don't we all sing. The Fairy boy out of respect to Anne if you take my meaning.

Soon the assembled mourners were singing the old lullaby.

A Mother came when stars were paling,
Wailing round a lonely Spring;
Thus she called whilst tears were falling,
Calling on the fairy King;
"Why with spells my child caressing,
Courting him with fairy joy;
Why destroy a mothers blessing,
Wherefore steal my baby boy?

O'er the mountains through the wild woods
Where in childhood loved to play;
Where the flowers are freshly springing
There I wander day by day;
There I wander, growing fonder
Of the child that made my joy
On the echoes, wildly calling,
To restore my baby boy.

"But in vain my plaintive calling,
Tears are falling all in vain,
Now he sports in fairy pleasure,

He's the treasure of their train.
Fare thee well my child forever,
In this world I've lost my joy;
But in the next, we Ne'er shall sever
There I'll find my baby boy.

The Fairy Boy (Trad.)

The house fell silent as such sweet music passed through the house and out through the chimney. They listened as the music seemed to circle the house. Slowly it died away beyond the river Camog.

As the music faded, there was a great speaking outside the door. This was followed by the three dead knocks.

"It's the Buachailleen from Lough Gur." A nervous voice called.

"Whist! whist in God's holy name, before he recognises your voice."

Should the Buachailleen hear a voice he would remember the owner. He would wait until a fairy child was born deformed and dying. At midnight he would take the dying child to the home of the person who's voice he remembered. Once there he would steal the spirit from the person and leave the dying fairy spirit in it's place. This action would result in the death of the person.

The house remained silent as they waited.... Then she came, the Wailing Woman. The Bean-Sidhe who was guided to the house by Aine of Knock- Aine and the Sideog Ri. Past the window by the light of the coinneal Mor came the great procession. It was led by Geroid Irla, The son of Aine mounted on a white swan. He was leading his army of Tuatha De Danann. Last came Aine and her husband, the Earl of Desmond mounted on their white stallions. This was their tribute to their departed friend and seer, Anne Griffin. The mourners swore to all this and confirmed that it took a full hour for the ghostly procession to pass.

Castlelurgan too braced itself for the inevitable on the night that they screwed the lid down on Anne Griffins coffin.

The moon rose that night like a huge golden sovereign in the sky. The villagers on hearing the keening, which was coming from the direction of the river Camog on the banks of Lough Gur, rushed to the sanctuary of their homes. Once there, they sprinkled salt on the threshold before blocking their windows and slamming their door shut.

They waited in fearful anticipation for the Coming.

Soon they heard the keening of no less than four Bean-O-Sidhes with the Buachaillini in attendance and he scratching on each door. This was indeed a very important wake for four Bean-O-Sidhes to attend.

They heard the headless coach coming down the street. They heard too the Dullahan and he sitting on the high seat in his coatamore. Swishing his whip as he thundered on his way to the bridge at Thomondgate. He had to make the river Shannon before dawn in the hope of finding his head. The coach they knew would be his black coffin brought annually from the depths of Lough Gur. No sound would come from the iron clad wheels nor from the headless black horses as they thundered on their way. Time was the essence to his tormented soul.

Any house holder caught with their doors open or on the streets or looking at him would have a bucket of blood thrown at them. No prayers, no exorcism would nor could wash away the blood. The persons would die and their homes be abandoned before the next Samain. No Christian priest would dare walk the streets on this night, for this was the feast of Samain, the night of the dead.

Whatever praying that had to be done would have to be done within the sanctity of the church.

Outside there were far more ancient customs to be celebrated. To night the Tuatha-de-Danann would leave their forts, their Dolmens and their Cromlechs and travel to the Boireann. They would gather from the four corners of the earth and once again rule Tir-na-nOg. There was no surprise within the company at this phenomenal happening.

Within the house the wake of Anne Griffin continued. A remarkable character who had the gift. It was also a gathering of friends and neighbours all come to pay their respects and renew old acquaintances.

Phelm looked around the gathering and was pleased to see that they were respecting the occasion. His mother would have expected no less.

This was the custom and although the Bishops condemned it under the pain of mortal sin, it persisted.

Phelm honours his promise

It was early next morning that Phelm left Bridget to look after the mourners and went to the home of his brother -in -law.
"Patrick, I've come to ask a very special favour of you. I ask this of you as a relative and esteemed friend." Patrick noticed that he was rather tense. He put it down to his being upset at the death of his mother.
"Will you come and help me exhume the bodies of my grandfather and grandmother?"
"Have you lost your senses man, we cannot just go around opening graves. Why in God's name would you want to do such a thing?" Patrick was shocked.
"I never told you before but they were buried in the bottom field, down by the stream. I want to give them a proper Christian burial. It was mother's dying request to me."
"I never knew that, but if that is what your mother's wish was then you won't find me wanting."
Next day they went with a dray drawn by a horse to the bank of the stream where the graves were located and on the dray were two new coffins.
Having exhumed both skeletons they placed one in each coffin before sealing them and taking them back to the house.
There they placed the coffins one either side of the body of their daughter Anne.
"Your mother would be proud of you this day and that's no mistake Phelm." Bridget laid her hand on his shoulder.
"It was mothers dying wish and my duty." Phelm ran his hand across the three coffins.
Phelm accompanied by Patrick went to the graveyard where his father was buried and opening the family plot they prepared it to receive the coffins.
"Here they will lie side by side in the grave that mother bought for them. Near enough to God, yet not too far from

the Sideog Ri."

Patrick cried unashamedly, letting all his pent up emotions and sympathy be seen.

"Give me your slan, Patrick." He took both slans and placed them on the grave in the sign of the cross, as custom demanded. There they would remain guarding the open grave from evil spirits until the internment.

On the morning of the funeral four close relatives of Anne all bearing the same surname came to lift the coffin and carry it to its last resting place.

Having lifted the coffin by its brass handles, each kicked one of the chairs on which the coffin had rested across the floor. By their action they would release the spirit of Anne from the house. This would also confuse any evil spirit hiding within the confines of the house.

With her spirit now free, the mourners stood clear of the door. Phelm opened it wide and shouted aloud to his mother's spirit.

"You are now free of the house mother. Go in God's holy name and join Father."

The mourners clapped their hands, they rattled pots and pans and shouted as they encouraged Anne to leave the house and take her place in the spirit world.

The men preceded the women in a long procession behind the coffins. The infirm the old and the children were carried in pony and traps. The coffins were taken by the longest route to the graveyard in order to thwart any evil spirit lurking around trying to steal her soul.

At each and every cross roads they were taken a short distance up each road where a short prayer was said. This was to delay the progress of the devil as he followed the cortège.

Neighbours meeting the cortège on the road joined the funeral procession and followed it for three divine steps to prove that they were indeed Christians.

Although they could have reached the graveyard quicker by crossing a neighbours land, this was frowned upon and would not be allowed by the community.

Anne's coffin was taken a few steps down the path to the fairy fort. There it was placed on the banks of the stream.

The gathering left the coffin and returned to the road.

Anne Griffin would have her final meeting with the Sideog Ri beside his Crainne Mor in secret, as she always had. After a short period the mourners returned and picked up the coffin .The procession continued to the graveyard.

The Priest made no effort to stop them partaking in what was a pagan custom.

At the grave side, Phelm removed the crossed slans and helped to lower the coffins into the open grave.

With the funeral service over Phelm spent some time alone at the grave side. He was glad that he had carried on with the old traditions. His mother would have felt proud of him.

His mother had now gone from this life and left within him and the community a vacuum that would be hard to fill.

The day following the funeral he went into Limerick and made arrangements for a memorial of finest Connemara marble to be made and attached to the monastery wall above the grave. It would be eye high so that all could see it. Of their compassion they would pray for the souls of the Griffin family.

On the foot of the memorial under their names he had them inscribe:

> Of your mercy pray for the souls of the deceased members Griffin family of this parish. This would be his final break with his native land.

Then as an after thought he had inserted in Irish Slan Leat Sideog Ri (Good Bye my fairy King)

The memorial lettering was chiselled deep into the stone and covered in lead.

"I want the names engraved deep in the marble and covered in best lead." He remembered his mother telling him.

Nor had he forgotten his promise to Philomena Carey and her children. He ordered a slab of granite some six feet by three feet to be dressed and inscribed with the names of the family. Phelm returned to his farm and awaited the arrival of the monuments.

There was little else to keep him in Ireland, apart from what to do about the farm. He could dispose of it by auction. Were he to do this then his last link with his native land would be severed.

Had not his father and his father before him, going back generations fought and slaved to keep the land in the family. They had made sacrifices to keep the farm within the family. Sacrifices to which he was a part as was his wife Shelia.

More the pity, he thought that she was not here to help him make up his mind.

He looked around the empty kitchen and thought of his childhood days. He prayed to his mother and father for guidance. Finishing his prayers he concentrated for a moment and then he decided on what to do.

He went to see his brother in law the following day with a proposition.

He was willing to give him a lease on the farm until such time as his own son came of age at eighteen years. There would be a peppercorn rent of £1 per annum to protect the family rights. Then it would be for his son to decide, if he wished to keep it or sell it. Should he wish to sell the farm them Patrick would be given first refusal.

Patrick was most grateful to Phelm for the magnanimous offer.

"That is more than generous of you Phelm, are you sure now"? Patrick could hardly believe what was being offered to him.

"Of course I mean it, why else would I make the offer, do you accept?" Phelm spat on his hand and held it out.

"God bless you Phelm Griffin, I'm indebted to you and that's on your mother's grave, God rest her." His voice was filled with emotion as he spoke.

"At least it should stop you going to church next lent with the two chalk crosses on your back."

"What do you mean, are you trying to marry me off now as well?" Both men laughed as they shook hands.

"It is agreed then, so get the trap out and we'll go to Limerick and have the lease noted."

"Come up to the house and have the drop to seal the deal, I want to tell my parents." Patrick walked towards the house.

"Oh very well then, but just the one, the quicker I get my business concluded the quicker I can get back to my family."

It was midweek when a large cart drew up outside the farm house carrying the marble memorial and the granite slab, both covered in hessian sacking.

"Mr Griffin, I believe these are for you." The driver pointed to the rear of the cart with his whip.

"They are indeed, wait until I get my cap and coat and I'll accompany you to the graveyard."

"Are they both for the one burial"?, the mason asked.

"No! The marble one is for my family grave, the other has to go across to Tipperary. You don't mind do you? I'll make it worth your time." Phelm stepped on the running board and sat next to the driver.

"That's more than generous of you, not too far into Tipp I hope. Old Bess here is not one to tolerate long journeys."

"No, taking the road it would be the best part of an hour." He calculated the distance in his mind.

"Well seeing that the marble one is going on a wall, we'll have the holdfasts in to hold it in two shakes of a lambs tail. Then we can be on our way, no disrespect now."

He helped the mason to erected the memorial to his family. he was impressed with their efficiency and with the speed at which he worked. Soon the memorial was erected to his satisfaction and after a short prayer in which they all joined. Them were once again they were on their way.

"This is the boreen, turn left here."

"Are you sure, I never heard of a graveyard down there, did you Tim?" The mason asked his driver.

"Sure there are graveyards all over the place, this must be one that we missed."

"I can tell you now that it is not a graveyard at all." Phelm interrupted them.

"Not a graveyard, then where in the name of heaven are we going"? The driver stopped the horse.

Bess was glad of the rest as she moved into the verge and began to chew what little grass there was to be found.

He briefly related the tragic story of the Carey family. Both men shook their heads as the story was unfolded.

"Mister come on, let us put that stone where it belongs, and it's an honour to do just that, is that not so, Tim?"

When they reached the track through the woods, Bess found the going too much for her. so the three men pushed and heaved the cart from the rear.

"Come on Bess old girl, we're near there." The driver encouraged the horse as the cart slowly moved forward.

"Stop! stop here, This is the grave." Phelm went ahead of the cart and stopped at a spot where the primroses and cowslips grew.

"Ah God be with them!, they could not have chosen a more peaceful spot."The driver removed his cap and looked down at the outline of the grave.

Soon the large granite slab was set in place and again the three men knelt in prayer.

With the load removed from the cart, the driver turned the horse around and waited as Phelm knelt alone beside the grave in final farewell.

A curious Robin came down and hopped along the newly laid grave. Looking thought Phelm for her supper.

"Look away little bird, I hope that you find food, for it was for want of it that they died." He rose from the grave side, said his final farewell. He left the Carey family to their God and the tranquil peace of the lonely hillside in the county of Tipperary.

The final calling on
the Sideog Ri

Having completed his business in the city he arranged for Patrick to take him to the coach station next morning, where he would board the mail coach for Queenstown.

That afternoon he returned to the old graveyard to pay his last respects and offer his prayers for the blessed salvation of his parents souls and those of his grandparents.

Leaving the graveyard he crossed the street and went over the old stile. He followed the long disused track to the Fainne Sideog. There he stood for some time looking at the pile of stones before he adjourned to the stream nearby and picked up a stone from the babbling waters. Returning to the Crainne Beag he placed his stone next to the one he believed his mother had placed there not so very long ago.

Making his wish to the Sideog Ri, he asked permission to remove a handful of earth from the ground and a cippeen from the Crann the one with the uil 'ic growing in its crown. He watched intently to see if his stone would fall and be rejected. To his joy his stone remained cheek to cheek with the stone of his mother.

There would be no mallacht an Cranda. Going to the Crann he took his knife and making a clean cut removed a branch. Then scooping up a good handful of earth he placed it in a leather bag.

"I must inform you, Sideog Ri, that my mother, Anne Griffin will not be calling ever again. No disrespect to you. You see she passed away some ten days ago, I asked the bees to give you the sad message."

A zephyr whistled through the old spinney, rustling the leaves on the trees. This was followed by a stillness in the air. The Sideog Ri was thanking him and knew that there would be no more mortal visitors to come and pay their respects now that Anne Griffin had passed away.

Phelm listened to the rustling of the trees and a calmness overcame him. He was convinced that his mother's spirit was present guiding him.

"Why did I tell you all this Sideog Ri, for it matters not, you knew all the time, did you not?"

He turned on his heel and left the secret spot. It would be many the long year before any living soul visited the spot again. Should God spare him in the new land. He would return and pay his respects as did his mother before him.

He returned to his house where he spent the last night alone with his memories.

After a restless night within the house, he dressed early and returned to the kitchen. There was a distinct chill within the room. It was the first time since the house was built that it had been without a fire. Gone also was the smell of newly baked scones and the aroma of smoked bacon coming from within the chimney stack. These were changed times indeed. This was indeed a deserted house, nothing remained but fond memories and the ghosts of past generations.

He looked around the kitchen, then at the leaba shuidheachain, now folded back into a seat. The bed in which his father and mother had died.

Entering the scullery he removed the salting barrel, from above his mother's hiding place. Removing the family deed box he opened it and withdrew the deeds to the farm and the deed to the burial plot.

Alone now with his memories he crossed to the bedroom. He packed what mementos he wished to keep inside his portmanteau.

The earth and twig from the fairy fort he placed on the top and closed the hasps.

He sat on the settled bed and awaited the arrival of his brother in law to take him to the Cork coach.

On hearing the horses hooves in the lane, he rose to his feet and for some unknown reason crossed the floor to where the old eight day clock was hanging on the wall.

Opening the door he stopped the pendulum. The room was now silent.

With one last look around the room he heaved a sigh, picked

up his portmanteau and left the house for the last time.

As he stepped aboard the trap he was sure he heard someone rattling the latch on the door.

He would liked to have thought that it was his parents, giving him their final blessing.

"Good Bye and may God bless you both." He looked back and blessing himself said a silent prayer.

Sin Deire

GLOSSARY

ACT OF UNION. William Pitt had the Irish parliament dissolved in 1800. It was replaced by the Act of Union. Ireland was supposed to be represented in this new assembly by 100 M.P.'s. Catholics would have no members by law although four fifths of the population were Catholics.

AGUS MHAIRE SE AG SCARTHEDTH TO RAB PIACHANAM. Shouting himself hoarse.

AGUS TITIM MISE AR AN TA LABH. Falling on the ground.

AISY. Easy.

ALLANAH. Term of Endearment.

AMADAN. Fool.

AMERICAN WAKE. A going away party given to members of a household emigrating. It was called a wake because it was unlikely that the emigrant would ever return.

BEAN-SIDHE. The Banshee.

BENNACT DE AIR AN AINM. The blessing of God on her soul.

BENNACT DE LIB GO LEIR. God's blessing on them all.

BODHRAN. Irish drum.

BOG DENS. Hovels built in the bogs by evicted tenants.

BOIREANN. Rocky land. Also known as The Burren.

BOOLEY. A rough, makeshift shelter.

BOREEN. Small access road.

BUACHAILLEEN (The). Deformed fairy child.

BURREN. See Boireann.

CAILIN. Girl.

CAIRN BEAG. A small mound of stones built as atonement to the Fairy King.

CAIRN MOR. A Big mound of stones dedicated to the fairies.

CANTING SYSTEM. A system where the lease held on a small holding was auctioned to the highest bidder when the lease expired. The peasant living on the small holding would have no rights of tenure. He would have to bid for his own farm and crop.

CAUBEEN. A flat cap.

CEAD MILE FAILTE. A hundred thousand welcomes.

CHALK SUNDAY. The Sunday two weeks before lent when all bachelors had two chalk marks put on the back of their coats to remind them that only two weeks remained to wed before the 40 days of lent.

CIPPEEN. Stick.

CIPPINS. Branches of the tree.

CISCEAN. Basket.

CLAMPING. Covering a crop to protect it from frost.

CLOONE SIDHBAIR. Field of the fairies.

COATAMORE. Big overcoat.

COHULLEN DEARG. Red cap.

COINNEAL MOR. The big holy Candle used at Easter and Christmas in the window to guide strangers on their way. Also used to inform travellers that there was a wake within the house.

COIRCEOG. A dome shaped mound.

COMINGS THE. The feast of Samain (Halloween) when the dead arise.

COMMALLIES. Old songs.

CORN LAWS. Laws that protected the high price of English corn against foreign competition. I.E. American and Canadian corn.

CRANN. Hawthorn.

CRANN BEAG. A small crown.

CRANN MOR. A large crown.

CREEL. Woven basket made from willow used to store peat and logs.

CROONERS. Women who chanted in sorrow at wakes.

CURRAGH. Light weight boat made of a willow frame with stretched canvas or hide over and covered externally with Pitch to make it water tight.

DIA UILECHUMHACHTACT. Almighty God.

DIARMID AND GRAINNE BEDS. Megalithic pre historic Irish graves consisting of a large slab sitting on three legs.

DRAGGING THE CLOTH. On May Eve a person having spite against a neighbour would drag a cloth secretly over their fields. It was believed that this action by removing the May dew would destroy all the milk and butter yield for the following twelve months..

DRUABUS. Mistletoe.

EIREANN AGUS CONNDAE LUIMNEAC. Ireland and Limerick.

EMMET. Robert (1778-1803). Irish patriot. Led revolt against the English in 1803 was captured and hanged.

FAINNE. Ring.

FIRE AND WATER CURSE. It was believed that anyone occupying land confiscated from the church would die by fire or drowning.

FUM. The clearing from the bog before cutting. It consists of reeds and grass with a poor showing of turf underneath.

GARRYOWEN "OWENS GARDEN" Suburb of Limerick. The tune 'Garryowen and Glory' was adopted by General Custer and played a prominent part in rallying the cavalry at the battle of "The Big Horn" and many subsequent battles) It was adopted by the American calvary as their military tune and is played by them to this day.

GEAL MO CROIDE. Joy of my heart.

GOLDEN VALE. Rich pasture land in the east of Limerick Ireland.

GRA GEAL MO CROIC. Love of my heart.

GREGORY CLAUSE. William Gregory. Member of Parliament (Dublin). Stipulated in the Poor Law Amendment Act of 1847, that anyone holding more than one quarter acre of land would not be deemed to be destitute. No member of the family could claim any relief nor would they be accepted into the poorhouse.
The landlords used this act to evict their tenants.

HEADLESS COACH. The story is told that a coachman on his way to Limerick came across a detachment of Raparees near Cratlow on scout duty for General Patrick Sarsfield during the siege of the city in 1690. Passing by the Lax (Salmon) weir on the river Shannon he encountered the Dutch troops on their way to attack the city. He betrayed the Raparees to them for reward. All but one of the raparees were butchered,he escaped to Limerick where he told of the betrayal. The coachman unaware that his foul deed was known continued on his journey to the city.

Once he arrived within its confines he was beheaded and his head stuck on a pike in the centre of Thomondgate bridge as a warning. There it was left to rot, until on the night of Samain it was unceremoniously thrown into the fast flowing river. A curse was then put on his spirit that he would travel the earth forever more. Of their charity the citizens conceded that should he find his head in the River Shannon on the feast of Samain then and only then would he find eternal peace. On the night of halloween he travels to Limerick in search of his head. Dare you look at him and you will have a bucket of blood thrown at you and you will die.

HALLOWEEN. The feast of Samain when the Tuatha-de Dannan return to rule Tir-na-nOg.

HOOLEY. A gathering.

HOUSE BLESSINGS. It was the custom to call on the blessing of God as one crossed the threshold of the house. At the same time taking the holy water from the obligatory font at the door. This was done out of respect for the household and to prove that one was a Catholic.

HUNGRY GAP. The gap left bare by the corn fiddle between the rows when sowing wheat or corn.

IDLE BACK. An iron crane used to hold pots and pans over an open fire.

JACK -O- LANTERN. Bog gas.

JARVEY. The driver of a pony and trap.

JUMPERS-PERVERTS-SOUPERS. Catholic's who converted to protestants in return for food.

KEENERS. Mourners at a funeral.

KILLEELY. (LIMERICK) known as the haunted glens. In the fields surrounding the old cemetery, the dead of the great hunger of Limerick and Clare were interred. Near here lie the fairy forts of Ballynanty Beag and the haunted woods of Cratlow. Here too the poor and destitute were buried in the Paupers field. The devil is seen on the Long Pavement where it is crossed by the old Clare Railway. Across the river Shannon lies the Lax weir where the raparres were murdered. The quarry road is said to be haunted by the Sean-Bean-boct.(The poor old woman of the roads)

LANAB. Child.

LEABA SHUIDHEACHAIN. A settled bed common in all Irish country houses up until the 20th century. It was used by day as a settee and at night as a refuge for stranded travellers.

LEACTHA. Cairn.

LEACTHA AN RI. King's cairn.

LEVELLING BOX. Long rectangular wooden box containing stones. It was used to bury the seed and level the ground.

LIMERICK. Founded in 155. A.D. by Immar. Cormac Mac Airt fought his first major battle here. St. Patrick baptised the Dalcassian chief, Varthann. In 795, the Danes came to Limerick and used it as a base to plunder the surrounding countryside. They particularly liked its fertile lands (The Golden Vale) and easy access to the ocean, that they decided to fortify the city. They plundered the monasteries throughout Ireland from the city. In 843, they captured the Primate of Armagh and his people and took them prisoners to Limerick. Brian Boru marched on the city in 967, and drove out the Danes. More battles have been fought for possession of the city than any other. Yet no power has ever been able to hold it to itself. Limerick had its own mayor and corporation ten years before London.

The coat of arms of the city in latin reads:

Urbs Antiqua Fuit Studiisque Asperrima Belli Dives Opum
Translated it reads:

An Ancient City Highly Skilled In The Art Of War And Rich In Resources.

LOUGH. Lake.

LUCK PENNY. A token sum of money returned to the buyer/ seller to bring good luck.

MAIGHDEAN MHARA. Mermaid.

MALLACHT AN CRANDA. Curse of the Leprechaun.

MASS ROCK. Flat rock used as an altar for secret worship by the Catholics in the 18/19th century when Catholic Priests and bishops had a price on their heads.

MATCHMAKER. A person who arranges marriages.

MHUISE. Myself.

MINTO (LORD) Sent on secret mission to Pope Pious IX. The purpose of which was to extinguish all plans for a revolution in Ireland against the crown. The mission was successful.It was declared any Catholic planning or taking part in any subversion against England would be excommunicated. This one act crushed at a stroke any thoughts of rebellion in Ireland.

MOLLY McGUIRES. Agrarian secret men's society. They were anti gentry. As their membership increased they exported their defence of the peasantry to the coal fields of Pennsylvania. There they instigated the first American strike..All its members were Catholics and for some peculiar reason dressed in womens clothing when committing their outrages. Thus the name.

MUIRE NA SNEACHTA. Mary of the snows.

NAIL. A stone pillar with a brass top where the merchants paid their bills in the eighteen/ninetieth century in Limerick before written receipts became common practice in the late nineteenth century. thus the phrase "to pay on the nail".

NEDDY. Donkey.

NIL AON TINTEAN MAR DO TINTEAN FEIN. There is no home like one's own.

O'CONNELL DANIEL. (1775-1847) 'The Liberator'. Born in Caherciveen Kerry. He was elected M.P. for Clare although a Catholic. He was denied his seat. Catholics were forbidden to sit in the houses of Parliament.He opposed the Union. When the Catholic emancipation act was passed in 1829, which he advocated, he devoted his life to the repeal of the Act of Union which was imposed on the people without their consent..

PEEL. Robert (1788-1850). English premier during the Great Hunger in Ireland. He finally repealed the corn laws and was ostracised by his party.

PEELERS. Constables named after Robert Peel who founded them.

PEELS BRIMSTONE. American yellow corn purchased during the Great Hunger to feed the people. It was only ground once and caused great pain and suffering as the people tried to digest it.

PISHOGUE. Curse.

QUARTER DAYS. The days every twelve weeks when the rent on the small holding was due.

RACK RENT. Rent in excess of the value of the holding. Used when the landlord wished to evict the tenant.

RAPAREES. Irish soldiers mounted on swift horses for scouting and harrassing the enemy. Successfully used by general Patrick Sarsfield during the siege of Limerick when under the command of 'Galloping Hogan' they attacked and successfully blew King Williams munition train to pieces at Ballyneety.

RED COATS. English soldiers given the name because of their red uniform.

RIBBON MEN AND WHITEBOYS. A secret society formed in the 19th century to protect the Peasantry from the State and Church. Although they worked for the common good of the people, they were outlawed not alone by the State and the landlords but also by the Catholic Church. Not because they attacked and burnt the homes and barns of the gentry, rather that they beat up any Priest charging high fees for performing their Christian duties. I.E. Baptisms, Funerals, Marriages etc;

SAGART. Priest.

SAGART AROON. Parish priest.

SAINT BENEDICT. Saint who could stop a curse having any effect.

SAMAIN. The feast of the dead. Halloween.

SARSFIELD. Patrick (1644-1693) Earl of Lucan. Successfully defended Limerick against the mightiest armies of England and Europe. He thwarted King Williams efforts to capture the city by blowing up his munition train at Ballyneety Co Limerick, IN the year 1690 thus saving the city.

SCAILPEEN. Dug out made in demolished homes where people hid.

SEAN BEAN BOCT. Poor old mother.

SEAN SCEAL. Folk tales.

SEED FIDDLE. The seed was held in a small bag under the arm of the sower. The Bow of the fiddle rotated a metal disc. As the seed fell from the bag onto the disc it was thrown to the left and right of the sower.

SHANNAGIN. Blackguarding or troublemaking.

SIDEOG RI. Fairy King.

SKIBBEREEN. Village in the south of county Cork which became the focal point for all the austerity suffered by the Irish nation.

SLAINTE LEAT. Greetings to you.

SLAN. Single bladed spade.

SLAN LEAT. Goodbye.

SLEADOIR. Turf cutter.

SOUPER. A catholic who converted to protestantism to obtain food.

SPALPEEN. Blackguard.

SPITTING ON THE HAND. The acceptance of an offer.

SPLEEN. Torch

SPONGING HOUSE. Secure room built to detain Felons awaiting transportation to jail. More commonly known as Sweat Boxes as they had no windows and little ventilation.

STEPPINGS. Steps cut in the side of the bog.

STIRABOUT. Porridge.

STOLE. Sacred Eucharistic vestment worn over the neck and containing the relic of a saint.

STOOLEEN. Little stool.

STRICKLE. Honing Stone.

SUGAN CHAIR. Easy chair.

TAE. Tea.

TALAB NA H-EIREANN. The land of Ireland.

TESTING THE WATER. Finding out how much the market price was.

THRIE-NA-HELAH. Higgledy piggledy.

THYME. Worn by maidens to denote that they were virgins.

TIR-NA-NOG. The land of youth.

TREVELYAN. Sir George 1838-1928. Chief Secretary to Ireland (1882-1884) Not sympathetic to the starving Irish.

TUATHA De DANANN. Now called Fairies.They dwell within the Cromlechs, Dolmens, Menhirs and Tumuli of Lough Gur in Limerick. From there they travel throughout the country. Their queen Aine has her castle at Knockaine. Be bold enough to sit on the shore of Lough Gur on St. John's night and you will see the fairies but beware that they don't see you.....

TURF. Turf or Peat, decomposing forests cut and dried as fuel.

TURF SLAN. A spade with an L shaped blade used for cutting turf or peat.

UIL'IC. Mistletoe.

UISGE BAUGH. Whiskey.

WAKES. The mourning for the dead person within the house for three days. This custom came about to prevent anyone being buried alive.

WALKING THE LAND. Confirming continued ownership of the land and that the claims made by the suitor were genuine before the dowry was handed over. Many the bride was cheated out of her dowry and marriage by rogues who vanished after the wedding.

WHIN. Gorse bush.

WINDOW TAX. A tax imposed on the number of windows in a house. Many houses bricked up their windows to avoid the tax. This caused disease within the household and became known as 'Typhus Tax.'